The Imperfect Guardian:

A Novel

Stevan E. Hobfoll

To Jim, my friend & colleague

All about
fatherhood &
becoming a man.

Steve

Chicago
November
2012

For My Grandparents

Tzvi Joseph & Chaya

The Letter Delivered

It has been many years since I have come to America, the Golden Land, as we called it in the *Shtetl*, the Jewish villages of Eastern Europe. There, a letter would arrive from a relative in America, already old from its journey. A mother cherished such a letter, carrying it in her smock for her private link with her son in America. She would take it from home to home and read it to those she loved. She would read it to the dairyman and to the butcher and to those who she hardly knew who waited in line to make their purchases. When everyone had read and heard and checked back with her on details and compared it with their letters, she would put it in some safe place. And when her heart was longing for her *kinder*, her children far away whom she never expected to see again, her grandchildren whom she had never seen, except in a picture, she would take it out of the drawer and read parts out of order, going from one letter to the next, imagining the hand that wrote it and touching it as if to touch that hand. She would weep as I am weeping.

But the letter before me is such a letter and it is not. This letter has also come from across the ocean. It has taken until now, 1956, to gather news of my family in Europe and this letter contains the official response of my inquiry. It is written by a caring hand, from a person who never knew me and whom I will never meet. A person who searches for families devastated and torn apart by the war. Many families have still not found their loved ones. Most never will.

In 1926 America closed its gates to those huddled masses yearning to breathe free. The gates were shut and locked tight, because they didn't want more Jews, more dark-skinned brunettes, Eastern European, Mediterranean, calling us mentally deficient, criminal types. I pledged to get my family out. I knew what was coming. Oh, not the proportions, but what does that matter? We knew a horror was awakening and we had to save our families. And they locked the doors.

And now this letter, with its official seal, will list the final solution found for my family. Had they escaped to Palestine I am sure I would have heard. But there is a chance they escaped into Russia as the Germans' death machine advanced. They would not be free to write so easily. They could be alive in Russia. They would not know my address. They would not know how to write.

As I feel the envelope I can tell it is thick with pages of names. I asked of the lives of fifty-six relatives. I did not know all their children's names, so this list may contain more.

Survivors from my town have told me some of what transpired. Uncle Yosl found his old gun and waited in his parlor until a German brigade entered the town. Already an old man, he charged the advancing Germans alone on horseback as they entered the town. He was shot from every direction. A woman told me she saw Aunt Miriam shot in the back of the head and thrown into a pit. She was sure Miriam had died because she lay for hours under her body, until the Germans thought everyone in the pit had perished. The woman kissed me, saying that my Aunt had saved her life, even in her death. Survivors tell of the horrors of the first days, especially. Of the times that came later they cannot speak. When the soldiers entered Kalushin many of our Polish neighbors aided the Germans, throwing children out of windows to waiting bayonets for sport. Before a Jewish family was cast out from their home or business, a Polish family entered and took over. If the Jew begged some bread from his own stores he was denied. The town was liquidated by the Germans in December of 1942. Most met their death at Treblinka.

I know they are mostly dead. But what if ten are alive? What if five? What if one of my loved ones is alive? Is one life not precious? If from something larger comes something smaller, is it not concentrated and rare? Perhaps it is my sister Rachel's youngest, or little Rayzella's. Perhaps she has married and has children. Perhaps they need my help, need their uncle who has done well in America. Perhaps I can get them out of Russia. I can send money. I can arrange for them to have clothing. I can arrange for food.

There are miracles, living miracles. I was walking hand in hand with my little grandson from Temple on Rosh Hashonah, the Jewish New Year. I heard two men speaking Yiddish behind us. I held my grandson's hand more tightly and slowed my pace. I recognized the dialect. It was my dialect. At first I thought it was just the sound that was familiar. But then I could envision my childhood friend Gedaliah, a huge behemoth of a man, who was always falling in love with some girl who wouldn't have him. I turned and Gedaliah stood right in front of me, but as a young man, and I became faint. Gedaliah would be older, like me, and this man was in his prime, with Gedaliah's body and voice.

"Are you alright sir?" he asked me in heavily accented English.

"Yes, only startled." I answered in Yiddish.

"Here, sit down on this stoop. Can we get you something? Do you need an ambulance? You don't look well."

"No, no that's alright. It's nothing. I already feel better."

"Are you sure?"

"Well, your voice. You sound so much like a friend of mine from the Old Country."

"And where are you from sir?"

"From Poland."

"I am from Poland."

"Yes, I could tell from your Yiddish. I am from Kalushin."

"I am from Kalushin."

"Yes, but of course it has been years. I left in '39."

"Perhaps you knew my family. The Apfels."

"There were many Apfels in Kalushin."

"My friends name was Gedaliah Zeidnoff."

"My God! I am Shlomo Zeidnoff. Gedaliah was my father, bless his memory."

It took me a minute to sift through my thoughts and emotions and what this young man was saying. I felt as in a dream, unsure where my next step would take me, no longer on solid ground.

"Then he is no more?"

"He was taken by the Nazi animals. He was murdered in Treblinka in '43. "

"He was my best friend."

"And that makes you Tzvi Apfel, no?"

"How did you know?"

"Tzvi Apfel the soccer player.   The warrior."

"Only in Gedaliah's eyes I'm afraid. But yes, one in the same. Although now, here, I am called Joseph. This is my grandson, Stevan. His Hebrew name is Shlomo, after my father."

"This is a miracle."

"Your father would be very proud of you. I can tell you that."

"Thank you Mr. Apfel. But how would you know what kind of man I am?"

"Because that became my profession. Knowing people. It is how I survived."

And we talked and exchanged numbers and promised to stay in touch. He was only visiting Chicago from Philadelphia, which I guess makes it more of a miracle.

We spoke on the phone once or twice when he was visiting Chicago. I met his children. His youngest looked like Gedaliah when we were in *Cheder*, learning with Rav Pinchas, being rascals. I told him of his *Zadie* and what a wonderful man he was. I told him he was a boy who could take on five boys and how he protected the religious Jewish boys from the non-Jews who would prey on them.

So, if Gedaliah could live in this young man, and be him to me, then my sisters and brothers would be alive in my nieces and nephews if they survived. A young cousin would carry the face of an aunt or uncle. And they would pray from their grave that I found their child or grandchild, that I acted, that I sought, that I hoped.

And if they have not survived, then there are obligations as well. Someone needs to light candles of remembrance. Someone must say the *kaddish* prayers for the dead. Someone living must remember their names. It is so very long ago, and it is yesterday. Such is the way of time and of life. If I close my eyes I am there.

Part 1

Searching

Chapter 1

Trouble in the Town

In March came my Bar Mitzvah, with winter still in the Polish air and onions and potatoes our only remaining vegetables on the table. I knew everyone was looking forward to my big day, but so much grief and threat surrounded us that the days were coated in what remained of the winter's gray sadness. There was actually little to prepare. I knew Hebrew as a second language. It was not a living language, because it was not a spoken language, but I read and understood it. There was little ceremony, only that I would be called to read from the Torah before the congregation. I was to deliver no speech. Even the Rabbi only gave sermons twice a year, before Yom Kippur, our holiest day, and before Passover. There was to be a gathering of family and friends at our home. A small gathering would have to do, because that is mostly how it was done if you were not a rich family.

With Mameh's death the spirit which had vitalized our home vanished. Much of this change was due to my Tateh, my father who had been warmed by my mother's glow and in her reflection had been larger, more alive. With her gone his tendency toward silence increased. He would come home and touch each of us, kissing the little ones. He would stroke my back as I sat at the table reading. But he was going through the motions and became smaller before our eyes. More and more, he spent time alone, sinking into his silence and separateness. I spent more time playing with friends or visiting my aunts' and uncle's homes. Had our lives been a painting on the wall that you had never looked at carefully, you would not really have noticed the change. For our lives inside the painting, it was profound.

The town was alive with rumors of demonstrations against the Jews. We had heard of such things recently in Russia, but although Poland was Greater Russia, our living with 'the others' was filled more with little hatreds than widespread violence. Still, extra tension was in the air and Jews stayed off the streets as much as possible.

Always the time before Easter was a mixed time of joy and trouble for us. The joy came from our celebration of Passover, the remembrance of our exodus from Egypt. The trouble came from the fact that Easter commemorates the time when our Christian neighbors were reminded that the Jews killed Christ. The cries of "Christ killer" would be heard each year by a fresh new crop of younger children. They did not have to learn this hatred along with dirty talk in the schoolyard. It came directly from the pulpit.

This only fed on their fear and jealousy of us. The fear was learned in the cradle. You would overhear mothers tell their children on the street, "Be good or the 'Yid' will get you." The Jew to them was the bogeyman. "Get to bed now before the Yid steals you and eats you!"

If the bent over Jew they knew in the street was so powerful as to steal them in their beds in the night and to even kill their God, he was something truly to be feared. Feared on some deep level like snakes, darkness, and the sounds that frighten children in their beds in the night.

And there was jealousy. Jealously, the adults would say, because we were unlike them. We were mainly poor like them. Mainly with little to spare. We lived in homes like theirs, often worse. We wore clothes as simple as theirs, even if of a different cut. But Jewish men were not spending money drinking or losing work the next day because of it.   A Jew would not be found drunken on the street in the morning. Jews could read, and write, and knew their numbers. Even the girls were educated. There were no Jewish robbers, or prostitutes, or God forbid, murderers. A Jewish family held together and the community supported one another. The poorest Jewish child might be learning the violin.

We also spoke in what was to them a secret code. We spoke their language and our own, which meant that we could always understand them, but they could only understand us when we chose. A Jew could meet another Jew from America or England or Hungary and talk. I had even heard it with my own ears from some Jews that came from Russia to talk to us about Palestine. It made us dangerous to them, and us apart from them.

These are the things that make two nations living side by side seem like one is rich and one is poor, even when it was us who could own no land or profit by many professions.

Perhaps too it was our own feeling of otherness toward them. We were the Jews of their town. They were 'the others' of our history. On Yom Kippur, our holiest day of fasting, I would read of the Jewish martyrs who were tortured and killed for their faith. Killed in Babylonia, killed in Judah, killed in Germany, killed in York. Killed in the Crusades by crusaders who never made it out of their own country, but could kill the Jewish infidels in their own midst. Somehow this liberated the Holy Land for them! On Passover we would read, "in every generation they have risen up against us." In *every* generation, and that meant in this generation.

These were the feelings below the surface always. The stories on which I and all children of my community were raised. Our stories and their stories. In times when there was real fear of their hatred being unleashed our angst only increased as did our vigilance. This was such a time.

My Bar Mitzvah was to be the *Shabbes* after Easter Sunday, 1907. I was excited about becoming a man, receiving presents, being the center of attention. Even my teachers began to treat me differently. They spoke to me, instead of at me. The younger children in *cheder*, the Jewish school, would listen when I had something to say, or so I imagined.

On Thursday my brother Isaac came to walk me home from school. He hadn't done this since I was little, and really even little children would walk alone from one end of our town to the other. That he should do so today was odd. He said it "happened to be on his way," so why not walk together. But he was not the only brother or father who came by the school that day. I knew it was that thing in the air.

"Are you really worried something will happen?" I asked.

"No, they're probably making something out of nothing. Its really no big *megillah*," which literally means "not the reading of a long Hebrew text from our time in ancient Babylonia," but that is how we spoke. "Still, why not be a little cautious? It couldn't hurt."

On the way home we passed Uncle Mayer's fish stall, no accident on our part because this was not the fastest route. Uncle Mayer sold fish in the street from a push cart. He said that it was a good business because people always liked a nice piece of fish. He would have liked to have a store, but this way he said that his house didn't smell, because even the stores of those who were rather well to do, like the butcher, were attached to their homes. Aunt Miriam said it smelled enough from his clothes, better he should have a cart. In any case, the fish didn't smell so bad today because it was still cold. Each day he had a different spot for his cart depending on from which direction he thought his business was coming. It was a small town, and truth was you didn't have to look far for him, that and with the smell of fish.

Uncle Mayer pulled out a large piece of pickled herring. He cut it in half with a sharp knife which he pulled from several tucked in the belt he wore over his coat and gave it to us to eat. With his sharp knives I always thought that he looked more like a Cossack than a fish monger.

"Sit down on the step here, a Jew shouldn't eat standing up like a goy." I told him that I didn't remember reading a commandment against eating standing up, and anyway I never saw 'the others' eat standing up. He told me not to be so smart as I wasn't a Bar Mitzvah yet. "On *Shabbes*, you'll know why you shouldn't eat standing up." I was happy with the fish, happy with his kidding me like usual, and I knew that the piece of fish, and my getting the bigger half, was a special extra something because next week was my Bar Mitzvah.

He told us to say a special prayer for the new fish of the Spring. It looked like any old herring to me. However, if he knew anything, Uncle Mayer knew his fish, so I said a *Shekheyonu*, the prayer we recite for all new beginnings, for the new season's fish and savored the sweet-sour taste.

He pulled my cap down hard over my ears, gave me a kiss on the head and told us that we better get home, and not to dawdle. "They don't even know that their God's Last Supper was a Jewish Seder? Could they really know so little about their own God?" Uncle Mayer knew a lot about 'the others.' I didn't have any fathom of what he was talking about.

Walking home, we passed a group of men and women. They were well dressed, people from the better part of town. Having been taught respect we stepped down from the path into the mud to let them pass. We lowered our heads, recognizing that they were above our class. Eye contact with 'the others' only invited trouble anyway.

Before looking away, I did not fail to notice a young girl, maybe a year or two older than me. She was a beautiful girl with long blond hair and wore a coat with real fur on the collar. Perhaps I stared for a moment too long, but she did not look away either. With my own blond hair and blue eyes I likely did not look like the Jew she had come to expect. Maybe I was handsome to her. Probably I was just a curiosity, as I am not sure that she could have seen one of us as handsome.

As they passed, we heard a woman's voice, "Dirty *sheenies*." It startled us, this filthy, hate-ridden term for Jews, catching us off guard. Adults like them talking so to children. These were not the bullies, the trash of the town. This was not a drunken group of young men coming home from a tavern, thick with vodka and the smell of women. These were not men from whom you knew the words were coming before it was ever spoken and so were not braced for the expected.

I looked to see who of them had spoken. They stared at us with daggers in their eyes. Only the girl had looked down and blushed. Then they walked on as if nothing had happened. We walked on unable to speak to each other. Stunned. Saddened.

Further on we crossed the path of a group of boys from the Yeshiva. These were the young religious Jews of our town, always looking like boys dressed as old men. They wore black hats, trimmed in fur, with long black gaberdine coats. Their hair, cut short elsewhere, showed long curls streaming from their temples like noodles. On any other day we would have passed them with only a nod and greeting. We were not close to them, although one of my aunts had married such a religious Jew, a *Chassed*, and moved to the next town.

Today they walked hurriedly. One young man had an eye already turning black and blue. Another had blood on his collar and cheek. There was no need to ask them what had occurred. They would never in a lifetime have raised a hand against each other any more than they would have eaten a plate of pork. They had been attacked and were lucky to have gotten away with so little hurt. Their pride, however, was deeply wounded and they could not even speak to us words of greeting.

Isaac squeezed my hand and we walked faster, hurrying to get home.

My father was already at home with Uncle Shmuel, Aunt Eti and their family. Uncle Mayer came not long afterwards with his family. The looms of the small factory where my father worked had already shut down, although Thursday was the late night of work to make up for closing early on Friday afternoon for the Sabbath. Likewise, Uncle Mayer and Uncle Shmuel would have worked late that night, especially Uncle Mayer, because women would buy the fish to prepare for the Sabbath and maybe half his weekly business was done on Thursday.

We told them of the *Chassidic* boys in the street, but did not mention the name calling.

They were not surprised. Some Jewish store owners had been bothered. Windows had been broken. Harsh words had been spoken.

Uncle Shmuel said that Reb Jabotinsky's store had been vandalized. "Could you believe such a thing!"

Many in the town owed money to Reb Jabotinsky, Jew and Gentile alike. He was a generous man, and neighbors knew that if they were short on money, he was long on kindness. Sure, wouldn't he always say, "What, do you think I am, such a rich man?" But you knew he would give you the credit, even if you couldn't say when he would see his money. Many women would find extra potatoes in their bag or an extra measure of flour, as he was a man who could not give two potatoes or a single cup of flour to a family of seven.

"And on such a man's store they would paint such words?"

"A *shanda, a shame*," and shame was no small thing. It was hard to have worse than shame. That something I did was a *shanda* was about the worst words my parents would ever say to me.

As the day progressed, word of atrocities came. Two young girls, not twelve, were caught in the street by a group of men and raped. They were left alive, but barely. What kind of animals could do such a thing and what kind of religion would sanction such behavior? These men would be drunk on Saturday night and heroes in Church on Sunday. They might only change their story to suggest that the girls were a few years older. Among the Jews it was quickly agreed that the girls were only molested, not raped, so that they would not live in shame and could someday find husbands.

As darkness grew, worry increased to near-panic that my sister Rachel had not yet come home. She had gone to the butcher and should have already returned. Afraid to wait longer, my Tateh and uncles with Isaac went out to look for her.

Arriving at the butcher, Reb Cohen was just closing his shop.

Reb Cohen was a large, powerful man. Afraid of nothing, so he had stayed open later than the others.

"Yes, your Rachela was here. I gave her a nice piece of meat. Something special before your Bar Mitzvah Sabbath. Mazel Tov! Maybe an hour ago she left."

With this, their fear grew to a frenzy. How could she have thought to go out this day alone? She should know better. God forbid something has happened to her!

They split up in twos to take the possible streets she might have walked home.

By a tavern Uncle Shmuel and Tateh saw two men with Rachel held up against the wall. They were kissing her and she was struggling. They rushed at the men, not caring the consequences.

Startled, the men drew back from the woman, but she was a *shicksa*, a girl of theirs not ours and one who was not minding the attention she was getting.

They apologized, and the men shrugged them off and went back to their celebrating.

They arrived home besides themselves with worry. "We must go out again and search."

Just then, Rachel came in the door, her face flushed. Ten voices spoke at once.

"Where were you?" "Are you okay?" "What happened?"

"Nothing happened. I stopped by Lena's house to visit for a little. I haven't seen her with her family busy for her sister's wedding."

"Don't you realize the kind of night this is?! Don't you know what is happening in this town?!"

My father's harsh voice, so seldom heard, betrayed his fear.

She broke into tears and he held her and sighed.

"That's okay Rachela. Thank God nothing happened. Next time use your head."

All evening we sat and talked, with the lights dimmed and most of the family gathered. Tomorrow was their Good Friday, a holy day for them said *Zadie*, but tonight men were drunk in the street, shouting and cursing. We could hear the breaking glass and the taunts for us to come out. Tonight no Jew should be caught out on the street.

"And this," said *Zadie* "is how they celebrate their God. How did we come to live among them? You boys, you should go to Palestine. Make a new land. Here we'll never know peace. Not if we live here another thousand years."

Chapter 2

For Love of Christ

Men dominated the synagogue world. Today, however, my sister Rachel would not be left behind. She was desperate for escape from my new baby brother Jacob that was left from my mother's parting life for her care, and my little sister Rayzella, who was still not ready for school, and angry over her mother's death. In *Shul* she could sit with the other women and catch up on all the news, or at least the news that was worthy to hold the high status of *rechiyles, gossip.* Not that gossip was women's domain alone. Rather, they orchestrated the symphony of stories and their families waited eagerly for the morsels they were willing to share.

Something more powerful also seemed to draw Rachel to the house of God. Sitting warmed by the coals at home, she immersed herself in the same few pages of the Bible, studying the text with a determination unusual for her outside of her romance novels, but registering the same flush around her neck and cheeks. In a house full of prying eyes she foolishly left her ribbon where she most reverently read, and she was only fortunate it was I, and not Isaac, who followed her tracks.

> *By night on my bed I sought him whom my soul loveth;*
> *I sought him, but I found him not.*
> *The watchmen that go about the city found me;*
> *Saw ye him whom my soul loveth?*
> *Scarce had I passed from them,*
> *When I found him whom my soul loveth;*
> *I held him, and would not let him go,*
> *Until I had brought him in to my mother's house,*
> *And into the chamber of her that conceived me.*

Whether my mother's loss hastened it or not, Rachel was aching for love. She was anxious to steal a glimpse of the object of her dreams at the

Synagogue through the screens that separated the men and women, although we could not for the life of us guess with whom she was smitten. Likely as not, he did not know either. Courtships were held at kitchen tables by parents with matchmakers, although young people often set the wheels in motion to encourage or force the hand of the matchmaker. This was a complicated chess game played by masters, but we could not see either side setting the pieces in motion. For her part, Rachel was offering no hints as to who had caught her eye.

"How will we eat when we get home if you are here with us?" Isaac, like my father, had his own best interests at heart and his bickering with Rachel had only increased since my mother's death.

"You don't have to be concerned. The *cholent* is warming since last night on the stove. God forbid you should have to lift a finger."

"Well, so long as you've taken care of it."

"Thank you your majesty. Your will is done. I hope it gives you gas."

Such does love show between brothers and sisters.

"So tell us Rachel, who is your knight in shining armor?" Isaac pressed.

"I don't know what you're talking about Isaac."

"Probably someone rich and if you think that some rich boy would ever look at you you've gone mad," he went on cruelly.

"No, actually I was hoping for someone from a good family, but with you as a brother all our dreams are squashed. I am destined to be a spinster, I'm afraid. Tzvi, I'm sorry to inform you that you must soon leave our town and find a place where no one knows our family and our shame."

And with this she had lightened the words that Isaac had used to sting her and we all laughed. But Isaac knew that he had hit his mark and that Rachel felt in many ways inadequate and awkward, while Rachel's words were just that, words. She lost the spring in her step and might have turned around, but we were almost there and Tateh would not have let her walk home alone.

Watching Rachel and her shy downcast eyes when young men were present, I knew she felt herself unattractive. I guessed that her fear was that she thought her true love simply too wonderful in his entirety, and that he could not possibly return her admiration. Rachel was modest and a romantic, which is a dangerous combination because fantasies that are never acted upon spiral into impossible standards. I doubted if she would care about money or status. No, when I gazed from face to face, I searched for a young man not so rich, not so learned, and not so attractive. My eyes rested on those who held something special that she would think only she could see. He would read modern books, or want to go to Palestine, or have revolutionary zeal lighting his eyes. And he would be in *Shul* today, or her pace would not have been so spry–nor slackened so instantly in defeat.

For my father's part, he needed Rachel at home just now, for she was playing not just mother, but also father, as he became increasingly detached, filled with his sadness. Tateh loved his children, loved them deeply, even if it was hard for him to display his love. But Tateh also saw the needs of others as revolving around his own. He would see Rachel as too young, the men as just not right, not good enough, too this, too that. He could not see that his judgments did not reflect the world; he expected the world to match his judgements. And if this fit neatly with his needing her at home, that was well enough. Having Rachel cloistered in *Shul* with the other women he felt safe-- poor judgement.

And she was wrong about her plainness. The young men stared longingly at Rachel whose full figure set their imaginations in motion. With their many layers of coverings our women were all but indistinguishable, swaddled from head to toe like infants sheltered from the window's draft. With all their shrouds, being buxom, *zavtig* as we called it, was a thing prized. Rachel may not have been beautiful, but she was pretty enough, with her haunting green eyes, thick brown lashes, and full lips. Heaven help me for talking this way about my sister, you could not help but notice her ample bosom. Her lack of outright beauty was even in her favor, for boys are afraid of the unobtainable, of the girl who will reject them, of the girl whom another will steal away.

I too was of course infected with this enchantment with girls' breasts, as much as I found it deeply objectionable when it pertained to my sister. My friends and I talked endlessly about breasts, noting those growing on Rebecca and absent on Sarah, pointed on Shula, and rounded on Bracha. At our age this was all the more interesting, because the wonder of puberty would constantly change the whole scheme of our admiration, as from one week to another the girls seemed to bloom, one after another like flowers of the field.

In school my mind wandered to thoughts of Leah Rosenblock, a girl developed ahead of her years whom I found a thing of perfection. I would get a swelling in my pants that sometimes caught my hair painfully. Nor could I slip my hands in my pants to liberate it. Once Daniel Shpielman was caught with his hands in his pants and our teacher, Rav Pinchas, had him stand in the back of the room with his hand left there for the remainder of the day. So all I could do was to squirm in my seat or try to turn my thoughts to something grotesque, hoping for spontaneous release from my entrapment.

Breasts kept me awake at night. Once at a *klezmer* dance, Leah Rosenblock rubbed against me, or more accurately did not move away too quickly as I rubbed against her. As her chest touched mine, she looked into my eyes and flashed a smile, but so quickly it was gone before it appeared. When she stepped outside for fresh air, I followed her into the street, took her into my arms, and kissed her. She turned her cheek, and I received a mouth full of hair and a slap. I wondered if I had only imagined her earlier response on the dance floor, but our bodies touched momentarily twice more that evening with the clarinet wailing its minor key of sorrow mixed with joy and the violin's plaintive response. The third time I was sure it was her doing.

With thoughts of Leah Rosenblock's bosom I rubbed myself guiltily under the covers at night, rather incessantly. I soon found that a small piece of soap and spit left me less pained in the morning. Unfortunately the soap would enter my mouth as one wad of spit was hardly enough, especially on the second or third turn of a night. Yet this was hardly a heavy price to pay for the enchantment of the feel of young breasts. With time I learned to like the taste of the soap.

A few weeks ago, Rachel had come to my bedroom when no one else was home.

"Tzvi, may I ask you something?"

Feeling a tension in my body that I could not identify, I tried to avoid her. "Not now Rachel, I'm just leaving."

"Oh...okay, I apologize, maybe another time." With Mameh's death she had acquired her annoying aptitude for producing instantaneous guilt. I was easy work for her.

"I'm sorry. Of course you can ask me something?"

"How do you think boys see me?"

"I have no idea Rachel. How would I know? You're my sister."

"But you are a boy, after all, and who else can I talk to and get an honest answer?" Which was true. Tateh could not be asked such a question and my aunts would have told her she was a thing of rare beauty without peer, or worse, that beauty does not matter. Isaac would only have ridiculed her mercilessly.

"Rachel, you look nice."

"Tzvi, that's a perfectly awful thing to say," and tears streamed down her face.

"Tzvi?"

"Yes?"

"Look at me. How will my husband see me?" and with that she slipped her dress from her shoulders and stood there before me. Her breasts were large and upright and her nipples were dark and thick. In clothes she looked heavy, but naked her waist was small and her ample hips spread to shapely legs. A large birthmark on her thigh was reddish, but instead of appearing like a blemish, it spread toward her groin as an added token of her womanhood.

She held her head down, unable now to make eye contact. She half covered her breasts with one hand and her belly with the other, but I felt dizzy

and leaned against my bed. I had seen her this way before because I was just
emerging from the age where there was little modesty over my sisters or mother
seeing my body or my seeing theirs. However, in the past few months this had
all changed, and I was afraid that being in my room she would somehow sense
the mischief that I was up to at night. I felt as if I might run that instant. Only my
love for her, and my doubt at my ability to move my legs, held me in place and
gave me voice.

"Rachel, a man would die for what you offer."

"But Tzvi?"

"What Rachela?"

"Aren't my breasts too large."

"Rachela, like it or not, that's what they'll die for."

And with that she held my eyes with hers and a smile crossed her lips as
she lifted her dress and slipped it on, knowing that neither of us would ever speak
of this again after her last words.

"I am sorry to have done this. I had to know." And she kissed my
cheek and left the room. I sat for a while to catch my breath.

Romance or not, I wished that Rachel had not come to Shul this day..
For those who work six days and save their pleasures for the seventh, the Sabbath
holds a special joy. Today anxiety lingered instead like the dread that cannot be
shaken from a nightmare that one wakes to find is less fearsome than the day that
awaits. Instead of going straight to *Shul,* as was our custom, we went by others'
homes and walked in small groups. Nothing needed to be said. There was safety
in numbers. Although it was early, a few hooligans might still be up and drunk
from the night before.

We saw no one but the occasional laborer, as Saturday was a normal day
of work for them. We passed shops just opening, but today we barely
acknowledged them, nor they us. Today the lines between us and 'the others'
were well drawn. Soon, it would be Easter and so already the storm of their

feelings toward us raged.

Passing the home of some, we found that they were too sick that day to brave the weather, illness being about the only acceptable excuse.

"Froi Finkelstein, is your husband coming to *Shul* today? We thought we'd walk together."

"No, Aaron is not feeling so well. It's a sin to go to Shul, only to catch your death of cold you know."

"Of course, that would be a terrible sin. We're sorry to hear he is unwell. Give him our wishes for a speedy recovery."

"Sarah, please move out of my way. I told you I'm going to *Shul*."

"But Aaron I just told the Apfels how unwell you are."

"Sarah, please. God has given me a speedy recovery. It's like a miracle. First I was racked with that cough and now I'm healthy as a horse. He works in mysterious ways."

"Aaron, I don't want you going to Shul and getting sicker," she insisted standing in her normally meek husband's way.

"Sarah, if Reb Apfel can go to Shul with his children, then I am suddenly recovered enough to go as well. Enough of this. Please don't make a scene."

And with that she moved however unwillingly from the doorway and Reb Finkelstein descended into the street, meekness and all, but with his chin upright and his feet already in motion.

"Nu? Let's be on our way before we melt in this rain," was all he said.

"A miraculous recovery, Reb Finkelstein."

"Yes, I thought so as well. Bless His name."

I was at my age expected to be in *Shul* and pray with the men, but I still was not counted among the *Minyan*, the ten men required for prayer. Once, that winter on a day thick with snow and freezing temperatures I had come to *Shul* with *Zadie. Zadie* would often cajole a grandchild or two to help him fulfill a task or one of our many commandments. In part it was because he was old and could use the help, but mainly he liked the company of his grandchildren and his joy in us made us want to be with him. He would think of a game to play to make the chore easier and to get away from the grasp of *Bubbie, grandma,* who would add to the errands she would place upon him without end.

"Come with me Tzvi to *Shul* before *Bubbie* has me peel those potatoes."

"But *Zadie*, I want to go play with my friends before supper."

"Come with your *Zadie*. It is hard for me in the snow."

Asked this way, I could not decline, so we bundled ourselves for the cold and off we went.

Trudging through the snow he held my arm for balance and we walked a bit silently. The snow was high and he became short of breadth, so we rested and then forged on.

"You know Tzvi the snow it didn't use to be so high. Or perhaps I was taller. In any case, if I stay in this world much longer you will only see my hat as I walk come winter. So, Tzvi..."

"What *Zadie*?"

"Remember my hat, because that way you'll always be able to recognize me so that you can come dig your *Zadie* out for *Bubbie* to send on another errand."

"I will *Zadie*."

"Tzvi?

"What *Zadie*?"

"How will you be different Tzvi once you've had your bar mitzvah?"

"I'll be a man *Zadie*."

"Yes, but how will you be different?"

"It means I have to fulfill the commandments."

"Yes, but you already fulfill many commandments. So, what will be different?"

"I'll be counted as part of the *minyan*."

"Yes, that is a way others will see you differently. But, how will you be different?"

I thought about this for a while, realizing that I was not going to be let off with an easy answer.

"Because God will hold me accountable for my sins." I was sure I had hit upon the right response.

"Do you think *Hashem* would not hold you accountable for your sins one day, and then accountable on the next? I don't think that *Hashem* thinks this way, although he has not personally informed me one way or the other I might add. So once again, how will you be different?

"I guess I don't know *Zadie*. How will I be different?"

"You will be different because you are expected to ask this question."

"What question *Zadie*?"

"The question, 'How will I be different?' *Hashem* will expect of you to think, to question, to ask more of yourself. To find how your path meshes with the path that we all must take together and what part will be your own. And speaking of paths, here's the Shul. There, help *Zadie* up the stairs. *Oy*, when did they make the stairs this high?"

And so the way to *Shul* had passed quickly and to this day I often think about this question that my *Zadie* asked me, although I do not believe that he expected me to find an easy answer.

It was a short service, and soon we were on our way back home.

"Okay *Tzvi*, now its back through the snow and don't let me forget to buy the sugar that *Bubbie* wanted. Heaven forbid I should forget and the woman will have me sleeping with the cow. And you know what Tzvikala?"

"No, what Zadie?"

"The cow snores worse than your *Bubbie*!"

"Oh *Zadie*!"

"What?! I am only teaching you a little about being married now that you're almost a man. Don't so much mind the cow and the barn, but the snoring is intolerable. Now come or we'll be late for dinner."

And now it was the Sabbath before my Bar Mitzvah. I was in Jewish no-
mans land, but soon to be forever a part of the men's side and the special things
that meant. The women sat separately in the synagogue with the children raucous
among them, behind screens or in balconies. No woman could touch the Torah.
My Tateh explained to us that this was because women may not be clean. They
always looked clean to me! Mameh used to chime in that it was because men
couldn't keep their minds on their prayers, and usually got the last word in on
that particular discussion.

My friends Gedaliah, Shimon, Micha and I sat together, but despite their
talking more than us, the *alteh kockers* in the row ahead of us kept shushing us
for disturbing them. An *alteh kocker* is an old man, especially one who is not at
that moment held in your fondest thoughts. These particular *alteh kockers* were
the bane of our weekly Sabbath experience. They would hold an unceasing
conversation, but our voices made it impossible for them to hear each other.
After *Shul* if someone held a reception in honor of a marriage or birth, they
would bar our attempts at drinking a little shnapps. They saw themselves as
God's sentinels expressly assigned for our behalf. Worst of all, they would fart
incessantly, but yell at us if we went to crack open the window. We could have
sat elsewhere, but we were unwilling to admit that we were outmatched, and our
dueling with them helped the time pass. Such was our hopeless state.

With the Torah now out of the Holy Ark, our attention was momentarily
returned to the Sabbath service. Removed from the ark, it was dressed in the
finest velvet and adorned with silver crowns and breastplate. The very reverence
with which it was treated drew awe, as does a king who is attended by many,
even in the face of a fool who does not know the rituals of court. We sang
together the song of joy as the Torah was marched around the room, with young
and old reaching out to kiss it as it passed.

I watched as men were called for the honor of coming to stand by the

Torah while the reader read from that week's portion. Each man would come

and bless the Torah, "Blessed art thou oh Lord our God that chose us from all the

nations and who gave us his Torah." I could say the words by heart, and could

hardly wait until the following Sabbath to be called for the first time to make this

blessing. This, my teachers told me, was the essence of being a Bar Mitzvah.

Today, my *Zadie* and Tateh were called to the pulpit just to stand beside the

Torah as it was read because of the honor of my upcoming Bar Mitzvah and the

donation they had made for the privilege.

 With the droning on of the service I quickly lost interest again and

became involved with my friends in our weekly searching for the most sexual

passage we could find in the Bible held between us. I found *"Don't let your*

cattle breed with other animals. Don't sleep with another's bondsmaid,"

Gedaliah outdid me and we read the passage over and over, not believing we had

missed it before. We assumed we should *"not uncover our mother's nakedness"*

and what moron would want to *"uncover their father's nakedness?"* But *'Thou*

shall not uncover the nakedness of a woman and her daughter' gave us ideas we

had never considered and probably would not have without this inspiration.

'Thou shall not take a woman and her sister to uncover their nakedness beside

each other.' "What, did they know the Zlotkin sisters?" cracked Shimon and we

burst out in laughter that met the quick derision of the *alteh kockers* and won us a

sordid look from my father at the pulpit.

 But Gedaliah would not be deterred, and he said to Shimon, "With you

liking Sarah, you better read the next line," and we all read *"Thou shalt not lie*

with any beast to defile thyself," which we found appalling, although we had

heard of older boys going to the fields to visit with sheep. We all avoided our

greatest fear, *"Thou shalt not lie with mankind as with womankind,"* because this

was territory we could not even approach in jest.

 So, with everyone's attention turned toward the pulpit at the center of

the room, ours deeply involved in the obligated exploration of timeless scriptural

debates, and the *alteh kockers* torn between their conversation, Torah, and chastising us, no one noticed until 'the others' were through the door. And there were many others, and they had with them a Priest and hoes and axes.

We were naked before them. We were aware that trouble was brewing and that danger surrounded us. But, we could not carry a stick or hoe or axe for protection. A Jew cannot carry a handkerchief on the Sabbath, but must tie it around his neck like a scarf because it is forbidden even to carry something so insignificant. So, we stood there with nothing and they stormed in angry and mocking with rods and axes.

I had seen the Priest in town, but he looked wild and transformed. If not for his white flowing robes, one would have thought him a drunkard with his shaved head and crazed look. He yelled to the men, "Check the closet for blood," meaning the Holy Ark that held the Torah scrolls.. On this command, men came forward to the Ark, as a collective gasp was heard that they should approach such a holy thing with weapons.

They rummaged about until one pulled from the ark a bottle of the type that was used for our wine for blessing. Like wine it was deep red in color, but this red was darker and clotting.

"This is the blood of our missing child," the Priest yelled. "See, I told you, they use it for their Passover just as they took our Jesus's blood! Imagine how this poor child suffered at their hands! They surely defiled her as God is my witness. You must only look at them to see their guilt!"

With this the men started beating the congregants–bludgeoning them with fists and clubs, and mercifully not with the axes. But the axes were destined for another sacrilege as they tore into the Holy Ark, smashing the doors and ripping the red velvet cloth that covered it.

I thought that men would fight back, and some young men did defend themselves. But this was a lesson deeply ingrained as well I was to find. The men covered their heads and were beaten with only their cries as a defense. Others used their bodies to shield the old men and the children who were wandering about and took the blows to their own backs.

The most annoying of our *alteh kocker* brigade slapped at one of the
intruders with his cane. "You should be ashamed of yourself Wladyslaw. I have
known your family for sixty years." The young man turned on him sneering,
"Shut up *sheeny* dog," and hit him so hard with a staff that it broke the old man's
jaw and shattered his few remaining teeth. He collapsed unconscious at our feet.

One Jew seemed to lose the courage to be still and yelled back with a
rage he could no longer control. Reuven Applebaum was a tall, dark-haired,
intense young man. I had always liked him, the older brother of a friend. My
Tateh would say, "That Reuven is a dreamer. A socialist." But what I think
many did not like in Reuven was that they saw that he stood erect while they
walked stooped in the streets. At over six feet and broad he looked 'the others' in
the eye. "We feel as he does," they would say. "But that Reuven goes too far."
Well, here was Reuven going too far.

"Get out! Leave us alone! Who are you to come here and desecrate our
Shul?!" he screamed.

He probably hoped that other young men would stand with him,
because men will rally around a show of strength. He was wrong; the other young
men were frozen in a thousand years of practiced servility. For his temerity, four
men attacked him with staves and although for a few moments he stood his
ground, he was soon beaten to the ground and his blood flowed freely. With the
blows came the cracking of his ribs and his screams became silent moans. This
only enraged them further and in their fury they kicked and hit him without
mercy. A woman thrust through the partition screaming and threw herself onto
him not caring for her own life, and maybe her courage made some small
impression because only with this did they turn their violence elsewhere.

Rachel lay prostrate over her *besheret*, her *destiny*, so that mystery was
solved. Indeed, if Reuven was alive, their marriage betrothal was thus pledged
and sanctified for their courage had in those quick moments fused their souls like
so much molten iron at a forge.

Everywhere there was blood and weeping and a new smell that I had never known, but that I would learn in the coming years again. This was the odor of blood mixed with men's fear and it has a smell that is unforgettable once you know it.

My Tateh stood before the Rabbi with three other men. In his arms the Rabbi held the Torah tightly to his breast, the aged yellowed parchment sheltered in his beard and his coat. No one dared approach this one huddle of strength at first. But then perhaps they realized that these men were little match for them and their weapons and they charged.

A man struck my father with a stick and he only raised his hand in time to protect his head from the blow. A second blow caught him short in the stomach and I could hear his gasp over the tumult and chaos. I ran toward him, seeing my brother Isaac do the same from where he stood. Three other intruders rushed forward and one slashed at the Rabbi with a short whip meant for horses. The whip splattering the Rabbi's blood onto the rolled parchment which he held tightly as one would a bride from men's spoilage.

And just as suddenly from behind was odd Pesach, the retarded custodian who followed the Rabbi and his wife and did small chores for them. Pesach was madly swinging a large shovel. He lashed out at one man and then another. Most of his blows swung wild, but one met iron with bone. The man with the whip turned and looked at Pesach as if stunned that someone had just told him something that he could not fathom. Then just as suddenly, he fell to the ground like his legs had been cut from beneath him. Pesach stood before the Rabbi and only another death would move him from his station, for in Pesach's eyes was the look of a rabid dog whose master was under attack. Blood and brains swelled from the man's skull at this feet.

They left as quickly as they had come, carrying the dead man with them, called off by some signal. They left a frightening scene. Pews were overturned and covered with blood and men lay with broken, twisted bones. The scene left behind was like the carnage of the slaughterhouse. Yet, 'the others' could have done much worse. The axes could have been used on human flesh instead of holy wood. The attack could have lasted until no Jewish man stood upright. Women could have been beaten. Children could have been killed, God forbid. One man might never walk again, another would never work, but most would heal, heal physically from this assault. They could have killed men and if it had continued they would have.

But this was not their main purpose, not this time, and only the most ignorant of them truly believed that the missing child was any more than a runaway and that the blood was any more than that of a pig's. One or more of them must have placed the blood in the Ark the night before, perhaps the Priest himself. This was meant to be a demonstration of wills. A warning of who was master and who was servant. A reminder that this was Christian Poland. This was a behavior sanctioned by a Russian Czar who turned a blind eye or worse used such things for his own purposes in faraway St. Petersberg. For the Priest, this was a reminder to his flock who these Jews were and to remember that they had placed Christ on a cross to spill his blood. It was less than the punishment that the Jews deserved. For the men it proved to them that although serfs to Russia, there was something else still less than them.

Chapter 3

The Apprentice

My father and others wanted to take the Rabbi to his home to tend his wounds, even as they ignored their own. The Rabbi resisted and shook himself free. Hurt and bleeding, he would not be deterred. Instilled by the violence he had just beheld, he yelled at them vehemently.

"Idiots! Leave me be! Stop that! Get your hands off me! Find Pesach! Find him before they do! Oh that poor fool. And you three. Yes you, who do you think I'm talking too? Moses, Aaron, and Joshua? O f course you. Bring Reuven to my home and you better bring Rachel with him. I don't think you'll wrench her off him in any case." And falling to his knees with his head buried in the Torah in his arms, "My God, forgive me for not stepping forward to protect them." And with this he collapsed with men reaching out instinctively to prevent him and the scrolls from hitting the floor.

After the doctor did what he could, Reuven was sent to heal in our home. Rachel would not let him be taken elsewhere nor would she leave his side. The word 'beating' sounds so innocent next to 'knifed' or 'shot,' but a beating breaks a man. Reuven would walk with a limp the rest of his life. He lost his sight in his left eye and most of his hearing on that side. His scars would heal and his ribs would repair. He drifted in and out of consciousness for two days, and cried in his sleep. He tried by the second day not to fall asleep, as his own crying would wake him and it embarrassed him that he could not be stronger.

Pesach was not found until late Tuesday. He was left on the steps of the Shul. He was so disfigured as to cause those who found him to wonder who he was. Any of one hundred blows to his body could have been the one that killed him. The Star of David was burned into his chest. His belly was split open and filled with animal dung. His genitals were in his mouth. The funeral was the Thursday before my Bar Mitzvah.. Many who came for the funeral, stayed for my Bar Mitzvah.

It was a full week.

Two men had died, but there was little in the way of an investigation. The police spoke to a few and officials came from the government, but no charges were made on either side. An eye for an eye. The papers wrote the following.

A group of unidentified men, apparently under the influence of alcohol were involved in a brawl. Several men were hurt, two seriously. Police investigated but were unable to identify reliable witnesses. It is believed that the culprits were from another district. No charges have been drawn up.

On separate pages were reports of two deaths. One man was killed by unknown assailants. Another, a day later, was reported killed after being trampled by a wagon. "Those with information leading to the arrest of the wagon driver should come forward to the police to make a report."

****

My Bar Mitzvah was celebrated with the heart of a wounded animal. On a humble *Shabbes*, every Jew in our congregation filled the room. On Yom Kippur it would have been easier to find a seat. In the center of the room I stood next to our bandaged, but not broken *Rebbe*. Next to him stood the *Rebbe* of the nearby Yeshiva, who stood beside the wealthy Jewish owners of the local factories, who stood beside a Chassidic *Rebbe* and his band of followers. Many showed bruises and broken bones, some had to be carried, but would not be left at home. Around this center were Jews from the other Shuls in town. With them were Jews from nearby towns. With them were Jews from as far away as Warsaw. The crowd flowed out into the street.

No one asked me how I felt. No one anticipated great things of me. My voice did not need to be sweet. No speeches were given. As it could not be expected that my father could pay for a dinner for these hundreds, it was arranged that food would be served in a hall paid by a few contributors who would not be named. No music was played. No one danced. No one sang. It was a day to be proud that we could stand together, that we would not be beaten down. It was a day of intense sadness.

We are after all a people expert in coming together in tragedy. When God invented the word Jew he invented the word *tsouris*, troubles. Never try to tell a Jew you are worse off than he is. You will receive the argument of your life. Of course Jews know this, but among ourselves we are at least willing to compete over the matter of who is the most miserable. "You think that's bad, well let me tell you what happened to me. You shouldn't know from it." We are masters at misery and at wearing our misery on our sleeves.

However, this means that we are also masters at not being broken by misery. And such was the feeling this day. Our misery was great. It was real. It cut deeply. But what each person there was offering to the other was that we were not broken. "Oh 'the others' will bend us, but we shall not break. Look how we spring back. This is nothing compared to the pogroms of Russia, the massacres of the Crusades, the Spanish Inquisition, to marrying into my wive's family." Yes, the worst tragedy is mixed with humor and us laughing at ourselves.

At the time I was disappointed that I could not be a more inspiring emblem of the day. As the Bar Mitzvah boy I was, well, average. I made no major mistakes. I sang moderately well. My voice broke a few times, allowing the necessary comic relief of embarrassed laughter. My aunts cried from pride and my Tateh and uncles and brother stood next to me as a family.

Afterwards, I remarked to my grandfather, "Zadie, it's not how I imagined my Bar Mitzvah to be."

He answered with a remark that I often heard spring from his lips.

"*Man tracht, Gott lacht, Men plan, God laughs.*"

****

By the following spring I was fourteen and ready to work with my brother and father. What education I was to receive was to be found in Reuven. Reuven's thoughts shook my world, just as people thinking his thoughts were shaking the greater world. I often accompanied him to his never-ending meetings, traveling around the region. I had always envisioned us as one people. Reuven opened me up to our differences; God save us!

We were divided between political Jews and non-political Jews. Jews had led the barricades in the 1905 uprising in areas like Lodz and almost toppled Czarist Russia. But the politicos were divided into one hundred disagreeing camps. There were even Jewish anarchists and one had shot a wealthy Jewish industrialist, a certain Shmuel 'Amerikaner' Vayner, so nicknamed because he once visited America. "What Jew could actually be such a complete ignoramus as to go to America and return to Poland? He deserved to be shot," was Zadie's opinion on this affair.

There were Jews who wished a return to Israel, and others who thought such ideas were sheer fantasy, or even apostasy. And, of course, the Zionists were as divided as well. There were even those who favored building a Jewish homeland in Africa, in Uganda, for God's sake.

And each group had a song, and Reuven taught me each and every one. We sang them on the cart in our political wanderings. Many seemed like silly children's melodies, but the spirit behind these songs, lest we forget, was about to topple much of the world, not just my own.

Some Jews were certainly more religious than others, but he explained how many of the deepest differences lay here. There were the wild Chasidem with their dancing Torah and romance with God, and ultra-Orthodox who only valued strict learning of Torah and Talmud and thought the Chasidem were superstitious heretics. Did I know that Yeshiva students from one Yeshiva had only recently attacked another and pulled their Rabbis' beards?!

"But the worst, Tzvi, is that in the large cities many Jews exclude other Jews from their *Shuls*, and won't even allow others outside their group to come and pray? While some Jews are praying in *Shuls* that are adorned like churches, others are in dirty apartments and storefronts. This is what capitalism does to people."

"Reuven, why do you fill Tzvi's head with all this nonsense?"

"Rachel, it's good he knows of the world. He wants to learn."

"If Tateh hears you're filling his head with your socialist ideas he'll have a fit."

"I'm not filling his head with anything. He has a mind of his own. Don't you Tzvi? Of course he does."

One day I asked him, "So with all these groups Reuven, what am I?"

"Quite clearly you're a *maskeel* Tzvi," he answered without a moment's hesitation.

"And which part of Africa do the *maskeels* want for a Jewish homeland? Or should I ask, which buildings do we want to bomb?"

"*Maskeels* are not really political Tzvi. *Maskeels* believe that you can mix Judaism with modern advancements, with science, and with the occasional *shiksa*. That's right, don't look so indignant. I've noticed you looking at those pretty blonde-haired Christian girls lately. Don't deny it."

"There are Jews that allow you to mix with *shiksas*? Do the *shiksas* come to the meetings" I asked gullibly.

"No, just kidding. The *shiksas* angle you'll have to develop on your own I'm afraid."

Still, I somehow felt better belonging to some group, even without the *shiksas*, as I had been nonplused realizing that being just a plain Jew left me in a kind of limbo with all our internal divisions. I was a *maskeel*, and although I can't say I understood what that was, it was good to belong once again and to be someone.

"Oh, and by the way Tzvi, don't mention to the Rabbi or the anarchists, for that matter, that you're a *maskeel*; they hate *maskeels*."

So much for my peace and tranquility, short-lived.

There was also another part of my education with Reuven and Rachel living in our home. It was one thing for my parents to occasionally hug and kiss, but newlyweds deeply in love share a different kind of passion. Reuven would graze his hand across Rachel's backside when passing in some tight spot in the kitchen. This was tolerable, but Rachel would actually do the same to Reuven if she was sure no one was looking. How could no one be looking in a house our size filled with as many people as it was?

We had enclosed a porch for them, which I thought was cold, but they obviously discovered how to warm it. Divided from my room by only a window that was now covered with an old sheet, I often heard them during the night. What usually woke me was Rachel admonishing Reuven to be quiet, "Shah, or someone will hear us." Once awake, I wrapped a pillow around my head to shut out the noise which made breathing difficult, but I preferred suffocation to hearing my sister's moans.

I took to pleasuring myself with the occasional rat peering at me in the outhouse. I assure anyone that it is easier to remain sexually excited in the company of rats than your sister's sexuality.

And sexuality emerged in the house in other ways as well. "Rachel, are you losing weight?" asked aunt Rivkeh one Sabbath dinner.

"She looks fine to me, although I always like a woman with a little meat on her bones," threw in Uncle Yosl. The size of Aunt Eti, and his adoration of her, spoke to the veracity of his remarks.

Before Rachel could answer one way or another, Bubbie quipped, "Of course she's thin as a wire; why should newlyweds bother eating?"

"Bubbie, how can you talk like that?" responded Rachel blushing a deep shade of crimson.

"It's nothing to be embarrassed about Rachel. Your Zadie and I were just the same when we were young. He couldn't get enough of me." This was

more than any of us wanted to hear and so there was a unanimous outcry.
"Bubbie!!" Zadie sat in a certain shade of pink himself and shook his finger at
Bubbie like a parent at some wayward child.

   "Its only natural," was her reply. "One of God's gifts, and he certainly
handed out enough *tsouris* because there's always plenty of troubles to balance
the scales. That's why it's a *mitzvah*, a commandment, especially on the Sabbath.
Or at least that's what your Zadie always told me." To which Zadie began a
coughing spell and Rachel jumped up to get him some water.

   We were looking forward to the Passover holiday and the family being
together. When Uncle Yosef and Aunt Hannah finally arrived it was a sign that
the holiday had begun. My cousin Chava, beautiful and about my age, and I
were always close, but I no longer had her undivided attention. She was more
interested in Rachel and Reuven and in helping with little Jacob. And Rachel
was pregnant now, which interested Chava to no end. It also explained why she
had lost weight with morning sickness.

   The days before Passover were the busiest of the year. Everything
needed to be cleaned, dishes for Passover had to be brought out, pots and pans
had to be taken to be scalded to remove any trace of leavened bread or that which
had touched leaven bread, or that which might have been suspected of touching
leaven bread. The house was scrubbed clean to the smallest crack and crevice.

   It was every young woman's task to help in the kitchen with cleaning
and cooking. It was every young man's task to drag all manner of things about,
for there was much heavy work involved as well. So I was glad when Uncle
Yosef asked me if I would go with him on an errand.

   "Tzvi have you thought about what you would like to do?"

   "When Uncle Yosef?" I could not imagine what he meant. No one had
asked me this. I was doing what was expected of me.

   "With school. With your life, I mean."

"Tateh says I am to be an apprentice in his factory."

"Is that what you want to do?"

"I suppose."

"You sound tentative."

"Well, I don't much like the mill. And I'm not very good at it."

"What would you like?"

"I really don't know. The butcher has no one to take on the business and I know he talked to Tateh about my coming to work for him."

"Ah, a butcher. A good trade. Respected.. People always need meat. That would be some opportunity. Would you want to be a butcher?"

"Well, better a butcher than the factory. People come and go, you get to talk to them."

"Would you prefer to continue your studies instead?"

"At the Yeshiva?"

"No Tzvikala, not the Yeshiva. I don't think you're cut out to be a Torah scholar."

This I took as an affront, as not being a Torah scholar was a way of saying someone was not cut out for learning. I guess my reaction showed.

"No, no Tzvi, I don't mean to insult you. I just mean that you could learn business. You are very good at figures and I noticed you pick up languages quickly. Your Polish is excellent and I saw you are even reading a little German."

"It's like Yiddish, and Reuven gave me some books in German. And everyone speaks Polish, or at least the young people."

"Yes, yes of course everyone does. But your Polish is not Polish-Yiddish. You can read and write and you use it correctly. No one taught you that at school. You may not realize it, but when you speak to me in Polish sometimes, you switch from village Polish to educated Polish and there's a big difference. I wouldn't be surprised if you were also picking up a little Russian...Yes? I thought so."

This was all quite amazing to me. These were mostly things that I thought everyone did. They were not things that were appreciated in the village and so I had never concerned myself with them –more organ grinders' monkeys and trained bears.

"But where would I learn commerce?"

"In the city. You would live with us in Warsaw."

"And Tateh?"

"Just leave my brother to me. Is this something you want?"

I often dreamt of life in the city. Maybe that dream had more to do with my being deeply in love with my cousin Chava, but in it I always imagined myself as a young clerk in a bank wearing a fancy suit behind a polished wooden counter. In my dream, Chava always entered arm in arm with a girl who looked just like her, the same thick dark braided hair, the startling blue eyes, and the hourglass figure. After our meeting they would turn to walk out, but their dresses were such that their buttocks and legs were exposed from behind. Recalling this recurrent dream as much as any thought of learning something, my answer was obvious and exuberant. "Of course I would love to learn commerce!"

"Good, I'll talk to your father tonight.... And Tzvi."

"Yes Uncle?"

"There's more than pretty girls in the city."

"Who's talking about pretty girls Uncle Yosef?"

"Oh, I believe you were. But there are worse things to think about at your age. Come. We have a big package we have to pick up from the butcher and your Uncle Mayer has some fish for us. And since you've been working so hard, maybe he could cut you a *shtickl* of herring."

For the Seder we had tables set up from our house and my uncles'. The furniture was stuffed in the bedrooms to make space. Everyone was in a festive mood. Neighbors visited for a few minutes with everyone busy cooking and preparing, but unable to miss the opportunity to wish one another a *goot yontov*, a good holiday. My Tateh and uncles were also busy with the committee that provided for the poor. Although we had little, others had less, and others still had less than that.

Thinking about going to study in the city, I was so excited I could barely contain myself. I told Isaac about Uncle Yosef's plans for me. How wonderful it would be to learn in the city, to be in such a modern place, to work someday at a bank like Uncle Yosef or in *industry*, the last word said like something sacred and mysterious.

"Tateh won't let you," was his only reaction.

"Why not!? I'm no good to him here."

"Because Tateh is Tateh. That's why. He doesn't like the city. When did he ever take us there? And the way he is now, he's scared of every shadow."

"You're jealous. You just don't want me to go because you'll have to work harder."

"Tzvi, I hate to tell you this, but you're about as much help as a second shoe to a man with one leg."

"Then, you'll help convince Tateh?"

"It won't help, no matter what I say."

I could only hope that Isaac was wrong, or that given family pressure that Tateh would cave in. Family was a powerful thing, and what the family willed was difficult to resist.

Around the Seder table that night we once more recalled our exodus from Egypt, as we retold the story of Pharaoh and Moses. The children did not have to be convinced of the truth of the Seder's message. We had lived it during the past months.

In every generation enemies have risen up against us. In every generation it is everyone's duty to look upon himself as if he personally had come

forth from Egypt. And thou shalt tell thy son on that day, saying: "This is done
for the sake of that which the Eternal did unto me when I came forth out of
Egypt."

"Does God place them on earth to actually torment us?" asked Reuven sardonically.

"They should only be cursed," was Tateh's reply.

"They are only victims themselves," argued Uncle Yosef, "they are tools of the Czar and their Priests. Men do not do evil like that on their own."

And to this, nearly everyone seemed to agree and the storytelling of the exodus from Egypt continued. But Rachel interjected with an anger that had hardened her soft demeanor since "our pogrom" as it had come to be called, ours as to mean not someone else's pogrom, as there were enough to go around. "They should die in their sleep. No, I take that back. They should die painfully with their parents who created them and their children before they become Jew haters too."

"Rachel!" admonished Reuven.

"No, she's right," said Bubbie, "Only it should happen with boils and with vermin."

"From where did you get such a terrible idea Mameh?" Uncle Yosef responded sharply.

"From page twenty-four in the book in front of you. 'Boils. Hails. Locusts. Darkness. Slaying of the firstborn son.'" Bubbie was still plenty sharp.

"Tateh, tell Mameh how wrong this is to say such things. What kind of example does this give the children?"

And Zadie looked to me and to his other grandchildren thoughtfully. He was not shy of this stage that was set before him, but neither did he ever take his words lightly. He spoke as if Rachel and Bubbie's words had just tipped the scales in his own head and he was for the first time forming the thoughts that could mold his words.

"I think Rachel's right."

"What on earth do you mean, 'Rachel's right?!'" cried Uncle Yosef, his liberal tendencies incensed.

"I mean simply that she's right."

"Where is your *rachmonos*, your *mercy*, aren't we supposed to have pity even for them?" entered Uncle Mayer to the fray.

"Hmmmm....No," answered Zadie.

"What do you mean 'no!' This is absurd." Uncle Yosef was turning colors.

"No means no," Zadie answered once again.

"But Papa, isn't that *their* way? Doesn't that make us like *them*?" insisted Uncle Yosef.

Zadie was gaining momentum now. This was going exactly as he had hoped. He was like a deep pit that a tiger enters chasing the bait, sure that at every next step the meat is his, but at each step getting more hopelessly trapped. With everyone talking at once, they believed that they had the upper hand and that Zadie was all but vanquished, ready to surrender to their moral high road. Instead, he calmly rose and got his Bible and read. The pages he had already marked with two black ribbons. He was not being as spontaneous as he pretended.

Thus saith the LORD of hosts: I remember that which Amalek did to Israel, how he set himself against him in the way, when he came up out of Egypt.

Now go and smite Amalek, and utterly destroy all that they have, and spare them not: but slay both man and woman, infant and suckling, ox and sheep, camel and ass.

"From *Amalek*," *Zadie* continued, "there must be no life allowed to survive. For you see children, the *Amalekites* followed us as we came out of Egypt and attacked our rear, the old and feeble and children. From such evil we should not turn the other cheek."

Aunt Miriam was not about to let this go either. "So here's a knife Tateh. Who would you kill? You know where they live. We'll hold dinner until you're done fulfilling commandments. Everyone, no one eats until Zadie returns and has time to wash up."

"Miriam my darling. You're no dummy."

"Zadie are you going out to kill *goyim*? Mameh, is Zadie going out to kill 'the others? Can I go too?" asked Aunt Miriam's youngest, only four.

"No tataleh, Zadie is not going to kill anyone. Your Mameh has caught the one weakness in my argument."

"Because you wouldn't really kill *Amalekite*. This is all just exaggeration," said Uncle Yosef, sure that they had won the argument and exposed Zadie's foolishness.

"No, that's not why. If I could, I would kill *Amalekite*. No, to fight *Amalek* we need a real nation. A nation and an army. So these *Amalekites* among us will live on. And their seed will infect our world. The pogroms are only a beginning. We've gotten off easy."

How can you say we've gotten off easy, Zadie?" asked Isaac, bewildered. "Pesach is dead, Reuven here will never see out of one side, can barely hear. Others are cripples."

"Isaac, if this is easy, can you imagine what hard would be?" Zadie responded.

"Perhaps many would be killed, I guess."

"How many?" Zadie pressed Isaac.

"Maybe a dozen, maybe a thousand like in the worst pogroms in Russia."

"Why stop at one thousand? Who stood and complained? Who stands in their way? Why would they stop at one thousand?"

"Mordecai, enough!" said Bubbie. "You're scaring the children now."

"Then let them be scared. We must leave this place. We must find a place without Amalekite."

And out of the mouth of babes, "Zadie, is *Amelkinipe* everywhere?"

"Oy Rayzella, I hope not. Maybe in America there is no *Amalekite*.

Maybe in America."

And with that came the bitter herbs in the Seder ceremony, but we did not need to be reminded of the bitterness of our people who had been cast out of Zion with *Amalekite* set free.

After dinner we sat drinking tea and eating cake. Uncle Yosef took this chance to open a new topic of conversation.

"I've been thinking Shlomo. Tzvi is a good student. He should continue his studies."

"He's not much of a Torah Scholar," was Tateh's reply.

"No, but he has a good head for numbers. And have you noticed he's good with languages."

"Yosef, beggars here speak three, four, five languages. The more language, the more people they can ask for money."

"That's true, but not in the way Tzvi does. He has a good head on his shoulders."

"Of course he does. Otherwise his hat would fall off."

"Shlomo, I'm serious. He could learn business in the city like I did."

"He's not that smart. He was never that good in school.."

Reuven threw in on my behalf. "No, he's smart Tateh. I've given him some of my books and he finishes them as quickly as I can find new ones."

"Oy, now I'll have another socialist in the house. Thank you Rachel for bringing me this Reuven. With good deeds like that we can look forward to having the Czar's police at the next Seder to remind us of their rising against us in every generation. In any case, there's no place to learn business here."

"We thought he could come live with us in the city."

"No, that would be too much to ask of you and your wife Hannah."

"We've talked about it. In fact, it was Hannah's idea. Right Hannah?"

"Yes, Shlomo," answered Hannah according to script. "The city would be good for Tzvi. He would fit in well. With only one child, I think I would like to have a son for a while anyway. And Chava would like a brother."

"I couldn't afford it. The business you know isn't going so well."

"Shlomo, you know that's not an issue. Tzvi is my nephew and it's as easy to feed four mouths as three. Another bone in the pot, after all."

"You know very well that such schools cost money, a lot of money. I can't be such a *shnorrer*, I can't be a leach even from you."

This was more than Aunt Eti could stomach. "That's ridiculous and you know it, Shlomo. Don't insult Yosef like that. You would do the same for him. Would you not take Chava into your home if there was something calling her here in the village? Of course you would. Family should not talk like that."

"Thank you for answering for me, but this is different."

"How is it different? It's no different." Now Uncle Yosl was into the mix, with our family's penchant for always answering the question they asked, in case the answer might be otherwise.

"This is very kind of you two, but I need him here. Anyway he never took to his studies in any case. He never worked hard at it."

"Tateh I would like to study. I would work hard. I promise."

"No. Its out of the question. I need you here."

"But Tateh, I hate the factory and I'm no help anyway and you know it."

"Isaac, what do you think?" asked Tateh, knowing that Isaac would back him.

Now I was lost. Isaac was jealous of my going to the city. He was forever fighting with me and Rachel. I should never have told him. Maybe caught off guard he would have sided with Uncle Yosef to show he had a mind of his own and could stand up to Tateh and to impress Chava.

"I think he's a big help with the looms. He's strong as an ox." I knew it. That was that. He was even willing to lie to do me in. "But, we don't need him. It will be a year, maybe more, before he can contribute fully and this year is critical. It would be better if we hired a man who already could weave. It would be much better for the business. No, Tzvi would be a drain on the factory for a good time to come, even if I'm sure he would eventually be good at it."

Tateh was trapped now. Uncle Yosef had played his cards well and I was all but the rage of Warsaw.

"I can see what's going on here. Isaac, that is really so good of you to be willing to sacrifice for your brother, and Yosef, Hannah, you're being very generous. But we need Tzvi here. I'm sorry Tzvi, but this just isn't the right time."

"But..."

"Tateh, maybe there's another way," Isaac spoke up. "If Tzvi apprenticed with the butcher, we'd have money for a new loom. I know a man in town who worked looms like the one we looked at in Warsaw. The new loom would pay for itself and him. And maybe in a couple of years Tzvi can go on to Warsaw to learn commerce."

And before Tateh could say no, for he would have said no to this as well, Zadie finalized the deal. "So, it's settled." And turning to his son, "And that's my word Shlomo as your papa."

Over the next weeks we adjusted to our new circumstances, as if with each turn we could fit the mold of each change. I began to learn the trade of being a kosher butcher. Reuven was delighted in his new job traveling to buy cattle to bring for the *shochet* to slaughter. Each day for him was an adventure and meeting new people from the surrounding area he could talk politics to his heart's content, if not theirs.

The new loom and Shimon were quickly operational, and the mill would soon be producing double its former output in the best of days. Isaac was confident. People had a little money and Jews were getting work so they could buy. Even the little ones seemed to respond to the new sense of order and enterprise. Rachel kept a brave face, and tried to appear optimistic about the more positive upturn of events, if only father could recover.

Even with the business doing well, Tateh sunk deeper into his abyss.

He seldom arose from his bed and rarely ate more than a morsel of bread and a little soup. The doctor came again, but with the same conclusions. Tateh was weak and suffered from exhaustion. He had what the doctor called simply 'a condition.' I heard in whispers that they were glad that father at least was not experiencing the attacks of mania that he had in earlier years, which evoked vague memories for me of chaos and tumult in the house that I somehow knew we were never to mention. Now, we often heard him quietly weeping in his room. When he emerged from his bed, which took great coaxing, he sat in a chair and peered out the window as if waiting for someone to come down the street. He was waiting for someone to come and take him.

Finally the *Rebbe, the Rabbi,* came.

"Shlomo its time to get out of bed."

"I can't *Rebbe.*"

"And why not Shlomo?"

"Can't you see I'm sick? I have no strength. The doctor says I have a weak heart."

"Shlomo, listen carefully to me. What you are doing is a sin. You're a father of children who have no mother."

"I know *Rebbe,* but what am I to do?"

"Shlomo, what does the Torah say about what a child owes his father and mother?"

"It says a child must respect his father and mother, of course."

"Does it say a child must love his parents?"

"No *Rebbe,* I don't think so. Does it?"

"No, it does not. And why do you think that is?"

"I don't know *Rebbe.* I guess I never thought about it."

"Well, many Rabbis before me have. The rabbis say that your children owe their love to you no matter what you do here. Even if you die they will love you. But unless you get up they cannot respect you. So, what do you think is your sin?"

"That they cannot respect me?"

"Yes Shlomo, that is your sin. That your children cannot fulfill this commandment. So Shlomo, I am going to go outside of this room and you are going to get yourself dressed and together we will have some soup. Tomorrow Shlomo, I expect to see you in the morning prayer *minyan* before work."

"Yes, *Rebbe.*"

"And Shomo."

"Yes, *Rebbe.*"

"The Rebetzin will find you a wife. You cannot be so long without a wife and these children cannot be without a mother."

"But..."

"No buts. You are unable to act, so I have taken things out of your hands. What is needed for all is simply what will be done."

Chapter 4

Tears in the Fabric

We began at dawn and worked into the evening without respite, for the meat not only had to be cut, but salted and washed according to the dietary laws. Reb Cohen was built like a steer. He sank his hook into a quarter of beef and swung it onto the block like so much laundry. In a few yeears I had grown to nearly my full height, and gained new muscle as well.

From *Shabbes* to *Shabbes*, the butcher shop bubbled with life, helping pass the long week. Customers lingered on uncomfortable bent-wire stools, with hard wooden saucer seats, *kibbitzing* as neighbors came and went, drinking sweet tea from greasy glasses. Reb Cohen was not so much in the business of selling meat as providing a passage to women's lost youth. The women laughed and shook their heads at his exaggerated compliments, sounding deep sighs and smiling with those around them and the distant memories of when his words were perhaps half true. "You are such a *katchke*, someone will steal you away." Now a *katchke* is a fatty duck, but with us this was a great compliment. So be it.

After working some years and having a little of my own money, I summoned the courage to court Leah Rosenblock. Her mother was a widow whose only son had left for Paris and from whom they never heard again. They had come down in the world since the death of her husband who had been the cattle buyer some years earlier, a good job now held by Reuven. They lived meagerly in two rooms, a living area with a small coal stove and a bedroom that they shared. Froi Rosenblock made what little money that supported them with the sewing machine tucked in one corner. She was a good woman and encouraged the relationship because she said that I was from a respected family.

Froi Rosenblock would sit in the bedroom with the door open as Leah and I chatted in the parlor. I struggled to impress her with my knowledge of politics and my increased leanings toward socialism. The *maskeels* to which

Reuven had assigned me seemed too tame, and although I was not willing to identify myself with communists or anarchists, I thought that the banned socialist Bund held just the right romantic flavor. Being part of something that was forbidden was obviously attractive to Leah and it drew her closer to me when I spoke in hushed whispers of the many dangers I faced by going with Reuven to their meetings. I believed myself to be exaggerating about the police in the shadows. The opposite was actually the case.

Leah hung on my every word. In turn, I afforded her little time to talk. She would, however, share with me her drawings made of charcoal burned at the stove. She was wonderfully talented and her sketches of townspeople held a measure of life, portraying a sense of each subject's soul. One felt their movements and sensed their bodies beneath the folds of their garments. I set aside zlotys I earned and bought her a fine set of colored pencils, which was an extravagance. When she unwrapped them, she ran to the bedroom in tears. I was puzzled as to the nature of my crime. After composing herself, she kissed me for the first time fully on the mouth, biting my lower lip with the strength of her passion. Without a father, such a gift was a kind of attention she had neither come to expect, nor felt she deserved. From that moment, I could do no wrong in her eyes.

With her mother in the bedroom we sat on the small, over-padded, worn sofa and stole kisses. Snuggling, my hands brushed against her breasts, those breasts that had long been the objects of my fantasies. Leah no longer objected. As her mother seldom interrupted, we became increasingly bold. Instead of becoming more attentive, her mother responded over the next weeks by closing the door behind her. When we saw that she would not reemerge once the door was closed, I ventured my hands beneath Leah 's blouse to feel her ample breasts.

When I grew daring enough, I placed my hand beneath her dress. She did not resist. Not expecting her acquiescence, I was stymied as to what to do next. Reuven had told me that a woman should be handled gently, like a violin. I improvised a concerto, if not a symphony. For weeks I explored her body and ruminated over a plan to move her hand to feel me as well. I hesitated, fearing she would think me a deviate, be repelled, end our romance, inform the *Rebetzin*, the feared wife of the Rebbe. The *Rebetzin* would post notices attesting to my depravity.

As I equivocated over the how and when, by instinct she sought me on her own one night. I exploded almost immediately, smelling the soap from the sink nearby. These games went on for weeks. We talked, or I talked, she showed me her art, and we frantically learned the melodies of each other's bodies.

"Tzvi, I love you so much. I love the time we spend together."

"I feel the same Leah. You make me feel good."

"I think perhaps I make you feel too good Tzvi."

"Is there such a thing?"

"There is if you're taking advantage. A girl has only one reputation you know."

"I would never tell anyone what we do Leah. You know that."

"Tzvi, you miss my point. Your actions speak for you. Who you are and what you do tells others what you're about. I want you here more, not less. But our actions are interpreted by others. Don't take that lightly."

"I won't," I assured her, but of course, I did.

I got in the habit of staying so late that her mother would call that she was going to sleep and that I should say goodnight to Leah and make my way home. But she did not come out to check. We waited and petted through a week of this routine. One night as we lay feeling each others' bodies, our breath became so loud that I was reminded of Rachel and Reuven keeping me up at night in the next room at home, and I began to laugh. Leah gave me a look showing her displeasure and gagged my mouth with her hand. But, instead of rejecting me for the night, she deftly removed her underwear and pulled me on top of her. I awkwardly guided myself inside her and as I entered she let out a small cry. She pulled a blanket over us, lest her mother emerge.

We always made love covered in that blanket. She would stare at me as if searching for some answer. With her black braided hair and crystal blue eyes, I believe she was unwilling to let go of the attachment of our souls that existed between our eyes. We made love twice that first night. In the weeks that followed we made love two, three, and four times in a night. I would go to the butcher shop so exhausted that I once fell asleep on a slab of beef, my head pressed against the cold flesh. It soothed my crushing headache.

We shared the deeper feelings that two young people talk about when the barriers crumble between them. She began to sketch me on benches or sipping glasses of tea in her kitchen. Once she drew me naked, which she saved below her other drawings, hidden. It was the only time that either of us saw the other naked, as our lovemaking was between a jumble of clothes and coverlets, rumpled and askew.

We spent much of the time together when I was not working. She was with me when we stopped by my house one day. Entering together, there was a woman sitting drinking tea with my father. Two children, a little boy and girl were playing with my sister Rayzella and Jacob, and as I entered, the little boy ran to hide in the woman's skirts. I recognized her as Froi Seiznovitch, a woman who was the daughter of a sometime acquaintance of my mother's. Isaac and Rachel sat on the sofa with an odd look on their faces.

Father rose and introduced me to my new mother. I had never exchanged a word with this woman, never heard my father speak of her. I asked, "Tateh do you mean you are planning to marry?'

"No," he answered, "we were married by the Rebbe this afternoon. I left work early."

He did not even take the day off for his wedding. The extent of his explanation was that "we thought it would be better."

Froi Seiznovitch, who I supposed now was Froi Apfel, tried to make the most of it and had obviously practiced a small speech, which was more than my father had thought through to sooth the obvious discomfort that this situation would cause.

"I know that I can't be a mother for you; Isaac and Rachel, you're already grown. But I will be a good mother for Rayzella and Jacob. I hope we can be friends, and maybe even love each other one day. My children Benjamin and Reyzl will also be pleased to have a father, and lucky to have so many brothers and sisters."

Her words seemed genuine, but I was discomforted seeing that, although she was perhaps only thirty years of age, she looked haggard and drawn. I remember hearing that her husband had been conscripted in the Russian army, the family being unable to pay the tax to keep him out. He had died of some disease, a more common occurrence than being shot in the Czar's army. Coming from such a family that did not even have the means to pay the tax I saw this arrangement as a good deal for her indeed. My even crueller side thought that with this wife he may have volunteered. That much I held my tongue.

Still unsettled, I spoke words that should have waited. "Where will we all sleep?" As usual of late, Tateh had no answer and it was Rachel who spoke up and tried to ease the tension.

"We'll be fine. We're after all *mishpacha, family,* and Friya and her children are now part of our *mishpacha.* She'll sleep in the bedroom with Tateh, of course, and her children will sleep in the bed with Rayzella and Jacob. It's a big bed and they're only little. Reuven and I have been planning to move into our own place and Reuven is looking to make arrangements. Then Isaac and you can move to the porch and there'll be plenty of room.

At first we did try to get along. However, as Friya became more secure in her position, and I more entrenched in mine, we started to openly lock horns. She missed no opportunity to admonish me to my father for not coming home and being wild. She would do this pretending I was out of earshot, but in a voice loud enough so that she knew I would hear. I yelled that it was none of her business what I did. She was not my mother. Tateh took her side, telling me not to speak to my mother in that tone. By calling her my mother he incensed me further and I returned a torrent of angry, hateful words.

To avoid home more my friends Gedalyeh, Shimon and I began to frequent a certain tavern. It was, in part, a right of passage, and, in part, a protest with the smothering ways of our Jewish world which held you so tightly to its path. Between the time I worked, visited with Leah, and spent at the tavern I could also avoid home almost entirely.

The tavern was run by two old Jews. They looked to be in their nineties and they may well have been. Everyone, even the non-Jews called them *Bubbie* and *Zadie*. He remembered next to nothing from one visit of a customer to the next, and she had a memory for each debt owed them, despite her advanced years. Neither had any teeth. He could barely see and she could barely hear. They were so shrunken and moved so slowly that one could order a drink or two and fill an evening from the time it took for them to go from table to kitchen and back.

It was one of the few places where Jews and 'the others' both ventured, although always at separate tables. The tavern keepers were known to be scrupulously fair and never watered down their liquor, or, God forbid, cheated a drunk, which attracted 'the others.'. They kept a kosher kitchen, which attracted the Jews. Beef tongue was their specialty and it went down especially well with a slice of dark bread and schmaltz, chicken schmaltz, it goes without saying, because butter could not be served with meat.

This is the first time I ever got to know any of 'the others.' Although we did not sit together, we mingled between tables and sometimes bought one another drinks. Despite the ongoing tensions between Jews and gentiles in the town, relations were good at the tavern. This may have received a certain guarantee because of *Bubbie* and *Zadie's* grandson, or perhaps he was their great grandson. He was a man of enormous proportions and legendary strength. He was literally the size of an ox, weighing nearly 400 pounds and standing well over six feet tall. He carried barrels of liquor under each of his great arms that another man would have rolled across the floor. Of course he was called Bissela, which means tiny in Yiddish, as in give me a *bissela* cake. I never learned his real name.

No Jewish women came to the tavern and if Leah was to meet me she sent someone in from outside. However, some *shiksas* came with the men. These were not the kind of women that went to the other taverns. Between Bubbie and Zadie's reputation and Bissela's guardianship young women could come accompanied without shame.

One pretty blonde, well they were mostly pretty blondes, caught my eye. I must have also caught hers as I often looked up and caught her looking my way as I tried to sneak a furtive glance. I would arrange to sit with my friends at the table next to hers and we talked between groups across tables. Her name was Catherina. We became comfortable conversing, which was a wide bridge indeed given the gulf between us.

"You're not like the others," she said one day.

"What do you mean? I'm just like my friends."

"Yes and no. You're a Jew like them, if that's what you mean, but you're different. You have a head on your shoulders. You often look as if you're thinking. And..."

"And there's something else?"

"You don't look like your friends. You look more like a Russian."

"We don't all look alike you know, with long noses and dark hair."

"I guess not," was her reply, "but you look more like a Christian than many of us. From where did you get your blonde hair and light eyes?"

"Probably from some Russian," and we laughed. "And so I am different because I look differently?"

"No, it's not just that. You're unhappy with your lot, with being here in this town. They could live here forever and not know the difference."

"And you?"

"For me there is no choice. I am twenty and have no education. I have no options. My world is closed."

"But you're a thinker too. Many people with an education know nothing."

This may have been the highest compliment ever paid her and she leaned over and kissed my cheek, which did not go unnoticed by her brother.

Over the next weeks we often spoke, but had nowhere we could go. I could no more visit her home than she mine. One evening I asked if she would meet me at my family's factory. I actually said that I would like to show her the looms, but as I said, she was an intelligent woman.

I waited there with a lantern dimly lighting the room. An hour went by and I was certain she was not to come. Maybe she had changed her mind. Maybe something had prevented her from coming. Maybe she had only been toying with me. When I had given up hope and was getting ready to leave, she rapped at the door.

We kissed passionately. Saying nothing, we undressed. She first removed her blouse and stood for a moment as if unsure what to do next. Then, she loosened her skirt and let it fall to the floor. She wore no undergarments, and it was the first time I had ever seen any woman who was not my sister naked.

She was thin with small, pretty breasts and long legs. She was almost my height. Her waist was so narrow I could fit my hands around it, and her hips were full. Blond hair sparsely covered her, which was so unlike the full black bush on the women I had seen, another species. Few Jewish women had this kind of figure, being typically built fuller and closer to the earth.

She stood naked before me, unashamed. Forbidden fruit is always sweetest. We made love on some old fabric I had laid on the floor. She took me in her mouth to bring me to fullness a second time, which was something I had never imagined. It was not even one of the sins we would read to each other secretly from the Bible. Afterwards we laid together naked in each other's arms and slept.

We often met like this and I saw less and less of Leah, or my friends for that matter. Leah and I began to argue, which I to some extent encouraged to have an excuse to separate and go my own way. The forbidden sex with Catherina was impassioned and she would scream out when she reached a climax. The first time this happened she seemed to collapse and stop breathing, and I truly thought I had killed her. Then she opened her eyes and smiled wickedly at me. I tried to kill her again.

Once, after gaining comfort with each other's bodies, she climbed on top of me. I was not even sure what she was doing. With her above me, passion filling her face, she looked like some Norse goddess bathed in the incidental light of the lantern. I held myself back for as long as I could, an idea that had never crossed my mind before, trying to both pleasure her and record the vision of the moment forever in my memory. And so it has remained.

More striking than our sexual contact was our conversation. We explored our separate worlds, just as we explored the bodies that came from different peoples. She wanted to know all about Judaism and found it incomprehensible that Christ was not our Savior. She assured me that most Poles had no idea this was so. I explained that we were still waiting for the Messiah, especially in times of pogroms, and she showed an understanding over this that was endearing.

I also asked about her religion, which to her was something told to her as she could not read. She explained that Bibles were forbidden by the Church in any case and that Catholics were not allowed to read them. That 'they' would not read or study divided our worlds in my mind as much as having different Gods.

She was also fascinated with my circumcised penis and would turn it every which way to examine it. She said it looked like a small Jew with a yarmulka on his head, which made us both laugh. When we would have talked enough she would order me, "Now bring that little Jew to Church, he has some praying to do for his sins. Bad boy, *shtupping shiksas*."

My world was split between the kind of satisfaction a young man feels with two women sharing his bed, well we never actually had a bed, and the discomfort I felt at home. At first I thought that most of the conflict came from me, but as time went on Friya's true colors showed as well. She was manipulative and favored her children over Rayzella and Jacob. She frequently slapped her children as well as my brother and sister, but Rayzella especially received the back of her hand. My parents had almost never struck us. Tateh watched in silence.

For *Shabbes* night dinner she would fail to set the place for Reuven and Rachel, saying each time she forgot they were coming, and rush to correct her error. She left Isaac's laundry unwashed, saying he was old enough to do his own, despite the fact that he labored long hours and his work more than Tateh's was supporting her.

Tateh entreated her, "Friya, I know how much work you have. But won't you please wash his clothes as a favor to me? It would mean so much."

And honey would not melt on her mouth, "Of course Shlomo. What was I thinking?" But Isaac's good Sabbath shirt was ruined in the very next washing. She would send me to the dairyman for milk or cheese and always complain that something was not right, "Can't you even do such a simple task? Shlomo, I tell you he does this just to irritate me." And Tateh would make some excuse, like "Oh, that dairyman could never be trusted."

The worst was yet to come, however, as she began to spread rumors that I was breaking the Sabbath. This was not necessarily an untruth as my friends and I often ventured to a far off field to play soccer before sunset on the Sabbath, but some things that are done are known by many, but not truths unless they are on people's tongues. She did not strictly observe the Sabbath herself and regularly lit a fire before *Shabbes* ended. She had little religious education or spirit, but this did not keep her from talking.

Within a few weeks of her talebearing, Reb Cohen called me aside and told me that he would have to let me go if I did not stop breaking the Sabbath. A kosher butcher, he reminded me, is especially commanded to observe the Sabbath. When confronted, she of course denied that it was she that had begun the rumors, or had any part in them.

Unfortunately, Friya had found new fuel to fan the flames of rumors she had begun about me. How she found out I don't know, but a gossip always has her informants. Others learned from her that I was seeing a *shiksa*. This time she spoke openly.

"Shlomo, I can't have that son of yours, who is no son at all, ruining our family's reputation. He is meeting openly with a *courva*, a known prostitute and out drinking at all kinds of seedy places. And I'm not only thinking of us. What of that lovely child Leah that Tzvi is seeing? Mustn't we think of her reputation and feelings as well?"

This time my father tried to defend me, but when he asked me to confirm that it was a lie, that she was somehow misinformed, I could only say, "She's not a prostitute. She's a nice girl. Intelligent."

"You see, he doesn't deny it. Nice girls don't allow boys to do what you two are doing."

I have never forgotten the look on my Tateh's face. His whole face contorted as if a great pain seized his gut. He understood what Friya was doing, but could not condone my behavior. This was truly a *shanda* on the whole family, and a shame they would all have to live with. He pointed to the door as if to tell me to get out, but then hesitated stroking his long beard nervously and only said, "Tzvi, this will cost us all," and retreated to his room.

"I'm so sorry Tzvi," Friya continued, as always loud enough to be heard throughout the house. "But in such situations a family must protect itself. You are ruining us. I wish it wasn't so. I hope you understand that."

The ramifications from this were worse than even I expected. My entire family outside of Isaac, Rachel and Reuven would barely speak to me. When I went to visit Leah to seek solace and somehow explain to her, Froi Rosenblock told me that Leah would not see me, that she wasn't home. I could hear her crying from the bedroom of their tiny apartment.

By mid-week Reb Cohen said he needed to speak to me and asked me to come to his home after work. He told me to remove my apron. That I did not need to work that day and that I should take my things.

"I'm sorry Tzvi. We'll talk more later."

Chapter 5

Secrets of the Flesh

I could neither face Reb Cohen that evening, nor the weeks that followed. I was a leper, as much avoiding infecting those I loved as they avoided me. My friends were more understanding, although we seldom talked heart to heart. They were jealous of my having a Jewish girlfriend and *a shiksa* on the side, and were foolish enough to admire me, such is the shallowness of the relationships of young men and why they need wives.

Rachel and Reuven remained steadfast and welcomed me with open arms. They even offered to take me in, but I didn't want to invade their hard-won privacy. My bond with Rachel grew ever stronger and it was not her fault if she chose this time to have her baby, a beautiful little girl named Naomi after Mameh. The newborn brought the family together, forcing me to withdraw further from my main source of solace and comfort. They sent messages for me to visit when the coast was clear, and we carried on a kind of clandestine affair.

I wanted something special for Rachel and Reuven and on market day I went to the town square. It was filled with every manner of carts and wagons and makeshift stalls where Polish peasants and Jewish peddlers displayed their vegetables, poultry, and wares. Today, perhaps a hundred sellers crowded the area as I wandered among them, trying to avoid the hobbled chickens and ever-present manure. Most of the goods were used and broken, but there was an occasional 'find,' someone who fell on hard times selling their jewelry, a set of dishes, a crystal decanter, a clock, or even an entire bedroom set. I found a peasant woman sitting alone against the wall of the Church, wrapped in her shawl and babushka, with a few items spread on a blanket at her feet, layered in dust from the surrounding wagons' motion.

Kneeling, I saw that she held her handkerchief to hide a deformity, having only two holes where once was a nose. She was wary at my approach, obviously not used to strangers or perhaps the bustle of the town. Nor did she know of my world as she blessed me in the name of our Lord Jesus Christ. I tried as naturally as possible to avert my eyes and spoke to her in peasant Polish. We both knew that I could only be interested in the pair of tarnished silver candlesticks that lay half exposed and half tucked under her skirts as she sat cross-legged. I pretended to look at a few cracked plates and a crude wooden painting of Mary beseeching heaven.

I inevitably pointed to the candlesticks, which she gave a final rub with her sleeve and handed me. They were obviously meant for the Sabbath and had Jewish art inscribed at their base. I asked from where they came and she said they had belonged to her mother's mother. I hinted about their design, but I did not get the sense that she knew of their Jewish origin. I asked her their price and she named a figure that would have been stealing for me to accept. I hesitated, not sure I understood her slurred speech, and she named a figure lower still.

Two weeks earlier I would have offered her still less and bartered her to an even more unfair price, but I could not saddle Reuven and Rachel with a stolen gift of this sort. I took out most of the money I had saved, which I thought was a fair price and several times more than she asked. She became confused and suspicious, but I assured her that they were more valuable than she imagined and that I could not offer her less than a fair price. She tucked them back under her skirt and refused to speak to me further, turning her head as if she could be done with me like an unwanted apparition, no matter how I implored.

I needed a trusted arbiter, and thought to find one in the Church. I stepped inside, fighting the fear that this in itself meant certain damnation. I was dazed by the silver and gold and fantastic stained glass, so different from our stark, wooden *Shul*. So intent was my reaction to the painted life size statue of Jesus with the blood dripping from his wounds that I collided with the parish

Priest. Dusting him off, I begged his indulgence for the sake of a good Christian woman who needed his aid.

Caught off guard by any request from a Jewish youth, let alone one knocking him down in his Church, he returned with me to where the woman sat. We found another already in her place. The Priest was angered at my prank and conveyed, with a virulence that reestablished our expected distance, that I should learn respect. I apologized profusely, but he was dismissive and obviously chagrined to be duped by a worthless Yid.

Without hope of finding something to match the candlesticks I set off on my way, but saw the woman had stopped for water from the pump. Seeing me, she made her escape as from a madman. However, with one hand holding her kerchief to her face and the other grasping her wares in her upturned apron, she could only hobble a small distance before I caught her arm. Luckily the Priest had stopped for a parishioner and I was able to convince her that she could best be done with me by indulging my request, madman or otherwise. "What harm could come of talking to the Holy Father?" She herself may never have spoken to a Priest other than in confession and, given her rural life, perhaps not then. But a Priest she trusted and bowing her head she rendered to his hands the hidden candlesticks.

I explained what she had asked for them and what I was offering and he looked at me with renewed curiosity. Deciding, however, that it was not worth further discussion, he told her that this was as far as he could see a fair price, and that these were after all Jewish objects that were sin for her to own. She withdrew her hands as if burned and gladly took the money and the Priest's blessing and scurried off.

He told me that if all Jews were as fair as I that there would be less trouble with the Jews, not 'no trouble' mind you, but less. I thought to remark that if more Priests were like him we would be as one happy family, but had the rare sense to hold my tongue. Instead I thanked him for his help and offered some zlotys for the Church which he refused.

I took my prized find to the silversmith and for a ten groshen he polished them like new.

"These are fine pieces, and quite old," remarked the jewler. Holding them to the window's light, he asked, "Perhaps you would like to sell them," and named a sum that was twice what I had paid.

"No, thank you Reb Kaplan. They're a gift for my sister Rachel and her husband Reuven."

He walked me to the end of the street offering blessings for my family, and probably hoping that I might have a change of heart. He wished me good health and that I should soon find my own bride and happiness, although he could not say that marriage ever brought him personally much joy.

"Make sure you tell Rachel and Reuven about my offer. Someday they may have a change of circumstances, God forbid, but you understand what I mean. It's good that they know what they have here. A Jew can never be sure in this world."

I gave them to Rachel and Reuven Friday before that *Shabbes* with the note describing them provided by the silversmith. I told the story of how I acquired them and said I could take them to the Priest if they thought I was lying.

"Oh Tzvi," said Rachel, "there is no need to check your story. We know what you're made of. But how did you get the courage to actually enter a Church and talk to a Priest? What was it like? I just can't imagine."

We had both grown up on stories of Jewish children kidnaped to save their souls, not least of which in an account concerning the Pope himself that had covered the world news. But, more than this, there was the ingrained fear of 'other' that was embodied most deeply in the symbol of the church itself. I dared not tell her of the painted, bleeding Jesus.

"Your Reuven is rubbing off on me," I told her. "He would have had the

Priest speaking Yiddish and coming to the next meeting of the Jewish Bund," and I laughed for the first time in weeks. Rachel beseeched me to stay for the Sabbath meal, but I left before *Bubbie* and *Zadie* arrived. Of all people I could face them least, so Rachel released me with a tin of her chicken soup and several *kreplach, Jewish soup dumplings*, as my bond.

After some weeks of purgatory, a concept I learned from Catherina, I received a note from Reb Cohen that if convenient he wished me to come to his home that evening.

His wife greeted me at the door, although one could never call her demeanor welcoming. Reb Cohen was seated at a table drinking tea with sad eyes. He did not appear so large without his great apron and I was unaccustomed to seeing him without the smells of sawdust and meat of the butcher shop. He was studying from a large Hebrew tome, and closed the book and set it aside as I entered. His home was larger than most and his furniture finer, but its appearance was as disheveled as his wife. The table was in its own room, separate from the kitchen or living area, which I found remarkable. He wore a black silk robe and I had the sense of appearing before a judge in the ancient Jewish *Sanhedrin* court more than a butcher at his home.

"Tzvi, please sit. May I offer you something to drink? No? Well tell me if you change your mind. It's no problem." He waited until I sat and seemed to search for the right words.

"Tzvi, I have always liked you. You must understand that. And you are not a bad butcher. Not an artist with a side of beef, mind you, but in time you will be more than adequate. You're good with the customers, too. I dare say the women come as much to look at you as anything, but I was a looker in my day too. Yes, we've had a few good years."

I gave a half-hearted smile at the compliment and his attempt to ease the tension and this allowed him to say what was on his mind.

"Tzvi, given the situation, I can't keep you any longer. I know it's only part your doing and part this person living now in your home, but I cannot speak evil about her without her here to defend herself, and that would not help in any case. I do not abide *leshon hara*, talebearing about someone without them present."

"I know that Reb Cohen. I understand."

"A kosher butcher is like a *Rebbe*. It does not matter only if he's pious or not to people. He must also appear so. Although I think that you are a good boy at heart, the appearance of your behavior has crossed a certain line."

I was crying at this point, but trying to hear him out to show my respect.

"Tzvi, there's another thing that I must tell you."

"What's that sir?"

He got up and brought a bottle of good schnapps from the cupboard with two glasses and poured a glass for us both. Large for him, small for me. He filled his twice and looked at me inquisitively, as if the words he needed to say were inscribed in some strange tongue on my forehead, and he had only to decipher them.

"Tzvi, there are things I want to say that cannot leave this room. Can you agree to that? Yes? Good, then let me just say them. Tzvi, I loved your mother. In fact, I asked her to marry me, but she chose your father. Or rather, her family chose your father. Your mother, Tzvi, I think wanted to choose me. At least this is what I have believed all these years. I can't be sure, because she would not break my heart by telling me that this was so. She knew I could not have lived knowing that she loved me, but had to be with him. She was the kind of woman that would have held this to herself, so as not to hurt me more. Her family needed the bride's price at the time, and they were willing to take her without bringing a dowry in return. That is the way things were done. I never held a grudge and I have a good wife and we have fine children."

There was nothing for me to say, so I just sat and looked at him.

"Tzvi, when I took you as an apprentice I was hoping that it would somehow make me closer to your dear mother, bless her memory. I had hoped even to someday have you take over the business. Oh, I'm not naive; were it not for the person about whom we cannot speak, this would have probably all blown over, or more likely never come to light. That is not to say that you did not do wrong, but after all, who of us is perfect? *Emmes? Emmes.* True? True."

"This money Tzvi is for you. I am part to blame for what occurred as I recommended a certain woman to the *Rebbe* and spoke up for her. I was trying to do a *mitzvah, a good deed,* by helping to provide for your mother's children, especially the little ones, but you and Rachel too. You must believe this is true. I thought she would be a good mother for your father's little ones. I knew she wasn't perfect, but again who is? *Emmes? Emmes.*" And taking another drink, "Your father is a fine man and a good friend. But he was so sunken at the time that even the *Rebetzin* couldn't arrange a better match. Or so we all thought.... and Tzvi, you had a part in this, but we did as well, even the *Rebbe,* and I have seldom known him to err. We're older than you and are supposed to know better."

"This money is the price I wish my parents had possessed to pay your mother's family, bless their memory, as a bride price. It is not a small sum. I know this is a lot for you to take in at once, but it is also a lot for me to say, and what I don't say now I may not be able to say later. Reuven will introduce you to a man who will teach you the business of buying cattle. Yes, that's right. Reuven's job was my doing as well. We couldn't very well wait for him to get himself arrested by the Czar's secret police, God forbid, could we? And we had to find him work to support Rachel and the new baby."

I was so stunned as to be entirely unable to speak, so Reb Cohen continued the conversation for us both.

"Don't look so shocked. There's no job in this town that anyone ever got on his own. No Jew anyway, and probably no Goy either. In any case, this money is to get you started with Reuven in a business of your own. It's not uncommon for an apprentice who is sent out to receive a sum, although we will keep the exact amount between us. Yes? It is as if I have broken my end of the promise and must buy you out. In any case, that will be our story."

I sat there, trying to take it all in and Reb Cohen just watched me, waiting.

"You forgot my Zadie's first rule, Reb Cohen."

"Oh, and what's that Tzvi?"

"There's no need to invite misery to the table. He will always find a seat." And he and the others knew they had erred most terribly, and that I was only the first of other casualties to come.

In the weeks to follow, I traveled with Reuven and met the many men with whom his business transpired. Mostly we roamed the countryside and spoke to farmers, striking up relationships that led to our purchases, if not on that trip then on the next. Instead of buying for others, we were able to buy for ourselves. The profit was not always great, but it was clear that we could in time make a good living as our own contacts increased. We went northeast till Bialystok, south to Kurow, and to all the little towns and hamlets and farms in between.

Even given my good fortune, I felt ashamed at what I had done. My family continued to ostracize me, I could not see Leah, who turned and cried if I happened upon her in the street, and I was a stranger in my own home. Most painfully, my father hardly looked at me. Even when I had made my peace with *Zadie* and *Bubbie*, Tateh and I could not bridge the distance and hurt that had grown between us.

At first I had stopped seeing Catherina, but without Leah and with no Jewish girl willing to look at me, I longed for female contact. I missed Catherina for who she was as well. In another world, another time, I suppose we might have married, rejected as I was wherever else I turned. The world forced us into one another's arms, but at the same time forbade that union–a rose by any other name.

Catherina and I returned to our rendezvous, although we no longer spoke at the tavern or acknowledged each other in public. If anything, this made us closer because we shared our world with no other. We would meet at the factory as it was out of the way and deserted at night. I continued teaching her to read and brought her books as she progressed. At numbers she drew the line. "I can add and subtract in my head. That's enough. Women have no need to know more. No man will want me when you're done with me." And saying this she looked at me strangely, as if another question that she could not speak was on her lips.

We joined our bodies with the easy comfort of lovers. She was sexually uninhibited and open in ways I never found with another. Her lovemaking was a gift that she bestowed willingly without guilt or doubt. Once in the heat of passion she asked me to make love to her from "behind," but I told her that the Bible didn't allow it. This immediately gripped us both in hysterics, that on this I thought to draw the line. "And on all the rest we are doing you think your Jewish God is smiling? If so, you are taking me to the *Rebbe* tomorrow so that I can convert, because I assure you the Priest has not been so approving of all the rest I have told him we have done, and I leave out half in confession and double the penance he gives."

Then she missed a few of our meetings. This happened from time to time as we could not always make exact arrangements, but I still worried that there was something wrong. Waiting one evening, I was relieved as the door opened and she entered. I was about to scold her for her absence, when I took notice of her sad look and the fierce bruises welling up on her face. Before I could speak, her brother appeared in the shadows and hit me so hard that I collapsed. I rose to fight back, but saw that he held a knife in his other hand that he surely felt no compunction against using, so I simply stood and faced him.

Chapter 6

The Smuggler

Had he wanted to kill me, I figured myself already dead.

"Tzvi is your name, right? Well, you've gotten Catherina pregnant. How could you two be so stupid?"

I looked up to her, but she held her head down ashamed and I could not make eye contact.

"I will marry her," I said without hesitation.

"Yes? And you will be a Catholic?" for which I had no answer.

"No, I didn't think so. And I will not allow her to be a Jew... Don't look at me like that you hypocrite. I'm not being shallow, or some dumb peasant. I know what you think of us. With her hair and looks, where could you go that people would not know who and what she is?"

"What then?" I asked, resigned.

"What then? What then, you should have thought of before. Now, I will arrange for her to marry someone. She's a beautiful girl and, with the money that you and I will provide, we can find her a good husband who won't know any better, or at least one that will not know to count. You see, I am not some animal. I want what's best for my sister. That's probably why I didn't interfere until now, idiot that I am. You made her happy, and our life hasn't known much happiness. She has shown me she can even read and write. I know that you meant well and what that meant to her."

I looked to Catherina. "Do you agree to this?"

"I'm afraid Titus is right Tzvi. We've gotten ourselves into a trap."

"So, what now?" I asked. "What can I do?"

"Well, we'll need money. Unfortunately, the parents of the man I have in mind will expect more than I have. I have known that he had his eye on her for a while, but the family expects a woman of a certain standing and that would require money. She would be expected to come into such a marriage with a good dowery to set up their home."

And he proceeded to explain his plan. It was a complicated one and not without danger, but he assured me he had thought it through. With his contacts, I was to buy cattle cheaply from a man he knew, and we would both benefit from the profit of their sale. The cattle were actually already paid for by the Czar's army. It would be a "good deed" to steal from them, any real Pole or even Jew could see that. It was not even stealing, it was political sabotage. With the money we would soon have enough to pay for Catherina's needs.

I felt trapped and unable to disagree. I understood what I was getting involved in, but saw no other way. I could not give Titus money that was now half Reuven's that we needed for the business. Even now, when I look back, I do not know what else I could have done.

He left me with Catherina and I gathered her in my arms. I stroked her, and gently touched her face, lightly kissing her bruises. After crying and apologizing and trying to find another path we made love for the last time. We would marry. We would run away. We would go to America. We would go to Paris and have no religion and live by our wits.

We made love slowly and when we finished we lay weeping. For the first time and last, I walked her home and kissed her goodbye. Through a certain clarity that comes with all these years, I have come to believe that we were as one person looking at the other through a mirror. Her soul was the other half of mine, not so much in that we were meant to be lovers, as much as we each completed what the other lacked.

I did not hear from Titus for a time and Reuven and I continued our work. I thought perhaps that Titus had given up his plan and I was not about to go to him and find out. I was not to get away so easily, however. One day I was approached by a man who told me he was sent by a mutual friend. He offered to sell me ten cattle for no more than the price of two. It was understood that I was not to refuse.

We arranged the exchange, but upon receiving the cattle, I was startled to see they already were branded with the army's mark. "So whose mark did you think they'd have?" was the extent of his reaction to my surprise. I had not figured on this further complication, nor for that matter thought too much ahead. So much for that, it was now my problem and he departed with the money and left ten tethered animals in a barn where we kept cattle that we bought.

I knew a non-Kosher butcher in a nearby city who had tried to cheat us on a number of occasions. We avoided further business with him, but it was not an altar boy who I needed at this moment and so I rode to seek him out. His wife said that he was in a nearby tavern which was named Warm Rivers, which was strange because it was neither near water nor especially warm in any way I could discern. He was surprised to see me on my Sabbath, and more so when I suggested that we share a drink.

"So, have you invited me for this drink to convert me to your Jewish faith? I have often considered it with the tits on your women. Doing a pair of those would be worth burning in hell for."

I took umbrage at his coarse words, but thought a smuggler should not judge another man's sins so quickly. So I responded instead in his own coin.

"That's true Stanislawski. We like our women with breasts and teeth. I just came from your wife, so as your luck finds you a woman with neither, perhaps we can get on with the business at hand."

His hand went to the knife in his shoe, but having better prospects with money than women, and seeing my hand already bearing a razor, he decided to hear me out instead. "I see you have been to school Tzvi since we last met. So yes, why don't you tell me what has brought you out on your holy Sabbath."

"Let us imagine that someone had received from our goodly Czar a gift of his cattle. To whom might he go to bestow such a gift and do the Czar further favor?"

That depends on how kindly our lord Czar has been."

"Ten now, maybe more later. The Czar is a generous man,"

He looked at me with newfound respect.

"Ten you say, and do they know that they have lost their way?"

"The cattle are aware of their plight, but the Czar believes them already on his army's table devoured."

"Nicely done little Yid," he said taking a deep drag from his cigarette.

With this he gave the matter some thought. "Ten you say? And this man that has them now could bring them to someone who would take them off his hands? Yes? Well, I think that for these first cattle such a man could gain half the market price. If the first shipment presents no problem, more in the future. I suspect that this would bring a nice profit for both the one who may possess such cattle, as well as the one who had them slaughtered. Such an arrangement would be greedy for no one, which insures that everyone wishes it to continue without having others involved."

It impressed me how fast he calculated and considered all the angles, but each man to his trade and its intricacies. I might have struck a better deal, but realized that he did not want me to take my future business elsewhere. So, although perhaps not the best price, I figured he was offering me a fair price, complete with the relief of my burden, having sensed my anxiety as well.

We arranged a time and place for the cattle to be delivered the next day. With this settled, for better or worse, worse I suspected, I accepted from his a second vodka that I drank in a swallow.

Having made the deal, I became overcome with anxiety. Worry had me up the entire night turning our conversation over and over in my head. What did I know of such deals and to the extent such criminals will go? Where did I misjudge? I did not know, but Titus would. So in the morning I asked Reuven if he could do without me for that day and sought out Titus at his favored haunts.

"Humph, I'm only surprised you sensed a trap Tzvi, even if you could't see what it was. Not bad for a novice. I don't think that your man will arrive wanting to hand over his money. Better to ambush you and wack you on the head and take the whole profit for himself. You're inexperienced and so he probably doesn't believe there will be more from where these have come. Take him half the animals and demand from him half the price. This way he knows that five more are already available. Each time do the same. Now can you write me a letter? I can't go to my sister and have her think me ignorant."

The next day, Stanislawski awaited with a dangerous looking crony and wondered after the rest of my herd. "Tzvi, I believe some of your cattle have lost their way, no?"

"Yes, I received a better offer, but brought you these so you wouldn't go hungry."

"Little Yid, we both know that no one offered a better price than mine. Oh well, I'm a better thief than a murderer in any case, not that anyone would look so hard for the killer of a Jew out here. Very well. Here's the money for all ten, I will take these for now. Bring the others when you will."

"And you aren't worried I'ill just steal your money?"

"My little Yid, you are no more a fool than I am a murderer. Let us consider each other partners and live well off the Czar's bounty. Christ knows he won't miss them."

Through that fall and winter I lived well and gained knowledge of worlds before unknown to me. Women were available at Warm Rivers for a price, and I prayed my contact with them would not kill me. Fights were an everyday affair and sometimes just for the blood sport. I used my razor more than once. Reuven attributed my occasional absence to womanizing and youthful vigor, and I am sure used the opportunities to advance his own revolution against the Czar. Friya I bought.

"Friya, I have a problem that I need your advice on."

"Yes, Tzvi, and what could that be?" she asked suspiciously.

"I don't think its fair that I live under your roof and don't share in the expenses."

"I told the same to your father," was her retort, unable to let down her guard.

"Yes, that's right. I mentioned it to Tateh, too, but he wouldn't hear of it. And you working so hard with so many mouths to feed."

"I don't overspend."

"No, no of course not. It's just that there are four little ones and me and always more dropping by. I thought that I could give the money directly to you. It would have to be our secret though, because Tateh would feel ashamed."

"Yes, I see what you mean."

"And I would want it to be fair, as I'm making a man's wage. You won't argue me out of paying my part."

Each week I gave her a generous payment, clear to both of us that I was buying peace. I noticed that the cut of meat she bought improved and a new dish appeared here and there. Still, she was saving for her own rainy day as well. I dare say that her entire tone changed. Had someone suggested that I move out, she would have served as my sword and shield and argued my finer points to the entire family.

"You see, when you draw the line in the sand, a young man responds. Tzvi is so much improved, he's lucky to have a mother now in the house."

What guilt I had over my affairs was at least partially salved by the change in my father. He was still wary of Friya's tongue and she practiced it with him in much the same spirit as before, but he lingered now at his own table. Friya kept him at a distance from me as there was a certain intimacy she would not tolerate between us, but as long as we each played our roles there was peace in the house.

Bubbie and *Zadie* invited me to their home for tea at least once a week, if I would only come, but I could hardly risk their scrutiny. They placed you between them in their tiny apartment and through kindness and love you were picked apart to your most basic elements. It was they and not this new Roentgen fellow from Germany who learned the art of seeing through people to their bare bones. I was forever promising to come and always finding reasons to avoid their loving grasp. Often I made it as far as their doorway, but lost the courage to enter. Once, making my about-face, I was startled by *Zadie* coming behind me from still another errand.

"Nu? You forgot who lives here?"

"Oh, it's you *Zadie*."

"You were expecting the local governor-general maybe? He's coming tomorrow. Today you're the guest of honor. Nu? Bubie's waiting and she made a strudel, with apples like you like."

With things eventually arranged so that a third person could sit in their crowded rooms, and my running to the dairyman for cream, we sat down for tea and strudel that melted in your mouth. I closed my eyes with each bite, fearing that I was reaching some crossroads where they or I would not be there to share such small wonders.

"Something hurts you Tzvikala?"

"Oh no *Bubbie*. I was just enjoying the strudel."

"I didn't think it turned out so good."

"No really, it's wonderful."

"I thought it's undercooked."

"No, it's perfect."

"But the apples weren't so good this time."

"Really *Bubbie*. It's your best."

"You're right. Last time it wasn't so good."

"No, last time was perfect too. I remember." Knowing that this could go on endlessly, I started small talk about the factory and how well Isaac was doing with his many new ideas. We talked about Rachel and the baby and *Bubbie* and *Zadie* gave me the news about their children and grandchildren, here and abroad. *Zadie* was fascinated with America and an ardent Zionist. He was also excited about the new Yiddish literature. He approached each day with wonder.

"I wish when I was young we could have had all these things to read, but you were lucky then to have a good Bible in the house, and how many times can you read that Enoch begot Irad, and Irad begot Methusael, and Methusael begot Lamech? That's all we had, a few religious books. I worry that *Hashem* will take me before I can finish reading everything."

"Don't talk that way *Zadie*. You'll live like Moses till one-hundred and twenty," which is the most a Jew is allowed to expect.

"*Halevai, will it were so.* But, in the meantime, I'll count on reading faster. So, how is your new business with Reuven? You seem to be doing quite well."

"Yes *Zadie*. Reuven has a head for business."

"Reuven is a good boy, but he says that you're the one with the business head. He's really impressed with your wheeling and dealing. Are you being careful?"

"Careful? What do you mean *Zadie*?" I could already feel the vise closing.

"You know with taxes and everything. Everyone skims, but you have to be careful. If we all gave the government all the taxes it demands we'd be eating turnips and onions, but still you need to be cautious."

"We are *Zadie*."

"Of course you are. So, to change the subject, you seem to be doing better with your Tateh's bride lately."

"Yes, we're getting along better."

"And she seems to be nicer to everyone," added *Bubbie*.

"And serving better food," entered *Zadie*.

"And on nicer plates," noted *Bubbie*.

"And has a new mirror in the bedroom so she can fix herself up nicer," mentioned *Zadie*.

"And did you notice her nice new dress for Shabbes?" asked *Bubbie*.

And I knew that they knew that all was not kosher and hoped that all they suspected was our being light on taxes. On parting we kissed and hugged and I received a package of strudel in newspaper, tied with string, that I was to be sure to return the next time I came because string you can always use again.

"It was so wonderful to see you Tzvi. You're good looking like in a painting. And Tzvi?"

"What *Zadie*?"

"Watch the company you keep."

"*Zadie*, I'm not seeing Catherina anymore."

"And who's talking about that nice *shiksa*, may she live and be well with some nice husband?"

So, in addition to Roentgen's x-rays, they were obviously employing the Czar's secret police. What was I to do with them?

It was an odd dilemma that confronted me over this period. Money was coming in from my legitimate business with Reuven and from my illegitimate dealings with Titus. My limited ability to spend this money without drawing attention was akin to fitting into a pair of pants that was now many times too small without bursting at the seams. How could others not notice?

My business with Reuven also flourished because of my extra cash. Some of this I was able to offer over the table, telling Reuven that since I did not have a family to support that I could reinvest more in our joint venture. Other monies I paid under the table to sweeten the deals we received. As astute as he was, he was unsuspecting of why we should get our cattle so cheap or the best of the pick, instead of the worst they often left for Jewish traders. I also offered more money for Titus to channel to Catherina, and although a hardened criminal, his love for his sister insured that the money saw its way there. I wanted to help my relatives, but only the legitimate earnings could be used as such.

I began to invest the money by giving credit and loans to farmers or the people with whom we traded. This could be kept private because they no more wanted their debts known than did I.

One merchant who had a run of bad luck left town during the night, owing me a tidy sum of money that I had lent him when his business collapsed. He was an inveterate gambler and once even tried to bet away his debt with me. "What do you say to double or nothing with the dice Tzvi?" I was almost relieved to see this sum of money lost, less to hide. But the dice landed in my favor, and he owed me double. I assured him that simply paying the original debt would be adequate. I could wait.

Upon returning, I learned he had skipped town. His neighbor asked me to wait, that the merchant had left something for me. She produced a picture or photograph wrapped in cloth that I simply threw into the cart, thanking her for her trouble. At the end of the day, unloading the cart, I came upon the forgotten picture. What was this man leaving me? His photograph to enjoy? Instead I found a Russian icon with Jesus's crown encrusted in gold and jewels.

I thought to pawn it at the next opportunity and eventually found a dealer who might deal in such objects.

"Good day sir. How may I help you?"

"I have here an icon for you to appraise."

"Not a bad piece. How did you come by it? I am sorry to ask, but I prefer not to deal in stolen goods."

"It was paid on a debt."

"You have some proof?"

"I have the man's mark and a note saying that the icon is mine to do with as I need. He even had his neighbor witness. A bad business man, but honest."

"Maybe that was why he was a bad business man. But that's another conversation. Let me take a look. Fair art I should think, and it has a weight of gold. The jewels are real, if not the best. Let's weigh it against this old photograph. It looks to be about the same size. That way we can get at least a rough estimate of the gold. The gold weighs about a 100 grams, more or less. And the painting is probably worth half of that in addition, I should think. The jewels worth that much again. How about you take something in trade? I can give you more that way."

"I would rather have cash, unless you would give me the same amount of gold. The additional worth of the jewels can be your fee."

"A smart fellow you are. I can see you've done this before. Less haggling this way, I agree.

But maybe you prefer these loose gems I have? Even more transportable and who knows when one might need to travel quickly in the night in such times."

"And what makes you think that I might have such a need?"

"Ah my young friend, because that is my trade. Half is to judge the item and half is to judge a man's need. You're a Jew. Don't worry I hold no prejudice. My grandfather was a Jew in fact, but you would not know that of course. As a Jew, you would feel safer going to a Jewish pawnshop. You would be less afraid of being cheated and you would be right. So, you come to me and that means that you have something to hide. A man that needs to hide, often at the next step needs to run. Voila!"

Once again I learned the lesson to respect each man at his trade. You will no more trick a butcher over a piece of meat than a tailor over a cut of cloth. Each learns his trade to survive. I sensed that the more I learned from each, the greater my own chance of survival. The pawnbroker showed me about diamonds and explained.

"Leave your cart here and go down to the jeweler with these two stones and ask him their value. I will watch your cart and horses."

"That won't be necessary. If you wanted to cheat me, you wouldn't send me down the street. My wagon is poor collateral after all."

"Come. I will show you how you sew them into your pants."

So, even through the pawn shop who took such items the man's debt was repaid with a handsome profit. What was I to do? What's more, I now had a way to transfer my cash into something more easily hidden. We became friends and from him I learned to judge a diamond or ruby. We often exchanged stories of our *Zadies*.

His was also the first home of 'the others' that welcomed me, or for that matter that I ever entered. His wife would serve me cheese and bread, knowing that I would not eat meat in a non-Jew's home. We would sit in his shop or his parlor and exchange stories. He was a worldly man who had for some years lived abroad, escaping the police during the social unrest of the end of the last century. He was not the first man of relative wealth that I met who talked of socialism and the oppressed poor, apparently oblivious to what such revolution would mean to their own wealth.

"Its funny this love and hate between Poles and Jews," he said one day. This was news to me, as he was the first Pole to ever show me anything like love.

"I see you doubt about the love. Have you never heard of Mickiewicz's *Pan Tadeusz*. He was our greatest poet and this was his most famous work. It is an epic of Polish patriotism. And who do you think is the main character? A Jewish innkeeper named Jankiel, who portrays all that is honest and wise and patriotic."

"It's too bad then that most Poles cannot read," was my response.

His most prized possession was a plumed helmet and leather-encased epaulets of a cavalry officer that had been worn into battle for Napoleon by his grandfather.

"My father said he was a great hero and here are his medals awarded by the Grand Duchy of Warsaw to prove it. The English infantry had formed great squares of men with their bayonets held out like thorns, thwarting the Polish

cavalry. This way, they were slowly devastating the horse soldiers with rifle fire.

Cavalry, you see, cannot charge an infantry square, but must catch them out in a

line or spread them out somehow, and then it's a matter of slaughter. My

grandfather charged a square like a madman, forcing his horse against its will

into the block of men. He fought like a demon right through the square and

emerged from the other side with his sword covered in blood and a British flag,

his legs bleeding from a hundred wounds and a bullet in his side. He made it

back to his line and collapsed handing the flag to his colonel. Seeing his bravery,

and emboldened by winning a battle flag, which you know is the greatest thing a

man can do in battle, his comrades would not be outdone. The Polish horsemen

threw themselves into the British squares with abandon. Hundreds died, but they

won the day. He was made captain, and so you see a Jew can fight if given the

chance like any man. Better I would say, because he always feels he has to prove

himself."

As a token of our friendship and our Jewish link, he gave me a silver

mezzuzah.

"He lived as a Catholic, but always kept this on his door. When I was a

boy I thought it was a whistle and only on his death did I find this scroll with

Hebrew writing inside. I think it should be owned by a Jew. What does it

mean?"

"Its from the *Shema*," I explained, "the holiest of Jewish prayers. It

probably predates the time of Moses." '*V'hayu ha-devarim ha-eyleh asher anochi

m'tzavechah hayom al l'vavechah.*'"

"Thou shalt teach them diligently onto thy children," he replied.

"How did you know?"

"Because he would tell me these words in Polish all the time. I guess he

wanted me to know."

"Are you sure you don't want to keep this?"

"No, all the more reason it should be in a Jewish home."

"Yes, it should. For the prayer ends, 'thou shalt write them upon the door posts of thy house and upon thy gates."

And so, I lived my life. Taking small steps more backward than forward.

And then, came my Bubbie's murder and Zadie's death.

Chapter 7

Eye for an Eye

The *Rebbe* spoke of a *tzaddick*, one of the thirty-six souls upon whose value the world is allowed by God to exist. Our family was touched by his words, because we believed this to be true, so holy and without blemish did we hold this man. We understood that most of what was good in who we were and how we behaved came from and were sustained by this man.

For all matters he was sage counsel and open arms. He could speak with his combination of love and wisdom, and no one was capable of keeping him and his insights at a distance. Indeed, if you did not arrive at his doorstep, he would know to come to yours.

"So, you have a glass of tea and a *bissel* cake, just a tiny bite, for an old Jew? I'm hiding from *Bubbie*. You have to help me. Sixty years and I'll never understand that woman! But I didn't come here to complain. You know, come to think of it, we haven't talked for a while."

And within the hour your troubles were poured out and your pain was diminished, salved, halved, understood.

As always in such times, I thought of Mammeh and how she would feel.

"Mammeh, *Zadie* died."

"I know child. You are very sad, no?"

"Yes Mammeh, I am very sad."

"He was an old man and old men die *Mamehla*."

"Tateh is lost in his own world too Mammeh."

"Father loves you."

"Yes, I know he does, but he cannot reach out to me."

"He loves you no less."

"Yes, but he is trapped inside himself and inside his own sadness."

"He wishes to speak to you and be with you."

"Is that enough Mammeh?"

"It is all he has."

"And now *Zadie* is gone as well."

"He is within you and will emerge with time. You have his caring and his love. From *Zadie* you have wisdom and faith. This will allow you strength on your journey that others don't have. But there must be a journey. The *shtetl* cannot hold who you are."

"How can we go on without him Mammeh?"

"We find a path."

I asked the *Rebbe* later at the house of mourning if he truly believed that Zadie was one of the thirty-six.

"Let's keep an eye on how the world goes over the next few weeks," was his only answer. He took my hand and talked to me of his boyhood friend. "Actually Tzvi, as a boy he was much like you. In many ways you are more your *Zadie*'s son than is your father." With this he closed his eyes and drifted off in a murmur of verses from 'Wisdom of the Fathers.'

Zadie had died of a broken heart not a month after *Bubbie* was murdered. He could not survive, he said wryly as he lay dying, without errands to run. Oh, it could not be charged as murder, but everyone knew the truth. She had gone to the store late one Saturday after the Sabbath ended to buy a few things, as our stores could not open on the Sabbath and were not allowed to open on their Sunday, allowing only a few hours to purchase odds and ends Saturday evening after dark.

She was trampled by a droshky driven wildly by two Poles. They stopped some quarter of a mile further to check what was caught in the wheels of their carriage. They were so drunk that they could not even understand that it was a human life that lay mangled in the wagon works. They were relieved to learn that it was a Jewess, as had they killed a Polish woman they would have had to answer to the law. As is, it was recorded as an unfortunate accident.

The driver was a hooligan who was often in trouble around town and one who I believed was part of our Pogrom years earlier. The man accompanying the driver was from a wealthy family, semi-noblemen, and perhaps not wholly without conscience. His father came to make amends, finely dressed and clean shaven, driven by his man.

"Is Mr. Apfel at home?"

"I am Mr. Apfel. Who wishes to know?"

"I am Mr. Kowalski. I am sorry to say that my son was accompanying the man involved in this dreadful accident. It was my droshky, but my son you understand was not driving."

"And you dare come to my door?"

"It was, as I said, dreadful, but they were just being young men, and we've punished him accordingly."

"You have sent him to prison then?" asked Tateh.

"No, of course not. Don't be absurd. I wish to make some compensation. I came to discuss the terms. They after all did not commit a crime. It was an accident."

"It was an accident that they were so drunk that they were sure to kill someone?"

"We understand your anguish. We would feel the same."

With this Tateh exploded. "Don't tell me you would feel the same. If it was your mother, the man would be in prison right now. If it was your mother, you would have paid the guards to beat him so that he would have arrived at his trial as mangled as your mother. If it was your mother, you would act to break whatever business his family was in and if laborers, his father and brothers would never again work in this town. They would have to take to the road. If it was your mother and the boy's father came to you like this, you would beat him with a whip. That things are the way they are we will have to live with, but don't sicken me with your money or expect that I'll ease your feelings of guilt. For that you have your Church. I am sure that the donation of this sum will bring its blessings. Now get out from my house before I do something that I will live to regret."

"Just like a Jew, demanding an eye for an eye."

"Even on this you're ignorant. An 'eye for an eye' in the Bible means offering something of equal value, never revenge. What can you offer me of equal value for my mother? Please go now, from what I have seen of your son he will be punishment enough to you."

With this, the man left, but that was not the end of it. He returned an hour later still dressed in his fine attire seated in the droshky that had been the instrument of *Bubbie*'s death. His face was beet red and the veins showed in his neck. He methodically stepped down from the carriage, removing an ax from the floor board as he did. He detached the horses from their yolk and fixed them to a nearby post. For the next hour he hacked and chopped at the droshky until it lay in a splintered heap. Satisfied with his labor, he threw the ax in the dirt and walked away, leading the horses by hand. I never understood if he destroyed this costly vehicle as a sacrifice or as a demonstration of his anger at father. There were few such vehicles in town, with fine leather trim and lanterns. Many people came by to see it lay in effigy and weeks passed before it was removed.

I myself was drowning in guilt. I had dealings with the driver on several occasions in my interactions with the seedy element that I acquaintanced. I feared that this was some type of revenge that was calculated to cause me the most pain, but that he thought would offer me no recourse. Where he miscalculated was that I was no longer a docile Jew. Men changed when mixed in the vat of other worlds. For better and for worse, I had changed greatly.

Once again I sought out Titus at his favorite table running his labyrinth of criminal and revolutionary endeavors. Titus and a number of men were involved in heated discussion. One could always tell when these men were talking of matters that worried them as the amount of smoke that wafted up from the table became an impenetrable fog, masking their failed courage. I could also see that Titus had the upper hand, as he smoked his cigarette more leisurely, his chair tilted back, displaying a nonchalance that I doubted he felt.

Seeing me, Titus dismissed the men and beckoned me to his table. "Tzvi, come share a glass with me. I am sorry for your loss Tzvi. It was terrible that a good woman should die this way. Jesus bless our grandmamas."

"Thank you Titus. I appreciate your words. Titus, could I ask you something?"

"Of course Tzvi, what's on your mind?"

"Do you think that this animal could have killed my grandmother on purpose?"

"You have had dealings with him before?"

"Yes and no. We crossed paths several times without good will. On one occasion it had almost come to a fight, but I think he thought better of it, hearing that I did not hold back like other Jews. He's a coward, so this might well be the way that he would seek retribution for his damaged pride. He would not confront me directly, of this I'm quite certain."

"I'll ask around. If I offer some money to grease the wheels, we can get to the truth. He's a fool and he will have said something to someone along the way if he had any plan in what little brain he has."

"I will pay whatever it takes."

"Don't worry about that *żydki, my little Jew*, I have never much liked that braggart and if I find out that he did this on purpose I will have others deal with him as well. This is not a matter for the police."

I would not have been as merciless, as even with money spread generously it appeared that he was guilty of reckless manslaughter, not murder. He was too stupid and too cowardly they thought to plan a murder. But as the saying 'thick as thieves,' Titus's friends found him in a drunken stupor one night. They might have even bought him drinks to loosen his tongue. They placed him under the wheels of a carriage and broke both his legs badly, rolling over them back and forth several times.

"Don't feel too badly Tzvi. There were many debts paid with that. He crossed one too many individuals. I mean, he had it coming to him one way or another. You're a favorite around here Tzvi. Don't you realize that? He may not have killed your grandmother on purpose, but he did brag that he hoped to get good and drunk so he could go out hunting *Yids* again. He deserved what he got. And don't worry, it will not come back to you either. It is a perfect crime. No one will for a moment believe that good Catholic criminals would seek revenge for a Jewish grandmother's death. It's unimaginable."

Perhaps it is a good measure of how I had changed that although I could not for a moment have passed or carried out such a sentence, I was satisfied that it was just. I felt that my grandparents' deaths had been in part avenged. Speaking with Titus on this personal level, I was able to broach another topic that haunted me.

"Titus, I know you would rather not speak of it with me, but how is Catherina and the baby?"

"Catherina's doing fine. She's not in love with this man, but he treats her well enough. Don't forget, a Polish woman doesn't expect to be treated like your Jewish wives. She's happy enough having a roof over her head and books from the new library. He doesn't beat her and he wants a home and family. A good fellow overall. Better even then I'd hoped."

"And the baby?"

"Do you really want to know about the baby?"

"No, you're right, but perhaps only if it is well."

"It is well Tzvi."

"Thank you Titus."

"I won't mention to Catherina that you asked. You understand."

We had no sooner finished the *shiva* mourning period for *Zadie* when an army detail came to arrest me. Friends of Titus warned me minutes before they arrived. Titus had already gone underground. He was wanted for more serious crimes and sedition, but had a series of safe houses to hide in between his criminal and political ties.

An informer turned me in. A man who owed me a considerable debt that I had allowed to go unpaid for months without even mentioning it to him saw it as a way to end my eccentric dirty Jewish 'usury.' The report was indirectly confirmed to the police by the gossiping of Friya who had mentioned to any number of people that she suspected I was up to no good, and that she would have nothing to do with my money.

The unit that captured me turned me over to a unit that turned me over to a unit, following the Russian bureaucratic penchant for secrecy and a way of thinking in which no unit of the army ever trusted another and so was built on layers within layers, each watching the other. Some units beat me badly, whereas others merely passed me along like so much laundry.

For two weeks I lay in various cells, sure that I had been abandoned. "What else did I deserve?" I thought to myself. Look at the shame I had brought on the family, not to mention that the Russians might not settle for punishing me alone. The investigators hinted at exiling my family to Siberia, or depriving my father of his license to conduct business. Ours would not be the first family locked out of its business and forced to beg on the doorstep of their former establishment. Had they not taken away my belt, I would have hung myself.

The various cells were a taste of prison and were meant to loosen tongues in hopes of leniency. At first, I was placed in a large cell with a mix of criminal and political prisoners. The politicos showed solidarity, protected one another, and used their time in prison to further their revolutionary activity. They identified my crime as close enough to a revolutionary act and I was protected. Indeed, many of them were Jews, or one should say former Jews, as they had rejected religion to the man.

Later, I was placed in cells crowded with criminals, deviates, and madmen. Had I not been studying at their university with Titus, I don't know what would have come of me. Two approached me not ten minutes after I entered their cell.

"So, what are you in for?"

"Nothing, I'm innocent."

"Aren't we all? Any money?"

"And what's it your business?"

"We could join together, buy some liquor from the guards or some cigarettes. For the right price, they'll bring us one of the woman prisoners. Let's see what you got."

"Fuck off," was my response. "One step closer, you spend the rest of your time in prison with no teeth."

"Oh, so we have a tough one here. Let's just see how tough you are."

With that, I understood that they thought they had my measure. There were two of them and we lived in a world where a Jew did not fight back. I grabbed the larger man as he stepped toward me. I used his forward momentum and pulled him into the wall, slamming his skull against the stone. Not letting go of him, I brought my knee up into his face, most likely breaking his nose and rendering him too dazed to stand.

I readied myself for his partner, but he didn't bother. He let his partner lay where he dropped, having no more use of him. He walked back to his corner and slid down the wall next to another fellow, lighting a cigarette with no more to say, but the words "dirty *sheeny*." I would live through his astute religious commentary, however. I had grown up with it on the streets from a better class than him.

The next day they shook another man down for some rubles that he had hidden in the lining of his shirt. The guards did not consider it enough to bring them a woman, but instead threw a peasant boy into the cell. "Consider it a favor," they said. "He's prettier than any of the women right now and has a nice fat ass." The lad knew what awaited him as testified by the bruises on his face. He submitted with only token struggle and much pleading to being raped by the three criminals. Two others took the opportunity when offered them, as long as it was available. The boy simply closed his eyes and cried out to Jesus and Mary through his tears. The only blessing he received from his Lord was to lose consciousness before the last two men took their turns.

Eventually, I was brought to a more permanent headquarters. Here, there were only two or three to a cell which meant some safety from other prisoners if you were lucky with the cell mates you got, and terror if you were not.

I was led from my cell into a sparsely furnished room. Three men entered in uniform and, without so much as a word, violently stripped me of my clothes. I do not know if it was expected that they beat me or just humiliate me, but as if an afterthought the roughest of the men hit me in the kidneys. The pain sent me from the chair to my knees.

At this point an officer entered with another man in a suit, sending the soldiers away. Instincts told me that I had more to fear from these refined men than from the coarse soldiers. The officer was of middle rank, a captain I believe, and the man in the suit was young and had the look of an intellectual with pale skin, thinning hair and wire-rimmed glasses. He seemed to fit more the part of a school teacher than an intelligence officer in a police unit. The strapping officer clearly was subordinate to the thin, anemic-looking civilian and deferred to him. I knew from whom I had most to fear.

The room was well lit with large windows, which I thought served as some protection, until I realized that this in fact meant that they did what they did with complete impunity. I was at their mercy. At first the questions were mundane, my age, name, town, religion. Then the questions moved to other areas.

"And what are your politics?"

"I am a *maskeel*." I was sure they knew nothing of such Jewish matters. More naivete.

"Then why do you attend Bundist meetings? *Maskeels* are not political, and you are not so scientific." They showed me the list of meetings I had attended and dates.

"They are just places to meet people."

"Aha, I see."

"And what was your involvement in the breaking of the legs of this man who killed your grandmother?"

Had they known of my placing a skinned cat in the *Rebetzin's* soup at the age of ten, I would not have been surprised, so many details did they already have of my life.

"What is your relationship to this Titus fellow?"

"He's an acquaintance. As you know, he arranged for me to buy cattle."

"What else?"

"Nothing else."

"Strange. He also seems to have arranged to break the legs of this other fellow. Perhaps you share a grandmother as well."

"I didn't know he had anything to do with that."

My only respite came in the academic's incessant coughing. He had the weak lungs and body of someone who had survived tuberculosis, and the anger of someone who has experienced the sharp end of life's stick. I had known children like this, who looked out from their illness at the world casting blame on those who were not bedridden, who did not lag behind with a limp, or who merely expected that tomorrow they would be well. This was one who survived and was taking his retribution. You knew it in the officer's fear of him as well as in my own.

The danger in these men lay not in what they said, but in the implied threat of their knowledge. Imagine men that know the intimacies of your life, the people whom you love. Imagine that these people hold the power to do as they please. You may take no refuge in that they are not God; God knows mercy.

Between their inquiries the soldiers would return and I was beaten randomly, sometimes hard, sometimes so hard that I lost consciousness, but always as if they did not care if they beat me or not, or for that matter if I talked or not. At times they would not strike me at all. At other times they entered and beat me until they again left and the interrogators returned.

"And you did not know that he has a sister I suppose?"

There was no use in lying, but nor did I bother to answer.

"Your brother-in-law, Reuven, seems to have had certain interactions with him as well."

"And what of these fires set at the munitions factory?" This startled me, as I knew nothing of such activity. I believe they saw that I could feign nonchalance at questions that deeply disturbed me, but that I reacted with surprise to questions about which I knew nothing. I also understood now that the beatings came when they were unsure of my answers and on such occasions they would leave to have their coffee or a meal and that the soldiers' sadism was carefully calculated.

My only small advantage was that I had acquired quite a bit of Russian, with my penchant for language, and although the officers were more careful, the soldiers spoke among themselves assured that a Polish Jew would not know their tongue. It may have saved my life, because it gave me just enough knowledge to keep my wits about me and anticipate what was known and what was not.

I was kept awake seated naked in a cold room as various men, the original pair and others, came in and out and questioned me, as if one had not spoken to the other. I became confused and disoriented, but of course could tell them little, for all I knew was about cattle and a few horses that came my way. I tried at first to withhold the names and places of men who were involved in the buying and selling of the stolen cattle, but some they already knew and other names I told them when the pain and disorientation got the better of me. It did not take long and I hoped that by telling them the truth, I could avoid speaking of those whom I truly must protect, Reuven especially.

Returned to my cell, without my clothing and with only a thin sheet, I swung between periods when I could not sleep and would lay awake with tortured thoughts for what seemed like days, followed by days when I could do nothing but sleep. When I awoke, I was so covered in bites from the infested straw that the scratching would not allow me to sleep again, until exhaustion overcame me.

What I could not know was that my family had been looking for me this entire time. Finally, having spent no small sum of energy and money, they located me. Isaac and Reuben appeared like apparitions at my cell door. They brought as much money as the family could raise to attempt a bribe. Even Reb Cohen and the *Rebbe* had added a considerable sum. Such was the way the world usually worked and there were few circumstances for which a bribe could not make amends. It meant that our crimes were of a more serious nature that they could not find a path to see me freed.

The soldiers who guarded my cell did not treat me roughly, as they were a regular regiment and even had several bearded Jewish fellows from one of the far Russian provinces. We conversed in Yiddish and they apologized repeatedly for having to keep me under lock and key to await trial. They accepted kosher food from the family, and it was the first meat they had allowed themselves to partake for some time, it being easier to keep kosher with cheese and bread.

My family was frantic and my aunts expressed their anxiety, as was their way, by sending me food to feed an army division. Isaac said that only Friya was full of "I told you sos." To every ear that she could bend, she told how if the family had listened to her that I would have been cast out long ago and that she always knew I would drag the family down. To many she said that perhaps it was a mistake to lend her good name to such a family.

Tateh pulled his hair out of his beard and rent his clothing on hearing the news of my arrest and could not be consoled. He sent his heaviest coat so that I had something to sleep on in my cell, despite it being early summer, and knowing it would be stolen by some soldier. He had tried to give Isaac his only boots to take as a bribe, saying that every soldier values a good pair of boots.

The political tracts that were always being published and distributed to further the revolution made matters worse. They spoke of an anti-Russian conspiracy, with Jewish and Polish partisans working together for the good of greater Poland. These were the liberal elements of Poland who were looking to

offer a partnership with the Jews. They were a small but vocal group throughout
Polish history, and as in my case, their cause often had the opposite of its
intended effect. Their writings saved my family from some of the shame, but
meant that the Russians were forced to treat the matter more seriously. Had I
smuggled cattle for mere profit, the number of cattle stolen could have been
minimized and I might have been saddled with a fine and short jail term and then
set free.

I might even have ironically been offered a place in the Russian army, a
common punishment for any crime short of murder, and actually more than a few
murderers filled the Russian ranks as well. This only meant that you received
worse duty, some regiment in Siberia or a grave digging company. Branded a
revolutionary, one paper even said there was "a young Jewish ringleader," I
found myself facing a show trial and long prison sentence or even the gallows.
Tateh returned to his bed.

My immediate guards took none of my alleged revolutionary activity
personally, having no fond feelings themselves for the Russian army and forced
conscripts to the man. They allowed Reuven and Isaac to sit in my cell. We
played cards and passed the time with small talk. One day I lay sleeping and my
cell door creaked open. It was midday, but I had taken to sleeping at odd hours,
often up at night and sleeping by day. Reuven stood before me with Rachel at his
side.

I could only turn my back to her, so worried did she look, pregnant with
another child. She kneeled beside me. With her body held against mine, she
cried tears that I could not release, until I turned to face her and we cried
together. She covered my head with kisses as Mammeh used to do to all of us
when we fell or had some hurt to which only love was a balm. After we drained
much of the water of the River Vistula, we sat up and talked.

"Your uncles tried to convince Isaac and Reuven that they could break
you out of jail Tzvi. Can you imagine Uncle Mayer leading the charge with fish
knives, flashing a large whitefish and Uncle Yossl and Israel coming armed with

aunties' brooms as weapons? Uncle Yossl dug up some ancient weapon that he had buried years ago. He just buried it in the dirt like that. So, of course, when he dug it up it just about disintegrated in his hands. The Russians would run from fear; they would be so sure it was a demon coming after them."

She paused to catch her breadth from the laughter mixed with tears and wiped her eyes to dry them.

"Uncle Yosef sent a telegram that he is working with a lawyer in Warsaw to see what can be done. He's the only one who understands these modern times. He knows how things work. Are you managing to eat? You must eat to keep your strength up."

Rachel lingered as much as she could, but they had a long road to return. She personally thanked the Jewish soldiers for their acts of kindness. Although they would not touch a woman, they could not take their eyes off of her, so long had it been since they heard a Jewish woman speak to them in their own tongue and with gentleness. With her large bosom, warm smile and eyes that looked into your Jewish soul, it broke their hearts that they had any part in her pain and suffering. It was the fissure that enabled my escape.

Rachel insisted on seeing the Colonel of the Regiment before leaving and the guards jumped at the chance to help her in any way and pleaded her case to their lieutenant. She spoke with the colonel respectfully, but did not demur from using her feminine charms. He invited her to return and have dinner with him on the occasion of her next visit.

The family, of course, was against this and I more than anyone. Rachel, however, would not be deterred once she had an idea in her head, however, and Reuven only agreed knowing that he would be just nearby.

Rachel arrived on her next visit in her finest clothes, with her hair swept back showing her strong profile. Her breasts, already swollen with pregnancy, accentuated her figure and she wore make-up, which I had never known her to do. Unfortunately, not knowing Russian, a mix up occurred and the soldiers thought she had come only to see a prisoner. The two soldiers led her to an anteroom, with the excuse that she needed to be checked for contraband.

When she arrived at my cell, some twenty minutes had passed, and she was clearly shaken and perhaps in shock. Her clothes were disheveled and her undergarments were in her hand. She tried to put on a brave face, but broke down in my arms. She barely spoke in the half hour she spent with me and had the strange reaction of falling asleep in my arms, the body's way of committing a living terror to the world of mere nightmares.

I insisted she must leave with Reuven and forget this whole idea that had already gone terribly awry. She would not hear of it, and swore me to silence. Before the guards came to get her, she did her best to regain her composure and fix her hair.

When the two soldiers came to escort her to their commander, having gotten the story straight, they were penitent and clearly frightened. Rachel showed them no emotion. She acted as if nothing had occurred. Raping visitors was fair game, but molesting a visitor of the commander in any way would mean a whipping, and their commander would be judge and jury. Whatever, the soldiers' offence, however, the colonel could not have dinner and whatever else was planned with a woman who had already consorted with his men.

The soldiers escorted her with what deference they could muster to the commander's quarters. The spotless room smelled of leather, polish, and horse liniment. A large photo of the Czar in military dress hung behind the desk and oil paintings depicting military scenes adorned the room. She was served tea from a silver samovar that stood on the massive sideboard. Soldiers came and went performing official duties, barely paying her notice. She thought she was forgotten.

The colonel entered, tall and proud in his dress uniform as if on parade with his silver sword hung at his side. His greying mustache was well-trimmed and although not particularly young, he cut a handsome figure.

"I am sorry madam. I must apologize. I had unexpected business. I would not keep a lady waiting. I have seen to a kosher meal, Froi Applebaum. I have a gramophone and have secured some Yiddish records for your enjoyment. I think you will find them, well....curious at least. I have also a very good bottle of French wine from my cellars if you will partake with me." He spoke well, but somewhat awkwardly mixing his excellent Russian, with good Polish, and a few words of broken Yiddish.

Seated at the mahogany table and having had a dinner of the sort that she had never dreamed, they talked more freely, but under the shadow of the threat that I was imprisoned only one hundred meters away. Soldiers, smartly dressed, served an exotic dinner of grilled meats of a type known in Turkey, but entirely foreign to Rachel, and made to impress. "It is food from my previous posting that I have grown fond of. Do you know Baku...Azerbeidshan? No? No matter."

"I trust, Froi Applebaum, that you are not of the Jews that consider tomatoes *treyf*."

"No, I'm not so strict, and I always thought that interpretation extreme at best. But this has all been very thoughtful of you, your honor." And after an interval that gave her time to collect some nerve, "May I ask sir from where does your very fine Yiddish come and from where do you have such knowledge of our dietary laws? Your soldiers?"

"No, I receive the soldiers because, although I have long been a Christian, there are always some of my superiors that do not wish me to forget my Jewish origins. My Yiddish, as you well know, is almost nonexistent."

"You're a Russian Jew then?"

"No, closer to home, I'm from near here, the Eastern Provinces to be more exact."

"Then how have you come to be a colonel in the Russian army?"

"I was conscripted like many in my time."

"Then why, might I ask, did you become a Christian? Did they force you? Please forgive me for asking, your honor. It is of course none of my business."

"That's quite all right. It is not a story that I often tell, so it weighs heavy on my chest. You see I left the faith because of what they did to me."

"Who, the Russians? How terrible."

"No, Froi Applebaum, you don't understand. The Russians set a quota of conscripts. But it was Jews who had to deliver the numbers. In the end, Jews were paying Jews to release their sons from service and in my town even the Rabbis had a hand. My father was a lowly tailor. He had paid the bribes to the Jewish elders, but obviously not enough. One day the Jewish press gangs broke into our home. The press gangs came from another town, but they could have only received the lists of names from Jews from our town."

"I was just Bar Mitvahed. My brother was only six, and my sister was seventeen. She argued, and cajoled, and fought for them to release me, but they were not to be deterred. I never saw my family again. When I returned to the town years later, I learned that they had emigrated to America, but I don't even know the name they took or if they arrived. One or two members of the *kehila*, the Jews who ran the governance board, were still alive. They were, to say the least, surprised to see me alive and in my current reincarnation. I exiled them from the town to a new business harvesting salt in the far reaches of greater Russia."

"How dreadful. I had no idea such things happened."

"Yes, it's not a pretty story. But you see why I have no great place in my heart for Jews. How could I? Still, I'm good enough to my Jewish soldiers and some of them guess at my origins, even if it's in everyone's best interest that the truth not be known. I am in the kind of unit in which there is generally little interference. On most matters, my word is law."

Unpracticed at such affairs, Rachel was still a woman and understood that she was fighting for her brother's life, however civilized the dinner. She took the officer's last words as meaning he wished to bargain. She leaned forward bearing as much of her bosom as she might. She was unsure how to act for fear that the officer might take offence at her actions, or even prefer to find satisfaction in her innocence. It was possible that he was aware of her pregnancy and that the violation of a Jewish housewife was a kind of retribution for the wrongs done him as a child. He did not seem that way, but he was formal and distant in a way that Rachel did not know how to read.

"And what would you like of me? I would do *anything* to help my brother." And with this, Rachel saw that the man was shaken and that some deep emotions were welling up behind his powerful image of high leather dress boots, brass buttons, and polished sword.

It took him some time to speak.

"I did not know what I wanted when you came, but I know now. Those were the last words I heard my sister speak. She told them she would do anything to save me. Anything. Although I cannot remember her exactly, I believe she looked much like you...I would like your photograph. There is a shop here in town where it can be arranged and if you do not think it too bizarre I would ask also for a piece of your clothing. Perhaps your shawl. Is this too much to ask? Can you understand?"

"And that is all you want?"

"I thought I wanted more. But no, that is all. My soldiers will untie your husband now. Don't worry he was not to be hurt, just incapacitated."

Rachel came around the table to the seated officer and held him to her body and stroked his hair, as might a mother to her small child. He called her by his sister's name.

My sister mentioned nothing to the colonel of her treatment at the hands of the soldiers. But you do not become a colonel in a Russian police unit without knowing everything that goes on. The day after her visit, the two soldiers were served fifty lashes each directly outside of my cell block so that I could hear their cries until they collapsed, which occurred already by the twentieth stroke. From fifty strokes a man, if he lives, is broken for his lifetime. I only wished that I had been given the privilege of administering the blows.

With this link made with Rachel and a sudden turn of events, a plan was arranged over the next few weeks. The colonel met with Reuven and explained. Titus had been captured and had testified that he had threatened my life if I had not helped. He claimed that I received no profit whatsoever. As he turned in others that were involved when 'persuaded,' the officials believed that he was telling the truth. He would not speak further because he died from 'unforeseen circumstances.'

I could not, however, just be released and it was likely that I would be given some token sentence of a few years imprisonment or sent to Siberia. Either, however, might in reality mean my death, so for the Russians it was a just end to the affair. The colonel let it be known that he understood there was more to the story, but allowed this version to be transcribed as the official account of the affair.

"This means that your brother-in-law's case has been relegated to a much lower profile and there will be little follow-up, whatever I do. A colonel in a police unit like mine has broad discretion and few have the stomach to ask what really happens to our prisoners for fear that someday it will be their own turn. Still, you understand, I must cover my own tracks as well."

The colonel did not have to threaten his Jewish soldiers too harshly. They were to take me toward Warsaw and 'lose' me on the way. From the investigation it would appear that they had done away with me, but without a body it would remain an open file. As the punishment for their incompetence would be severe, they were to then desert across the border. With money in their pockets and the chance to avoid years in the Russian army where they might in any case never see their families again, this was a soldier's dream. Chasids in Antwerp were known to help such Jews.

Reuven arranged for a group of Jewish peddlers to supply clothing and a cart. As for me, I would have to disappear as well. If I was captured, it would not go well for me. On one thing the colonel was insistent. No one could come to say goodbye to me. That would be too suspicious.

On the road, the escort of three soldiers released me with our mutual expressions of safe journey, with *mazel und berocha, luck and blessings*. And so passing not far from my village, I went off in the night.

Chapter 8

Outcast

I could not risk returning to my family as patrols would be set out to investigate my escape or demise. They would, of course, expect that if alive I would return to my home directly. I looked into the windows of each of my family, like a burglar under the cover of night. I believed I might never be with my family again, so I have preserved this strange memory of them framed in windowpanes through wavy glass.

My father lay in bed behind a cobweb-ridden pane of glass, reading a holy book. He appeared broken and sunken into himself. Rachel and Reuven sat at their table not speaking and holding hands staring occasionally at each other's eyes. I almost tapped the window to tell them somehow that I was well, but I heard the police patrol and darted back into the bushes.

I dug up the gems and money I had saved, which reached a considerable sum. I took a horse from the barn where Reuven and I kept our livestock between buying and selling. He would understand. I traveled the road at night and lay many times in the brush when I thought I heard men in the distance. Once, a group of soldiers passed on horseback, but they were too great a number to be looking for me I thought.

The next day I stayed hidden in the forest and at nightfall returned to my good friend, Krzysztof, the pawnbroker. He was aware of my circumstances, but without fear took me into his home.

"So why did you come to me?" he asked when I had slept and eaten.

"I'm sorry I did not mean to endanger you."

"I know that, and that is why I don't understand why you came. I suppose you wish a favor. That's the only explanation."

"Yes, as you have always said, reading people is your trade."

"It's the only way a man in my business survives."

"I have these gems and cash. Can you convert the cash to a few more stones and get them to my sister Rachel? Can you do that?"

"Consider it done. Can I do anything else?"

"No, if you do this you've done more than enough. I'm so grateful."

"I was afraid it might come to this or worse. You were in over your head."

"What was I to do? You know the circumstances. I had to help Christina and had little choice."

"No, few could take my grandfather's path. You could not give up your faith. You're simply not built that way. It's your *Zadie*'s doing I'm afraid," and with this he smiled. "In an odd way your sense of honor made you a criminal and now a wanted man. What now?"

"I will take a few stones and some cash and get lost in the city. I believe that they'll not be able to find me in a place like Warsaw. One Jew looks to them like another. With a little money I can buy identity papers that are good enough."

"Perhaps you should leave the country altogether. It may be best and you have the money to start somewhere else and more education than most. You could do well if you could get to Vienna or Berlin. Your German is more than adequate. They are no more anti-Semitic than the Poles and more modern. You would find opportunities."

"I'll sleep on it. The borders seem so foreign. Even Warsaw feels to me like another country. I am not sure how I might fare in another land altogether."

"Tzvi, one last thing. How are you sure that I will get the valuables to your family? You will not be able to check."

"Because I have learned from you how people are made. It has become my trade. I'm afraid."

"Yes, I think it has Tzvi."

On the next night I set out. Krsysztof insisted that I accept some extra money, which I at first refused.

"Please Krzysztof, you have done enough. I can already never repay you for all you've done."

"Tzvi, don't worry. I will probably earn money from this whole affair. I
will collect the debts still owed you with the markers you've left me. I will make
the bastard who turned you in bleed through the nose. That you can count on.
He'll wish for the return of his Jewish moneylender, I promise you. Remember,
this is my stock in trade." And with this he laughed, obviously relishing the
opportunity to seek my revenge.

On my departure he insisted I wear around my neck an exotic amulet
which he told me was from Jews in Morocco. He said it represented God's hand
which would shelter me.

"It is not something known here, so you will not be taken as a Jew
unless you choose so, yet at the same time you will be guarded by God as you
know him. Unless they find you swimming without your trousers, no one will
suspect your bond with Abraham."

As before, I traveled by night and slept in the forest by day, avoiding
people on the road. Krzysztof had exchanged my horse for another, so it could
not be linked to my family and his good wife gave me plenty of food for the road.

On the road the second night, I became frightened when I could not feel
the gems in the lining of my pants. I ripped them open frantically, only to find
that they had simply shifted. My momentary relief was quickly lost when I saw
the small pebbles substituted for the precious stones. I was dumbstruck and fell
down sobbing at my misfortune. This was truly too much to bear, that a good
friend should do such to me. I lay like this despondent, unable to think as if
drunk or drugged. I simply could not believe what had happened. There had to
be some mistake, some words that passed between us, some greater plan that I
could not see. Finally, I slept.

I dreamt a version of Joseph's dream. My brothers had cast me off in a
pit for wild beasts to devour. Regretting their murderous desires, they recanted
and sprung me from the pit and traded me into slavery to some traders, but these
men were crossing Poland and they looked like Chassids. They were carrying

the holy Tablets of the Law of Moses and it was inscribed in bold letters, "Thou shalt not steal." Instead of saving for seven years of famine, I spent the Pharaoh's wealth in the years of plenty. All was lost and I was again imprisoned, naked and cold despite the great heat outside. One friend came to me in the form of Krzysztof, but now he was circumcised. I pleaded with him, "Krzysztof, friend, why did you betray me as the Jews betrayed your Christ?" And he answered, "I could not betray you for you are my son and I am your brother."

I awoke disturbed by the dream, but knew that Krzysztof had no more betrayed me than a loving father could betray his son. I went to put my pants back on. I had might as well be on my way. I believed he had devised some greater plan that was beyond my comprehension, but that would unveil itself in time. I was not thinking logically. Shock and fear overcame any rational thought.

Dressing, I noticed other lumps in the waistband of my trousers. Looking carefully, I saw where these were sown in a much more exacting manner, with the mark of a professional seamstress, obviously Krzysztof's wife. I thought I felt the stones underneath and knew I should not break the seal, because I could never match the artistry of their concealment. Krzysztof had indeed tricked me, but his plan was that I should myself think that the poorly concealed hiding place I had constructed held the gems. That way, when robbers attacked me, they too would look there and find only pebbles. I would give no sign of the gems' true hiding place, as I was to be as ignorant as them. There is no actor better than one who believes the part he plays. They would not think to look in the craftily constructed underseam, and would be satisfied with the theft of my money, a considerable sum, but nowhere near the value of the jewels.

I sensed that I should trust him, but distraught and lacking courage, I lacerated the stitching with my pocket knife. Cutting the seam, I found that he had replaced my gems with larger, better stones wrapped in an ancient piece of parchment with the Hebrew words, *Lech b'shalom, Shuv b'shalom*, "*go in peace, return in peace*," written plainly above a miniature inscription of a traveler's prayer so tiny it might only be read with a magnifying glass. My emotions being at my fingertips, I cried more over this than at my discovery of their loss.

Removing the cheese and bread from my satchel for a final meal before starting off into the night, I found that he had bestowed one final gift, a tiny Hanukkah Menorah made to light the Hanukkah lights for some wealthy Jewish traveler. I sat for the remaining hour of twilight playing with the delightful miniature device which folded and unfolded to hold either Sabbath candles or the eight lights of Hanukkah, not three inches in length and finely etched with the blessing of the lights. In it was the last of his messages. "Also my grandfather's."

On the third night it rained and the temperature dropped to an unseasonable cold. I tried to make a fire to warm myself and dry my clothing, but was as incapable as a child. I found a small cave in the hillside, but falling asleep was awakened by the growl of what I was sure was a wolf. Actually, I was not sure, because I did not hesitate to ask his name or nation.

Cold and damp, if I remained in the woods I was destined to die of pneumonia, if not eaten first. As there were inns on the road, and many of them run by Jews, I returned to the main highway where traffic meant an inn sooner than later.

I decided it prudently and even interesting to play the part of a non-Jew. The innkeepers and their daughter who tended table were polite but distant. I longed to use my Yiddish to evoke the comradery that it immediately elicited. I spoke in Polish to a group of religious Jews at the next table, but they either did not speak Polish or pretended not to. I knew that whatever I ordered would be kosher, but despite my growing hunger it was best to be modest, so I ordered soup and bread with schmaltz, a poor man's hearty meal.

A group of young Poles invited me to join their table, but I politely deferred using only few words as would a peasant. A Jew I thought would have made a dialogue of declining, learned of their origins, discussed politics at home and abroad, argued a point of The Law, and eventually found a connection of families that would have forced them to sit and eat together and share news.

I must have fallen asleep at the table, but they left me undisturbed for a time and I awoke no longer chilled and somewhat revived. I realized that what had awoken me was the rustling of a rather pretty woman who had seated herself at the table next to mine.

She was friendly and we talked. As we spoke, I found myself attracted to her and she apparently to me. She was more or less my own age, and at seventeen in the full flush of young womanhood, aided perhaps by a touch of rouge. I ordered a drink for each of us, careful still not to display more than a few coins. Our conversation found us drawing closer together and I moved to sit next to her in her more secluded booth.

I longed for the warmth of a woman's body and the shelter and peace it brought. There was that precious moment when you for the first time entered a woman that seemed to make everything else possible and worthwhile. As I had sought the warmth of the fire, so I sought this passage now. We began by speaking of the chill outside and soon enough she had steered the conversation to the chill within.

"We are all alone, one way or another," she said. "Some of us are only more alone than others. You think you are alone too, but I can see that you have those who love you. You have been cared for, although you see yourself as some tragic figure in a play."

"You sound like a gypsy. Do you wish to see my palm madam? Here's a coin. Read my future," I answered playfully, not wanting to affirm her insights.

"My mother said I have some gypsy in me, yes. But it is not so hard to read men, although you act so stern and unfeeling. No, I am only a woman who must use her wits."

Our flirtation moved to innocent touching and then not so innocent. I brushed my hands against her breast, obviously enough, but not so that she might not think it perhaps an accident, or at least excusable. She talked to me with her eyes locked onto mine and her tongue frequently wetting her lips. I could smell her more deeply, as excitement opened my nostrils to her womanly aroma, melding with the odors of the fire. I recognized this sign, as before love's piercing our eyes, nose, mouth, and feelings become more sensitive, more sensitive to take in all that is wished to be seen, smelled, tasted, felt. She placed her hand on my thigh, making no great display of it one way or another and with no break in her conversation. Before long she was stroking my swollen member through my pants and nibbling at my ear.

We were half in shadows and others seemed to simply go about their own business. She inquired if I might like to spend the night or part of it with her, unveiling an ample portion of breast and nipple. I reached out to her to stroke it, but was abruptly interrupted by the innkeeper who shooed her away, as a cat from a kitchen counter.

"Out, out with you. Take your business elsewhere."

And then to me, "I am sorry if that is what you came looking for sir, but we don't abide by her type here." *"Kurva,"* he then said under his breath, using the Yiddish for prostitute, thinking I wouldn't understand. I had honestly not known. She was not the obvious type I had encountered before. And here I was sure that she had so quickly succumbed to my wily charms and handsome face. It was not only for the woods that I was ill-prepared.

The Poles at the next table found the entire incident quite humorous and good-naturedly informed me I could find her or another better still at a tavern just down the road if I pleased.

"These Jews are a strange sort, aren't they?" said one of the revelers without malice. "They seem to live on wives and food, instead of whores and liquor! No wonder Christ turned his back on them." And I laughed with them until I thought I would burst, because as a Goy I understood their point of view perfectly.

My body longed for hers, but with her departure the spell was broken and good sense returned. As long as she was present, I am sure she could have guided me by my "little Jew," but gone, the leash by which she bound me was cut. I paid my bill and departed once again on my journey.

I rode for a few hours, finding the road deserted and I free to follow my thoughts. For a young man, the sequence of sex once initiated is hard to silence. In the saddle I dreamt of being close to Leah and then Christina. I tried to force myself to recall specific times when we were together. I wished to remember events as they were so I could store them for harvesting at some future time when I would like my father be old and married. The time passed quickly as I was once again on Froi Rosenblock's sofa wrestling under the blanket with Leah, sucking at her ample breasts. With Christina I was exploring yet untried positions. With one hand on the reins and the other in my pants, I masturbated for a long while until I came into my handkerchief. I collapsed against the horse's neck and more or less slid from the saddle to thump onto the moist ground.

I thought it a good time to stop and clean myself and rest before daybreak exposed my flight.

Absorbed with fantasies of the woman back at the inn and preparing my pack for rest, I did not hear them approach. I was knocked unconscious before I knew what hit me.

I suppose I was lucky not to be murdered, but you would not have convinced me of this at the time. I never saw my assailants, but they obviously had time to go through my things thoroughly. When I regained consciousness, I could not remember who or where I was. In time I became more oriented and pieced together what had befallen me.

At first I had a moment of hope because I was still wearing my pants, but then I saw that the waistband was cut out. They had left me the small Menorah, perhaps thinking in the dark that it was a child's toy, but had taken most of my food. My hand quickly went to my neck, and I was somehow assured that the amulet hung there. They were probably afraid to touch it in case it was cursed. I realized that the Hebrew writing on the Menorah might have frightened them as well, not wanting to touch Jewish things. My horse, of course, was gone. I was devastated to the point of numbness, and blamed myself for all the past sins that made me deserve such a fate.

As I was nearest Warsaw, I decided that I had no choice but to make this my destination, at least until I could make other plans. I had no thoughts of approaching my Uncle Yosef and his family, as I would not for a moment endanger them, but I needed a city's anonymity. I walked for a while, but became dizzy and puked. I managed to seek the shelter of a forest and laid for what must have been two days coming in and out of consciousness from what I guessed was a concussion or perhaps even shock at my plight.

It was not so easy entering Warsaw as the roads were watched and papers were examined at various checkpoints. With the hundreds of men evading conscription, abetting revolution, and the various and sundry criminal element, the police officials had their work cut out for them.

Walking into town on foot and alone I appeared most suspicious and so I tried to devise a plan to join with others. I came upon a group of Chassids in a wagon with their *Rebbe*. The wagon had four horses and must have held eighteen men and one goat perched on two levels like an enormous open stagecoach. Of the number of goats I am certain. I spoke to them in Yiddish saying that I was a lost Jew. Without a beard and in peasant's garb, they were too suspicious to do more than answer me gruffly that "A man without a beard or a community is no more a Jew than these horses," mean words that struck me like a fist.

I cursed them as best one can in Yiddish, which has no curse words at all, and ended my diatribe by yelling rather biblically in Hebrew "May God curse your blessings and rebuke your seed." They pitched back with a joint gasp as if I had fired a shotgun in their direction. I stepped to the side of the road despondent, and their wagon lurched ahead with them silenced at least from the droning singing that announced their coming long before I could make out their likenesses.

I was startled when a young man came running back toward me with his long black *kapote*, the coat they wore no matter what the temperature, fur-trimmed hat, and sparse blonde beard with side curls longer than a woman's hair.

Out of breath he spoke to me with a pleading tone.

"The *Rebbe* sent me back with this small *Sidur* book of prayers and this bread, asking if you would be so kind as to remove the curse. He promised, without an oath, to pray for you and his prayers are answered where I have witnessed. He is good to his word, even if the Law forbids his making oaths."

"Tell your *Rebbe* that I will do so if he will pray for my soul and for my children, born and unborn, to be healthy and to learn Torah. My name is Tzvi Yosef ben Shlomo," I said, giving him my Hebrew name. "Remember, born and unborn."

"Yes, of course. Born and unborn. I will tell him." And with that I had bread for the day at least and a *Rebbe*, of some mystical sect or other, praying for my well-being and that of my progeny. I felt the day had taken a small upturn.

I found an active set of train tracks, and nursed my small portion of bread. Luckily, many of the trains at that time went so slow that as children we would step off to the side and play, keeping pace with our parents watching out from the third class cars in case the train would miraculously increase its pace. The latter never occurred to my knowledge.

In time, I heard a train in the distance. I hid in the brush by the trackside to avoid the scrutiny of the engineer and his helpmate, and was able to jump into an open box car as it passed with no great difficulty. The train stopped frequently and on one such occasion, several cars were uncoupled and I feared I was now traveling in the wrong direction. I passed people and villages that looked one like the other, but thought it best to remain on the train because this was at least going somewhere. As to which somewhere did not matter all that much, I tried to relax and accept the destiny of my journey.

Uncoupled again, my car with several others stood in a small town and I descended and found water at a pump. Before I could find food I was discovered by a large anti-Semite of a dog if ever there was one. Better hungry than eaten alive, I lay trapped on the train for two days until it finally resumed its tedious journey which took me eventually into the great train yards of a city.

I had fallen asleep on some loose packing straw and was rousted by two Jewish porters who yelled at me in Polish that I had better be on my way before the police found me. I could not figure why these bearded, stocky men with their prayer shirts worn under their jackets with the fringes hanging out of their pants did not speak to me in Yiddish, until I remembered that I was dressed as a Pole.

"This is Warsaw?" I asked in Yiddish, unsure of where I was.

"No, it's the Garden of Eden and we are angels of the Lord. You slept longer than you anticipated."

And with this answer I understood as clear as day that this was Warsaw and I best be gone. I listened to their advice and descended the train into the bustle of the freight yard with thousands of people coming and going and slipped into the city.

The area around the train station was filled with warehouses and seedy establishments. I was almost run over by a horseless wagon carrying some hundred chickens in cages stacked ten high. I was dumbstruck by the noise it made which alerted me to its coming well in advance, but paralyzed me in awe. The combination of the cackling fowl and the truck's engine was more than I could quite comprehend. The driver was sure I knew to get out of his way and only at the last moment averted the wheel, causing many chicken cages to fly through the air, and a nearby horse to draw up on its rears and bolt. Everyone around simultaneously yelled that I was an idiot and deserved to be run over. I ran to avoid being beaten.

Against a building in a quieter street, I took what little bread I had left from inside my shirt and scraped off the growing mold. I could smell the food from the carts from which people sold all manner of delicacies. I was so hungry that I would have eaten anything. I found some rotten fruit against the building and ate what I could salvage, but the smell of meat was more than I could take. I was still somewhat faint, which I attributed to my hunger, having all but forgotten about the recent blow to my head.

I wandered the area until I found a sheltered doorway. From the shadows I watched a group of Jewish peddlers on the curbside selling used clothing, pots, and odds and ends. One hawker chose to don his wares, four or five coats, despite the day's warmth. To allow customers to inspect his goods, he would shrink from a man of huge dimensions with a tiny head, to a fellow who was skin and bones, but proportional. As each prospective buyer declined to make a purchase, he would repeatedly be transformed again from weakness to great stature.

A tailor had a sewing machine attached to a cart which, like my Uncle Mayer and his fish business, he could wheel from place to place. He sewed for passersby. He had a sign that read in Yiddish and Polish, "Suits Tailored While you Wait." I wondered if anyone ever brought him a whole suit to fit up on the street, as his few customers came with torn trousers and shirts that were ready for the rag pile. For a man who needed the pants sewn that he wore, the tailor held a blanket around him, so he could disrobe with due modesty. He waited wrapped in the blanket like a Hindu until his pants were repaired and repeated the ritual in reverse.

Setting old cans on boxes around me so that anyone who approached would make a warning racket and covering myself in newspapers for warmth, I cried myself to sleep. I awoke in the morning sore from the pavement and ravished with hunger, but without a groshen in my pocket and having eaten the last of my bread. I thought to sell my tiny menorah, but felt that would be bad luck. Venders had set up all around me with bagels in baskets, pickled fish, and steaming sausages cooking over hot coals. I approached a bagel seller and asked if I couldn't do some errand in exchange for a bagel. She could not disentangle my appearance as a Polish peasant and my Yiddish. She decided it best to ignore me, but then as an afterthought reached into her basket and threw me a broken bagel without a further word and was on her way.

I went in and out of sleep for much of that day and the next, eating scraps and wandering about a few block area. The following day I felt some return of strength and tried to work helping people with crates and boxes. This earned me a powerful box on the ears from some rough looking porters who told me in no uncertain terms that not just anyone with arms could help with a box.

Exasperated, I yelled back at them in Yiddish that I was hungry and if they had a Jewish soul that they had not sold to the devil that they might think to help a poor Jew. They were startled at my speech and softened, sharing with me some bread and a piece of meat that they cut from a roll of salami. From their earlocks and prayer fringes sticking out of their pants, I knew it was kosher and gorged myself, which they found for some reason humorous and soon had me encircled by a group of their fellows, each offering me something to eat from what there was.

They explained, however, that they still could not allow me to work as the porters were organized. If I tried, I would receive a beating and even have my hands broken if I came upon an enforcer. Not being without hearts, they asked if I was willing to load and unload at the stock yards. This was the dirtiest work that porters did, and there were sometimes openings at the bottom of their rungs for someone with initiative that was willing to work hard and didn't mind the stench of animal offal.

"Wait here until the end of the day," one told me. "You don't look strong enough just now to work in any case. Eat some more and get some sleep and I'll take you to a man on my way home."

Good to his word, he brought me to a man sitting in a cheap café dressed as were the porters. He sat with a ledger in front of him and a large sum of money in a cash box on the table. He drank an endless glass of tea and smoked incessantly, lighting one cigarette with the next. Porters came and left with money. Everything he recorded in his ledger in a careful hand as if he was a scribe writing religious text on parchment.

"*Nu? Bistu a Yid?* You're a Jew?" He asked me in Yiddish.

"Who else would have this luck?" was my response, more as a way of convincing him of the veracity of my reply than being a smart mouth.

"Another country heard from! So, you are not a *Litvak* are you? I don't

abide by Litvaks in my *artel*. Those Lithuanian Jews aren't to be trusted, Jew or
not."

"No sir, and I'm called Yosef, I lied."

"Don't call me sir; we are all the same here, workers, that is, except for
the *Litvaks*. Mendel tells me you're willing to work in the slaughterhouse. Have
you any experience?"

"I'm an apprentice butcher."

"That won't help in our line of work. From the looks of you, you're not
afraid of hard work. Be here at six in the morning. Do you have a place to sleep
tonight? No, I didn't think so. 'Yenta,' he yelled. 'Give this one some soup and
bread and show him where he can sleep in the back.' It's not too comfortable but
there are some mattresses back there. You are not the first to wander into Warsaw
from the *shtetl*. Have you no family here? Don't answer that. Either you don't
or you do, but can't go to them. Don't worry. We take care of our own. We're
like family."

I ate three bowls of soup, and with each my hunger and sense of dread
diminished. The first was a thin chicken broth, but having *rachmones*, *pity*,
Yenta made sure the second and third bowl contained pieces of fat and skin from
the chicken. She was a slovenly woman with dilapidated shoes with the backs
broken down. She wore heavy stockings and her legs and buttocks were massive,
despite the fact that her upper body was average size. She did not so much walk
as shuffle, dragging her legs beneath her. Her teeth were so crooked I wondered
if she did not have trouble eating. She had the appearance of someone assembled
with unmatched parts. She barely spoke, but to ask me if I was sure I had eaten
enough. She called me "*mein kind*," my child.

When I finished eating she showed me to the back where there was a
large sink with running water. I smiled inwardly to think that if this was my new
family, how strange were my adopted mother and father.

"I'll bring you some clothes. You won't look like Rothchild, but those
things you're wearing need washed. I'm not sure if this blood will come off this

jacket or your shirt. From the looks of it you lost a liter. There's plenty of soap by the sink and you can wash yourself as best you can. In a few days you'll have money to take a bath. The men will show you where. The food today was on the house. The artel will pay for it. From tomorrow you'll have to pay me if you wish to eat here."

And so I began my illustrious career in the porters' artel of Warsaw.

Part 2

Finding and Losing

Chapter 9

Warsaw

I did not wake on the next morning without rousting. Yenta had allowed her early morning chores to proceed around me. Finally, I was shaken out of my stupor by Mendel, the same Mendel who had brought me the evening before.

I slipped into the pants that lay next to me. They were so large that I had to shimmy out of the cubicle, holding on to them so that I did not emerge undressed and make an altogether wrong impression.

"You're a hard one to wake. My sons were like that when they were your age. Young people. Humph! They sleep as if they have not a care in the world. It's a blessing. What's the matter Yosef? You don't look altogether well."

"No, no, I'm fine sir. I don't know if I thanked you for the food yesterday and for bringing me here. I was done in."

"Yenta, you won't believe this. A boy with manners. Not like our city boys, I'll tell you that."

"What time is it?" I asked.

"It's almost nine."

"*Vey is mir*! Nine! I was supposed to report to work at 6:00. I'm done for."

"We tried to wake you. I came by at half past five, but you were dead to the world. Also, at six and seven. No matter how I shook you I couldn't rouse you. I wanted to throw cold water on you, but your guardian angel over there, Yenta, wouldn't hear of it. Said I wouldn't eat here in a month if I did."

"Leave him alone," yelled Yenta from the next room as she served some customers. "I've got some work for him to do here if he expects to eat."

"*Nu*. So, who's keeping him from working? I just said he had manners? Didn't I just say that Yosef?"

"I didn't hear you say anything of the sort," yelled Yenta back to him. "And if I hadn't stopped you, you would have doused him in a cold bath. Shame on you. Look at him. He needed his sleep; now he needs to get up and get busy. Hershl and Menachem-Mendl said they found him in a railway car yesterday all mixed up and starving. And today you're throwing cold water on him. You make him sick, what help is he going to be to me?"

"I can see Yosef that you have a way with the women. I've never seen Yenta show this much attention to a man. Usually you're lucky if she shows up at your table with your coffee or your soup."

"*Nu* already? I don't have time to waste like the two of you. Come here to the table. There's coffee, bread, and jam waiting for you. I made an egg for you too. Here, eat while it's hot. You need your strength. I didn't do all this for nothing you know."

Yenta more or less yanked me up and shoved me to the table, so strong was her need to nurture this poor orphan waif she had found in me. I had clearly become a private project for her. However, I was not sure that I would survive her aid.

"Thank you," I said, "but only the coffee...okay and perhaps a little bread. I have to get to work, if they'll still have me, that is," I said looking inquiringly at Mendel for an answer.

"Don't worry. It's okay. Everything's been worked out."

"Wonderful! You mean they've found me a job already?!"

"No. I mean there's no work for anyone today. Chaim and the other chiefs called a strike."

"A strike? What's that all about?"

"It means there's no work today. That's all. And maybe not tomorrow either, who knows."

"So, what happened?" I sat at the table and ate, feeling that no matter what I consumed I could never fill myself.

"Well, it's complicated. You see the merchants got together and decided that they would have the wagon drivers unload the railroad cars themselves. Normally the drivers only drive. We load and unload. They don't like that we charge them for one porter to load the wagons and another porter to unload the wagons at their shops and factories. But, you know, we have to make a living, and as is half of us aren't working at any one time."

"So, what happened?"

"What happened? I'll tell you what happened. Yenta, can I get a little tea please. And a little bread and jam? Well, the merchants hired their own men to unload the trains that came in late last night and early this morning. Chaim and the other headmen came over to take a look. Before the police could be called in, they beat some heads and had the men reload the train cars and lock them again. Right now the food is sitting there rotting. They won't even allow water for the cattle cars, which I personally don't think is right. Not that anyone asked my opinion, God forbid. An animal should not suffer like that and maybe die. There are too many people starving right here in Warsaw."

"Why don't the police unlock the cars and allow the merchants' men to unload? I'd think they'd be on the side of the merchants."

"Oh, so you're a political expert on police tactics then."

"No, it's just that..."

"Don't interrupt if you want to learn something. You see, what do the authorities care? Most of the merchants are Jews. Most of the porters are Jews. For all they care, they'll let us eat ourselves alive. Plus, they're a little bit afraid of us. You don't want to get on the wrong side of ten thousand porters who live with you on the streets."

"Most of the porters and merchants here are Jews?"

"No, who said anything about them all being Jews? You're here a day and already you're an expert?"

"No, it's just that you said..."

"Never mind what I said. That's a bit of an exaggeration. But enough of us are *Yiddin,* that everyone says we all are. Actually, I think about half. The others are just guilty by association so to speak."

"What are you filling the poor boy's head with politics? Don't *ferdrey a kup*, don't mix up the poor boy's head. He needs to eat and regain his strength. He's skinny like a rail." And with this Yenta gave me a second egg and more bread and cuffed my head as she passed, as if to say, "Pay attention when I'm feeding you. I'm not this nice to everyone."

"Thank you Yenta," you're a *malach*, an angel," I said, giving Mendel a look like, "help me out here before I perish at the fountain of her kindness."

"Sure. Why not? To you she's an angel, but have you seen her bring me my tea yet? Here, let me take a little bread and jam from you."

"Leave his food alone, you big oaf. I'm bringing yours. I'm just adding a little fresh arsenic. I want to get it just right."

Order here was like the menu, nonexistent. You told Yenta what you wanted, she had it or she didn't, and she brought what she pleased. You ate, or the next time you did not get served. You might not get served in the best of circumstances, but if you were to reject her selection or preparation, her judgement and sentencing were immediate, without mercy, and irrevocable.

It was a popular café.

This is further testimony that much of the world is not given to understanding. During the time I lived in Warsaw cafes and restaurants of excellent quality and reasonable prices came and went, but Yenta's place was an institution. It somehow fit the crowd that frequented it in some intangible way that they themselves could not describe, because they spent much of their time complaining about it.

If a sign was in front of the café, there was none, it would read,

Yenta's Café.

Unattractive Waitress

Belligerent Management

Virtually Inedible Cuisine, Not Always Available

Service, Don't Get Your Hopes Up

Not Terribly Clean

Insults Provided Freely Without Charge

Talk Back Once, You Can Take Your Business Across the Street

I suppose that Jews are attracted to unknowns and puzzles and things that cannot be explained. Take the dietary laws. The choice of what animals are kosher and those that are not is never justified. Sure, you can say that pork can carry trichinosis, ugly little worms, but why a deer yes and a camel no? Why a fish with scales yes, and a fish without scales no? Why can you eat a meat meal directly following a milk meal, but have to wait five or six hours to eat dairy after meat? Like an army prepared for battle, we were taught that about many of the most important things there is no rhyme or reason. Without rhyme or reason there remains two things, the opportunity to argue and the need for faith. With one comes the other. We Jews were consummate experts at both. As I was lost in these deliberations, I realized that Mendel was trying to talk to me.

"Yosef. Yosef. Yosef!"

"What? I'm sorry, I didn't hear you calling Mendel."

"We're going to a soccer match. With the day off we're playing the porters from the Iron Gate area. And the porters from Simon's Passage have challenged the porters from Jaruszewski's Courtyard. We'll let the *gantzeh machers*, the *big know-it-alls* work out this strike. They don't need us now. No one in their right mind will open those railroad cars until a deal is worked out."

"Do you play soccer?" asked Mendel.

"A little, but I have to stay here and help Yenta clean up at least."

"No, that's fine," said Yenta, acting perturbed. "You're probably worthless around a kitchen anyway. Like most men. Go on, play your games. But expect that you're going to help later if there's no work. This is not a charity I'm running."

"Yes ma'am, I promise."

With that and having eaten a loaf of fresh bread and butter with jam and seven eggs, and Mendel never receiving his tea, but sneaking from some of my coffee and bread, we set out. Before we made our escape, however, Yenta gave me a sack with sandwiches handed to me in the manner of "take this you good for nothing." The bright daylight hurt my eyes and brought on a slight headache. So I half listened as Mendel explained about the politics of the porters as we made our way.

"Actually, you were fortunate to stumble upon Jewish porters at the train yard Yosef. The *goyim* have most of the train yards covered and we just have a small portion of that business. We're organized in groups, and you were lucky to find a good group, because we need to strengthen our numbers a bit right now. That is for someone willing to work hard and do the shit work."

I was amazed at the city and all the people. We walked through boulevards with automobiles and horses and the red cable cars. Most were still drawn by horses, but many of the cable cars were electric, although they seemed to stall more often than not, detaching from the wires above. People were dressed and mingled in all manner of clothing. Women and men, finely attired with silver tipped canes and leather bags. Women with great hats with feathers and what looked to me like gowns for a ball. Others looked more businesslike, like my Uncle Yosef who I wished at all costs to avoid. The businessmen moved at a dizzying pace, hurrying here and there as if all were late for the same appointment.

There were also any number of police and military. Most were standing around or going about their business. Others, however, were checking papers and staring at people passing them. I tried to meld with the crowd. I was glad for the change to city clothes that Yenta had arranged. I looked like many of the porters and walking with a porter, talking like old friends, was not the description they had in mind. Nevertheless, I could feel my palms sweat and I could not stop my shivering.

Everything was for sale and we passed stores that sold every manner of goods. In the village one store sold a little of everything, but here were specialty shops. On one street were fine cafes, with rich looking people, sipping coffee and eating cakes. On other streets I saw working men's cafes where the men stood at tables and drank their coffee and ate large sandwiches and argued.

Amidst it all were every variety of people, many of them Jews, with wagons and carts selling food and candy and hats and sewing things. One man sold used books from a wagon he drew through the street. Some of the books were in German and newer and I hoped to sometime have the money to return and buy one. Mendel said you could buy from this one and return them if you kept them in good condition, and he would buy back the books.

We stopped in front of a newsstand to read the news of the day. Mendel said there were so many Yiddish papers now that you could read the news from morning till night and not finish all of them. Others stood there like us, reading the papers in their rack, too poor to afford to buy one. There were indeed an incredible assortment of Yiddish papers. The news in each was the same, but once again Jewish opinion is as varied as the number of Jews. *Der veg*, The Way, *Der Telegraf*, The Telegraph, *Yidishes Tagelblatt*, Jewish Daily paper, *Morgenblatt*, Morning paper, *Di Nayettsaytung*, The New Newspaper. To see the news of the day, on time, felt like a miraculous pronouncement from above. Men stood in layers in front of the papers and it was remarkable that the owner made any money or that anyone learned about the stories beyond page one. A few men, however, did buy a paper and groups were huddled about them, reading together.

Just down the way, a family sang beautiful melodies while their two daughters played their sorrowful violins. The father stepped in for only a few songs, looking embarrassed at putting his family to begging on the street. He played a tune so mournful that a crowd was drawn and the street became silent. Tears rolled down his cheek and onto the clarinet at the saddest refrain, as the instrument wept. So deeply personal became his playing, that his family lowered their instruments, allowing him to conclude alone. As people placed money in the violin case, many touched his arm.

Children were everywhere on the street as well, hawking bagels, newspapers, and all matter of small things. One small child stood next to his basket of breads in jacket, knee pants, and cap. He constantly worked the toe of one shoe with the heel of the other, trying to uncurl the leather which looked as if it had bent upwards like a character in *The Arabian Nights* from a combination of its being wet and his father's.

Then, as if caught unacceptably in a good mood with no care in the world, an undertow of anxiety washed over me like the morning tide and I felt faint. Was that policeman looking for me? Was I acting too much like someone from the country, gawking at everything? Might I accidently stumble on my uncle or his family? I think from that time on, whenever I am beset with feelings of happiness, they are tempered by that same undertow of anxiety emerging from a deep dark place that I entered during those weeks as I lay naked in prison, not knowing my fate, life out of my control, fearing the next moment.

"Are you okay Yosef? You look a bit pale."

"Yes, fine I think. It's all so new, that's all. I only yesterday came to the city."

"Oh really. I would've never known. Come on or we'll be late."

In time we arrived at an open park with soccer fields and men already at play. We watched the game and cheered for our fellow porters. These were all strong men, hardened from carrying heavy loads, day in, day out. The older porters watched on the sidelines and made bets and argued. Many had brought food and made small picnics as they viewed the game's progress.

Mendel sat with men his own age and I drifted over to a younger group and tried to make contact, but they were uninterested in a boy from the *shtetl*. I drifted back to chat with Mendel.

"So, how did you become a porter Mendel?"

"Well, I was studying to be a surgeon, but I found the work unfulfilling."

"No, really."

"Really? Well, really I was born into a family with great wealth. We owned most of the banks in Poland. The Rothschild used to visit for the holidays. They were, how would you call it, poor cousins. From carrying the great bags of gold my father, sage man that he was, saw that I could best make my mark on the world hauling *chazerai, crap,* from one place to another."

It is not easy getting a straight story from a Jew. We are so skilled in communication that each interaction is an irresistible opportunity to display our prowess at wit, wisdom, and intelligent banter. Being no novice at the game, I recognized that the only way now to get the answer was not to ask again. Because we need to talk incessantly, Mendel could not resist the temptation. We have a deeply felt need to share our stories and they leak if stoppered.

"So, you're not interested in my story?"

"It's up to you. I plan to live one way or the other."

"Well, all right, if you insist. I did carry bags for my father, only not of gold. He was a peddler and a *nogoodnik* of the first class. He left my mother and me and roamed from place to place selling his wares. He would occasionally come home to Lodz with money and I wouldn't doubt it if he had wives in other towns. When I was ten, my mother died and I was taken in by a distant cousin who wanted little to do with me, but was not so unfeeling as to leave me to starve. When my father returned, I was handed him as an unwanted package returned to a shop. With little choice he took me on the road and I would *shlep* his goods from place to place. He was so unsuccessful that when his horse died he could only sell his wagon and we had to walk. When I was fourteen and we were in Warsaw he decided I was old enough and he up and left, giving the landlord a month's rent so that I could contemplate my future for a few weeks before being turned onto the street. He left one thing for me, his hand cart. I'll show it to you soon, as I still have it. It looks like a small wagon, but with room for a man to pull it instead of a horse. This was to be the means of my existence as with this cart I have made my living all these years."

"He sounds, pardon me for saying, like not the best of fathers."

"I suppose not, but it's funny because I can't ever feel angry with him. Whenever I was with him, he treated me like a good friend. Not as a son, mind you. But, he would share stories with me, talk to me like a man, tell me jokes, stories about women. He was warm and friendly, with an honest heart. He was always affectionate. He simply was not capable of being a father. In the end, I think he left me so that he did not burden me further, not because I would burden him."

"And you Yosef? What of you?"

"I also lost my mother some years ago. Let's just say that my stepmother and I did not get along. My father chose her over me."

Sensing my sadness, Mendel sat quietly, building his thoughts. I figured he had let my response pass for what it was. He could no more do that, however, than I could pass an old woman fallen before me in the street.

"Many men accept the will of their wives when they remarry, Yosef. I've seen it often. A woman will stand up to a new husband before a man will stand up to a new wife."

"I have to admit that I was no angel either. I did a lot to shame my father and make it difficult for him and the whole family."

"Perhaps you can go back and talk to him."

"I'm afraid I can't Mendel. I wish I could, but I had to flee my village and had hoped to escape the country altogether. I have endangered them and for that I can't forgive myself."

"I don't know what you did Yosef, but perhaps someday you can tell me. I can see, however, that you're in more than a boy's minor mischief, and so I won't treat you like a child and just say, 'Don't worry. It'll all be okay.' What I will say though is that if the worst doesn't come to pass soon, than the trouble will probably blow over. There are few things so large that time does not absolve them. I suggest you give it time. Here, have another sandwich." And then muttering to himself, "How is it possible for the woman to ruin a sandwich?

Eating her food is punishment in itself, whatever our sins."

A holiday atmosphere prevailed and I was quickly caught up in the
spirit, kicking a ball back and forth on the sidelines after we had won the first
game. The man I was kicking the ball with was a religious lad about my age who
apparently had never seen a ball in his life. I was therefore set to doing near
acrobatics to keep the ball from heading down hill, on the field, or into
someone's lunch.

"Hey Mendel, where did you find this one? He looks pretty damn good.
Anyone that can play with *Shmendrick* here is got to be a real player."

"We shipped him in from the countryside last night. He's a
professional."

"He is?! Let's get him in the next game."

"I don't know, I don't think he'll play unless he can make a few rubles
on the side. He has only just begun to work and now the strike. He needs some
pocket money for food."

"He's that good?"

Mendel pointed his upturned hand in my direction, as if to say "You can
see for yourself."

"Okay, ten rubles if we win. We have a lot of money riding on this
game."

Now in my experience Jews seldom drink, but gambling, Jews are as
bad as the rest, perhaps worse. It was a notable omission from the Ten
Commandments. Of course, who would have accepted God's offer to be the
Chosen People, had they not been willing to accept long odds? And with news of
a ringer playing for our squad, the betting increased rapidly.

I pulled Mendel to the side.

"Mendel, what have you started here? I'm no professional, I play for
fun like the rest of them and I'm out of training to boot. You've never even seen
me play. If we lose, I'm done for. They'll have whatever foreskin the *moyl*
didn't take."

"Likely enough."

"Likely enough! Then why did you do it?!"

"Listen, we can't beat this next team anyway. If you play well, maybe we can win. If you play poorly, I would advise you to fall down when someone fouls you and not get up."

"Thank you," I said with as much sarcasm as I could pack into the two words.

"You're welcome. Play in good health," Mendel answered me in my own coin.

After a suitable pair of shoes were commandeered from a man that was only too happy to be excused from the melee, I tried to prepare myself mentally. One thing for sure, my pants were not going to restrict my movements!

Had I not been through my own ordeal I would have perhaps excelled, as these men were unused to running and not in good physical condition. As is, I barely kept up myself. We played one goal to one for what felt like an eternity after two quick scores in the first half. Then the pace quickened as each team wanted a win. The porters from Jaruszewski's Courtyard scored with a couple of minutes left to play. It looked like all was lost. Mendel gave me a look like it was time I consider falling down.

With little time left, I took a pass that everyone expected me to pass back to the inside, as I had been playing cautiously. With nothing to lose, I darted inside instead, stepping between the first defenders. I took a long stride, as if preparing to kick with my right foot, but instead met the ball with a shot from my left. The final defender was completely caught off guard. The goal keeper, though first drawn to the wrong side, corrected his error and dove back deflecting the ball. As he, and it, lay on the ground separated by an arm's length, my teammate easily tapped the ball into the net. With no time remaining, we ended in a tie.

The railway porters went wild and swamped us as if we had just scored for the national team against the Germans. Our opponents argued that we had to play to break the tie, but the railway porters would have nothing of it. The chances of our surviving a tie breaker were slim, as we had really been outplayed most of the game. Men argued that "it was getting late in the day," "no time for the tie breaker," "never arranged before the game." Men who are raised disputing over the Talmud can debate to make your head spin on the smallest point, and a soccer match was no small point.

Despite our not having won, only tied, I received my ten rubles and tips from several ecstatic men -- almost fifteen rubles in all, perhaps two weeks wages for a laborer. "But we didn't win." I told one man. "Who cares," was his reply, "this is the first time in years we haven't lost." Someone offered me apricot brandy. I collapsed.

Chapter 10

Beshert, Destined Love

I could hear people talking around me, but could not understand what they were saying or where I was. I tried to move my arms, but they lay dead at my sides. I tried to speak, but no one responded. I recognized my cousin Chava next to where I lay and she stroked my forehead with a cool wet towel. I was thankful.

I dreamt I was being chased on horseback and on foot. Robbers were accosting me from all sides and I could not escape them no matter how I ran. One of the robbers was a Priest and he carried a bottle of blood that he tried to spill on me. "Here! Take your sins!" he yelled. I cried out in terror, "Leave me be! I am not the one! It is not me! I am alone, with no one. You have hurt me enough!"

"There, there now. Shah. It's okay. You're safe. There is no one to get you here," said Chava, tenderly. I lost consciousness again. I could hear them talking around me later. But try as I could, I was unable to speak.

"What do you think doctor? How's he doing?"

"Hard to tell. I don't know if he'll come out of the coma or not. The girl said he was trying to speak yesterday, but couldn't hear her when she spoke to him. Did you see him get hit on the head in the game?"

"Not that anyone remembers. He just collapsed, after it all."

"Well, my guess is that this nasty wound in the back of his head is the real culprit. He was still suffering no doubt from the concussion when he played in the game...well, you see the results. He also seems to be exhausted, and there are more signs of some bad beatings, terrible beatings. Had this been you or me, we would never have been in that soccer match, but who would want us playing anyway I suppose?"

"Micha, I'll win your ball back. The bastard *goyim* won't keep your ball. Don't cry Micha, we can get the ball. It's a Jewish ball after all. Mameh

I'm frightened. They took Micha's ball."

"Quiet *mein kindt, my sweet child*. No one will take Micha's ball."

"But I won't be there to protect the little ones, Mameh. I left Rachel and Isaac and the little ones, poor little Rayzella and Jacob. I'm sorry Mameh. I promised to watch over them. I can't die Mameh. If I die, I can't watch over them. How will I keep the *goyim* from stealing Micha's ball? It's up to me Mameh."

"Tzvikaleh."

"Is that you *Zadie*? How are you *Zadie*? I miss you. I'm sorry my friends punished that man that hurt *Bubbie*. Were they too cruel?"

"You got the right one Tzvi. The other one next to him was not so bad. He was of *Kenite*. The one you killed was of *Amalekite*. Remember, we are commanded to destroy all that is of *Amalekite*. That he was left to live at all was more than he deserved. He saw *Bubbie* and hurried the horses to trample her."

"I'm coming to you *Zadie*. I can feel it. I'm coming *Zadie*. I miss you and Mameh too much. There is no one here for me anymore. Anyone I touch is poisoned."

"Nonsense. This is just the way the world is turning now. Palestine or America, I told you. Palestine or America. Europe is rotten. You're going to live Tzvikala."

"How *Zadie*? I'm dying."

"Life is a choice at many points, and this for you is such a day. Now awaken and eat. You have much to live for."

"You promise *Zadie*."

"I promise without an oath. Now gather your strength."

"But *Zadie*, stop. How will I know the path?"

"*Hashem* will show you the path when you awaken."

And with this I saw a tunnel of light. But whatever force I gathered, I could not make it to the light. I was held back, fettered, bound. I knew I must try again. I gathered all my strength for what I felt certain would be one final effort, calling on a place from deep within. I ran into the tunnel and threw myself at the light.

"Thank God, you're awake. Someone get the doctor."

"Where am I? Who are you? You're not my cousin Chava."

"You're in a hospital. I'm Devora. Just a girl. I come here to volunteer," she answered nervously, caught off guard.

"A hospital? Where? What happened?"

"Well, I don't know exactly what happened. You'll have to ask the nurse or the doctor when he comes. This is a Jewish welfare hospital for the poor. I shouldn't have said that. I didn't mean to be insulting. Your friends, maybe ten of them brought you in four days ago. They have been coming and going to check on you, but they're not here now. Let me go get the nurse and tell her you're awake and talking."

"Well, look who came back. How do you feel? Let's see. No fever that I can tell. And your eyes look clear. I sent for the doctor and he'll take a good look at you. As soon as he says it's okay, we'll get some food into you. Here's the doctor now."

"Dr. Tobiansky, Reb Yosef has honored us with his presence."

"So it would seem, nurse Levy."

Dr. Tobiansky came to my bedside. He was an older man and a religious Jew. He wore a yarmulke and I could see from the strap marks indented on his arms that I had taken him from his morning prayers where he had been wearing his *tefillen*, the prayer straps a Jew binds on his left arm and upon his head for the morning prayers.

And these words which I command thee this day shall be in thy heart...thou shalt bind them for a sign upon thy hand, and they shall be as frontlets between thine eyes.

"How do you feel young man? Let me check your eyes. Very good.

Let's have a feel of your pulse and check your blood pressure. Hmm. If all my patients were young and strong I would be a very good doctor. With *Hashem's* help."

And I understood the sign that had been offered me.

"Doctor?"

"Yes young man."

"Can you bring *tefillen* so that I can pray? I don't have my own here."

"You want to *leyg tefillen*, to say the morning prayers?"

"Yes, please. But I need your help. It has been years since I put them on and I think I would get it wrong."

After examining me thoroughly, the doctor returned and helped me put on the *tefillen*, making the sign of God on my hand after wrapping them according to the tradition around my left arm. I prayed with the Doctor and *Zadie* for my recovery. The doctor promised to come by again later and the next day in the morning to help with the *tefillen* again.

"Doctor, can I ask you a question?"

"Surely, young man. What is it?"

"Who were the *Kenites*?" I asked recalling my dream with *Zadie*.

"What an odd question from someone who has been unconscious for several days. The *Kenites* were the tribe of Jethro, Moses' father-in-law."

"That doesn't make sense."

"Things are often all a jumble when you wake up from a hit on the head. Is something bothering you?"

"Not really, but that's okay. I was dreaming about the *Kenites* and the *Amalekites*. I remember the story of the *Amalekites*, killing our helpless women and children in the desert when we left Egypt."

"Oh I see. Then your mind has gone to a different part of the Bible. I hadn't thought about that reference. Strange how the mind works. That Freud fellow is no dummy. I might write him about this. Yosef, King Saul spared the

Kenites who were living among the *Amalekites*. It means that in searching out evil, one must take great care not to slaughter innocence. Does that make more sense of your dream?"

"I think I will have to think about it some more doctor, but I believe it does.

"Good. Now that we have finished our Torah lesson, I would like you to have some soup. Do you feel strong enough to sit up and eat a little? Yes, good. Devora here is helping us this week and she's been sitting by you most of the time in any case, so we might as well put her to good use. Devora can you please feed this young man?"

And I sipped at the soup, half of which Devora awkwardly spilled on my gown. With that I slept, but no longer with the nightmares and I knew even from my sleep that I was returning to the world.

It was a strange love affair, because I slept through most of it. They said that during the days when they thought I might be dying, Devora sat and read psalms. When I lay in a sweat, she cooled me with wet towels. They told me she held my hand much of the time and twice slept in the chair by my bed.

"You're not from here, are you Devora?"

"No, I'm from near Vilna."

"Vilna is a long way off."

"Yes, I came to visit my aunt here in Warsaw. She married a doctor who's here at the hospital in the children's ward. I want to be a nurse someday, so he allows me to come and volunteer at the hospital. A lot of people come to volunteer, as this hospital can't afford a big paid staff."

Given that most of the men on the ward were old and dying, it was no surprise that Devora chose to visit with me. The Torah says that seventy years is the length of a man's life, so these *alter kockers* were well past dead, or onto their second Bar Mitzvah at least. On my ward alone there were twenty beds crowded into the room and each of them full, but for the few hours after someone was sent home or to heaven.

Three times a day the men gathered in prayer, as there was always a
minyan of the required ten men available. Of course, they shuffled between
rooms if they were mobile because in a matter of a day they found the groups that
they liked to pray with and those with whom they would never consider doing so.
As each group prayed in a fundamentally identical manner, these divisions were
mainly along lines that were virtually indiscernible.

I did not feel comfortable praying with any of them, although they
welcomed me when they saw me put on the *tefellin*. I felt like God and I had
made some headway, but that I had remaining disputes with how he treated me
and my family that still required further negotiation.

I felt my thoughts were private and personal, so I was surprised when an
old Jew of imposing countenance despite his many years hobbled up to my bed
with his walker to invite me once more to join them. He was dressed only in the
embarrassing robes of the hospital which he had tied with a section of cloth
around his waist to keep from exposing himself, but it was clear he was a deeply
religious man from his long beard and yarmulke. He had a charisma that comes
from many decades of being used to having others' attention when he spoke.

"If it's all right *Rebbe*, you already have ten men. You don't need me. I
don't mean to be disrespectful you understand."

"You are working things out?"

"How would you know that?"

"Isn't it obvious? You were unconscious. Now you're awake. You put
on *tefellin*, but you don't choose to join our prayers. You're caught in between
places."

"I didn't think I was that transparent."

"Like glass I'm afraid. Not to worry. There are few souls that are strong
that have not been tempered by fire my son."

"I can't imagine a religious man like you having had such a period."

"Constantly...What is your name?"

"Yosef."

"Well if you say so, but you don't feel like a Yosef to me. More like an animal in flight, say, a Tzvi, a kind of gazelle, no? No matter. Yosef, if that is what you wish to be called, life is a journey, not an end for a Jew. 'The others,' may *Hashem* bless them, live for heaven if they are good men and women. We live for earth. If you do not doubt, how can you believe? To believe with never doubting is what an animal does with his master. A man searches and finds answers. *Hashem* is the question and the answer, so if you are searching you are with Him and if I have found Him I am with him just the same."

"Do you really think so?"

"I'm not talking to hear myself speak Yosef. I have too little time left on earth for that."

"I'm sorry, of course you think so. I was just using an expression. What is your name *Rebbe*?"

"I am the *Kozenitser Magid*."

I was awestruck. Although I did not know his exact origins, this man was even known to someone as ignorant as me as a great sage.

"May I have your blessing *Rebbe*? A blessing to find my path."

"Of course child. May He who lives forever keep you in His sight and show you light for your way."

"Thank you. And would it be too much to bless my children born and unborn."

"Hmm. Of course. May your children live, find joy, know their grandchildren, and recognize He who gives us life. Now I have to go join the prayers. I hope we can talk later and you can tell me your story."

The *Magid* was not the only one on the ward who read minds either.

"So, it seems our little girl from the *shtetl*, Devora, has a crush on you," said Nurse Levy, looking to stir up a little trouble in paradise.

"I can't imagine why. I must look like hell warmed over."

"You think so? You really don't know, do you Yosef?"

"Know what? I don't know even what you're talking about now."

"Yosef, if I was thirty years younger, I would be after you myself. You're a very handsome young man Yosef. And you have a look about you. A little like a pirate in one of those new cinemas, all muscle and scars. It's more striking I think because it's unusual on a Jew. And there's something else that would draw a girl's attention."

At this point I just gestured for her to go on. She was going to anyway.

"You look like you're pleading, but won't ask for help," said the old man in the next bed who I had not been so sure was counted among the living.

"Who asked you? And what does that mean anyway?"

"It means you have a look like a wounded deer who needs help, but can't ask for it," continued nurse Levy. "No girl can resist that. We're suckers for wounded helpless deers that won't ask us to help."

"I had no idea."

"That's the last part that gets us. Now get some sleep and get some fat on that muscle."

In the coming days I slept much of the time. By week's end, however, I was strong enough to walk the halls and then in the small garden. Always, Devora was there by my side. It was a sweet flirtation, because it contained an innocence that I had lost. I could not have imagined seducing this girl, even if I had the strength. She was the nice girl that you married--pretty, gentle, with a Jewish soul that felt and cared and gave. She would be the backbone of a Jewish household.

"Devora, can I share something private with you?"

"Are you in trouble?"

"Why do you ask that?"

"You seem pensive all the time, and constantly, well...constantly looking over your shoulder."

"It's better that you don't know. You would not think so well of me."

"And what makes you believe I think well of you now?" she said pinching my side.

"Enough of that! Can I tell you what I'm thinking or must you play these girlish games?"

"I'm sorry, I do want to hear what you have to say."

"When I was laying there unconscious, I had an epiphany."

"A what?"

"A vision. Like a religious experience."

"I saw my *Zadie* and he told me that we all must leave Europe and go to Palestine or America."

"I don't mean to minimize what you're saying Yosef, but many people think that. It's not quite what you call an epiphany."

"Of course not. But he said that I would know what to do, what path to take, because when I woke up I would receive a sign. He said that God would show me the path. When the doctor came, he placed his hand on me. The first thing that I saw when I could see clearly was the sign of God impressed on his hand, you know from his *tfellin*. The Hebrew letter, *Shin*, signifying God was the first thing I could see clearly."

"So God wants you to live."

"Yes, but more than that. I think that God meant that I should go to Palestine. America is the Golden Land, but Palestine is the Holy Land."

Devora looked at me with eyes that expressed deeper feelings than I could accept just then. I lowered my eyes from her gaze.

"Devora, I must tell you something else. I promised my mother that I would protect my family. If God is telling me that I must leave Europe because of danger and that I must go to Palestine, I need to bring them out as well. I have to find a way. *Zadie* did not act like the danger was imminent. But it is lurking in the shadows, in the way we are treated, in the way we are hated. He would say, 'Watch the Armenians.' He felt God was testing the world with the Armenians."

"What does that mean?"

"The Turks have been killing Armenians for twenty years now, and the world has done nothing. 'If Armenians, why not Jews?' he would say.

Another girl might have argued with me or patronized me for having such wild fantasies. Devora was of deeper spirit. All she said was, "Then we must prepare."

I was sure I would never see her again. She gave me her address to write to her, but even as I took it we both knew I wouldn't write. She could see that I was set on a destiny that would not take me to a farm near Vilna, or off with her brother to America. She was to become more a part of my life then I ever dreamed. Those long hours that we spent talking and walking and helping me gain strength formed a bond that would kindle a fire years later. When we parted, she kissed me fully on the lips. I am sure it was her first kiss and she ran off crying. I would find her through the horrors of war, or more precisely, she would find and shelter me. She placed one line on the note with her address. "You are my *beshert*, my destined partner."

With Devora leaving, I settled into a depression and spent my time looking out the window at the passing days. I had not seen Mendel or the others I had met. After all, I told myself, we hardly knew each other and there was little bond there. I worried that I would not have work. I worried that the police would think to search the hospital as they might have thought me hurt in the escape. I had no strength or choice but to wait.

Mendel did come.

"So Yosef, you look better already. How are you feeling?"

"Much better. Thank you. And thank you sir for bringing me here."

"I would leave you in the street? Of course we brought you. You were the big soccer star!"

"Yes, a star that collapsed."

"That's true, but we have never beaten those *mamzers*, bastards that they are, from Jaruszewski's Courtyard before."

"We didn't beat them this time."

"A technicality. They always beat us by two or three goals. We can walk with our heads held high until the next game and they are simmering in their piss."

"Mendel, I'm worried. Do you think there will be work for me when I get out of the hospital?"

"What day is today?"

"Tuesday, I think."

"And do you see me working?"

"Well no, now that you mention it you don't look like you came from work either."

"A genius. That's right. There's no work. The strike spread and the officials became angry, blaming the Jews as usual."

"And so what happened?"

"Are you always so impatient? Isn't it obvious that I'm telling you what happened?"

"Yes, I'm sorry."

"No problem. Where was I? Oh yes, how are you feeling?"

"Mendel, you were telling me about the work situation."

"Oh yes, that. Well, as I was saying before you interrupted, the officials are encouraging the non-Jewish merchants to only buy from non-Jewish suppliers. That might mean that the Jewish merchants could buy from Jewish factories, but they are not allowing suppliers to supply the factories with raw materials. The *goyim* are avoiding the Jewish stores too. There's hardly work for anyone. As for the porters, if there's any work and a Jewish porter delivers something to a non-Jewish merchant, he won't accept it."

I tried to take in what he was saying. I felt that I was getting back my strength, but without work there was not much I could do. My emotions showed on my face.

"You look worried Yosef." "Shouldn't I be?"

"Well, to be perfectly honest, we're all worried. But I get the feeling that somehow you'll land on your feet. Yenta told me to tell you that you can sleep in the back of the café on the mattress for as long as you need. You can help by cleaning up the kitchen, although she says she can't afford to pay you. Still, it's a bed. You can always make enough to eat. It's when you have to feed a family that times get rough. Children need clothes and shoes and warm coats and food and money for school. A young man can survive on the streets. Don't plan on buying a new suit any time soon."

"Thank you, Mendel." "Thank you! For what, being the messenger of doom?"

"For talking to me as a man. I have to know reality if I'm to survive."

With Mendel's leaving I closed my eyes and tried to sleep. I was awakened by Dr. Tobiansky who wished to examine me.

"Tired are you? Well that's understandable, but you're really doing well. In a few days we'll send you home."

I did not mention to him that I didn't have a home, but since everyone was reading minds around the place, I didn't think it necessary. He probably knew.

"Doctor, you know I met the *Kozenitser Magid*. What an honor, even for an ignoramus like me."

"It must have been Yosef. Where did you meet him?"

"Here, the other day."

"Really. You're quite sure?"

"Yes, of course. Why? Do you doubt me?"

"Who am I to know, but the *Kozenitser Magid* has been dead for nearly one hundred years, although the Chassidim still revere his name and his teachings. I do have to write to Dr. Freud about you. Most interesting. *Kenites* and the *Kozenitser Magid*."

As I dozed, the old man in the bed next to mine alerted me to the presence of two policemen coming down the corridor. I did not wait to see if they were coming for me. I grabbed my clothes which I had Devora bring me to hide under my bed and I was out the window before they entered the ward.

When they asked the old men where the young man was who was supposed to be in my empty bed, they told them I had gone to the toilet. "You better sit. With what he's got, it'll probably be a while? You've been in Warsaw long as a policeman?" And I was off into the night.

When I returned to Yenta's café, it was already dark. I hoped that the police hadn't been looking for me at the hospital, but simply doing a regular check of who was what and what was where. Had I been fleeing the Germans I was a dead man, but the Russians are less orderly and if there were ten kinds of police in the city, no one authority would share the smallest kernel of information with the next. It was on this I depended. I planned to sleep in the alleyway behind the café, but I thought to look for a window that might be open. The one over the storeroom gave way to my nudging and using a sturdy box left there, I was up and in and asleep in my cubby hole.

As before, I slept late, but this time no one woke me. The trip from the hospital had exhausted me more than I thought possible, but the dizziness was gone and my head felt clear. Clearer, in fact, then it had been in a long time. When I rose, I found Yenta and her 'cook' already hard at work.

When Yenta saw I was awake, she picked up more or less where we had left off. "I see you found the box in the alley. Good. Now get up and eat. A Jew should eat at a table, not on the floor like an animal. God divided between man and the animals and between Jews and 'the others,' not that they don't also have their place in the world."

"You sound as if you've been talking to my Uncle Meyer, Yenta."

"Nu? I don't have time to stand here yapping. Eat and then find a mop and a bucket. I'm not a charitable organization and you're not helpless."

I had not thought the food could be worse than before, but miracles never cease to exist. Yenta had made my last eggs. The chef was obviously her apprentice. Business had picked up, even though there was still little work, and after breakfast I found the mop and went to work. When a policeman entered and looked around I made to bolt, but a porter stepped on my foot holding me in my place as the policeman only sat down to get his breakfast and chat with the other men.

Life on the street resumed. I had to use it to find a path to my destiny in Palestine. I had to honor my promise to Mameh and protect my family from an evil I could not name or place, but which most Jews understood was lurking just around the corner. If a man tells you he has no fears, it is because he lives in a world where there is no evil that comes knocking on his door in the night. When this visitor walks the world, no one is without fear. It is only that Jews have developed a better acquaintance with the gentleman than most.

Chapter 11

Beast of Burden

With limited strength for work, I explored Warsaw. I could not get enough of the tumult, automobiles, and storefronts. Finding a stoop that allowed a gallery view of the street, I sat with other young men and watched the endless groups of young women walking arm locked in arm, laughing with gleaming smiles and sparkling eyes at their shared secrets, stealing glances at the young men watching them.

Often as not, I made my way to Yekezkel's book cart. The bookseller wore glasses so thick that his eyes were absent, until he looked straight at you, and then they materialized suddenly like dual sunrises. His glasses sank deeply into a nose made ponderous by God so that he would have something of substance upon which to support their weight. He had abandoned the Yeshiva, his wife, and children in order to read unencumbered. He apparently wore the clothes that were on his back the day he left his *Rebbe*'s study, although no longer religious. He sat silently reading in a wooden chair that he carried from place to place strung to his wagon. Only a handful of intellectuals were able to alter his single-minded focus, and then he would light up in discourse on Kant, Engels, or Freud.

I invested a ruble in a used book. This was a work by one of the Warsaw circle, Jankev Dineson. I traded this one in, adding a few groshen for a work by Mordkeh Spektor, and then on to Perets, who I sometimes saw at a café filled with writers where I took him a copy of the book to sign. He did so graciously, ignoring me.

Unfortunately, even as I gained strength, the economy did not. Yenta pretended to find tasks so that I could earn something, but I refused to take advantage of the hand that fed me. Nor was it comfortable for anyone that I slept in the back of the café. True to Mendel's word I did not starve and by lowering my standards I became inured to Yenta's cuisine. I lost all sense of taste.

I pleaded with Chaim for anything offered, but that was no news to him. A hundred men were after him who would do the same. Even the most terrible of jobs were taken with a second man waiting for a job even more terrible if it were to come available. The Jews were blamed in the papers for sabotaging trade.

As I accompanied Mendel one day on his route looking for work, we came upon some fellow porters standing outside an old factory, a load of machinery at their feet.

"What's the problem? Waiting for a circumcision?" asked Mendel, with the banter that passed as humor among us.

"It's impossible. They want us to carry this stuff up to the fourth floor. It's too tight for two men to lift these round the damn spiral staircase on the last floor. We thought we could get it up from the outside with a winch, but the window up there's not big enough. One man has to do it and it's too heavy. It'll kill a man. None of us are willing to die for this lousy job, work or no work."

"I'll do it," I said.

"What you? No offence, but you don't look like you're man enough."

These were not empty words as two of the five fellows were Goliaths to my David and hardened with years of this labor. Nor did he say it in a way that spoke of bravado. He was just stating the obvious, as you would indulgingly to a child who heroically wished to fill in for something that was beyond his father's strength.

"I'll do it." I said emphatically, "You have nothing to lose by letting me try."

"Yosef," Mendel intervened, "a load like this can kill a man, and that's only if you can lift it, which I doubt. If it doesn't kill you, you could be hurt so badly that you won't be able to work again."

"I must." And without further discussion, I climbed to the third floor and placed the worn carrying straps around the machine that lay inert at the foot of the spiral stairs. Two men helped me place it upon my back. The load was crushing and, as my legs gave out from underneath, they took it off of me before

I collapsed.

I insisted on another chance and braced myself as they placed it on me once again. I supported the weight with the straps, my anger, and my will. With slow steps I ascended the staircase, and at the top of the stairs two men helped me unload it from my back. I was not sure if I could repeat my feat, but seeing no choice, I descended again and again until I had lifted nine of the machines to their destination. The tenth I lifted onto my back, but my legs would no longer propel me up the staircase.

"Good enough," said the foreman. "Either you'll come back tomorrow or that machine will stay right where it sits for eternity."

When I went to help the porters with the remaining goods, they refused my services.

"What, I help you out of a jam and this is the thanks I get?!" I was furious.

"Relax son," responded one of the porters. "None of us would have worked today if we couldn't get those loads up there. With these jobs, it's all or nothing. If a crew can't do it, they'll find another. So, you did your part."

"You mean I get a share?"

"No you don't get a share. You get two shares, because that was the work of two, only the staircase made it impossible. Sit down and rest. If you can do that again tomorrow when the pain comes, you've got a job."

I could not straighten the next morning, the pain was so excruciating. They offered to transport me to a kind of chiropractor in a hand cart, but my pride was still greater than my pain and I walked the half-mile, crablike.

His patients waited in chairs amidst bins of Brussel sprouts and potatoes in the back of a corner shop, with a sign that read **Grubman and Grubman, Green Grocer and Anatomical Manipulation**. Another patient said he was the grocer's brother-in-law from his former wife. Despite a divorce many years ago, they continued their business arrangement. It was with his sister that he no longer spoke.

Many left appearing to me more twisted and pained than when they

came, so I was not inspired with confidence. His honor, the grand inquisitor had

no devices by which to put a man to the rack, only an old wooden table that was

half filled with yesterday's produce. He inspected me for a few minutes and

asked about how the injury occurred. He also inquired in much detail about my

relations with women and my marital situation. Having made his diagnosis, he

locked his arms around me and gave me a *kvetch, a twist*, that rather

miraculously eased the pain and allowed me to stand upright. He charged me

half, saying that in my new line of work I would be a regular. He suggested that I

consider buying some apples; they were especially good today and on special.

Before leaving, my curiosity got the best of me. "What did the questions

about my love life have to do with my back?"

"Nothing whatsoever. What could that have to do with your back? No,

you're a nice looking boy and I thought my niece might like to meet you. She's

here most days in the afternoon if you're interested. I think you'd like her, and I

don't have to tell you her father makes a good living."

"Is he the other Grubman?"

"What other Grubman?"

"But the sign said...never mind."

The next day I reported to Chaim.

"So, do you really have work for me?"

"There's always work if you're willing to repeat your performance from

Monday. Do you think you can? I may not look it now, but that's how I started

in this stinking business. I can tell you, many don't survive. It may be better for

you to keep looking for other work or wait until we have something else

available. Like Mendel told you, many of the porters could do it, but choose not

to. This work can kill or destroy a man. He was not speaking poetically."

"I have no choice. Is there regular work to be had?"

"Absolutely, and in some ways it's easier. On most days, there's a

couple such small jobs, or one big one like on Monday. You're on call for when we need you. You don't get paid if you don't work. You get double or triple when you do. You'll be lucky if you last a month, but some do. Big Eleazer over there is near sixty. He's been doing this so long he smells like a mule, even after he bathes."

And this is how I worked. Some jobs I could not do and they would call other men, still stronger and more wiry, or more willing to destroy themselves. One man, an Arab that had landed in Poland by some wrong turn in a war, was so powerful that he only needed to work a few jobs a week to earn his living. He would wait for a job that had to be done and name his price. Everyone called him Ahab, but his name was Abram, after our common father Abraham. I always called a man by his name. Being without mine, I realized how important it was to be acknowledged with the name that God had affixed to you.

Abram only spoke enough Polish and Yiddish to get by. They said his Polish wife was a schoolteacher, but I can't imagine how they conversed. I learned to say to him, *"Salem Aleykum," peace onto you*, which is so much like our Jewish *Shalom Alechem*. He would answer me *Aleyham Salem, onto you peace*, and smile at me with his two gold teeth, slapping me on my back with a force that hurt from back to front.

One day, on a whim, I saw a tin of Turkish coffee in a shop, with Arabic writing and I purchased it for him as a gift. Who knows how it had gotten there. The shopkeeper himself didn't, and so sold it to me for less than nothing. When I gave it to Abram, he shook my hand so hard that I had to grip my arm at the shoulder to keep him from dislocating it.

One day the next week, Abram came to a job removing a safe from a room that had been built around it. He declined the task. Asked if that meant he was pronouncing it undoable, his ultimate judgement and sentence, he responded, "No, it's doable. Get Yosef."

We did the job together, with my squeezing into the corner behind the massive iron box and lifting it with him until we could get it on his back. Thereafter, Abram and I often worked as a team. I became known as the "wiry strong kid who could get tight jobs done." It got me a lot more work.

With winter approaching and a steadier income, I decided it was time to get a place of my own. Yenta responded that it was about time I got out of her hair, by which she meant she hoped I would not forget her and still eat my meals at her café whenever possible, that she cared for me, and was a devoted mother-friend. I told her that I doubted I would survive her cooking any further, which she understood to mean that I cared very much for her indeed. Before leaving, I hugged her and gave her a kiss on the cheek. She slapped me with a dishrag and waddled off sobbing into the back, barking, "if I you don't come back soon, I'll poison your soup too," which only made sense if you knew her.

Much of the money I earned I sent home through trusted couriers going to Kalushin as part of their journey. There were always religious men who would take a letter if you would give a little something to their charity. Many such men, called *shlichim*, which literally means, 'one who is sent,' traveled the country from *shtetl* to *shtetl*. They would be sent raising money for a Yeshiva, a devout Rabbi, poor orphans, or a religious family whose father had taken ill and could not provide for themselves. I would also hear in this indirect way from time to time about my family's well-being.

"Reb Altler, I see you're back from your journey. Was it successful?"

"The *Rebbe* seemed grateful that there are so many that think his teaching important and support his work."

"And did you find my family?"

"Yes, of course. I saw your sister Rachel, who has two healthy children, *kine-ahora, phew, phew, phew*." Reb Altler had my father's habit of pretending to spit, thrice, when invoking against bringing on the evil eye. "They, of course, asked about your health. As you requested, I said that you are well and wished that your whereabouts not be made known."

"Can you tell me more, and please, you will not spare me by sweetening the story? I need to know the truth."

"Very well. It is always hard to hear news from a distance. Let' see.

They said your father is a little better, which I took to mean that he is not, or they would have said he is quite well. Your brother Isaac's business is thriving and he made a donation to the Yeshiva in your honor. This I took to mean that he forgives you and that the business is indeed profiting. Your father I could not see because the woman who lives with him cannot really be a Jew, as she is an anti-Semite if ever I met one. The children that ran around her in chaos seemed happy enough, however, which I took to mean that others in the family are caring for them. Your sister is a special woman."

"How do you know this, Reb Altler, although you do seem to have insight into everything else?"

"That's my business. How else would I know how much of a donation to ask? Your sister is special because she longs for you like a mother for a lost child. She wants to know everything about you. Yet, she barely questions me, knowing that I would have to lie to her, and she would thus place me in a position between two sins. She does not even attempt simple tricks, such as asking where I was last, or where I include in my travels. She understands that I could not break her heart further and I could not bear false witness."

"Was there anything else?"

"Oh yes, this package is for you. It's a simple prayer shawl, but if you look closely, the embroidery is as fine as I've ever seen. Look here. You can also see that several women worked on it. I count six."

"And you think this means..."

"That they wish you to wear it and not sell it, because it is not of great monetary value, only sentimental worth, and of that it is a shawl for a king. More than that, they want to be sure that you have something of them that you will keep and pass on to your children. And of course, they want you to not forget your religion. It is also especially large."

"I am almost afraid to ask what this means Reb Altler."

"I will tell you anyway. It means that they wish you to be married, because it is large enough to wrap around two."

"Thank you Reb Altler. Here, please take a little more for the Yeshiva. You were made to your profession."

"So I've been told."

I found a room on the fourth floor of an apartment block on Grzybowska Street. The apartment was rented to a widow and her two young sons, and I was offered a tiny bedroom of my own. The widow slept with her children and the remaining room served as a kitchen, parlor, and dining area. The bedroom had a small slanted window that let in a great deal of light, but leaked in the rain. Gain something, lose something. I could open it and sit out on the roof and watch the city. Froi Vorsky worked in a sweat shop and the children went to a charity *Cheder* that was known to produce children who were more ignorant on leaving than upon entering.

There was barely food on the family's table. I was not making more than a meager laborers' wage myself, but as a porter one naturally received a little extra fruit or vegetables from the grocer, extra meat from the butcher, or some cheese from the dairyman. I shared these with Froi Vorsky, who repaid me by setting an extra place at the table. I brought candy on Fridays for the children, so that they would have a little sweetness for their Sabbath. The children, lethargic when I moved in, like old people who had lost their zeal for life, gained color and played with abandon to make up for the period they had lost.

The greatest discomfort was that the toilet was outside in the tenement's courtyard. Luckily, this building had a strong, organized tenants' group, and took care to be sure that the hallways were clean and that children made it down the stairs and to the toilet or used a bucket in their apartment to be emptied in the morning. Great fights ensued when protocol was not observed.

The only non-Jews on the street were the janitors and their families, who resided in basement apartments, islands of mechanical non-Jewishness in a sea of Jews. Jews were somehow considered, and considered themselves, unfit for this work. In the small towns everyone was more or less of a type. The city, however, put pressure on people to change. Our street had its share of good families, criminals, bachelors, a handful of Rabbis, merchants, laborers, and men who never did a day of work in their lives.

In the *shtetl*, a package could be placed on a stoop and when the family came back from a trip it would still be there, or someone would have brought it in so it was not ruined. On Grzybowska Street, you dare not leave packages unattended, as they would be gone in a moment. One family, moving in from the countryside, had their wagon stripped clean of all their belongings, as they waited for the janitor to bring their key. When they stood crying by their wagon some of their goods drifted back to their doorstep, but only about half.

We even had a Jewish prostitute, which was as strange to me as if you said that a Priest was Jewish. Actually, for a long time I thought that this was the home of a Rabbi, because of the steady stream of religious men. The Torah does not forbid seeing a prostitute, for a man that is. Only that he should do it where it will not shame his wife. So, the men came to our prostitute from another street, and the men from our street likewise took their business across town.

During this period, I wrestled with God as well as his followers, and found as much testimony against Him as in His favor. One of the numerous sources of my questioning came from Froi Vorsky's two children, Pinchas and Zalmon-Dovid, in the form of the cruelty of their Hebrew teacher. Not only was this man lazy to a fault, the children were better off when he slept through their lessons as then they were at least spared a beating.

One day I came home early, as there was no work to be had that day. Zalmon-Dovid, only nine, was so covered in bruises that I was sure a group of *goyim* had caught him in the street and handed him the beating of his life. Welts were bleeding from where a hard object had been used to administer the blows. I could not get him to talk, but his younger brother Pinchas blurted out that Rav Weinmacher, their teacher, had thrashed him for not knowing the week's Torah portion.

This was too much. I marched into the *Cheder* with the children in tow. I did not have a plan, but just then Rav Weinmacher was in the midst of haranguing a cowering child, screaming in his face and slamming a wooden rod against the table threateningly. I lifted him, Rabbi or not, and held him to the hot stove. I was so enraged that he must have been sure that I would burn him to death, and I barely kept myself from doing so. I told him that if he ever used the poker from this stove, his weapon of choice, or anything else for that matter to beat a child, that I would come back and kill him with my bare hands. I went to leave, but returned to remind him that if Froi Vorsky's children were expelled from his *Cheder* I would kill him twice, once for each child. He did not doubt my sincerity for a moment.

But even in this, I could not completely find the fault in God, because the next day the wife of the poor, devout Rabbi in the next building brought the family a pot of chicken soup and a cooked goose, the latter being well outside of Froi Vorsky's means.

"The *Rebbe* asked me to bring this to your family, Froi Vorsky. It comes in fact from several neighbors who wish to thank you for dealing with Rav Weinmacher. The *Rebbe* himself was furious with the man, and tried to talk to him, but...well, you know. *Gooten Shabbes*, Good Sabbath to you."

Froi Vorsky was more cautious in her reaction.

"You know that Rav Weinmacher is the only one who will take poor children nearby. You should not have gone there without asking me."

"I'm sorry. When I saw the boy's injuries I exploded. I never saw a child beaten so."

"From beatings they will recover, ignorance is forever. I don't want to be ungrateful, but you must remember, you're not their father."

"I apologize."

"Enough said. I hope you're joining us for *Shabbes* dinner. You've provided us a special meal and with the Rabbi's backing and your threats, I think the children will be safe with that Torah sadist."

That night I could hear Froi Vorsky crying and I understood that I had thrown in her face what she lacked. She was not a very attractive woman and poor with two children she was unlikely to find an answer to her prayers. From that point, I let her be both mother and father to her children. She was not unappreciative that I was there to help and be a friend to the boys, and understood that if the boys were to learn soccer or how to box to defend themselves from the bullies in *Cheder*, which also came in boyish form, that a male friend could surely help out without shame to her.

During the next year, I buried myself in work, reading, and my Zionist aspirations. With my socialist leanings, I eventually found myself drawn to *Shomer HaTsayir*, *The Young Guard*. They were training young people to form kibbutzim, the collective farms that were springing up in The Land of Israel. It was a romantic notion as much as anything.

We trained in an odd combination of military tactics and farming techniques, generally using the same instruments. Our swords would more easily be turned to plow shears this way. I had grand plans that Reuven and Isaac would want to go to Palestine as well. But news was that Isaac was increasingly married to the business and seeing Chana Sarah Zeishaltz. I remembered her as a dark-haired, shy girl about my age. I thought she was a good match for Isaac, but with a big family in town, she was no adventurer. Rachel and Reuven were doing reasonably well, although buying cattle and fomenting revolution was more likely to get him to Siberia than the Promised Land.

One day, I was approached by a leader of my Zionist group.

"Yosef, we would like you to commit yourself to the sports club." Those involved in socialist organizations were always talking in terms of commitment, dedication, and sacrifice. It was tiresome. Nevertheless, I swelled with pride knowing that he had obviously heard about my soccer prowess, so I was able to forgive his condescending tone.

"Certainly, when does the team play?" I answered.

"Well, I'm not sure you're quite qualified to play for this team. We have many of the very best players in the city, after all. But I suppose you can try. Personally, I have little time for children's games when world events are demanding our fullest attention."

"What then are we talking about?"

"You see, we are dedicated to expanding the sports team and training in self-defense. With war in the air, Polish nationalism's on the rise. With no Germans to distract them, they're preying on Jews. It's gotten to the point that Jews can't take a Sabbath stroll. Last Saturday, a group attacked a number of couples, some of them elderly. They roughed people up pretty good. We can't tolerate this anymore."

"So what do we do?"

"We would like you to train others in street fighting."

"What? Me? I'm no street fighter."

"That's not what others say. Yosef, face it, we're mainly a bunch of intellectuals and spoiled middle class boys. We've never been able to attract people like the porters. Maybe a son of a tailor here and there, but tailors are good with needles, not knives. You've been in your share of scraps, don't deny it. Nathan says he saw you take on three Jew-baiting thugs at a soccer match the other week."

"Let me think about it, okay? I'll get back to you. I don't know if I'm cut out for this. I'll help out, but I'm not sure I can take the responsibility for leading."

I was not sure to whom to turn. Mendel thought it a good idea as long as I didn't get hurt, which was no help at all. I could not confide in Froi Vorsky either. She had her own troubles and we had never really been intimate with each other despite, or maybe to preserve, living together in such cramped quarters. Knowing of my doubts, God sent a messenger.

I was carrying boxes of books into a Chassidic *Rebbe*'s apartment. It was the winter and he wanted us to join them for *Purim*, the holiday that commemorates Jews being spared still one more time from destruction. I had

been shying away from religion and my Zionest friends were fervently anti-

religion, religiously so.

Still, an invitation for Purim among the *Chassidim* piqued my curiosity.
They would dance with joy and abandon and on this one night drink themselves
into utter oblivion. I returned the next evening and found the festivities in full
force. Food was in abundance and the *Chassids* were dancing like lunatics. As
they spun, their hats were flying in all directions and their sidecurls made them
looks like tops that children had spun with the string whipping through the air.
The *Rebbe* himself, a young man who inherited the position from his father, who
did from his father before him, stood on the table and made a speech that
everyone listened to with rapture, but that in fact was entirely incoherent, so
much had he already fulfilled the commandment of the day. Seeing that I was
not being made welcome, he sat me next to him and spoke to those around him
about their wrongdoing.

"I can see I have failed you," he said with dramatic emphasis and
slightly slurred words. *"The stranger that sojourneth with you shall be unto you
as the homeborn among you, and thou shalt love him as thyself; for ye were
strangers in the land of Egypt.* And this man is not a stranger, but one homeborn
onto us, for he is a Jew. All of us have a single soul that we share that the
Almighty has given us."

With this, the revelry only increased and the *Rebbe* seemed to himself
lose his concentration, but he returned after some time to his teachings as if he
had never stopped. He pointed to me as he spoke. "Who of us could support
Joshua in gaining Israel from the mighty nations? Look how frail we have
become in our wandering. Now look at this one. He is a protector of Israel and
blessed is his journey," he went on in the exaggerated way of someone who is
both drunk and a fanatic. "What risk do we take in our joy and love of *Hashem*?
Moses, our teacher, was a leader, but poor of speech. Aaron was his
mouthpiece. Joshua was his right hand. The Messiah will not come until our

three parts are one."

"And what of those who wish to establish a new Israel before the Messiah has come?" I challenged him when he sat back down.

"We cannot support this. We can only join you when the Messiah has come."

"If you are not too drunk, I would take your words to mean that we could go, but that you could not join us."

"You have learned in a good *Cheder* Yosef."

"But we may have to fight for the land."

He looked at me, suddenly sober and answered clearly, the slurring entirely evaporated from his voice and the hazy unfocused look vanished from his eyes.

"You would fight to protect yourselves, yes? And not only in the Land of Israel, but right here in Warsaw. So what choice have you? You are obligated to protect a Jewish soul if it is in harm's way, Messiah or no Messiah. Who knows, you might force the Messiah's coming, no one else has. But this is not what you are really asking, because you're already a fighter. You turn to me because you want to know if you must lead. The answer here is simpler. *Hashem* has picked you as a leader if others ask you with a true heart and in this case I think you believe they have."

"And what leads you to think so?" I pressed.

"Yosef, I was made the *Rebbe* of these families when I was fourteen, when my father had a massive stroke. I am only twenty-six now, not that much older than you, but I have been leading for half my life. I will tell you this; it's a fearful task. The fact that you resist, however, is a sign that you might in the end be a good leader. Those that rush to such a station are often in it for the wrong reasons. Whether or not you are capable of leading is more the decision of others. Let it be the will of He who lives forever."

And so our sports club was formed and I trained the middle class boys in the Young Guard in street-fighting. My message was simple. Only fight when you must. When you must, there is no halfway. Strike with intent to inflict the most harm with whatever weapon is within reach. The main thing is to strike quickly, mercilessly, and not to stop. The lesson lasted maybe fifteen minutes. A second man was therefore elected my committee co-chair and in the coming weeks he proceeded to lecture from a text on fighting techniques and strategies.

Several such sports clubs had formed, numbering a couple of hundred strong young men spread over the city. Although I put little effort into training these city intellectuals to fight, I put much thought into the system by which they would become a credible deterrent. We walked in pairs on the Sabbath, with other pairs within the sound of whistles we carried. This way we could cover large sections of the city with relatively few men, but were able to attract a strong response when necessary.

We intervened to protect people where we could. Seldom would these bullies stand up to even two men who stood up to them, and more often we responded quickly with six or eight men. The anti-Semitic newspapers, there was not another kind, decried the Jews' sports clubs as international agitation created to thwart Polish independence. The police aided the anti-Semitic gangs and followed close by to intervene on their behalf if we gained an advantage.

Jewish representatives of the community and Rabbis came to us pleading that we disband. We were only making matters worse, they insisted, but we would not hear them out. This was the chronic, timeless fear that we were fighting against. The only way to live among 'the others' they thought was with a bowed head. Nor did they feel shamed doing so, as the oppressed Jew would quote the scriptures that said the defiler only defiles himself. The Jews held 'the others' in such deep contempt that they felt no more shamed by him as would one by a rabid dog who attacked you. He was just being a mad dog, and it was no shame to cower from him.

With rising nationalism, the anti-Semitic attacks grew bolder throughout the countryside. Old Jews were caught in the streets by gangs and had their beards yanked or cut off. Women were molested and raped and mini-pogroms raged from town to town. Although we were relatively few in number compared to the endless horde of anti-Semitic gang members and general rabble that could be exhorted for a little fun and Jew-baiting, we were aided by the fact that Jews lived in circumscribed neighborhoods, branching out from the old ghetto. This was in part from a will to stay together and the fact that Jews were not allowed to rent or buy in Christian areas. This meant that the nationalist gangs had to enter the Jewish areas to unleash their Sabbath menace. With many out of work, however, they were only too happy for the diversion.

We entered a protracted war of attrition, but seemed to be gaining a space for people to go out for their stroll from one week to the next. Mostly, they would see us coming and be on their way. However, at other times a leader stood up among them, and they were not all cowards for a fight by any means. Still, only the most diehard among them was looking for even odds, and they lost from their ranks the drunks and lowlifes who they would drag from the bars to fill their numbers. This also meant that those who they could rally were the most committed and ready to do harm.

It was the end of the Sabbath and as the streets became more crowded I was on my way to a dance. I came across two of the worst sort, with their black armbands, signifying their allegiance to their cause. They were haranguing religious Jews that passed them, pushing some to the ground, pulling earlocks of others, grabbing their prayer books and throwing them in the gutter. I was ready to just leave it be, as the *Yeshiva* students were grown men and should have been able to stand up for themselves. But then the two started in on an old woman, taunting her. They drove her from the sidewalk into the street and a wagon almost ran her over.

I saw white. Grabbing a rod that hung to crank an awning, I tore into them. They tried to take me on, but they did not know the anger inside me. One ran, but I did not let the other out of my grasp and I was banging his head on the curb, my screams louder than his. I would have killed him if a group of storekeepers had not restrained me.

I was still kicking and fighting as they carried me to the curbside, allowing the poor devil to flee with his life. Although the men were gone, my demons were not. A restaurant owner let me hold my head under cold water to regain a semblance of composure and a clothier gave me a new white shirt and jacket to replace the one that was torn. A non-Jewish owner of a sweet shop gave me a box of chocolate wrapped with a bow for my sweetheart, had I possessed one. When the police came to investigate, with the two bloody and ragged men trailing in their wake making their case, the crowd surrounded the policeman and I slipped off, better dressed.

We had meetings and more meetings, but for all our talk there was little we could do that we had not already initiated. The cycle of violence continued, but life went on as it always did. Occasionally, the sports club actually played soccer and, of course, we socialized. I kept my distance from more than casual involvement with the girls, not wanting any entanglements. At work there was the occasional woman who invited me up to her apartment for a little extra tip after carrying her heavy parcels, but this was more myth among the men than common practice.

Another Sabbath, I was walking with one of our group, Moshe, as we made our patrol. The neighborhood was quiet and we flirted with the young women we knew who strolled along the boulevard in small ensembles.

About a block away, two men were harassing Jewish women who passed them. They hurled curses and grabbed at bottoms and made obscene gestures.

"Look at the tits on that Jew bitch. Husband not giving you cock lately? Come here *Sheeny* bitch and we'll slip into the alley where I can give you a quick fuck."

"You don't have to ask a Jew bitch for a piece of ass. All they're after is money. A few groshen is all it'll cost you. Just throw her a couple of coins and whip it out. Her husband will be glad for the money."

When one middle age woman answered them back, they slapped her once in the face and then grabbed her by the breasts and pulled her thus along the street despite her cries and pleas. Others beseeched the men to stop, but they were big fellows and no one was willing to risk a beating. We had arranged for boys who were too young to fight to blow whistles when trouble arose and we would come running. One lad saw them and at less than a safe distance, let out the call for help.

Seeing us coming, the two men took to a run down an alley and we followed them to take them on. The alley dead-ended and we thought we had them, but in a moment there were four more behind us with pipes and chains. The whole rouse had been a trap and I recorded the manner in which I had been fooled for future reference, even as I considered that my future might be short-lived. Moshe was inexperienced, and looked like he was a moment from panic.

"Moshe, we have to fight our way back to the street. Take your blows, give back what you can, but stay on your feet and keep working your way back out of this alley."

With this, we ran at the four fellows behind us. They fell on us with a vengeance and we took their blows hard. I felt a chain wrap around my neck, and dislodged it just as I was seeing black. We held our ground as best we could and by inches made it back toward the open boulevard and the slim chance of escape. Taking a hit to the head, I felt the blood flow down my face and begin to impair my sight. I had to keep pulling Moshe with me as the fight was almost gone from him and he could do little more than protect his head from the blows coming now from all directions. Another stroke felled me to my knees and I would have been a dead man, but Moshe rose to the occasion, and with more courage than strength, pulled me to my feet.

All the time, the youngster with the whistle stood his post and blew his whistle with all his heart, exposing himself to as much risk as us. Like a drummer boy at war, he played his tune to hearten the soldiers on and rally the troops. His call was heard and others came to our aid and the gang ran, not prepared for an even fight.

I took thirty-eight stitches and Moshe needed eighty and his arm set in a
cast with a serious break. We each lay several days in bed. The drummer boy
came to visit me with twenty-five stitches to the face that he wore like a badge of
courage thereafter in the street. Years later I heard he was a leader in the Warsaw
uprising against the Nazis. With few weapons and small numbers, they held off a
German army division before succumbing. I was not surprised.

For the most part we were able to protect some small areas and Jews
took to walking within those zones. It was the best we could do. For a time it
looked like the fun had gone out of the game for them and they would leave us
this small concession, but then it escalated once more. They could not be
satisfied until they could drive the Jews from their land, as if this would rid them
of us and Russia as well.

One Sabbath, several large gangs entered the Iron Gate area where the
Jews had felt relatively safe among their own kind. In the early afternoon, with
Jews taking their walks and religious Jews returning to their prayer houses for
afternoon Torah study, the gangs attacked.

One group surrounded three old men and were forcing them to dance or
be beaten. The old men danced and had their beards pulled as they were slapped,
punched, and kicked. A group of young women were followed and the men
behind them pinched at their backsides. When they went to break into a run,
other men came from their front and pushed them back into the others who pulled
at their clothing and ripped it from their bodies. In the cold of the day they were
stripped naked and pushed among the men who squeezed their genitals and
breasts and made vulgar humping motions at their backsides.

Another group surrounded a young, modern couple pushing a baby
carriage, just the type who would during the week have advocated that we can get
along with our Christian neighbors if we just didn't dress and act so differently.
They pushed at the man and grabbed at the woman. They beat the man to the
ground when he fought to protect his wife and child. Three men tore her coat
from her back and ripped her blouse to expose her breasts to the cheers of the

others. They pulled the woman to her knees and undid their trousers. "Here, you bitch. Have a taste of some cock that hasn't been cut in half." When she resisted, she received a kick to the side, but she fought back valiantly. Then, one of the men held the baby in the air as if to throw him to the ground and the woman submitted to their sodomizing her. The men turned her husband to watch, one man holding his face to the ground in her direction with his boot.

We had been ready for them and hoped that they would hit in the Iron Gate area where the narrow, winding streets would allow us to come upon them as if from nowhere. I had held our men from the streets to make us look vulnerable. I had not, however, anticipated the magnitude of their attack. They had come looking for a day of reckoning.

Many of our men hesitated when they realized the nature of the brawl that awaited them. I had learned, however, the cry that rallies men, and when faced with the rape of their women, they were emboldened with the primitive call to defend what was their birthright. The gangs were at least our number if not more, but we descended on them like locusts from all sides, armed with ax handles and lead pipes.

I directed our men to split into three large groups with ten of the fastest men held in reserve. We hit them first where they were congregated in larger number to break their spirit. We came down on them with a vengeance and without restraint. The reserve group turned the tide of small battles that began to go the wrong way. The clash held the violence it promised, but was over in half an hour. The police tried to intervene on the gang members' behalf, but they were few in number as they had vacated the area to turn a blind eye to the assaults. A group of a half-dozen young religious men, who had themselves been humiliated just moments before, joined the melee with their earlocks waving in the air and had to be held back from killing two men. In short order we broke some bones and sent those that could still stand running and bleeding back to their own neighborhoods.

Chapter 12

Bringing on the Messiah

In the weeks that would follow, The Polish press would decry the formation of Jewish anti-nationalist gangs that were under the influence of Bolsheviks, Germans, internationalists, or a Jewish Cabal, and sometimes all of the above. The Yiddish press would try to report what occurred honestly, but the Jews who would read it, would already know every detail, and of course, possess their own "insider version" of the "true story." From our own ranks there would be self-recrimination that we had not moved quickly enough. For now, during the brief, still moment as the victorious gladiator stood before Caesar and the crowd judged his fate, we could bathe in our glory.

Wet with perspiration and wide-eyed, one of the religious men tentatively approached us, as we sat in a café and recounted battle stories. He had the same flaring nostrils and wide-eyed expression of the dominant beast in the pack. Even as Jews, we seldom looked beyond their black coats and broad hats, anymore than one looks at the face of a nun. But face to face, this young man was an imposing figure. He was a head taller than me, with broad shoulders and handsome, strikingly so.

"That was wonderful! We really gave them what for."

"We certainly did. I didn't think you *Yeshiva* boys had it in you," I responded as others slapped the fellow's back and invited him to join us.

"That felt...I don't know...liberating. Like chains were removed from me. I felt free for the first time. You don't know how many times I've bitten my lip, sometimes until it bled as I endured their insults."

"So why did you never fight back?" one of us challenged him.

"I didn't think I could, quite frankly. And our Rabbis tell us that fighting makes us like them. They even argue that taking their blows will help bring the Messiah."

"And you, what do you think?" I asked.

"I think that we must fight back."

"I never imagined that any of you thought this way," I said incredulously.

"Oh yes, there are many of us. But let's face it, our kind and your kind don't talk much. I saw what they did to that young couple and I exploded. Do you think she'll be okay? No, don't answer that. It's a stupid question. How can you recover from such a thing?"

Nisan Eisen, as he was called, and I met often over the following weeks. Each of us was quite unwelcome in the other's circle, so we met in places where no one knew us. We talked of everything, trying to absorb each other's lives. There was an attraction that pulled to make us part of the other. Eventually, we realized that what others thought didn't matter. I no longer saw his long coat and beard and he no longer saw my short jacket and clean shaven face. This did not stop others staring at us as we walked together down the street, but we became enured to their reactions.

In many ways Nisan and I were from different worlds. He was the son of a well-to-do merchant, and his father was dedicating his life for two things, to have his one son study Torah and to marry off his daughters to religious scholars. He had lived a sheltered life of religious urbanity, wanting for nothing, sure of the place that had been chosen for him. I was to be the wrench in the works on more than one count.

One Sabbath he brought his sister to meet me in the park. Nisan was handsome and dark, with strong features. Hadassah was not so much beautiful, as exotic. She had the same dark cast as Nisan, but her slanted eyes hinted at ancestors of the far eastern provinces, a mixture of Europe and China. She was lithe, but in an almost masculine, athletic way. She had none of the shy reserve of young religious women and looked me in the eye and asked frank questions, which upset my balance.

Hadassah would sometimes join us after that when we met. As the three of us got along so well, it was only natural that Nisan invite me to their home for

Shabbes dinner. I demurred, not having proper clothing, but Nisan promised to bring me a jacket. It would have to one that had been his in a previous life if he thought it was to fit me.

"Now, you've no excuse," he said. "And I'll bring a shirt and tie, in case you think there's any way out of this."

Jacket or not, Hadassah thought it was a terrible idea.

"You know how father is."

We should both have listened to Hadassah's advice to avoid their father at all cost. She found him rigid and intolerable. Nisan, for his part, still had hopes of converting him to more modern thinking. In his mind, I was to be part of his father's reclamation.

As their father would barely speak to a woman, Hadassah recognized there were no inroads for her to make. Already she was only religious in his sight, and read widely and cultivated activities that he would have found of 'the others'-- plays and concerts and talking to men. As others waited for the third star to appear to mark Sabbath's end, permitting them once again to smoke, she would light her cigarette and puff away, having waited the rest of the day. Her point was that "I can do with or without this cigarette. I am not a slave to it or to the Sabbath."

On Nisan's assistance, and having run out of excuses, I was finally pinned down to a Friday evening. The porters always finished work early Fridays to prepare for Shabbes and I made sure not to dawdle and left time to clean myself up and make a proper appearance. I departed with plenty of time, but somehow managed to still lose my way.

I arrived at their door in a sweat, having run the last few blocks. To add to my discomfiture, I mistook the maid that greeted me for Nisan's mother, and trying to make a good first impression, went to kiss her cheek. Thinking that this panting stranger meant to molest her, she gave a shriek, slapped my face, and ran off to the kitchen in a state. Needless to say, the family and guests wondered what had transpired in the foyer as maidless I made my way into the parlor, but there was really no way to explain it. One cannot say, "Oh, it was nothing. Your maid merely thought I was sexually assaulting her." Nor would it have been any better to say I mistook the maid for Froi Eisen, worse perhaps. So, I merely let the matter pass, and tried to act as naturally as possible, dripping sweat, disheveled, with one crimson cheek.

Once the meal commenced, Rav Eisen let the matter pass and became more convivial. What might or might not have occurred with his gentile maid was of little moment to him.

"So, Nisan tells me you've made quite an impression on him Yosef," began Reb Eisen. "Better, in any case, than you made on the maid."

"I'm terribly sorry about that...I mean with the maid, but yes, with Nisan, he has also made quite impression on me."

"Where is your family from?" asked Froi Eisen.

"Yes, where are you from?" echoed Reb Eisen, as if his wife's question was invalid unless he sanctioned it.

"From a small town east of Warsaw, Karczew. I lived there with the Answel family after losing my parents." I had chosen this story because I knew enough of this town from visiting my aunt and uncle to answer the general run of questions if I happened on someone familiar with the town and its inhabitants. I swallowed the sin of calling my father dead in order to protect him, as people shied away from questions about an orphan's parents. The Answels had since left for America, so I was safe from their being contacted as well.

"And you work as a porter I understand," Reb Eisen went on.

"Yes, this is how I support myself."

"Any honest work is blessed," he went on, this said with little conviction, "but Nisan assures me that you are well-read and good with numbers. Wouldn't there be work that's...well, easier on your back and for better pay?"

"Father, you promised not to drill Yosef, and here you're doing it anyway," Nisan charged.

"I am doing nothing of the sort. I'm only showing interest in your friend."

"That's quite alright Nisan. Your father has every right to ask me what he wishes at his own table."

"Thank you Yosef. At least you have some respect for a father's place, not like the non-Jews I'm raising. Perhaps I should send Nisan to the street to work with you to learn a thing or two about manners. Now where were we? Oh yes, why do you choose to work in the streets?"

"I'm able to earn well as a porter, sir. If I were to enter a job at a bank or in a business I would have to serve an apprenticeship for years of little pay. I'm saving to go to Palestine."

"So, you are one of *those*," this word saying everything he felt about politics and Zionism, none of which was good. "I can't say that I rejoice living among 'the others' here in Poland, but until the Messiah comes the Rabbis say that a Jew should not return to The Land of Israel. Otherwise, I would be the first to go, especially if I was a young man like you."

"We cannot wait for the Messiah Tateh while we're killed off like flies and starved to death," Hadassah challenged aggressively.

"And since when are you a Zionest my little princess? You, who can't live without a new dress each week and dance lessons."

Although he played the patrician's part, you felt his desperation. He sensed that he was losing his children to the ways of 'the others.' In his eyes, I was no more than a non-Jew, and worse perhaps, because I was a bridge over which his children could divert from the path he had chosen for them. Had it not been for the other guests at the table the scene might have exploded, but for the sake of his Jewish guests, Reb Eisen showed restraint and allowed the talk to drift to politics of the day--as they related to Jews--and a discussion of the portion of the week from the Torah and its meaning. Cordial to the end, he made it clear I was unwelcome.

His disdain propelled Hadassah in my direction. His pronounced disregard made me a prize worth having. Still, she had a strange way of winning me over. She was not content to sit like the other young women and allow the men to take charge. She organized the women into vowing not to work in the kitchen when the group moved to Palestine to establish their own kibbutz. To emphasize the point, she had them refuse to prepare coffee and bake cakes for meetings, "better to start now and not set a precedent." She had them walk out of meetings when their voices were ignored. She drove everyone to distraction, except of course the women, among whom she was enormously popular.

She especially relished arguing with me and we became like oil and water. Wherever I would go I would find her there, and whatever I said she would take the opposite position. She would whittle me down like a teacher with an upstart pupil, tearing at my logic from left and right until I was forced to raise my arms in exasperation. We were obviously falling in love.

I gave her no sign that I was interested in her, in part because I believed I wasn't, and in part because I was fearful of letting anyone close to me. I longed for family and love, but whoever I touched was hurt. Even what little relationship I had with Froi Vorsky and her boys evaporated, as she came to feel that propriety required that she have a female boarder, and I found a room for myself that opened up down the hall.

For her part, I did not fit with Hadassah's life plan either. She intended to marry an intellectual who could earn a good living, a doctor or a lawyer. She had no use for the bohemian way I lived or the poverty that I accepted complacently. How this fit with her idea of joining a socialist collective in the Land of Zion, I cannot fathom, but many of those involved in Zionism were running their train on two tracks, one toward Zion and one toward the more probable destination at which their life would inevitably arrive.

I sensed that Hadassah was becoming infatuated with me, but the more I avoided any romantic involvement, the more she appeared. I believe that I also kept her at a distance because I saw her as too aggressive. Although I considered myself the epitome of all things modern, I was not prepared for my female counterpart.

After political lectures and discussions at the Zionist youth meetings, we learned the new dances that were being carried back to Poland from Palestine. Composed of a mixture of Polish *kleysmer*, with its weeping clarinet, infused with a slight Arabic beat, we whirled around the room and lost ourselves and our politics. It was here that I first saw Hadassah's beauty and grace. Her body was not manly, but strong and when she danced she was light on her feet. As her long dress lifted as we spun, her legs sent chills down my spine with their lissome strength. As we joined arms, she may have pressed up against me, but I did not retreat.

After one such evening when Nisan had not come, I accompanied her home with another fellow. She hooked her arms in ours as we walked as a threesome. I could feel the heat from her body and as she looked into my eyes, she silently pierced my remaining defenses. I went home to my bed late that night, as we were young and we would often go with a few hours sleep, or even straight on to work. When I rose for work in the morning it was later than I had planned and there was a knock on the door. I assumed it was the boys, Pinchas and Zalmon-Dovid, looking for some rough-housing before *Cheder*, but there was Hadassah rather flushed and out of breath. She threw herself at me quickly, before I could create the semblance of a defense, and we kissed with a passion that we had both saved in a world of dreams during that night. I tried to recover my senses and made a feeble attempt to convince her that it wasn't right.

"You're a religious girl. You know as well as I that your virginity will be checked by your mother-in-law after you lay with your betrothed on your wedding night as the guests wait for her announcement."

"But I will marry you."

"You know that's not possible."

"Then I'll use chicken blood like half the others. For my father's money, my mother-in-law will swear it's mine."

Half of me hoped that she would not be dissuaded by my argument, but half hoped she would have the sense of restraint that I lacked. She didn't, and we

collapsed weightless into my bed. From the crack of the window we heard
children laughing and playing, so different than the signature of nighttime love
making. It sanctified our union of the morning with its innocence.

I showered her with kisses and all the love that I felt for her for these
months, but had denied even to myself. She undressed herself modestly and
slipped under the covers, but I could see that she had small, shapely breasts with
nipples that were almost the color purple. Her waist was thin and her thighs and
calves were strong. I touched her gently, but she became feverish and drew me
into her. She let out a small cry, clutching me to her body. I moved almost
imperceptibly, but it was obviously painful for her. I wanted to pull out, so as not
to hurt her further, but her body would have nothing of that. I cried words of
love to her. She was "a flower,""a bird," "a thing of beauty," "my angel," "my
love," "my destiny."

I let her move as she could, her body being the judge of what it could
tolerate. Between us there was barely any movement beyond the throbbing we
both felt, but that was enough. I pulled out at the last moment, but she tried even
then to draw me within her and I barely managed to finish outside of her.

My impulse was to apologize.

"I shouldn't have done this to you." "I should have known better." "I
should never have let this happen." "I'm sorry I hurt you." "I'm terrible." "I
can't forgive myself. "

But Hadassah only looked me in the eye and put her mouth to mine and
kissed me in a deeper place than I had ever been kissed. As my penis regained its
erection, she again placed me on top of her and although I know it was painful
for her, she moved with me in a dance that ballet could not have taught her.

Her father wasn't sure with whom his daughter was involved, but knew
that it was best that they take steps to secure Hadassah's future. They increased
their efforts to arrange matches, but Hadassah refused to meet the men. Twenty
years earlier, and even at this time in the countryside, a marriage would have
been forced on her, but Hadassah understood that the family would not embarrass

itself with arranging a match that she would repulse. They tried a less frontal assault, and invited families and their eligible sons to dinner, as if merely guests of the parents. Hadassah responded by being churlish, and the families would see her as an unacceptable match. Her parents were exasperated, but however they threatened, she stood firm. The mistake they had made was to allow her to believe in her self-worth. With their younger daughter, they would not repeat the error.

Their father came to his senses and realized that I was in some way part of her and Nisan's fall from grace. He forbade them to see me. They bucked at his demand, but when he threatened to cut off their money Nisan crumbled and Hadassah broke free. She knew that she would not be thrown from the home, and unlike Nisan, she was not dependent on her father to enter the business, or be supported from it in the house of study. Nissan, having studied in the Yeshiva, was perfectly prepared for nothing except entering the kingdom of heaven. Nor did he really have the cunning required for business, so they would have to use his personality and good looks to barter for a wealthy bride. In their world and with their family's reputation, they would easily succeed. As a woman, the business was not open to Hadassah, although she could have run the largest factory in Warsaw province. The marriages that her family could arrange were intolerable to her. Ironically, being less valued made her free.

"So, you would rather be off with that *shagitz*, that non-Jewish heathen, than to heed the word of your father."

"He is not a *shagitz*, but a good man and a good Jew who wants to settle in The Land of Israel and build a Jewish homeland."

"Nonsense! He defiles the Sabbath and shaves his face. He probably eats pork on Friday night to celebrate the death of *Hashem* with the rest of the Bolsheviks. I forbid you to see him."

"You forbid! What a hypocrite! In your factory you won't even hire a Jew because they can't work on your precious Sabbath. You have a Christian for a mock partner, so that the Jewish court allows you to have a factory that runs on the day of rest, and your precious *Rebbe* makes the contract for you to do that."

"This is the way you talk to your father? I do what every man does for business. If I could operate on Sunday, I would hire Jews, but you know very well I can't and you can't compete working five days a week. Please be reasonable, or I will have no choice but to cut you off without a shekel."

"You can cower Nisan, but you have nothing to offer me that I cannot give myself. I love you Tateh, but the more you pull, the more you will push me away. Think for a moment Tateh. Could a Torah scholar live with me any more than I could live with him? Give up on that dream. The times have changed, or I have changed at least. If you want to support a scholar in your home for five years, you will have to do it with my sister, because I will not take such a parasite under the canopy."

"Hadassah darling, don't think I do not understand? This is only youth talking. We had infatuations when we were young too. You would learn to respect such a man and from respect comes love, just as it did with your Mameh and me."

"Like you have learned to love Mameh? Hah! You hardly acknowledge that she's alive. If you had it your way, you'd be at the *Shul* studying when you're not working. You haven't talked to Mameh in twenty years. You treat her like dirt, and I will not have such a life."

"And this Yosef, what can he offer you? If he received twice what he has, he would have less than nothing. He's a common laborer and if he loved you he would not let you sink down to his level. I have checked where he lives. The street is a hovel. They live like filthy animals."

"On this Tateh you're right. Yosef won't marry me, because he can't support me and he's ashamed how we would live."

"At least he has some sense. And he may even be a good man, but this is no life for you. You have no future with him."

Hadassah was as persistent with me as with her father. She would have me as I was, but I could not allow her to marry a porter. Nor did I feel that I could live without her. I swung between feelings that I could not possibly deserve her and joy that it could possibly be.

"Oh Mameh, she is so beautiful."

"Yes, she is very beautiful, my *kind.*"

"Mameh, she does not even know my real name. She knows nothing of the terrible things I have done."

"You have repented your sins. None of us are without guilt in what occurred to you."

"Mameh, how can she love me?"

"Because you are good and strong and caring. Because she has a rare depth and understands."

"But she won't love me when she knows the real me."

"She already knows the real you, Tzvi, and that is what she loves. You must move forward as a man. No more of this hiding and child's game of breaking your back to punish yourself. She needs a man who will stand tall. For your future, she will need you to believe in her and in yourself as well."

"Will we know joy Mameh?"

"You will know joy and pain my darling. That is the way of this world. Accept the joy as you do the pain. There is no measure of the one without the other."

Hadassah's father was more astute than he knew. After the harm I had done to those I loved, I could not bring Hadassah down to the way I lived. She would not have complained, but as I looked at those in the apartments around me, I saw how hard their lives were. Poverty breaks a man, but it breaks a woman first. It annihilates love, of this I had no fantasy. For a family, if I worked sixteen hours a day, I would make enough to starve slowly. When there was no work to be had we would simply starve more quickly. If I could not put shoes on my children's feet I could not respect myself, and with that loss of respect would come a hatred that would creep into our love.

I tried to push her away with my moodiness, which I did not have to feign. Hadassah would not allow herself to be rejected, and I could not keep up my haranguing her for long. She would leave me in a huff, exasperated with my immature behavior. Inevitably she would return, and we would both apologize, make love, and begin the whole charade once again.

I feared the end this would bring her, and so gathered my will and broke off our relationship. I could not drag her down into the gutter with me. Before knowing her, I was content with my bohemian existence. With Hadassah in my life, I knew my existence for the awful poverty it was.

For the leper is cut off from those he loves. He is cast out from the community because of the harm he can do them. Only the priests of the holy temple can declare him healed, and my priests were nowhere to be found and I did not know how to purge my wounds.

Command the children of Israel that they put out of camp every leper. And the leper in whom the plague is, his clothes shall be rent, and the hair of his head shall go loose, and he shall cover his upper lip and shall cry: 'Unclean, unclean.'

And so I cried, "Unclean, unclean."

I convinced myself that we were wrong for one another, and that ours was only an attraction of opposites. I found women more like me, base, common, shallow. I flaunted the affairs so she would see me and have to leave or hear of them and they would shame her. I found women who offered up themselves with seeming nonchalance, but deeper hopes of snaring a man in love, and failing that into marriage with a pregnancy. But Hadassah had opened a new part of me and instead of seeing them as cheap objects, there for me to exploit, I was confronted with their grace and delicacy and loneliness. Knowing this, I continued with them for the pain it brought me to prove to Hadassah what I was.

There is something purifying about working sixteen hour days, forcing the body to accomplish what is too hard on a beast. On *Shabbes* I looked for jobs among the non-Jewish porters. On Sundays I found jobs in warehouses away from the prying eyes that forbade desecration of the Christian Sabbath. I avoided the places where Hadassah could find me. I ate where I found food on the street and slept on the floor of Mendel's apartment. His wife wanted me to at least sleep on their sofa, but they were already crowded and I would not infect another family. I went back to carrying the heaviest loads. I tried to break my back.

I am a stubborn man. It is a hallmark of my being. I am stubborn even against myself and back myself into positions and feelings that I find intolerable. Like a bad horse, I cannot be trained to reverse a few steps no matter how hard I pull back on the reins. I am bullheaded, contrary, headstrong, inflexible, and obstinate. Compared to Hadassah, I was a rank amateur.

Nisan caught up with me loading cases by the railway.

"Yosef, I'm glad I found you. When you want to get lost, you do a good job."

"How are you Nisan? How is Hadassah?"

"That's what I came to talk to you about."

"It can't work Nisan. Your father's right. You were right to make the choice you made. I have nothing but harm to offer your family."

"I would not have believed that for a minute, but for your recent behavior, Yosef. Now I'm not so sure, but I think that ultimately you are a good man and as good a friend as I've ever known. Me? I am a hypocrite, but until I can figure out a way to support myself, I'm stuck with my father's abuse. Hadassah is stronger."

"Stronger than either of us Nisan, and she deserves better than I can offer. Our being together would destroy her. Look at that woman on the street selling whatever's in her basket. Every day it's something else. Whatever her husband can find her to sell. She's still almost pretty. But look at her hands. Look at her face closely. Look how worn she is, and I bet she is no more than thirty. With me, that would be Hadassah's life. I cannot watch that happen."

"Well, I'm afraid it's not so simple Yosef. Hadassah's on a hunger strike. She hasn't eaten for a week now. She'll only drink water. They're going to put her in the hospital soon if she doesn't stop. The doctor says she's permanently ruining her health."

"Then the hospital will save her life. With me she would starve for certain."

"Yosef, if you believe that, you really don't know my sister. When she gets an idea in her head there's no stopping her. When we were little, she once held her breath for three minutes to prove that no one could beat her at this. She passed out rather than stop. When she regained consciousness, you know what she asked. 'Did I win?' If she hadn't, I am sure she would still be holding her breath to this day. She will kill herself if she chooses."

When I came to their home, her mother was crying and frantic. Her father was chewing so hard on his Cubans that he was meeting the smoking end half way. He brought me into the parlor.

"Young man, do you see the harm you've done? I warned you both, and now you're killing her."

"I'm sorry. I've really tried to listen to you. I can't find a way out."

"I am a man who always has the answers, but when it comes to my daughter I lose my reason as well. I can't pretend that I approve of you. There's something about you that worries me. I can see that you come from a good family. I am no fool. I can see that you are a good man, as well. But you are the wrong man for my daughter. You have a streak in you that causes you to sabotage yourself. You will bring down my daughter with you."

"That is what I told Hadassah."

"She told me that as well. But now she's starving herself to death. I intended to offer you money to go away, but here you did it for free, and it may cost me my daughter. Yosef, I swear she has broken me. What if I agreed to pay for you to go to a college? Nisan thought that you always wanted to study commerce. If I can support a lazy good for nothing Torah Scholar who will probably suck me dry, why not a future banker?"

"I think you know that I could not accept that. I would have to meet you half way, and I cannot make it even a few steps close to earning my half of such a bargain. Reb Eisen, let me just go in to her. At least I think I can get her to stop this hunger strike. Perhaps over time, she will simply tire of me. I tire of me. I promise you this Reb Eisen, I will not marry her unless I can care for her, and I know that I can't care for her now... I do have one question for you though."

"And what is that Yosef?"

"How did you raise such a daughter?!"

I knocked on Hadassah's door, but she would not unlock it. She insisted I go away. She wanted nothing to do with me. I was a good for nothing. I was beneath her contempt. I was less than an ant that she would not bother to squash and dirty her shoes. But as I said, I am the second most stubborn person on earth, and so I slid to the floor with my back to the door and began to sing every song I knew. I went through the political songs that Reuben and I learned at his hundred and one political meetings, all of the songs of the prayer book, new catchy tunes, and old *Chassidic* melodies. Froi Eisen brought me something cold to drink, then coffee, then dinner. I sang some more and slept through the night. In the morning, Froi Eisen brought me breakfast so that I could sustain my siege, and I began singing again. By lunchtime she let me in.

Still, this was only the collapse of her first wall of defense. As I entered the room, she simply went back into her bed and lay face down with her head in her pillow. When I saw that further cajoling would not lure her out of her cocoon, I got up and locked the door.

I knelt on the floor next to her bed and rubbed my hand along her back. She bucked to reject me, but I persisted and her body rendered itself to my touch. I slid my hand underneath the covers and lifted her nightgown. I ran my hand slowly up and down her legs, squeezing as I was near her tender parts. I rubbed and squeezed her tight buttocks and she whimpered under my touch. I placed my hand between her legs and her wetness drenched me and she began to move her body in response to my urging. I rubbed her between my thumb and forefinger in the firm, gentle way I found her body to need. She came violently into my hand. I turned her over and lifted her from the bed into my arms and sat back down on the bed with her cradled to me. She shivered as if the warm room was exposed to the winds of the winter day.

"What am I to do with you Hadassah? You're impossible."

"Your only choice is to love me."

"I do love you. But I cannot be with you. I cannot bring you down into my world and I don't know if I can lift myself up to yours."

"We can just be together, Yosef. We'll see what comes later."

"This is what you want?"

"Want it or not. It is not only you and my father that must suffer from the way I am. I am a slave to my own emotions. Can't you see that? I have no more choice in this matter than I am giving you. I can't help the way my soul burns, or who it burns for."

"Will you eat now?"

"If you don't remove yourself from my path to the kitchen I will trample you."

As much as I feared losing her, I also was afraid that I could not make something of myself. Tateh was right. What head did I have? Half the class were better students than me. What did languages and numbers matter without an education? Someone of value would not have done the things I had done. There was already a child that I had left to the world without being there to watch over him.

But each night *Zadie* would come to me in my dreams. And he would repeat his chanting in an endless refrain.

"Tzvikala, you have family. Tzvikala we are family. Tzvikala we are everything with family and nothing without one."

I thought that perhaps enough time had passed that I was no longer a risk to my family, but I wanted to be sure. The porters were only a half-step from the criminal element of town and so I turned to Chaim, who knew the right people as the secretary of the artel.

"Chaim, *shalom aleichem, peace to you*."

"*Aleichem shalom, and to you peace* Yosef. What's up?"

"Well, I have a favor to ask of you. As I think you already know, I was in some trouble with the police and the army before I came. A small matter of some army cattle who preferred not to give their lives for Czar and mother Russia. Is it possible to check if I am still a hot item, or if everything has cooled down? I mean can this be found out without disturbing a hornet's nest?"

"I'll take care of it. Is it a girl?"

"And how did you know that?" I asked, but I knew from many others what his answer would be and each thought it was his personal answer and each was correct in their intimate knowledge.

"It's my business to know such things. Can a man be in my position with all these criminals around me and merchants trying to do me out of an honest wage for my men? I'll check and get back to you in a few days. It won't be hard to find out. The army needs things moved too, and we move a lot of things for a certain senior officer that he can't order his men to do, if you catch my meaning."

It took Chaim a few weeks, but the word came back that I was clear and the case long forgotten. "Best not to get caught doing the same thing," he told me, "as that might rekindle their failing memory, but they have bigger fish to fry."

So, the next morning, and then the one after that, I showed up at my Uncle Yosef's bank. I had come by occasionally to glance at him through the window from the street. It comforted me to see him and know that he was well. He looked so official and important, so self-confident. Once I saw Aunt Hannah come in. She passed within inches of me, but could not have recognized me in my current reincarnation.

I paced back and forth at the entrance for an hour, and only after walking half a kilometer to return to work did I steel the nerve to return and face him. When I approached him he almost did not recognize me in my porter's gear with a rope and handler's strap around my neck and shoulders like a Mexican bandolier. It had been two years since we had seen each other. I saw a quickly extinguished look of warmth pass behind his eyes. He kept calm and in a formal manner asked me to come into a more private office to speak to him.

I was certain he was planning to dismiss me as the miscreant I was. I knew he would berate me, call me a blackguard and a fiend, villain, scoundrel, rogue. He would rightfully charge me with having no shame, no integrity, no soul. He would upbraid me for turning my back on my family, for causing so much pain. He closed the door behind me and took me into his arms and cried tears of joy and relief.

My family, and most Jews for that matter, cannot separate tears of joy and grief. It is impossible to tell whether we are grieving or celebrating. We cried through one hundred questions and answers and within the hour he was on the telephone and by that afternoon had me together at his home with Aunt Hannah and cousin Chava and her husband and their son. When I held Chava and realized that I was not jealous of her husband, but happy for her and her good fortune, I knew that I had truly found love.

Before dinner, I bathed and Uncle Yosef loaned me some clean clothes. The sensation of clean, laundered clothing was other-worldly. I felt that I was putting someone else's body into them.

Over dinner we caught up on family news and the way my life had gone. There was good news and bad, but mostly things were as they had been. Rachel and Reuven were well. Yes, Isaac had married Chana Sarah and she was now pregnant. Father was perhaps a little better. It was hard to tell and Friya was squeezing what life was left out of him. Aunt Hannah showed me an affection that she could not express in our village, but was at home within the city.

When the others went to bed, Uncle Yossef and I sat up to talk.

"Remember Uncle Yosef that Passover when you proposed that I study commerce?"

"Of course, Tzvi. I'm afraid I didn't handle that very well. I never thought your father would react the way he did. Your mother's death, bless her memory, changed him. Or maybe she just always balanced his pessimistic tendencies. I've felt guilty over that whole ordeal for years."

"We're good at feeling guilty, we Jews, aren't we?"

"Professionals," he responded, with a wry smile. "But after all, God says we're responsible for the world, and so each of our sins is magnified. I 'm so glad you came to us Tzvi, but why now? Is it a girl?"

"How is it everyone knows everything about me before I tell them? You don't see me for years, and it's as if I had my life story written on my face."

"But it is written on your face. And anyway, life is not so difficult to figure out. It's usually a girl for a young man your age, even before we came to rest a night in Poland."

"It is a girl, and she's wonderful. You'll meet her. Soon. But there's a problem. As you saw, I work as a porter. She's from a good family and deserves better. I hope I deserve better."

"If she loves you, she will have you as you are. Never mind I said that; I already understand. You are so much like my Chava and like your sister Rachel too. If this girl insisted you had to go and become a *gonste macher*, *some big shot*, you would be out the door for the next street car. So, let me guess. She wants you anyway you'll have her. You won't have her unless you're a somebody."

"Why do I bother to talk?"

"Like the rest of us. So you can hear yourself. It's worse when you get married. Then, you're not only told what you think, you're told that you should never be thinking that way. But I don't know the details. How can I help, Tzvi? I'll do anything I can for you and so will your Aunt Hannah."

And I explained my plan. I would use the money I had been saving to pay for school, but that wouldn't go very far. I would need to continue working. I could go to school part-time and work part-time. They always needed a beast of burden somewhere. I would pay back every kopek I borrowed.

"Tzvi, I have other good news for you. First, your *Zadie* left you a little money. Actually, he gave it to me for you when you were ready to study. It's not much; it will pay for maybe a year of tuition. I also owe you money. Don't look so surprised. When I went to study, all the uncles, your great uncles, contributed. The understanding was that we would always help out each other. You're the first to call on me to fulfill my promise. You lift a burden off of me. And don't worry, for the rest, you can keep whatever account you like. Only I will not accept interest. You can pay me back the principal only, and only when you're ready."

That Friday, I brought Hadassah to their home for *Shabbes* dinner. It was awkward becoming Tzvi again, and from that day I was known by my first and middle names, Tzvi-Yosef.

The following Friday, we were invited to *Shabbes* dinner by the Eisen family. I was so proud coming to their door with my suave Uncle Yosef and sophisticated Aunt Hannah and with Chava and her husband. A man is nothing without family. My Uncle was not a Torah scholar, but he had a kind of success that Reb Eisen appreciated. He was an accomplished man of business, and although clean shaven, an observant Jew. His philanthropic work in the Jewish community was known to Reb Eisen.

Between the two men, it was decided that they would support my study for three years and that I would live with my Uncle Yosef and Aunt Hannah. Hadassah and I would marry after I completed two years of successful study. Reb Eisen was made to understand that I would not accept a large dowry, but that what money was due to Hadassah would be given to her directly. Divorces were not unknown, and this relieved Reb Eisen of any fear that I was out to exploit her for his money.

The following month, I took the entrance examinations and received an exceptional mark in mathematics and an outright failure in writing. After a few more months of study, I retook the examination in writing and passed, barely. In the fall I began my studies at the Warsaw Institute of Commerce. When I wasn't in class, I worked carrying everything that was to be carried around Warsaw, and saw Hadassah as much as I could. We were happy and I felt that I was climbing out of a pit and that I was on the path that could take me home.

Chapter 13
And a Man Shall Take a Woman

Between the burden of studies and the carrying of burdens, time passed quickly. Reb and Froi Eisen never accepted me, but they accepted the inevitability of my presence in their lives. Like a small nail exposed in a poor man's shoe, I was not going away. The man can dream as to the day he can afford a new pair. He can work the shoe time and again to remove the protuberance, but it prevails. Eventually he learns to walk without putting pressure on that part of his foot. After a while, it hardly disturbs his gait, and at other times he can think of nothing else. This is how I was to them.

In one sense they were relieved that Hadassah had found a match, because with her willfulness and non-religious ways, they had worried that she would live her life a spinster, "*Gott zol uphitin, God save us, phew, phew, phew.*"

I was a fair student. I had a knack for numbers, and struggled with business law. Living with my aunt and uncle was pure joy. I became the son they never had. My own longing for parenting made me the model child I had never been. Aunt Hannah was not at all cold, as I had sometimes experienced her. It was her city ways that I had found odd, but she was a *Yiddisha mameh* to her core. If I missed a meal, it was kept warm and she up worrying beside it. I was expected to eat it whether I was hungry or not. "Do you think I don't have better things to do than to make dinner for someone not to eat?!" If I had a cold, I was sent out with so many layers I looked like our neighbor, Reb Alderman, who was so fat that as a girl Chava thought that he was what they meant by twins. Reb Alderman and I would meet on such days in the stairwell and have to give one another unencumbered passage because two of us could not descend together in this state.

Hadassah visited often. Uncle Yosef and Aunt Hannah would sit with us and chat, and then excuse themselves to the sitting room. On one such occasion, our kissing and petting gathered momentum in a way that was going to be hard to derail. We were both afraid to be discovered in a compromising position and not wanting to undermine their trust. Rational thought notwithstanding, Hadassah unbuttoned my trousers and rubbed me like a lost puppy just found. My hand found her tender parts and stroked her, and discovered her already soaked with anticipation. She sat herself on my lap and covered us with her silky dress and I entered her as we slowly rocked back and forth in silent adoration. We tried to be as quiet as the night. Still, this was a fool's game. Our bodies were well in control and our minds were not.

Just then, Aunt Hannah uncharacteristically entered the room. My erection shriveled, as if like a turtle it could escape detection. Hadassah pretended to be bruskly shaking dandruff from my shoulders–why else would she have to be so close and have her arms flaying about me?! Aunt Hannah, ever poised, found her glasses, mumbled something about not being able to see without them, and talking as if to no one in particular, said "Isn't young love a glorious thing?"

The incident was never spoken of again. We became more circumspect, and Aunt Hannah never entered again without knocking.

By the second year, I had acquired the skills for an office job, which was called a "good position." I left the porters' artel. Still, my aunt and uncle made my street friends welcome despite the class difference and my uncle even took to lunching with me at Yenta's café. He too never understood the attraction he found there.

The estrangement with my own family continued. From Uncle Yosef's trips to Kalushin, I learned that Tateh and Friya continued to live in an unhappy home. I felt helpless that I could not be there for little Razilla and Jacob. It was sad that I had been able to grow up in a home so full of love and happiness, and that they, though born from the same parents, were denied even a portion of that knowing and being.

When I thought of home I became moody and difficult. My own tenuous self-esteem, and that nagging feeling of being guilty of some sin that I could neither exactly name nor recant, tore at the emerging fabric of my relationship with Hadassah. I accused her of wanting me more as the roguish porter than a successful student and clerk. In truth, I think she did lose some of her excitement when I was no longer the object of her father's outright disdain, but there was more than enough love left in her deeper feelings for me. Still, I was sensitive to the slightest alteration of love's tide, and if she withdrew some small amount, I pulled back disproportionately.

During the Spring of the second year of my studies, the Eisen family was overtaken with the joy and excitement of a wedding. A woman was found for Nisan. She was a beautiful girl, if a bit young and not of the greatest intellect. She was scared of the world and looked to Nisan as a husband and father, it seemed, more than husband and partner. Like many girls of her class, she was raised in a sheltered manner with no knowledge of the world. These peccadilloes, notwithstanding, Nisan was smitten with her, so Hadassah and I held our tongues. He was not by any means forced to marry her. Neither would she be the first girl who became a woman after marriage.

Shifra Reimwaart also came with a considerable dowry, and no one could really argue that they were mismatched if they felt they were each other's destinies. While love was a new concept for Jews of the Pale, destiny was not. Yiddish romance novels and tradition both spoke of the destined love that was somehow found in the match made by parents and matchmakers through the will of God. To be someone's *beshert, destined one*, was everything, and it was not assumed that human intervention played a role in this in any case, so it did not matter that it came from your parents, the *Rebbetzin*, or a professional matchmaker. It was touched by the hand of Him that knows. Shifra and Nisan felt that they had this connection and that was enough.

For all of Hadassah's modern notions, she too was infected with the
excitement of the wedding. She went with Shifra to pick out lace, choose the
flower arrangements, and select dresses proper for a married woman. Hadassah
claimed no interest in jewelry. How could she in our socialist circle? These were
the adornments born of the blood of the masses, after all. But she didn't miss the
opportunity to go with Shifra to the jeweler to select the diamonds that Reb
Reimwaart would bestow on his daughter for engagement presents, let alone
when they were married.

The engagement no less infected our relationship with each other. It is
easy to use the frailties and faults of others as a marker by which to judge our
own superiority. We could see the immaturity of Shifra and her shallowness at
times. We were aware of Nisan's lack of resolve. But we were also exposed as to
how they were more and better than us. They were gentle, where we were sharp-
tongued. They listened, where we wanted to be heard. They saw the faults in
each other, but did not react to them, whereas we wanted to "improve" each
other. They tried to fit into the world and others' needs, whereas we expected
others to make room for us. Their love had less passion, but more devotion. We
never spoke directly of these things, but I believe that our awareness of them
helped us change for the better. This also drew us closer to Shifra–we already
loved Nisan– because with all her immaturity, her tender, caring heart instructed
us about parts of ourselves that were more childish and self-absorbed.

If love was in the air, everything was business for Reb Eisen. His
wealth was understood by him to be a testimony to the validity and sanctity of his
religious fervor and he weighed one by the other. A poor week of commerce
caused him to search his soul for signs of sin in him or his household. What was
he doing or not doing that had brought God's wrath? What charity had he not
considered or considered not enough? What evil lay in his heart? A successful
week was a sign from God that he was favored and that his religious beliefs and
practices were judged and found acceptable in God's eyes. His was a
bookkeeper God and he kept Rabbis as his lawyers to keep him within the Great

Accountant's graces. That his good weeks were actually God's way of testing his insight that he was looking to the wrong God never crossed his mind. He had a system of record keeping which he held to and held the Almighty to with religious fervor. For him, Torah was a list of rules and he read nothing between the lines of mercy, love, caring, or beauty. It was a contract to be upheld scrupulously.

And yet, there was no denying that he was a shrewd man and he knew exactly what his son was worth. Many a father-in-law had laid out a small fortune for a daughter's betrothal to a young scholar who had nothing in his pockets and was ungainly and myopic. Nisan was an Adonis, a fair scholar, and had money in the bank. Moreover, Shifra was deeply in love with everything about Nisan and her father loved her and wanted her to be happy. The size of the dowry paid was so large that Nisan confronted his father.

"It's an embarrassment Tateh. You're extorting them. They have other daughters after all and their money is not endless."

"Ridiculous, it's a good match for the girl and I think she has weak lungs. They're lucky to get someone like you. Anyway, they have money to spare."

"That's the point Tateh. At this price and without your matching the sum, it's as if she is sickly and wanting and I'm David King of Israel."

"What! You expect me to match his contribution? It's unheard of!"

"Tateh, I don't want you to give more. I want them to give less. She will not be able to walk with her head up when this becomes known."

"And who said it will become known?"

"Oh, you will make it known Tateh. This is a coup that you cannot keep to yourself. Anyway, they will know it and it is a bad way to start a family."

"No matter Nisan, it's done."

"If it's done, I ask you Tateh, with all respect, to undo it." And looking at his son's eyes, Reb Eisen was surprised to find the glimmer of a resolve that he had not before seen. "I'm asking you to go to Reb Reimwaart and renegotiate."

"This is ridiculous Nisan. This money's for both of you."

"Tateh, either do it or we'll go to the *Rebbe* and be married ourselves. I will not have Shifra shamed."

"I'll leave you without a kopek. You'll be out on the street. Such disrespect!"

"Tateh, the worst that will happen is that I'll have to earn an honest living. I could study at the university and probably do very well. I'm leaning toward studying medicine."

"Medicine! A doctor is no more than a fancy tradesman. You couldn't make a tenth of what I earn in business. It's a noble trade, but still a trade. It is not your destiny. Anyway, how could you support your studies?"

"I have enough for that. Look how well Tzvi-Yosef is doing."

"Tzvi-Yosef, Tzvi-Yosef! I curse the day that *cholerya* came into our lives. He is truly a plague onto our house! Has Tzvi-Yosef put those ideas in your head? I thought so. May *Adoshem* keep me from the evil thoughts I have for him." And so saying, sidestepping that he did not wish *Adoshem* to keep me, Tzvi-Yosef, from the evil intentions of those thoughts.

Nisan had Reb Eisen in a bind. If there was one thing that he liked less than losing money, it was losing face. If his son was willing to play this card and take him out of the picture he would be a laughing stock. People would see that his son thought so little of him that even his money would not purchase his respect. A shrewd man of business, he saw that his only options were to call Nisan's bluff or to capitulate to his wishes. Part of him realized that he should capitulate. What harm would come if his son had less money? They would still have plenty. They would have a good life and Reb Reimwaart was weak and too generous. The fool would certainly give them more money if they needed it. Why, with their first child, he would buy them a mansion. The man had no sense of proportion. A grandson would cover his daughter's hand in diamonds the size of marbles.

But, no, a deal was a deal and he had only one son. Look how much was invested in bringing him to this point. People would be awed by the dowry he had achieved for his son. It was a sign of the family's status that so much was paid to become an "Eisen."

"No Nisan, you will not do this. It has been settled and undoing it would be an embarrassment. It would be a *shandeh*, a great shame, on the family. If you marry her without my permission, I curse your marriage."

And from this position he would not budge. He saw Nisan shudder at his curse and saw the tears come to Nisan's eyes and knew that he had won. He had called Nisan's bluff and the boy had once again caved in. This was why his son was just no good at business. He lacked backbone; he just buckled under pressure. Reb Eisen felt pride that he understood his son so well, as he understood others in all his business deals and that was why he was so successful. But the tears were the wellspring of a broken heart, not weakness, and Nisan walked out the door.

Nisan came to Reb Reimwaart who sat behind his large desk reading *Gemara*, the "ocean of Talmud." With over two and a half million words, he was not about to finish it that evening. He placed a ribbon in his place and left it open to show God that he meant to come back to it. He took off his glasses and pulled back his satin cap. He came around the desk to the two chairs positioned there and motioned for Nisan to sit, keeping his hand on his shoulder and offering a squeeze of affection. He lowered his own girth more slowly and sat with one hand on his stomach, like a pregnant woman above the shelf of her swelling.

Even before Nisan spoke, he searched for the real meanings that could be seen but not heard, because that is how Torah and people are intended to be read. They existed for him more between the lines than in the black and white of text.

"What is it my new son? You look troubled."

"You are very perceptive Tateh. I am not keeping you from your studies though?"

"And what are my studies for if not to talk to my children when they are troubled?"

"Reb Reimwaart, I've argued with my father. It's a sensitive issue. My father is not a greedy man. He has not asked for the dowry for him, but for me. But for him it is also about winning."

"Your father is a good man Nisan. He gives much to charity, follows the law, and shows respect to others."

"I knew that you would say that Reb Reimwaart and that you would not speak badly of him and neither will I. Still, I cannot accept the dowry you have so generously offered. It makes Shifra look undeserving. I would take her without receiving a shekel from anyone. I would especially do that if it made her realize her worth, because she herself is doubtful of it. I can see that."

"The money is no problem Nisan. What do I have money for, but to give to my *kinder*? It's best to forget this and just to go on as if the money is not part of it. Where is money spoken of in Torah? So very little—about paying a workman on time, about tithing. With family, it is other things we owe and must give."

"I wish my father saw it that way, but we are at loggerheads. I have tried to reason with him, but he won't listen. I've tried to be respectful, but he takes any disagreement as disrespect. I'm afraid to say this, but he has forbidden me to marry under such circumstances."

It took Reb Reimwaart some time to absorb and think about what Nisan was saying. "And what are your thoughts on this?"

"I know that, given these changed circumstances, you would block the wedding or at least hold us back until we could convince my father, so we've taken certain precautions. Please forgive me. We have already exchanged vows before witnesses. Out of respect for you, we have not been intimate sir, other than in our hearts."

With this, Reb Reimwaart sat and thought. He was a man that appreciated that not everything had a quick answer and that conversations often proceeded too rapidly because people feared the silence of thought. In time he came to his own conclusions, but wished to hear more from Nisan.

"What can I offer you son? Without your father's contribution, you will have still less."

"I would be happy with half of what you've offered and that Shifra and I have our own apartment. I think she needs to accept a home away from her parents if she is to be a wife. That is already a lot."

"But I sense there is more."

"Yes, Reb Reimwaart. I will leave my religious studies and enter the university. In the end, I'm not a great scholar, only a scholar. I think that what I know will help me in another area of studies. I wish to learn medicine."

"And you're sure of this?"

"I'm happy for the first time in my life."

"*Loybe tzu Gott, praise God for that.*"

Reb Reimwaart asked for some time to consider Nisan's proposal. After much thought, he called Nisan to his study to give him his decision.

"Nisan, as a young man I was at a picnic in the countryside. For some reason, I left the crowd and decided to take a walk alone. As I walked, I came upon a small lake and the peace of the day was disturbed by a child's cry. Two children were drowning in the lake and I jumped in to save them. In the end, I could only save one. In all my life I have done nothing greater than to save that life. For all the lack of choice that the circumstances allowed, I have nevertheless been troubled most by not being able to save the other. There is no greater blessing in *Adoshem's* eyes than to save a life that He has given to this world. To save one life is to fulfill all the commandments of Torah. I think you will be a wonderful doctor and that this is the true path for you to fulfill *Adoshem's* plan for you."

"I understand part of your story Tateh, but you couldn't save the other child. Why do you still chastise yourself for that?"

"Nisan, I, like you, could only choose a single path of the two that lay before me. Yet, we still mourn for the forced choice and the great loss that follows. In life we have both to celebrate and grieve, and often the one is the other's handmaiden."

His own father sat *shiva* for him, the ritual for the dead.. Even his *Rebbe* came to admonish him. "Such pride is a sin, Reb Eisen. To sit *shiva* in such a case is anathema. It cannot be done to count your son among the dead for this." Froi Eisen was too terrified to disobey her husband, and although she continued to see her son, it was at clandestine meetings from that day forward. Her heart shriveled to half its original size, for a son was equal to two daughters, especially an only son. In testimony of her loss, she never again could fill her lungs and became asthmatic. This gave the constant appearance of her being winded, as if she had just heard some tragic news that took her breath away.

No matter how they entreated Reb Eisen, no matter how they tried to show him honor, no matter that no one was told of the lowered bride price, he would not participate in the wedding or allow his family to attend.

And God in his wisdom frowned on Reb Eisen by increasing his business at every turn. He could do no wrong. Every investment was rewarded disproportionately. If he failed to invest, the bourse collapsed and the stocks others bought plummeted. If his workers went on strike, it was when orders were low, and he incurred little loss. When other men's workers' struck, his factory was running and the demand for goods was overwhelming. Then, the land he purchased for development, mortgaging most of what he owned, could not be used for the purpose he intended. This great loss finally satisfied him that his punishment was forthcoming. In his heart he was waiting for God's wrath at his abstinence, as much as knew he could not be otherwise. By the week's end, he was informed that the land was needed by the government for the railroad at great profit to him. His wealth grew tenfold. He lost all joy in his gold. "It is like a sumptuous meal to a man with no stomach, so my money has become to me," and still his wealth grew.

To Froi Eisen, we brought the details of the wedding arrangements. We brought drawings and materials and seating charts, so that she could have the joy of the wedding held closer to her bosom. Even as she cried, she insisted that we continue. "With what would I be left without this? Only the pain."

When Shifra went for the final fitting with her mother, Froi Eisen was there as well.

"I have something for you Shifra. I hope you like it," she said handing Shifra a small package. "Go ahead, you can open it now. I'm only sorry I can't give you more." The box held a necklace with a ruby placed between two emeralds. Its value was nearly equal to what Reb Eisen had offered the couple in the original arrangement. Hadassah placed it on Shifra's neck laying it on the gossamer thin lace that rose to her delicate chin. It shimmered against the white and reflected like a brilliant sunset over the green sea in the many-mirrored space.

"It is from money given to me in my inheritance from my grandparents. I hope you don't think it's old fashioned."

"Froi Eisen, it's really too extravagant."

"I want you to have it."

"I wish you hadn't given it to me though..."

"Oh, I hope you don't think it's inappropriate."

"No, I only mean that I wanted to speak to you about something first."

"What is it Shifra? I'm so sorry for all the heartache we're causing you. I know it must be making you very upset. If you prefer, I won't come any more and be in the way. I don't mean to..." She knew she shouldn't have come, that she was intruding and evoking in the girl the bad taste of the turmoil her stubborn husband had created for no good reason at all. She got up to leave, realizing that she had overstayed her welcome, that the gift was misunderstood. She was not trying to buy the girl off, only to offer something special from her heart. Why couldn't she ever express herself better?

"Wait! It's not that. I only meant that I wanted to know if I had your permission to call you Mameh. I have a very good one, but a girl like me needs all the mothering she can get."

Shaken, Froi Eisen was barely audible. "Of course my child. Nothing could make me happier."

"And do you bless our marriage then mother?"

Froi Eisen could barely speak. "You want *my* blessings *fageleh, little bird*?"

"Why yes, of course. Why wouldn't I?"

"Because this has always been my husband's role, to approve or disapprove."

"But your blessings are important too. Very much so."

And Shifra approached Froi Eisen and stood before her. Froi Eisen placed her lips on the girl's forehead and holding her so said, "May God make you like Sarah, Rebekah, Rachel, and Leah. May God give you children to so bless, sons and daughters both, and may they be as good and as loving as are you."

And Mameh Eisen knew that her son had the right woman for him, and sensed something potent in this overtly fragile container–like cognac in a delicate crystal. She could not hold the tears back any longer, and neither could Shifra, Froi Reimwaart, or Hadassah.

It is not permitted to have a wedding between Passover and the holiday *Shavuoth*, the Festival of Weeks, which entails most of Spring. On these days, Moses our father was on Mount Sinai and we were waiting for the Ten Commandments. I guess we are still either paying penance for the golden calf-- we and our God have a long memory. Still, since everyone loves a Spring wedding, a number of select days are permissible. On the first day of the new month, the wedding was held, made sweeter by having few other weddings that can be fit in during this time.

The wedding was a splendid affair, if marked by a certain sadness by the absence of the *chassen's* parents and many of his relatives, especially those financially beholden to his father. With the *ketuba, the marriage contract,* signed

in the presence of witnesses, the festivities began. The men came to congratulate
Nisan and his father-in-law. A kleizmer band played and the men danced around
Nisan.

In the women's room, the same ritual was going on, in feminine reverse.
As the women danced around Shifra and her mother, Shifra wondered how
anything as big as a penis, she had seen them in art books, could fit inside of her.
The thought terrified her, especially since Nisan was such a large man. There
was no one to speak to her in a loving way about sex. Hadassah could have done
it, but Shifra could not have accepted or approved of the fact that Hadassah, an
unmarried woman, was sexually experienced. It was all met with a light head,
however, by Nisan and Shifra, as they were fasting to sanctify the day, and so
their thoughts had a mystical, other-worldly edge that comes with the multiple
deprivations they were experiencing.

Following the separate festivities, the men danced with Nisan to the
women's room to escort the bride's party to the canopy. Shifra was a tiny queen
seated on her throne and Nisan approached her to unveil her face and be sure this
was the bride he had bargained for, according to tradition.

Our forefather, Jacob, did not uncover his bride's veil, and had been
deceived into marrying the older sister Leah, instead of his love Rachel.

"And it came to pass in the morning after going unto her chamber that,
behold, it was Leah, and not Rachel, and Jacob said to Laban, their father, 'What
is this that thou has done unto me? Why hast thou beguiled me?"

So, as not to be beguiled again, for three thousand years, we check.
Nisan leaned over and whispered to her, "Don't be afraid my darling," and her
anxiety was replaced by a quiet calm for perhaps the first time in her life. And
the Rabbi spoke the words, *"Our sister, be thou the mother of thousands of ten*
thousands, and let thy seed possess the gate of those that hate them." Something
about 'mother of ten thousands' drove her fears back up to the heavens
themselves.

Under the canopy I could sense Shifra's eyes look up to Nisan seven times, seven being a mystical number. Seven levels of heaven, seven levels of the soul, and seven times it is listed "and when a man takes a wife." Then, Nisan used my special prayer shawl and wrapped it around Shifra, placing the other half on himself to symbolize that they were one.

And the Rabbi gave the blessing, *"Bless are You, Lord our God, who has made us holy through Your commandments and has commanded us concerning marriages that are forbidden and those that are permitted when carried out under the canopy and with the sacred wedding ceremonies. Blessed are You, Lord our God, who makes Your people Israel holy through this rite of the canopy and the sacred bond of marriage."*

Each sipped from the wine. When Shifra received the glass, her hands shook and she spilled some on her dress below her belly. A small cry went out from the women's section and people's eyes closed, pretending not to see the bad omen. With this, Nisan said the only words that mattered, for with this statement, Rabbi or not, canopy or not, a man weds a woman, *"Behold you are consecrated to me with this ring according to the Law of Moses and Israel."* And placing the ring on her index finger, so she could point and say, "that one is mine," they were married, as they had been weeks earlier in my presence.

The old Rabbi wrapped the wine glass in a napkin and placed it under Nisan's foot for him to smash, but he hesitated. The hall held its collective breath. I looked at his face, and saw the heartache, and knew he was waiting a few moments to mourn the absence of his parents, and then his strong leg came crashing down, mixing the joy of the wedding with the sadness held in all Jews' hearts for the destruction of the Holy Temple in Jerusalem of old, shattering the glass. And the poignancy of his action and the power of its deliverance was echoed in the cry of the crowd, "MAZEL TOV!" a cry so loud that the chandelier swayed overhead not only in the wedding hall, but above the parlor of Froi Eisen where she sat in silence miles away.

With this, the dancing began in earnest, the men and women divided. I looked across to Hadassah and signaled her to meet me outside and we secretly made our exit and kissed in the hall. We were each longing for the other as with all the preparations we had barely time to meet and my moodiness had created some distance between us that we were not able to overcome completely .

She pulled me into a coat room and locked the door behind her. Hadassah was wild with romantic abandon. If anything, the canopy had filled me with trepidation at the awesome commitment it entailed. Still, Hadassah kissed me fully and took my hand and placed it on her breasts and then between her legs. I resisted, after a fashion, but my 'little Jew' was more powerful than my own *sechel*, for what is the worth of good judgment at such times? I took her nipples in my mouth, one at a time, as she demanded each receive equal attention. I knelt at her prodding and lifted her dress to reveal her strong dancer's thighs that so inflamed me. Smelling her scent, I had the sense of her being some powerful cat, a tiger from India, and that I was helpless in the face of her desires. With my tongue I gave her satisfaction and she held the fur coats, which as a tiger she grasped in her strong claws, to keep from collapsing. We lowered a few furs to the floor and made love quickly, with Hadassah straddling me, so as not to wrinkle her dress. She growled at me in her orgasm.

We returned to the main hall and by this time people danced with abandon on the men and women's sides. Navigating through the tumult, gloved waiters in white tuxedos and matching skull caps served the many courses prepared by a Parisian chef who had become known in kosher Warsaw. Fresh flowers were everywhere and the women were dressed in the most elaborate gowns that they could afford, and some more than they could afford, for this was an affair at which to be seen.

Nisan's Yeshiva friends lost all proportion and danced with abandon, lifting their great black coats like dresses and spun in each other's arms. Our political friends were more reserved. They sat smoking around tables, holding their endless cigarettes between thumb and index finger, talking politics and criticizing the obsolete, anachronistic nature of Jewish tradition. But they were after all looking through wire-rimmed glasses with optics the size of small coins, and these and the smoke obscured their vision. Even for them, the celebration infected their cerebral approach and soon they too were up and dancing arm in arm with the *Yeshiva bokhers*.

It took eight men to lift Nisan's chair in celebration and march him around the room. The *Yeshiva bokhers* and politicos intertwined their arms, because only then did they have the strength to steady the chair held above them.

The wedding was a great success, the nuptial bed was not. Nisan was a kind man and sensitive to Shifra's feelings. Shifra found his entering so painful, however, that they could not consummate the marriage. This only increased her worries, because technically and in reality, a man could cast out his wife in such cases. His word and her lack of pregnancy were enough. Nisan would not do such a thing, but anxiety is not a product of reality as much as its perception in a young, childish woman's heart. Nisan kept this to himself for a month, but having no one else to whom to turn, and at this point fearing for Shifra's well-being, he came to me.

"Tzvi-Yosef, I swear to you I was gentle as a lamb. I coaxed her into telling me funny things that happened on the women's side, and that seemed to calm her a bit. I held her hand and just made love to her with my eyes, as you suggested, although I suspect that came from Hadassah. She was a very long time in the toilet and I could hear her being sick. When she finally came out of the bathroom in her nightgown she was shaking. I laid down beside her and kissed her and stroked her arms and back. I whispered to her like one would to a child. She felt so guilty that she was being so silly, but I assured her it was normal. After all, you have never been with a man, I told her. I told her we could wait, that maybe she was too excited after the wedding and all the people. That it was okay. She insisted we go on, but she could not look at me. Her legs were locked shut. I could not open them gently and would not open them forcefully, although she begged me to keep going. It would have hurt her Tzvi-

Yosef." I held Nisan and his large body shook in sobs that had been waiting
since his fight with his father.

"Since then how has it been?"

"Worse, I'm afraid. We've tried to make love, but I can barely enter
her. She's trying so hard, but it is very painful and she cries out. I cannot hurt
her, so I withdraw. I will not go into details and shame her, but I've tried all the
little tricks you said, the stroking, the kissing, taking time."

"Have you talked to her about all this Nisan?"

"Yes, or at least we've tried to. Tzvi-Yosef, I don't think it's the sex
really. This may sound crazy, but I think it's that she's scared to be pregnant. It
slips out all the time about being fat. How disgusting she would be with a big
belly. She throws up all the time, even though she eats little. She fears becoming
fat like her mother and aunts. She talks about it all the time."

I suggested a little wine and that worked wonders for a week or two, but
then Shifra developed an allergy to the wine and broke out in hives when she
took even a small amount. The doctor was of less help and Nisan said he only
lectured her on a woman's duties. The *Rebbitzen* was tender and supportive. She
had talked to countless young women about the marital bed, but essentially gave
her the same message more gently wrapped. I finally had Nisan convince Shifra
to talk to Hadassah. Hadassah tried to be her sister and friend and mainly
listened to her worries.

Hadassah was the least hopeful of us all, but she did not tell this to
Nisan. "She is like a small child, Tzvi-Yosef. She's not a woman. The doctor
has given her something to calm her nerves, but I think she forces herself to
throw up. Have you noticed that if she eats more than a little, she is immediately
off to the toilet and often comes back with a change of clothes and the excuse
that she spilled some food on her dress?"

I told Hadassah that she was exaggerating. However, I suspected that I
was trying to convince us otherwise so as not to be too aggrieved at the
seriousness of her malady. Our teeth were already set on edge having to wait for

our own wedding, and this added worry created tension between us. A good outcome for them foretold of one for us and a bad outcome portended troubled waters ahead for us as well.

I also could not understand Shifra's coveting thinness. To me, to most of us, my sister Rachel was the embodiment of womanhood. Ample bosom and plentiful hips promised a warm bed and sexual comfort during cold nights. Thinness was seen as sickly, a sign of poverty. Even my Christina, who was slimmer and tall, had ample thighs that had haunted my dreams with the blonde promise that lay between. Hadassah's insight was the only answer. "She is scared of being a woman, Tzvi-Yosef, and all that entails. With breasts and thighs she is sexual and grown up, and nothing frightens her more."

God's will be done. In three months Shifra became pregnant by virtue of the second known immaculate conception, or more likely the painful sex that she insisted they have. Holding himself back so long, Nisan probably offered up the life that was held at bay quickly and she was fertile. Nisan came to me and we actually went out to a tavern and got drunk. Nisan bought drinks for some fifty people, Jews and 'the others' and they all blessed his good fortune.

Not eating well, Shifra was sent to bed and a nurse or her mother were assigned full time and the bathroom was not allowed to be locked when she used it, ostensibly to help her if she fell. Mother Eisen also came as often as she could and read to the girl the Yiddish romance novels that she so loved. The doctor had no remedy to offer, but he had seen this syndrome before.

Throughout the pregnancy, Shifra insisted that Nisan lay with her in her bed at night, and although the sex was painful she insisted on this as well. She told him, "You are my beloved and I am yours, no? Kiss me, love me, be tender with me. We will keep the painful part small and the fulfilling part large. I love when you whisper to me and stroke me. I love even when you enter me, despite the pain. I am not whole. I know there is something wrong with me. A part of me is missing. You be that part."

And so they lived, part broken, but who is not? Their love and caring and frailties were real, and they were much more together than alone because

Nisan learned that he was strong and that Shifra made him whole as well. He had

a broken part that her need fulfilled. He made her a woman. She made him a

man. I watched and learned things about love that I had not known.

But I didn't have long to watch. The telegram found me at work.

REUVEN ARRESTED IN THE NIGHT [STOP]

TRIAL BY IMMEDIATE ORDER [STOP]

PLACED ON TRAIN FOR EAST [STOP]

PRISON [STOP]

I CANNOT ASK BUT MUST [STOP]

SAVE HIM [STOP]

JEWELS SENT VIA USUAL COURIER [STOP]

GOD PROTECT YOU MY ANGEL [STOP]

LOVE RACHEL [FULL STOP]

Chapter 14

Into the Wilderness

"But how will you find him Tzvi-Yosef?"

"I will head east, Uncle Yosef, to the place they have informed Rachel about. You will have to telegram me when you know more. They may move him on. He may not even be there at all. In any event, I can't wait here or he may be dead by the time we find him. His health has taken a turn for the worse from his old injuries and someone needs to be there."

"Let me go Tzvi-Yosef. I can use my position and connections. I can get things done where you can't."

"That would be true here Uncle Yosef, but he has been sent to a different world. Official help will not be what he needs. I'm afraid I understand more of that world than you would like to believe. Anyway, we don't know how long this will take and you have a family to support."

"You have a family too, or at least are supposed to begin one."

"How can I begin one if I don't face this Uncle Yosef? My family has had to stand up for me so many times, and all I've done is fail them. Now it's my turn to stand up for my family."

"Tzvi-Yosef, you exaggerate your sins. And, I think you have to begin thinking for Hadassah too.'

"But I am thinking of her," I said emphatically. "There will be nothing of me to love if I can't help Reuven now. After my mother's death, and in other times as well, he was the one who supported me. Don't forget, when the pogrom came to our *Shul*, it was only Reuven who came forward. We all owe him for that. He was the rock that held our family together, too. In many ways he was also the one who opened the world to me. If not for him, I would never have been who I am, and mostly for the good. The bad I did behind his back," I added with a little laugh.

We sat quietly for a bit, looking out the bay window of the parlor onto the street below. We drank our glasses of tea, me slurping mine in the nonchalant fashion of the countryside that still marked me as not quite so citified as I wanted to believe. My link with Uncle Yosef was indeed deep and as we respected and loved each other enough that once something was said it did not have to be repeated every which way like in so many arguments.

"But really Tzvi-Yosef, what can you do for him?"

"I have talked to friends who spent a spell in Siberia. They think that given the nature of his crimes, Reuven will spend only a short time in prison. But, they say you can starve to death without someone taking care of the guards on the outside."

"So, what will you do? How will you live in that wilderness?"

"I'll find work. I only need to live for one. I'm told there's plenty of work to be had. Some even go there to make money to send home. Who knows, I may become a baron and send for all the family to come live on my estates. You can manage my bank."

The first problem, however, was finding out where to go. We had received an official notice of detention that gave the name of a town that could not be found on a map. It took weeks to discover the town's real name. I spent days sitting in waiting rooms for officials who met me with cold distance. Luckily, my Russian was more or less fluent, as most of these men refused to speak Polish. I might have made more headway as a Christian, but I met a different reality.

"Let me see your papers. It says here you are a Jew." This was always said as if it was the first time I had heard it. I wondered if they thought I should be surprised at the discovery. "What! Me? A Jew! Let me see that!" Why you're right. I was wondering all these years why my penis was missing that little rain hood and I detested the taste of pork. And this little hat on my head. Why that explains it. Now all the pieces are coming together. Why do you suppose my parents never mentioned this to me?" But, of course I remained silent and kept my head bowed submissively.

"What is your purpose in Krasnoyarsk? So, your brother-in-law is a revolutionary. Why on earth should I help you? You Jews suck the life of the land, rob from the peasants, steal from the landowners, and complain that you're oppressed and wish to overthrow the Tsar. Still, I can understand your wanting to help family. Let me tell you a little something. Family is everything to a Russian, but you Jews would sell your mother for a few kopeks. You have no sense of family and no ties to the land."

How this laundry list of Jewish evils came to be known escaped me. Jews had no land to suck life from, we dealt with peasants because we offered the cheapest prices, and no Jew I had ever heard from managed to steal from a landowner. Peasants would steal sacks of wheat and such, but Jews did not work the land and frowned on stealing in any case. I would admit that Jews were involved in the revolutionary movement, and God knows we complained we were oppressed, but who did not under the yoke of Mother Russia? And a Jewish man sell his mother? Why, he can barely leave her for a wife. These anti-Semitic ideas, however, were ingrained with mother's milk, so there was no use in arguing the point.

One just hoped that after venting, the bureaucrat would offer some help, and some were human enough to do so, for the Russians did understand family and they were not all without souls. Like this bureaucrat, some offered a little slip. I had not heard before of Krasnoyarsk as a destination for Reuven, and if this piece of information was accurate, it helped immensely to piece together the puzzle.

The father of one of my Zionist friends was active in the revolutionary movement and I went to see him. He was sympathetic and said that he would inquire and find out what he could based on the smattering of facts that I actually managed to glean from the endless waiting rooms. The movement was already strong and had networks in industry, city councils, and the military itself. They had been working for years, whispering in the Russian and Polish ear about the evils of Russia, the landlords, the factory owners, the capitalists, the bankers.

His first inquiries were to discover of what Reuven was actually suspected and how good was the evidence. They did not need good evidence to arrest and imprison, but they tended to give lighter sentences if the crimes suspected were not of the worst sort. With Reuven he discovered it was more complex. He was actually deeply involved and higher up in the revolutionary hierarchy than I had supposed, but he had been surprisingly careful. The authorities suspected his real crimes, but only had evidence of his smaller ones.

"We believe that he was held in Tiumén so that they could amass evidence for a better case. Depending on what they found out, they will know where to send him and for how long. They're arresting in such numbers that anything can happen. They can lose him on trains, they can imprison him for life, or he could be in prison a year and then set free, if you call having to work in Siberia for no wages, free. If what this official says is true, that he's to be sent to Krasnoyarsk, that means a long prison sentence and not supervised exile. It is not good. I hope this is not the case."

Hadassah at first took the news stoically, "You have to go. There's no one else."

This, however, was the calm before the storm. Following stoic acceptance, came a period of anger and denial. She could not see why I was the one that had to go. Reuven was a grown man and got himself into this mess with his eyes open. He was even glad for it; his arrest fed the flames of revolution. Didn't I have a wagonload of uncles who could go? What was wrong with Uncle Mayer and all his fish knives I was forever talking about (I had mentioned the knives once or twice). Why not Isaac? And what was wrong with Reuven's family? It did not matter that there were good logical reasons why each candidate had more strikes against him than in his favor. Nor could she understand that I saw this as a way to pay penance. To go to Siberia and save Reuven for Rachel and her children and the family was a script made in heaven for me. It was the act that could allow me to go home. It was the sacrifice I promised Mameh I would always be willing to make for my brothers and sisters. It would restore pride in me in Tateh's eyes, no matter what Friya said or did.

"*Zadie*, Mameh is afraid that I should go. What do you think?"

"It is far, no?"

"Yes *Zadie*, it is very far."

"And you believe Tzvi that you know what to do there? That what you know to do will mean something? You must not throw yourself in harm's way to sacrifice yourself for no reason. That is a terrible sin."

"I believe that I am the only one that can go. I believe that I have been destined to do this. I can speak several languages. I can handle people in positions of power and I can handle the lowlifes that crawl the earth on their bellies. I can live on nothing. I know how to fight and how to avoid a fight."

"You have truly grown up Tzvi. I am very proud of you. I remember when you were little and I would make a rabbit out of my handkerchief, tying it so that two ears stuck up from a knot. Do you remember? You would reach for it, and I would flick my wrist and make it jump and you would laugh. That is a long time ago. But now, this is not chasing fantasy rabbits and it sounds like you are already convinced that you are the chosen one."

"Yes, I guess it does, but what of Hadassah?"

"Well, you must act true to Hadassah, even before you act true to yourself. You must lift her burden even when yours remains a weight on your chest."

I understood *Zadie* to mean that I would have to promise Hadassah my love and that I would remain true to her until my return. I would give Reuven a year. At this point, even if my burden was not paid, I could not ask Hadassah to give up more of her life. In Warsaw she had her family and I was not the first man to be sent to Siberia, even if I was more or less volunteering.

The next problem was finding out how to get to this Krasnoyarsk. Traders were the best source of information and several had been to the place. They actually said that I was lucky, as he could have been sent much further. As one fellow put it, "You traveled in the general direction and eventually you got there." Despite the vastness of the region, there was one main route for the train, without a lot of tributaries. The main fear for finding him was that by the time I arrived that he might be sent away to Yakutsk in the north or to the Kamchatke near Alaska, where he might never be heard from again.

As the day of my departure approached, Hadassah came to another decision.

"I'm going with you."

"You're what?!"

"You heard me. I'm going with you. We'll be married at the *Shul* and we go together. I'm already mostly packed."

"You're what?!"

"Are you developing a hearing problem Tzvi-Yosef? Tell me right now. I'm not marrying an invalid. I said it quite clearly. I'm going with you. I've waited two years. That's enough. Who knows when you'll come back? Maybe never. Where do you men get in your heads that hardship is a man's job? A woman's as strong as a man. Stronger, because we can bear children. I can work, and two heads are better than one. Especially as addled as your brain seems to be these days. And now, add to this you're losing your hearing."

"Hadassah, you have no idea what you're talking about. The only women in Siberia are peasants and prisoners. There's no running water, no electricity, no comforts."

"Don't talk nonsense Tzvi-Yosef. Plenty of women are in Siberia with their husbands. Plenty of women have chosen to join them, rather than stay here."

"Hadassah, we've been through this, and you know that I'm the only one that can go. Who knows what awaits me there? But as a man, I have the best chance of surviving and helping Reuven. I want to be with you more than anything. I love you and care for you. You're everything to me, but for that reason I have to know that you're safe."

"I'm going and that's final. End of discussion. Good-bye, I'm going to the *Rebbetzin* to make arrangements for the wedding and then to finish packing. Today's Thursday, I expect the wedding will be on Tuesday. You'll need a new suit."

Everyone disagreed with Hadassah. Mendel, who had himself spent seven years in Siberia during military duty, pleaded with her. In his simple way, he was the most convincing as she knew he had no agenda other than our welfare at heart. Still, his words fell on deaf ears. Her parents forbade her even thinking about it. Her father demanded and announced edicts and sanctions and her mother fell into hysterics. Uncle Yosef and Aunt Hannah tried to use the common sense approach and appealed to her rationality. The *Rebbetzin* told her that the *Rebbe* refused to marry us under such conditions. "So then we'll be married by a Priest," she threatened. "You wouldn't!" "I most certainly would. I'm not letting Tzvi-Yosef go without me. He needs me and what's more, I need him."

She grew into such a lather that she couldn't sleep and became hysterical. The doctor was called and applied a sedative that might have put a horse down. Having been up for three days and nights, she finally fell into a deep sleep. When she awoke, she was calmer and seemed to accept the inevitable. Her parents left me alone with her and we talked and talked and she came to understand that this was something that our love would have to withstand.

Her surrender was bittersweet and we made love with her parents in the next bedroom, not caring what they thought should they stumble on us. It was tempestuous lovemaking, and instead of orgasm, Hadassah pounded at my chest with her fists saying that she hated me and that I was cruel and did not love her. I remained inside her and she began to lick my face and neck and chest, trying to salvage the last tastes of me as a starving woman would her last plate of food. I became aroused again and we moved to a slow rhythm, our bodies sensing that they might not meet again, perhaps not ever. We rocked our bodies like a raft on a slow moving river, endlessly traveling toward the sea. I whispered words of love to her, cupping her small, shapely breasts in my hand, trying to create a mold that I would carry in my head on my journey. "You are my one and only, my *beshert.*" "I am empty; you make me whole." "Your body is a gateway that I have entered and will never leave, no matter where I am." I searched for words that might bind our love and hold her fast to it, because I was not so naive as to think that such a woman would wait forever for one such as me.

On Tuesday, when she would have had us wed, they all came to the train to see me off. All except Hadassah. She could not bear to see me leave and feared that she would again become hysterical in public and embarrass all of us. "You don't need me fainting and making a scene at the train station. We'll say our goodbyes here privately."

By this time it was clear that Krasnoyarsk was my destination. Reuven, it seemed, was destined for a long prison term. The information was never entirely clear, which is hard for people from democratic countries to understand, but his sentence was set for "six years, and longer if deemed appropriate."

Aunt Hannah, Froi Eisen, and Chava cried enough tears to make up for Hadassah's absence. Among the women, only Yenta held back her tears, and instead chastised me for being such an idiot as to have a brother-in-law who gets himself arrested and then sent to a place like Siberia. Reb Eisen, for all his sullenness, had a money belt made for me, and had placed extra cash inside. "Come back to my daughter Tzvi-Yosef. She will make us crazy otherwise."

My Uncle came on the train with me and insisted I begin my journey in a second class car, despite my protests. "You'll have plenty of third class travel and worse, *tataleh*. Enjoy the first five hundred kilometers in comfort. Anyway, it's an easier memory for the women to remember you departing this way. "Here, you almost forgot your miniature menorah from your friend Krzyszstof. I noticed you never take his little amulet off either. He must be a good friend. He must have known you'd be going on a long journey and that you would need to remember that you're a Jew. Do you hear me, my little antelope? You are a man and a Jew. And you are a man with family. You hear me?" he implored, already in tears himself. "I hear you. *Ich bin a Yid. I am a Jew.*'

As the train pulled out, I looked back onto Warsaw. A number of porters stood by their loads and waved, and the non-Jewish porters I had befriended doffed their hats as a note of farewell. The air vaporized around the mouths of those at the station and in the distance the smoke drifted skyward across the grey skies as the smokestacks stood tall above the factories, hard at work into the evening air.

I was saddened to be leaving Hadassah and my Aunt and Uncle, but it would be dishonest to say that I was not excited as well. I was traveling into a wilderness and a great unknown. Had I been traveling for myself I might have felt more afraid, but like a soldier with a mission I was aware mainly of a sense of purpose and a chance to gain honor. I had made a promise to my mother to protect my brothers and sisters. I knew that my mother must be proud of me, a man of twenty, on a train with a single bag, carrying money and jewels sewed into seams that I would not open or divulge this time as to their whereabouts, and a razor that I would use if it was called into service, as well.

As I removed my coat in the warm compartment, I noticed through the reflection of the window that the young woman accompanying what looked like her husband, was staring at me. Her look gave away more than she intended, and she quickly lowered her eyes when she saw that I had caught her through the mirrored glass. I would never be tall like Reuven. But my chest and arms were expansive and my waist was small, a body created by grueling physical work and little food.

Her stare also reminded me that I appeared to all the world now as one of "the others" and had fake papers as well. Clean shaven, with blond hair, I looked more like a Pole than a Pole. By work of a forger who owed several favors to Chaim, the lead porter, I was now Joséf Apfel, which by only slight change indicated a Christian of probable German origin. With my excellent Polish, I was obviously from family who had come to Poland a generation or more earlier. To Jews, I could be a Jew simply by a few sentences of Yiddish and a change in the lilt of my voice. With my now excellent Russian, I could also play the obedient Pole who understood the ultimate superiority of Russian culture.

As evening came and the light faded I watched the small lights of the scattered farmhouses in the distance and the occasional village flash by the windows. In a few hours I passed by villages near my home town and longed for the time that I could enter my village with my head held high. Night came early in the countryside, I had forgotten, not having left the city for these three years. I recalled the boy-man who had entered Warsaw beaten, bruised, and without a groshen in his pocket, and shook my head in wonder at the changes that had occurred. I had been a street urchin, a porter and then a student and a clerk. I had womanized and settled with a woman who was beyond any fantasy I might have had about what I deserved. I had become a Zionist and gang captain, protecting Jews against the constant threat of anti-Semitic abuse, so endemic to Poland.

And then I was captured by the thought that a child of mine was also somewhere out in the distance and that I must trust in Christine to raise him well, with the love I knew she had to give. He would be a toddler now, probably white-blond like Christine, and one of "the others." I longed to extend myself to him, but understood that a mere change of papers was not enough to ever bridge the gap that lay between us. He was forfeit to me, and with that I must accept that a part of me was not dead, but lost, and probably lost forever. With these thoughts I nodded off, waking through the night to the occasional stop and alighting and disembarking of passengers. My second class ticket would take me to the Russian border and a few hundred kilometers into Russia. From then it would be third class, and I would not again sleep quite so secure and restfully.

Come morning, I washed and shaved in the miniature toilet. Fresh towels were laid out and the brass was shined and the oak wood polished. I remembered the excitement of first going to Warsaw as a child with Mameh and

Tateh and Rachel and Isaac on the train. It was slow moving and within their protection. This was rapid and out of control. I was passing into Russia and beyond. The view of the tracks through the small hole was dizzying, and I checked that my valuables were safely intact so that they might not fall and be lost to me.

The corridor outside the seating compartments was narrow and crowded with people, stretching from their night's sleep. In the opening between two of the train cars, a group of Jews were swaying to their morning prayers. Just then, a Pole in a business suit pushed by, muttering some obscenity and incidentally shoving one of the congregants. I accidently knocked the Pole down the few stairs of the exit, and gave him a small scare...well probably more than small. I gave him a hand back up and said I was sorry in perfect Polish, and he limped along his way. Looking back down at his prayer book, the man closest to me said in Hebrew, as if part of the prayers, *lache b'shalom, travel in peace*. I answered in a Yiddish whisper, *Gott willen*, God willing, and moved on.

Sliding open the door to my compartment, I was greeted by the young couple and merchant who shared the cabin, now somehow a unit having slept a night together. They invited me to breakfast, as the tables were set for four and this would avoid having to eat with "strangers." I thanked them for their thoughtfulness and said that I would be delighted for the company.

We were shown to a table with white table cloth and thick, slightly undersized porcelain dishes. The strong steaming coffee was served with fresh eggs and toast and clotted cream. Cooked prunes, fried ham, and potatoes were served in small steel containers, and again while not the china and silver I had seen passing earlier through first class, it was as fancy as any restaurant that I had ever visited. I hesitated with the ham, but decided that not attacking it heartily would signal my origins as well as might my appearing naked with the covenant of Abraham showing between my legs.

In the name of *pekuach nefesh, the saving of souls*, in this case mine and Reuven's, all is permitted. I used this codicil in the law, that over-ruled all but murder, idolatry, and forbidden sex, to justify my act, and hoped that my swallowing it almost whole was neither noticed nor harmful. I was no longer certain about the borders of forbidden sex, but surely my journey was for the saving of souls, a brother who came like a father and savior, larger than life in our time of need.

I was bothered by a sense of anxiety, feeling I was being watched or followed. Such feelings had accompanied me when I first moved to Warsaw fleeing the police. Chaim has assured me I was too small a fish to be followed all the way to Warsaw, and that anyway if they found me, why not just arrest me on the spot? But the feeling stayed with me, like when I awoke to Devora in the hospital, having felt her presence from deep within my coma. I thought this recollection odd, because if I was being followed, it was not by a benevolent beauty such as Devora.

I tried to nonchalantly survey the dining car as I asked the waiter for more sugar for my coffee. The tables were filled with a few families, some merchants, and two groups of young Russian officers. A young man with a group of Poles a few tables down looked vaguely familiar, but this was certainly no source for worry, and the soldiers were obviously too busy nursing hangovers to be any source of threat. I attributed my anxiety to the nervousness of the adventure and catalogued it as a signal to stay on guard in my current conversation.

I traveled this way without incident, and at the frontier my papers were reviewed with barely a nod. Russia was a great empire with people coming and going in all directions. My companions departed the afternoon of the third day in Minsk. This is where I had intended to move to third class, but I could not find a way to do so without their noticing and thought it prudent to purchase an additional second class ticket to Moscow. I proceeded on with a family with two young children and a mother-in-law, who were cordial but reserved. Seeing me as a foreigner, they might not have thought I spoke Russian. In time, we exchanged a few words of Russian, but they became only slightly more friendly.

I realized that their demeanor was to my benefit, as the less I spoke, the less would be revealed. Still, it made the hours pass more slowly.

Moscow station was enormous. The endless number of trains and people made Warsaw seem like a small town. Thousands of people milled about and goods were stacked everywhere. Army units slept on their packs, legions from distant regions of the Empire coming in and Western Russians heading East. Senior officers were arrayed in a brilliance of polished brass and silver, many in white that was miraculously clean given the sooty surroundings. Here and there I saw the entourage of lesser and greater nobles who walked as if not touching the ground. Here, waiting for the trains, the many social classes and ethnic groups that made up Russia were forced to brush shoulders, but there was no mistake where the borders remained, indelibly etched between them.

There were also many foreigners arranging business and politics with powerful Russia. Moscow was not yet, of course, the capital of Russia, but it was better situated than St. Petersburg for commerce with the East and greater Russia. Arabs in traditional garb, and Turks in Western suits, their identities revealed by their huge mustaches sprinkled the crowed.

I searched for the trains heading east, and bought a third class ticket. The ticket agent gave me a sad, knowing look, communicating his pity for anyone that was headed for that frozen wasteland. I nodded back, accepting his commiseration with a shrug that said, "what has to be done, has to be done." He pointed to the clock, indicating that I had better hurry. In a final gesture, he extended his hand through the wire cage and shook mine. No words passed between us other than the name of my destination. We understood each other completely.

As I hurried through the station with my canvas bag holding my worldly goods, I was again aware of the sense of anxiety that I had felt earlier on the train. I looked behind me as I turned a corner, but could make out nothing suspicious in the crowded vestibule. I thought that I had time to get to my train by a more circuitous route that might lose any pursuer. I hurried toward the exit and jumped on a droshky that was available for hire. I told the driver to take me around the block and that I would pay him for his trouble. With a shrug, he cracked his whip and we circled to where I could return through a different entrance. He was glad to earn a ruble for nothing from a crazy man.

Unfortunately, at the moment of re-entering the station my body chose to reject something that I had eaten or water I had drank and I barely made it to the toilets. Hundreds of men were in the third class facilities, most pissing from both sides into a large continuous trough. Fathers held their sons tightly, as had one fallen in, he would have been swept with the current and lost somewhere far downstream.

Luckily a stall was open, or I would have been in great trouble as my bowels were bursting. There was a hole in the floor and places for my boots to straddle it. The odor from the chamber was unendurable, and one could only use such a place in dire emergency. I crouched quickly, hoping to avoid ruining my clothing and emptied into the hole all that my body thought of Russia. I laughed to myself, even as my stomach heaved in painful spasms, that this was my first gift for the Czar upon my arrival in Mother Russia.

There is always a wry humor in the worst of situations. Grasping it seems to make people aware of their humanity, and at the very times when the justification for that humanity is often at its nadir. Perhaps that is why God imparted a sense of humor to humans, and gave an extra portion to Jews in His goodness. Had He, in His infinite wisdom, provided us less reason for this extra measure of droll wit we would have been equally satisfied I assure you.

I was weakened by the experience and felt that although temporarily offered a reprieve, I might be revisited with the same symptoms at any time. Still, I had little choice except to try to still make my train. As I hurried through the busy terminal, I was also relieved, in addition to my primary relief, that my unexpected interruption also probably confounded anyone that was tailing me, however remote the possibility. Although I tried to hurry, the horde of humanity and an army brigade that decided upon that specific appointed moment in my life to move en masse to their troop train, hampered my progress. I also made a few wrong turns, frustrated by the Cyrillic alphabet and multiple levels of the station.

Finally, I caught sight of my train and darted the last two hundred meters. The conductor was still taking tickets, and as I handed mine to him he told me that "I had no need to hurry." "Why?" I asked, "Was my train delayed?" "No, your train was on time, it left twenty minutes ago. The next train for you is tomorrow at the same time. Nothing to worry about though. You can use the same third class ticket. There're no reservations in third class."

Well, since there was nothing to be said or done I had to accept the fact that the first Russian train in history to leave on time was mine at this moment. I said something to that effect and the conductor agreed that indeed it may have been one of the first times in his memory as well, and he assured me he had more experience with trains than me.

I walked back toward the main terminal and found a corner to sit and think about what to do. I was certainly not hungry and at some point I must have fallen asleep. When I awoke it was many hours later and nightfall, my head resting on that of an enormous garlic-breathed Bulgarian, his head resting in turn on mine.

I noticed a group of Jewish families and men huddled in one remote corner that was a bit more exposed to the wind coming in from the open doors than territories that other groups had sequestered. They were talking among themselves, eating bits of food and beginning to bed down for the night. Gravitating toward their warmth, I dragged my bag among them and with my remaining strength found a small space against the wall. I received a few suspicious nods, as people wondered what this goy was doing in their midst. What kind of trouble was I about to make, after all who were they bothering? With two words in Yiddish, *Gooten auvent, good evening*, I distilled any harsh feelings.

After I settled in my place I began to shiver, and guessed that it was not the food but flu that had gotten to me. A woman, about the age my mother would have been and looking every bit her part, ordered her husband, "Find out where he's from."

"*A Rushisha yid? Russian Jew?* "

"*Nane, a Polisha yid?*

"He says he's a Jew from Poland."

"So ask him where he's going so far from home, such a handsome young man and alone, and here us with three unmarried daughters," the woman instructed her husband. The woman knew I could hear, but that after all was half the point, and it was not appropriate for a traditional Jewish woman to talk to a stranger.

"*Aha. Avi gait ir? Where do you head?* "

"*Sibeer.* "

"*Oy vey!* He says he's going to Siberia. "

And turning to her husband, but with her eyes on me mournfully, she added, tell him, "*Gait mit Gott. Go with God.* "

I nodded and told the man that I hoped *Hashem* would bring three Torah scholars for his three daughters, to which he nodded and his wife added, "*Aumein.*"

Seeing me shivering, the man sent his one son, a boy of bar mitzvah age, on a mission to find some old newspapers. Returning with a handful, I placed them under me, because the floor felt much colder than the air. They obviously hoped for some conversation. For *shtetl* Jews from some remote region such as these, this was a great adventure to be in Moscow, and this chance to talk to a Jew from another land was a great opportunity that could fill many years of conversation, added like spice from time to time. My fever, however, must have been increasing, and after politely declining some food, I fell into a restless, but long sleep.

When I awoke, it was morning. There were still a crowd of Jews around me, but the family had departed, leaving me some bread and cheese by my pack. I realized that I was covered with a warm woolen blanket that they must have left for me as well. I was touched by the sacrifice this meant for such a family, as a good woolen blanket was needed for any family who would have to provide dowries for three daughters who were not the most attractive in the world. Sitting up, I sensed that my illness was not entirely gone and that I should take things slowly. After drinking some weak tea that was offered to me by another family, I fell soundly back to sleep and awoke in time for lunch, for which I was alternatively starving and nauseated.

I asked about the family that had left the blanket. A family that had spent the night by my side told me that, no, they didn't know the family, but that the blanket had appeared on me after the family had left. Of that they were certain. No one else seemed to know to whom the blanket belonged. Someone thought they saw a young man leave it. Others thought it might have been a young woman.

I gathered my belongings to go look for the toilet and perhaps some hot soup. I continued to be bothered not only by weakness, but by that sense of foreboding that maybe just comes from being alone in a strange land. If someone was following me, why wouldn't he just arrest me and be done with it? Anyway, as Chaim said, who was I as to be so important to Russia? Rather than convincing me of my safety, however, the outcome of this logical analysis was my feeling that much more disturbed. From one minute to the next I tossed back and forth between paranoid notions that hinged on small pieces of rational thought, connected by a fabric of fear and fever.

Why was this man following me, and what did he want, if not to bring me harm? Could it have been the same man on the train? He might have even put the blanket on me in a sick show of his power to invade my world.

Finding the toilet I was able to purge my bowels and with it at least some of my distress. I found a kiosk that sold hot soup to poor travelers, but those not so poor as to be entirely without resources. I stood around a high table with several other weary travelers and the hot soup comforted me. I nibbled at the hunk of black bread that came with it, but decided the better of it and stuffed it into my jacket for later consumption.

As I returned with my bag to the huddle of Jews, I saw them in the afternoon light through a different filter. Whereas they imparted an aura of safety during the night, in the daylight they looked exposed and victimized. Passersby made their objections noticeable as would people exposed to a garbage heap or a house of ill repute. Their noses would turn up, or they would take closer hold of their children, so that they were not kidnapped and their blood used to make their unleavened bread. I thought better of rejoining them.

Instead, I found a wooden bench and wrapped the strap of my bag around my leg, so as to keep it from being stolen if I dozed. I slept much of the day, and awoke to find my head nestled once again against the huge shoulder of my three hundred pound Bulgarian who reeked so badly of garlic and onions that I almost returned his kindness with my lunch. Looking up at the clock, I realized that I was again about to miss my train if I didn't hurry, so I grabbed my bag, said excuse me, and bustled off to make my train. The Bulgarian waved as if saying goodbye to an old friend.

How is it possible that a few days of comfort can allow a person to forget a former misery? Adults, children, and not a few farm animals filled the third class carriage. Looking for a seat on the hard wooden bench, I found a spot at the border that had already been created between the Jews and "the others." I was lucky to still get a seat next to the window, as others avoided these seats because of the wind that made its way through the cracks. Pressing the side of my head against the window, it felt like a cold ice pack that Tateh used to make in winter if one of us were sick. I placed my face against the crack of the window to take in as much fresh air as I could. As the train pulled out from the station, I drifted back to sleep. It was perhaps four in the afternoon when the train pulled out. I awoke once during the night dreaming that I was in a barn, but it was only the mass of humanity and children's urine and feces, and the bleating of a goat nearby. I fell back to sleep until after dawn.

In the morning, the Jewish men were gathered for their first prayers. I had not been praying regularly for some years, but I said the prayers to myself silently, so as to be part of the congregation. I always said the *Shema* when I went to sleep and upon rising. It was a habit that was as much superstition as comforting. As the *minyan* spoke the holiest of words, I covered my eyes, pretending to concentrate on some distant thoughts, and said them as well, *Shema yisroel, adonai alohaynu, adonai, achad, Hear O'Israel, the Lord is our God, the Lord is One.* At the appropriate moment in the prayers, a small voice behind me among "the others" responded, *Awmein.* There were probably more of us secret Jews in the world than I had ever considered. I took out my bread and bought some hot tea from a woman passing through the train with a small cart, and ate as if it was a breakfast for a king.

I settled in for a long ride, switching trains several times. We often stopped in remote towns or at track sides for interminable hours. At other times, the train picked up speed and went without stopping for many hours, covering enormous distances. The people changed, the faces changed as well. Many of the passengers now had slightly slanted eyes and flat foreheads. Some had dark skin and eyes pulled like slits across their broad, round faces. Not only the Jews prayed now, as Muslims knelt for their prayers even more often. One nation turned toward Jerusalem, one to Mecca. One stood upright and bobbed back and forth, one knelt and prostrated.

A small group of us became veterans of the trip and were obviously headed in the same general direction. We gravitated toward each other over time, and began to sit together as the car emptied and others came aboard. Always, however, the separation between the Jews and 'the others" remained, and always the invisible border between us. I spoke only in Russian or Polish, but, of course, understood the Yiddish spoken between the Jews. We chatted about politics, the weather, families. I learned all I could about Siberia from those who had experience. As I journeyed eastward, the mention of places no longer provoked such mournful replies or pity. Many of these people had made a life here, one way or another. For some, the trip meant going home and they looked to the signs of barrenness with joy that they were ever closer to their loved ones.

The Jews in our little entourage pegged me for a classic anti-Semite. It was in "my look," one of them said. He could spot a Jew-hater anywhere, however, politely I acted. I had to keep myself from arguing with them, and kept a blank expression on my face. Still, there must have been trust on some level, as we shared stories and food, the Jews accepting cheese and bread, but no meat. Our comradery offered some measure of safety, like we were from a neighborhood within a larger city.

Dozing in the dim twilight, the man beside me, named Ivan of course, nudged me. He signaling quietly that I pay attention to something going on across from us. A thief was positioning himself to pick the pocket of a sleeping Jew, an older man with sad eyes and a long beard, still black. I went to intercede, but Ivan held me back. Of course, why would we intercede on behalf of some old Jew? Let the thief take from him. After all, hadn't Jews constantly been taking from us?

Still, I felt compelled to act, despite the fact that it would probably expose me as another Jew. I simply could not allow the man to lose his purse. Before I could make my move, however, Ivan whacked the pickpocket with his walking stick so hard he surely busted a few ribs. The old Jew woke quickly and added a kick to the man's backside that sent him flying down the aisle, and those all around broke out in laughter and passed vodka to toast the good deed and the entertainment it provided. The world, as always, was more complex than any simple explanations can make it.

At times food was hard to come by and we shared our meager provisions. At other times, a peasant would board as we waited in a station with whole chickens, or loaves of fresh bread and cheese. Nothing was organized, nothing was to be depended on. With the clicking of the wheels, as we moved east, the bureaucracy and hold of Imperial Russia changed to something more simple, harsh, and unsupervised.

Like the food, it became impossible to depend on what might occur next. In Kazan, police boarded the train and went from car to car checking people's papers. They seemed to be looking for someone. I froze in my seat, as there was no escaping them if I was the object of their search, as officers came toward me from both sides. They stopped beside four men who apparently shared no language in common with them. Not getting answers to their questions, the police responded by talking more loudly, as if this would overcome the language barrier. Finally, in despair, they unleashed their batons and beat the four men to a bloody pulp. They arrested no one, and left as if they had no more than checked papers and thanked everyone for their cooperation. The bloodied men returned to their seats after the police departed. One man's jaw was dislocated and another had a broken arm. They were obviously pleased it had not gone worse.

As the train rumbled east everything was stranger, more primitive and wild. As we passed rivers, the barges were cruder, like ones that might have traveled one thousand years earlier. They were stationary, locked in the ice, as the rivers were mainly frozen. As we passed villages, peasants were dressed in brightly colored costumes, with designs that were exotic to the Western eye. Young men were dressed in blue, crimson, pink, purple and violet shirts. Women wore lemon-yellow gowns, scarlet aprons, and donned short pink jackets with colored head-kerchiefs. Many had removed their dirty sheepskin overcoats to enjoy the mid-day sun, but more likely to attract young members of the opposite sex, given the chilling temperature. This region gave away nothing of the promise of the Russian frontier that was just off in the distance, as the area was still rather populated and villages well-developed. In its own way this land was as removed from Russia as I imagined America could possibly be, and much less Russian than Siberia where Russia had transplanted itself, stepping over this middle region.

The train barely stopped in the city of Perm, or I slept through much of the stop, and when I awoke we were almost departing the city. I barely managed to buy some food from the peasant children at the track side, but received great quantities at cheap prices because with the train leaving bargains were available as people didn't want to be left with their wares.

Leaving Perm I had the sense that this was the end of Russia proper, at the crossroads to Siberia and the Ural Mountains. Still, I could see it was a fair city, prettily set on the water of the river Káma with many churches and public buildings and a bustling traffic. A fellow traveler remarked that although it did not look like much, that it was a city of great wealth, as all of the riches of Siberia and the mines of the nearby Ural Mountains passed through its gates into European Russia.

From Perm we set out for Ekaterínburg. The railways stations here appeared better built than earlier, a sign of the importance of the region's trade. Even the verst-posts marking the distances were set in neatly fitted mosaics a full meter in diameter using colored Ural stones. Ekaterínburg's wealth was almost gaudy in parts. The signs of the mining industry were apparent and many houses were grand and public buildings were spacious. The streets were not paved, but the houses were well maintained. Most structures were of wood, log cabin style, but tightly made and well set for winter. Most had pretty ornamental window casings. The *gastínnoi dvor, city bazaar,* was active and as we were told that a change in schedules was to result in our switching trains, I had time to wander about the town.

I still had the sense that I might be trailed, so I wound my way through the streets and doubled back several times to allude any pursuer. I picked up some sunflower and pumpkin seeds, and as was the custom, consumed them as I strolled through the bazaar, spitting out the shells. Being winter, the bazar was not as crowded as it would be on a summer day, but the break in the weather had brought in more sellers and buyers than usual for the season. Some of the peasants had come in on their *tárántas*, the large heavy wheeled carriages, but more had their sleighs for there was much accumulation of snow.

Toward a side street off the bazar were several taverns. I was caught off guard by the moans and screams of women, and thought for a moment that a rape must be occurring. On closer inspection, I saw that it was merely the goings on in a tavern. The door to the alleyway had been left open and I could see where men were chasing women whose breasts were exposed, and several were having sex on tables. I stood mesmerized watching one attractive gypsy-looking woman who was being pummeled by one man, while sucking on the exposed member of another. I had never seen anything like this and stood staring. I became aware of feeling very warm and sweaty. She looked over toward me and with her free hand beckoned me to enter. I shook my head no, but managed a smile in return, as if I was saying no thank you to the offer of some nice oranges or a pair of shoes. I picked up a considerable handful of snow and dabbed my neck, trying to cool the burning embers that were welling up inside me.

I found a more tame tavern and ordered a meal. Still, a number of women propositioned me and it was clear that where there was gold, there were men with extra cash, and where there were men with extra cash the oldest profession was busy at work. I declined, feeling rather virtuous, but I must admit that I might have been more tempted if my stomach was fully recovered and I was back at full strength.

Returning to the train was like returning to old friends. As we rejoined each other's company, we shook hands hardily and asked about everyone's escapades of the day. Several men had taken up with women where I had left off and were full of talk of the virtues of the city and what it had to offer. As I by now knew all the "regulars" on the train, my sense of anxiety at being followed was beginning to wane. None of them matched the suspicious faces I had taken pains to note through the journey. Perhaps all my concern was for naught.

I should have remained more watchful. Making my way to the toilet in the early morning, I sensed I was again being followed. I ducked into a cabin in the second class compartment, and being better dressed than the typical third class passenger, the occupants took me for a late arrival, or someone who had slept in a berth, but now had to take his regular seat. I faced the window, using the reflection to study the passageway. Sure enough, the young man from days earlier passed with his cap pulled down almost over his eyes, stalking his prey. I remained in the compartment, hoping the conductor would not check tickets until later in the day.

So, my fears had been justified after all, a lesson I would never forget. Knowing the truth, my survival instincts quickly replaced my fear. Identifying the object of my distress, it was no longer time to worry but to plan and to act, as Reuven always taught.

I decided on a dangerous and in retrospect foolish scheme, but I was after all in dire straits. I would exit the train at the first station it was to stop for a prolonged period. I would head down a deserted street outside the station and duck into the first hiding spot. If the man chose to follow me, my razor would find his neck and that would be the end of his life. I would return to the train, and no one could connect me with the crime. I only had to be sure that I was not seen. I would take his wallet, as if he was robbed, and throw it somewhere that it would not be found. The razor I could leave in his neck. From the butcher shop, I was sure I could make a clean cut, and avoid covering myself in blood.

With my strategy set, I felt secure that this was my only remaining course of action. Having been the assignment of so diligent an agent, who had taken such pains to follow me, my ultimate demise was nearly a foregone conclusion. If it were to come in any case, better to take the initiative. If I could use this aggression to gain time to get to Reuven, I could at least settle his needs before I was ultimately arrested. Clearly, I was lost in any case. I could only possibly prolong my journey so as to accomplish my mission. With great luck, I might both provide for Reuven, and make my escape, continuing east, but this much luck was unreasonable to expect.

Before we reached a town where we would stop, I made it back to my compartment and my bag. The young man was small in size and had his hat pulled down over his face a few rows behind me. Given his size, I wondered if he might have an accomplice. I told myself to be doubly watchful. More than once I had fallen into the trap of underestimating my enemy.

My bag was where I left it, and the Russian family that had been next to me had spread out in my absence. They grudgingly relinquished my spot, with the father offering me a tip of his cap. This was the way of the Russian peasant. They understood that I was dressed above their class, and that it was their duty to give me my due. It was also their duty to leak their sense of hatred for my position, however only slightly above their own. Had they known me a Jew, and therefore lower on the pecking order, my bag would have already been rifled and pilfered and I could have as soon asked them for a hundred rubles as the return of my seat.

The landscape became increasingly barren and covered with snow. I hoped that the storm would continue as it would cover my tracks after I dispatched this nuisance to his maker. A convenient snow drift might even give me some days before he was even found. The way the snow and ice accumulated, he might not be found until Spring's thaw. There were fewer signs of population as we traveled east, and even the landscape became barren and hostile. After some hours, the conductor announced that the train would be stopping for a few hours to load coal and resupply provisions. The timing was perfect as this far north it was already dark by early afternoon and in the twilight I would have the best chances of success. Darkness serves the one being tracked, when he is on to his pursuer.

I made no sign of my leaving the train until the last moment, hoping to gain some extra meters from my stalker. After those who were descending for this God-forsaken destination departed and had cleared the station, I took my bag and walked quickly past him and to the exit from the car. I descended into the station and hurried through the small terminal, no more than a few benches and a ticket window, and out into the street. I saw a church ahead and thought this might be an appropriate spot to leave my first sacrifice to Russia's evil. I emboldened myself thinking that this was a revolutionary act and that many more lives would be lost before the turmoil that was brewing everywhere had ended.

Indeed, this death would be more justified than most.

I turned down beside the church into a narrow footpath where stalls would be opened during market day. I walked ahead a ways and then doubled backed on my own tracks and slipped into a small passageway and waited for the agent to come. My heart was beating so loudly that I thought its pounding might alert him to my hiding. Moments passed and I hoped that I had not unintentionally alluded him. Then, I heard him coming. I would let him pass to be sure of not murdering some innocent in the split second my attack would require. But I could not wait too long either, as he was certainly armed. Then he was there. He passed me obviously bewildered by where I had gone, and was about to turn and retrace his steps.

Before he could make his turn I was upon him. I grasped his head and took the razor to his neck. In the instant that I began to slice his jugular vein I hesitated with a sense of some inner knowledge. My hand felt a smooth face that I recognized in some deep place. I resisted the hesitation, but in the same instant dropped the razor from my hand and fell to my knees with Hadassah in my arms. I had come as close as possible to ending her life. Even now, I had wounded her, but prayed the cut was not mortal. As she dropped in my arms, I felt her belly and understood.

Chapter 15

Finding Reuven

Hadassah's wound was ultimately superficial. There was much blood, but little injury. Her image recalled a female partisan of the French Revolution, ready at the barricades with her beloved. Her equanimity at almost being dispatched by her betrothed was more than compensated for by my agitated state. At no time did it seem that we were both on an equal emotional plane, but played a seesaw game of up and down between our two emotional states. I was reeling from the fourfold shock that I received. To find my life's love in the wilderness, nearly murder her, learn she was with child, and nearly extinguish that child's life before it could draw breath was more than I could handle. I entered into a waxy twilight and could not place together a coherent string of words–for two days! The train departed without us.

We had the chance fortune to be stranded in a barracks town, not even identifiable on a map as a town. These were like many towns on the Siberian frontier, erected in a period of days to house the military at chance points for possible war on the Chinese border, to refit troops sent to fight Japan, or to keep order in the provincial wild west that Russia had made of Siberia.

In 1904, Japan attacked the Russian stronghold at Port Arthur. The world expected Russia to easily defeat backward Japan, but someone forgot to inform Japan. Well-disciplined and closer to the fighting, they beat the Russians in a series of daring and well-organized land and sea battles. Russia did not go home with its tail tucked neatly between its legs. Siberia's enormous wealth, and the promise of China, could not be abandoned so easily. Rather, it had learned that to exploit the richness of Siberia and the East, it needed open supply lines and available troops nearby. Muscle flexing requires soldiers and the vastness of

Russia demanded that soldiers be stationed across much of Siberia. This was such a place.

We entered a tavern looking for food and a chance to more closely examine the source of the renewed flow of blood from Hadassah's neck. The innkeeper and several soldiers were friendly and curious. In a few words, it was clear that my uncle's family was from a town only a hundred kilometers from the place called home to three of the men. One had actually heard of our Kalushin, although he had never been there, nor known anyone that had.

This made us at least cousins, and the men sent for what stood for a doctor in the form of a medical orderly. Better a battle-hardened medic, however, than a professor of surgery from Moscow for a wound such as Hadassah's, as this was the kind of trauma he had dressed in many battles and dozens of soldiers' brawls.

They immediately discerned Hadassah's injury, but could not decipher the nature of my seemingly more severe condition. Hadassah, always quick witted, explained that we had been attacked by two men and that I had driven off the assailants, but had received a wound to the head. Searching my head they could find no bump, bruise or cut, but were sufficiently appeased with the story and the chance of some excitement that a platoon was dispersed by a young lieutenant to round up the criminals.

"Do you have any food we can purchase?" Hadassah, introducing herself as Natalia, asked. "I'm really quite hungry and my husband, Jósef, could use some food I think as well, and maybe a little vodka for him too, or whatever passes for liquor here."

"We have potato soup, with a little meat in it. And homemade potato vodka. I'm afraid it's the best we can do," answered the innkeeper. "So you are a woman then. They said you were."

"Of course she's a woman. And clever too," affirmed the young officer. "You're not the first, madam, to travel as a man. If those criminals had known you were a woman, it might have gone a lot worse for you."

"Thank you for your kindness. It's good to meet an officer who knows how to take charge." Hadassah had again with a few words won over still another knight errant ready to do her bidding, if he needed any more winning. A table was set for us, strong drink provided that was also used to cleanse Hadassah's wound, and a tablecloth dug up which was as white and starched as if had come fresh from the Paris Ritz.

After we ate and rested, the young officer arranged with his major to billet us in the lieutenant's own quarters. We slept through the night in each other's arms and although by morning I felt over my shock, my ability to perform anything but simple speech was quite impaired. Except, of course, for sexual performance, for which my own soldier was immediately able to mobilize and respond to his call for duty. This call came in the early morning with revelry, as I awoke with Hadassah's mouth stimulating me to battle.

Eventually, we had a chance to talk through what had occurred over the past weeks of intrigue.

"I guess I can see why you came, but why all the secrecy?"

"Isn't that obvious?"

"Perhaps it will be when my head clears, but all I can see right now is that you endangered yourself and almost got yourself killed, and by me no less."

"Well, quite frankly I didn't think you were so quick with that knife of yours, but I guess I should have known better. Still, this is not my daily trade, following someone."

"You seem to have done pretty well getting this far."

"That wasn't so difficult. After all, I knew where you were going and I just went to the ticket agent or the conductor after you left the area so you could not possibly have seen me."

"I did see you quite a few times on the train Hadassah."

"Yes, there was no hiding from you there. I had to eat, and I thought my disguise was pretty good. I would make a fine Russian policeman at my size. How could you have thought I was a big tough policeman?"

"Hadassah, the man that interrogated me in Poland when I was arrested years ago was no more than your size and not your strength. He was the scariest man I have ever met and the subject of most of my nightmares. Size isn't the essence. Evil is. But I still don't understand why you didn't reveal yourself to me."

"Your brain is rattled Tzvi-Yosef. Because you would have sent me back of course."

"And why wouldn't I send you back now?"

"Too dangerous. We've come too far."

"Oh."

"And anyway, this is where I choose to be. I could not bear if something happened to you and I had not been there. So there it is."

Having landed in a barracks town might seem like we were thrown directly into the lion's den. But the situation was quite the opposite. Conscripts were never happy with their plight, but even officers were angry with Russia and the Czar. Some were stationed in Siberia for past offenses or lack of family connections. Others were disgraced in the Russo-Japanese war and felt abandoned by the government for not sending the necessary troops and supplies, with which they felt they could have won honor and the war. Many in the town were former or current prisoners on parole to serve out the end of their sentences in hard labor and exile. In short, everyone was willing to help us locate Reuven and his exact location was identified and tickets on the next train that was largely a military transport were obtained. Two dresses were found for Hadassah and we attended several dinners and gatherings in our honor where we, rather she, was the center of attention.

As our train awaited provisioning, we had the further good fortune, or so we thought, of being introduced to the company of a colonel of the elite Lancers. He graciously invited us to dine during the journey, but our lieutenant friend quickly begged off the invitation. He let slip that we were going to visit a brother on trial, at which point the colonel unceremoniously dropped his invitation and departed.

On our own again, the lieutenant reverted to his solicitous self without otherwise referring to the incident. He arranged our seating, and asked some fellow officers of his own rank to look after us for the journey. We thought his abrupt and even insulting actions with the colonel strange, but decided later that he was perhaps piqued by not being more affectionately treated by Hadassah. Or perhaps, we thought, he was worried that should the colonel find out about our tainted mission later, that he would be held accountable. Nevertheless, in relative comfort, and with good conversation, we began the three-day journey to our destination.

Before dinner the first evening we were therefore surprised by the receipt of a written invitation to dine with the colonel, whose wax seal and stationery indicated that he was a baron as well. Hadassah felt it was odd that he would bother with the likes of us, but I thought she failed to realize just how striking she was. Even looking more tired now, and strained with pregnancy and her chase, she was a startling woman. We responded to the colonel's adjutant that we did not have proper dress for dinner, but he assured us that proper dress would not be necessary. After, all, certain formalities had to be suspended so far from home.

The colonel's dining car was elegant. What we now recognized as his family seal was posted, inscribed, and embossed everywhere. The colonel welcomed us and took us on a tour of the compartment, with its many ingeniously concealed panels to make best use of space. He was most proud of his sword, a family heirloom that, he said, had been used to fight in the Napoleonic wars.

The problems soon began, as with each drink Colonel Lvov became more sexually provocative. This was obviously his intent from early on, and we were not so much naive as having little room to maneuver. His adjutant sat me at opposite sides of the small table from Hadassah, with the colonel next to her. As the wine and liquor flowed, so did his hands. It was all innocent enough, however, and offered in the best of spirits and good cheer. Luckily dinner was ending by this time and we were able to retire to his salon for drinks where I was able to place myself between him and Hadassah until we could successfully disengage from his contact.

My mistake was to excuse myself to the toilet, but nature called demandingly. No sooner had I entered and lowered my trousers, the door clicked from behind. I fumbled with the lock for a time, but making no progress decided that I would have to risk our transport and break down the door or Hadassah would fall victim to this lecher. As I lowered my shoulder, the door swung open of its own accord and I stood facing the colonel. He stood nonchalantly swirling his crystal snifter filled with what he had told us was the finest French cognac, naked as the day he was born. I don't know what would have made me more upset had I had the choice, but it turned out that it was my body and kisses this decrepit degenerate of a Russian noble preferred.

I had thought that there was something uneasy transpiring all evening between the colonel and his adjutant, and then it dawned on me. The adjutant had placed Hadassah in the colonel's grasp hoping to bait him with feminine odors, and not masculine ones. They were lovers and I was the object of the adjutant's jealousy, not Hadassah. And, of course, our friendly lieutenant, either by reputation or a sense developed in the military, had immediately understood the colonel's proclivities and tried to steer us from harm's way back at the station, but we had been too dense to see the signs.

"I take it young man that you do not especially find me appealing," he declared with one eyebrow raised, a smirk on his face, obviously enjoying my discomposure.

"I apologize colonel, but you can understand that one either has such inclinations or one does not. I simply don't, no insult intended."

"Ah, all the better. There are any number of willing young men on this train looking for promotion or favoritism, or who even like aging men."

"I don't think I quite understand."

"Well, Joséf, I take it you're a virgin . . . Oh not that way silly . . . with men. You can understand that every man wants a virgin, especially at my age. And in the army, virgins can be hard to come by." These words brought on a fit of laughter, and then coughing, and he had to sit and take several sips of brandy to regain his equilibrium.

"And what makes you think I will do this? I'm obviously much stronger than you."

"Oh yes, indeed you are, and I long to see those muscles that your clothing only promises. But to your question. The answer is simple. If you don't, your wife will be deposited from the train, as it is moving, I should add. You will be kept here for a time and then deposited likewise. Neither of you will be too badly hurt, perhaps some broken bones, but no more than that. But still, the chance of your finding each other with even twenty versts of ice and snow that I will place between you will make your reconnecting, alive, quite a formidable challenge. Oh don't look so glum. I'm quite healthy, despite my body's sinking in places that it used to swell. In the morning you'll have no more than a memory of an adventure and the knowledge that you saved your wife's life. Oh come now. Here, drink this, it will make it go down easier, so to speak."

I was set to rebel and risk it all, but I recalled Rachel coming to me in prison years earlier and risking her own pregnant body to the major to obtain perhaps what was likely to amount to no more than better conditions for me. The colonel was right, in the morning I would be disgusted, but we would be alive. Nothing more to be said, the colonel approached me and began kissing my neck and biting at my ears.

I worried that I would not be able to perform, and that he would take his frustrations out on Hadassah. My penis had entered a cavity in my body seeking shelter and in full retreat. I took a large glass of the cognac and then another and tried to imagine a beautiful woman as I removed my trousers and underwear and stood before him as naked as he.

His reaction of disgust was palpable in the air and he fled from me to the other side of the salon as if I was rabid.

"You sheeny dog. You're a Jew. You're a fucking Jew dog and I nearly tainted myself with touching you. How could you think that I would ever touch a Jew? How totally revolting! Get out, and not a word of this to anyone. You fucking degenerate!"

And then, just as suddenly, his anger and disgust transformed to a look of fear. "Listen very carefully," he said speaking in a frightened whisper. "No one is to find out you're a Jew. You are to stay in my compartment with your fucking whore of a wife for the night and you'll be deposited at the first town in the morning so that no one finds out you're a Yid. Do you understand me? No one on this train. They will have assumed that I seduced you. My proclivities are known, if not openly discussed. There's nothing I can do about that. But first thing in the morning, the very first town you will make your departure."

With this he took his clothes in hand. He walked into the corridor, still naked, making his exit to whatever other compartment he frequented, perhaps with his adjutant to sink his troubles and whatever else he might raise to the occasion to salvage his ruined night. I found Hadassah locked in the next compartment. She had heard the whole interlude, and we could only stare at each other in wonder over the entire episode.

In the early morning, two soldiers came to "escort" our disembarking from the train. The station looked foreboding, no more than a few shacks and some buildings for grain storage and warehousing. It immediately struck me that trains might not even frequent this same route and we would be stranded. I looked around for wagons and horses that we might purchase to make the remaining leg by road, but from the weather it looked like a sleigh was the only means, and how would we even find the way with the roads covered in snow and ice. Even experienced travelers can lose their way and their lives in such conditions.

In this miserable state, glad only for our lives, and my virginity as it were, the train began to pull out of the station into the dark, snowy morning.

Suddenly, a soldier emerged from the blizzard, grabbed Hadassah, and was off. I jumped to the chase, sensing that I must not lose them in the blinding snow. Just then, strong arms encircled me, and when I struggled I felt a stunning blow to my head, and lost consciousness.

I began to revive with snow pressed to my forehead, only to find Hadassah perched on some boxes, laughing with several men. I thought I must be dreaming, a sick hallucination, but as my senses returned I realized that we were back on the train with the young officers. As I looked around, I saw that we must be in a supply car and the atmosphere was more party than panic.

A young captain, who looked like the heart of Russia with his broad forehead and deep-set eyes, spoke up with a look of great amusement. "Oh Jósef, here, have a sip of this. It will relieve your head a bit. We're sorry for being so rough, but we only had very little time. We couldn't leave you at that station, no train would have stopped there as the colonel had this one diverted to pass this outpost during the night. We didn't see another way without alerting the colonel or his flunkies. You began to yell out and so Yuri here had to quiet you down."

"But how did you know?" I asked, still bewildered at the turn of events.

"I'm afraid we've had to live with our colonel for some time now. He knows not to touch most of us, or he will one day receive a bullet in the back of his head. Anyway, he's not the worst of colonels. He's well-connected and gets us good conditions. He's mainly ceremonial, and connected to the Czar himself. It could be worse."

"Then thank you," answered Hadassah.

"So, he wouldn't have a Jewish lover? That's no surprise really. We have no Jewish officers or non-coms, and any Jewish soldiers are made miserable."

"You knew we were Jews?"

"Yes . . . I mean, no, not at first. The colonel's adjutant told us."

"But, we thought the adjutant was . . . "

"Yes, he's the colonel's lover, and a deviate of the worst sort. But didn't want to see you two stranded and pregnant. He didn't want to feel responsible for your lives."

I shook my head in wonder. Every time I thought I understood people, this task that I had set as my business to understand, some new twist on life presented itself. It was as if God had sent me a great, never-ending test.

As I sat there absorbing these thoughts, I noticed that Hadassah looked weakened by the experience. *Mameh* came to me and spoke into my ear.

"Look at Hadassah. Look closely. I don't like her pallor. She's exhausted from all this. And maybe more. Get her rest. If you're to be a guardian, you must guard to your left and to your right, in front, and behind."

"I am a guardian Mameh?"

"Of course *mamaleh*, isn't that obvious that this is what you have been shaped for?"

"But Mameh, I cannot save all those around me."

"No, and many will die in the course of your life. Still, many more will be saved, and even now would not have lived, if not for you."

"But I cannot do this alone."

"Who asked you to do this alone darling?"

And with this her image was gone, and I finally understood. I was the imperfect guardian. The prodigal son sent out not to return home and receive gifts, but to shelter my family and my people, imperfectly, with the help of others, with the pain of partial success.

With these men, who were not always good, who could be lecherous with Hadassah at one moment and perfect gentlemen at the next, who were ready to kill and were ready to sacrifice their lives for their comrades and country, who could be good with us, while they detested Jews, who had families and loved their children, who whored in drunken revelry when given the opportunity, who were themselves sons and fathers, we traveled to Krasnoyarsk. We left them in good cheer, given the names of several friends who might have influence at the prison.

Krasnoyarsk was a large town, with perhaps ten-thousand inhabitants. As we exited the station, we found ourselves in a long, wide street, bordered by unpainted log houses, with closed shutters. Their steep, pyramidal tin and thatched roofs loomed high and dark in the last light of the short day.

The richness of some of the houses spoke to the wealth that Krasnoyarsk derived from the Czar's gold mines and commerce in fur trading. We passed several houses which would have been considered lavish anywhere in Russia, and by their gates and decorations they spoke of fortunes that might not have been so easily gained elsewhere. These were the reward for those families of standing that were willing to make their homes so far from European Russia and culture.

The tallest building was the police station. Many structures were of stone or stucco, but the police station was wooden with four stories and a high pitched roof. Upon this was placed the fire tower which stood another two stories above the main edifice. Other homes were less grand, but even several peasant houses had multiple buildings for the family and animals, surrounded by gates and log fences. These houses were more roof than house, with thatched roofs pitched so steeply one wondered how a man could ascend them to make repairs.

At last, we wearily arrived at a place where we were told we might find rooms. We entered the tavern to find ourselves in a pleasant room. A large stove was burning brightly with coal and the room felt oppressively hot in contrast to the freezing cold outside. Most notable were the books on the shelves, and seeing my interest the proprietor explained that as a former university professor he had brought many books over the years of his exile and that others knowing this left their books through the years, establishing the tavern as a lending library.

"We have books in Russian, Polish, German, and English, and even some American magazines. They are quite old, but everyone finds them interesting. You can browse if you like, we're preparing your rooms."

"How is that possible? We have not yet mentioned that we were looking for rooms," I answered.

"From Tyumen to Yakutsk, what is done, and even what is not done, is known. You cannot sneeze in Siberia without word traveling about the nature of your malady."

"You mean you already knew us to be looking for rooms?"

"Of course. Now sit down and have something warm to drink. You look frozen. It's minus fifteen already, and the thermometer is dropping rapidly."

"But what of the price?"

"The price will be the same all round. We have already determined what you're worth and what you're not. Don't worry, you'll be here for a while. We must be fair or we cannot share the household. You will be sharing many of your meals with my family. We can work out the details later."

We were famished. We ate a zakúska, rye bread and pickled fish. This was followed by vegetable soup with small crescent-shaped meat pies; mashed potatoes mixed with spinach, cutlets of brains; small birds on toast, and chocolate cake. For drinks we were given a kind of homemade rum. It was more than we had eaten in weeks and the best home-cooked meal we had enjoyed in several months.

I took the occasion to look through the books. There were perhaps five hundred in his collection. All the great Russian writers were represented. I was more surprised to find books by Spencer, Lewes, Dickens, Poe, and Harte. There were also many Russian books on science and engineering, but these were less enticing to me. I hoped to learn some more English and wondered if I might actually be capable of reading some of these English books before we departed. Part of me hoped our departure would be immediate, but the library itself made the possibility of a long, drawn out affair more palatable.

In the morning, we presented ourselves at the prison and made our wishes to visit with Reuven known to the authorities. We were insulted, ridiculed, forced to wait, and in the end asked to return the following day. Through it all, I watched carefully for signs who I should approach. I chose a mid-level prison officer and a desk sergeant, letting them know that we were ready to "help out" those who were able to help us. I was quite confident I had chosen the right men, these two looked the most hardened and the healthiest. They were men who were prospering in this environment in which there was only one way to prosper.

"What do you think this means?" Hadassah asked the army captain, one Lavr Kerensky, whose name we had been given by one of our saviors on the train. The two had been at military academy together and were, he said, closer than brothers. His help seemed forthright and unconstrained.

"I'm not sure. The police keep us regular army pretty much in the dark about the prison's affairs. We've been called in a couple of times to quell riots, but day to day, we're glad to keep our separate ways. Still, if they asked you to come back, I would be cautiously optimistic. They may wish to clean him up a bit, so that you'll be more likely to see it worth your investment to start paying for his . . . his welfare. If he was too far gone, many families would just up and leave, understanding that the situation was hopeless.

We were given extra furs to cover over our coats and heavy boots for the snow and ice. Any part of our faces that were exposed were likely to develop frostbite in minutes. In the few minutes it took to walk from our rooms to the prison, the cold penetrated us, even bundled as we were. I spit in the air and heard it crackle. I was taken with an urge to try to pee into the snow to see if it would freeze in the air like they said. I told this to Hadassah and received one of her "go grow up" looks and a swift elbow in my side. And so it was in the early morning when we presented ourselves again, looking like two bears come out of hibernation by mistake before winter's end.

After being gruffly received, and giving a small packet of money and a blanket for Reuven to the sergeant of the guard in the outer office, we were placed in a bare room. We waited in an anteroom on hard, worn wooden benches that were not much more than boards nailed together. We sat for hours with no one acknowledging our existence.

Having waited nine hours, we were without hope and quite starving. It was also very cold in the room, and the stove in the corner had burnt down and gone cold hours earlier. Here too we were being given a message as to what the costs would be to restore Reuven to an environment in which he could be comfortable enough to survive. I was also becoming more worried about Hadassah. Dark bags lay beneath her eyes. I knew that pregnant women could go through such stages and that Hadassah was a strong, young woman, but I also understood that this journey had been arduous.

As Hadassah slept on my shoulder, a deep sleep that had overcome her off and on for the past three hours, the door opened and Reuven stood before me across the room wrapped in the wool army blanket I had brought that day. He was gaunt, hardly his robust, larger than life self, but neither did he look broken. His usual gleam was in his one good eye.

My desire was to rush to him, but I felt it better to appear nonchalant. I also needed to extricate Hadassah from my arms, and did so slowly, waking her gently. My slow actions were done shaking, as I was holding back so many emotions–fear, love, anxiety, joy, sadness. I had to force myself to remember that I was playing the part of a concerned brother-in-law. My wife and I were Christians, a Jewish brother-in-law was a family obligation, not an object of my love. Hence, there were limits as to what I would do and what I would pay.

It was all I could do not to reach out to hug Reuven closely. I was overcome with the need to check his wounds, reassure him, tear him from this place. I thought he did not fully recognize me at first, or perhaps did not possess the energy to show signs of that recognition. But then it came to me that I must not underestimate Reuven. I sensed that he had quickly observed my reaction and had intended to follow suit. The less intimate our connection, the less likely they would exact small tortures, and larger ones, to increase the cost of his deliverance.

The guard unshackled his fetters and walked from the room, saying only, "You 'ave a half hour. That's all."

And with the guard gone, I enveloped Reuven in my arms and we wept, but silent tears, trembling, so as not to be heard.

Even through the weeping, Reuven began to ask questions about Rachel and his children, and me and Hadassah. He never shared with me all that he had been through, but fresh scars, and some already fading, told much of the story. Yet, he was immediately concerned for us, and I could see in his eyes his disquiet over Hadassah's state, as he held her in his arms.

"Don't offer them too much Tzvi. Just enough to keep me alive and well in here. Already yesterday I knew someone was here as there was a little extra bread and soup. I need to get stronger."

"But what if we can get you out of here? It may be possible."

"More than you know Tzvi. With war brewing in the West, they can't afford all the men in prison and all the men watching the men in prison. War will begin soon, it's only a matter of time. Or the revolution will begin, and then if we're not murdered, we'll be set free by the revolution. Either way, the wheels are in motion. Those that watch well will survive."

"Reuven, I don't think this is time to become philosophical."

"Philosophical is practical right now. It's in the air. The men who are in better health have been receiving more food and much of the harassment has ended. Those who have minor sentences have been paroled to work in the factories and mines. They're spread out here in the East, Germany and Austria are strong, and the revolution is infiltrating the countryside, and not just in the cities any longer. Wealthy landowners and the aristocracy have been murdered and their homes burned. Worker committees have been dictating the terms by which estates are being run and strikes have hit the factories and are winning better terms."

"Reuven, I believe that might be the big picture," entered Hadassah, "but we have to be concerned with you."

"Yes, you're right Hadassah, but that's the point. If I can just remain well, and get a little stronger, I'll be released to work. They'll need every able-bodied man."

It was not time to remind Reuven that with one good eye and a limp he was not likely to be thought in the category of able-bodied. He also had a hacking cough that was disturbing and he carried a rag that had brownish blood mixed with phlegm. I would have to get a proper doctor in to see him. But maybe this was the time to support his plan even if just to make him feel in control.

"I see your point Reuven. And this will also allow us to gauge the guards and what they want."

"Tzvi-Yosef, if Reuven is right, then the guards will also be sensing that their years of plenty are ending and that they have this last chance to gain. If we can be there at the right moment, they may accept one large, single payment for an ultimate favor." Hadassah's sharp mind was working quickly.

"So, you're Tzvi-Yosef now. I see also that you've found a woman with a real head on her shoulders. We need women like this in the revolution."

"Thank you Reuven, but I'm committed solely to the reform of Tzvi-Yosef, and perhaps Palestine if we can find our way. Those are revolutions quite large enough for me."

With this our time was ending. We kissed and promised to return. As Reuven held me closely, he whispered in my ear. "Watch out for her. She's ill. Get a doctor at once." Reuven had grasped clearly what I had been fearing. Reuven was to survive, for no man could be so perceptive when he himself was in such conditions, unless he was endowed with a powerful soul and spirit. "Go with God," said this revolutionary who was helping orchestrate the revolution from his small cell in this far off wilderness.

Chapter 16

And Two Shall be as One

Hadassah experienced somewhat of a recovery and the doctor felt that she had probably just been exhausted. During the next weeks, we settled into a routine, visiting Reuven, arranging for our food, and finding a small circle of friends. As Christians, our friends were from 'the others." This meant there was more liquor, more gaiety, less complaints about bodily pains, and less intimacy. Still, when the liquor flowed our friends opened up and spilled their wounds and their pain freely. The next day with the return of sobriety these intimacies were never mentioned, but a closeness grew that came from an inner acknowledgment of these shared moments. As there were mostly men, only a few women accompanied us and then only occasionally. Typically, Hadassah was the only woman and if there were others, they were of another calling. The men accepted us as a married couple, and although they were flirtatious with Hadassah, they formed a wall around her to separate her from the commonness of the tavern. Truly, they were so thick sometimes around her that she could not have seen what was going on behind them.

With our plan to give little money at first to the guards, we were in good shape financially. Luxuries were terribly expensive, but we needed few of them and everyday items were cheap, provided with government subsidy to keep workers happy. Much of the meat we ate was hunted by natives who came into the outskirts of town to sell their kill and the skins they obtained. Bear, all sorts of large deer and caribou, and an occasional seal found its way to the table. Fresh vegetables were almost impossible to obtain, and near rotten at the best prices, but pickled vegetables were plentiful enough. I began a small trade in buying skins and furs and arranged to have them warehoused for the journey west. I saw how this could be an endeavor that could make us wealthy, but mostly dabbled for something to do with the extra hours.

Making love with Hadassah during these weeks was wondrous. Her budding pregnancy made her all the more desirable to me. Her belly swelled, and we spoke of the need to find a Rabbi, but in the meantime I could not get enough of her. I chased her around our small rooms and she would pretend to run from me.

If I did not chase her, she would chide me that I found her obese and ugly, and that I should just discard her like a charwoman, and I would cover her in kisses and assure her of my ardor. "Then prove it Romeo," she would say, and we would make soft, sweet, always gentle love. Her breasts became enlarged and sensitive, and her nipples darkened. She had not been very excited by my playing with her breasts before, but this became a source of great passion for her. I was careful not to press against her stomach, so as not to hurt the child. This led to our finding different positions to caress each other. She enjoyed best when we made love with me behind her and we both laying on our sides. I would reach around and play with her pert nipples and she would purr like a kitten or growl like a great cat. She always achieved orgasm easily, but with time on our hands we learned, to both of our amazement, that once she had an orgasm, she could continue to have more for a long as I was willing to keep up my end of the ceremony! This could last for an hour or more, and afterwards she would sleep soundly nestled in the bow my body would make for her.

Then, her health floundered once again. This time there was no mistaking that she was ill, and she wished to stay in bed and only left to sleep. Her face became ashen and lost its vibrancy and she developed deep dark pockets under her bright eyes. I found the doctor again, and he came as quickly as could be arranged. He was clearly a competent man, and when asked he explained that he was Moscow trained and exiled for an affair with a woman whose jealous husband was a little too well connected. "So I used to treat the aristocracy, now I treat the outcasts. A body is a body. Actually, my work here is more satisfying, and in truth I am comfortable enough. People with the means are generous when they receive proper medical care."

I understood the hint, and was more than glad to oblige, as we were indeed thankful to receive first class medical attention so far from European Russia. In the coming weeks we were to quickly learn that much of Russia's intelligentsia, in addition to its large criminal class, was in fact settled here in Siberia. Great minds and talents were a threat to the archaic Russian system that was crumbling during these times. The punishment of dissent was robbing Russia of its greatest resources at its time of greatest need.

"Has there been any bleeding?"

"No," answered Hadassah, looking embarrassed by the question.

"A little spotting maybe?"

"Yes . . . that . . . I suppose a little."

"Well, to tell you the truth, I don't have much experience with pregnant women. Not since medical school. But I think it would be prudent for you to be on bed rest."

"I told you that you needed more rest Natalia."

"No, not *more* rest. Complete bed rest. That means you're to be in bed all the time. You may get up to go to the bathroom, for now that is, and if the spotting gets worse, then not for that either."

Seeing the look of alarm on Hadassah's face, he became less harsh. "I'm sorry. My bedside manner is something . . . well, of the distant past. By bed rest we should hope to stop the spotting and the pregnancy will proceed normally and come to term. I want you to eat plenty of meat and you will have to spend money to buy vegetables. Make them into a soup. They can't be eaten any other way in the state you will find them in any case. And blood sausage."

With this word, Hadassah proceeded to puke into the bucket that we stationed next to the bed. The doctor could not have known that as Jews we were forbidden to eat blood and that the thought of this "delicacy" was enough to turn the strongest Jewish stomach."

And whatsoever man there be of the house of Israel, or of the strangers
that sojourn among them, that eateth any manner of blood, I will set My face
against that soul that eateth blood, and will cut him off from among his people.
For the life of the flesh is in the blood; and I have given it to you upon the altar
to make atonement for your souls; for it is the blood that maketh atonement by
reason of the life.

On the way out, the doctor wished to speak to me further.

"Mr. Apfel, I was a bit disingenuous with your wife. I don't wish to
alarm you, but even if she is in fact in her fourth month, then this pregnancy is
not proceeding well. Typically at this time women have renewed strength and
good color. There is a midwife in the next village, I will alert her and have her
come and check as well. She is a rather primitive woman, but can out birth me
with her eyes closed and drunk. Not that she's a drinking woman. I am. I mean,
not that I'm a woman. Oh, of course you knew . . . No, I mean I do drink, but
that is of course another matter. In any case, I will let her know."

When I returned to Hadassah she was already asleep. I found the
innkeeper's scullery woman and asked that she sit outside of Hadassah's room
should she awaken and went on my next mission. She was a kindly childless
woman and was glad to oblige. She already called Hadassah "daughter."

There was no actual *Shul* in the town, but there was a Rabbi. It was to
his home that I went. I knocked at the door, but there was no answer. I poked
my head in and given the cold outside, I was forced to enter and just wait. With a
few coals I fed the fire in the main room which obviously served as the
sanctuary, his study, and their living and eating area. The door of the stove was
rusty and it was probably unsafe. I picked up a *chumesh*, a book of Torah and its
interpretation, and leafed through the pages, seeing if I could still read the
commentaries in the sidebars by the great *Rebbe* Rashi. With the strain and the
heat I dozed off and when I awoke the *Rebbe* and his wife had returned and a
glass of steaming tea and a piece of *Mandelbrot*, a kind of twice baked cake that

seems to improve with hardness, were placed before me.

"Nu, you know then to read that thing you hold?" he asked in Russian.

"And why should I not know?" I answered in Yiddish.

"Why does a Jew then always answer a question with a question?"

"Why not?" I answered. And with this any question of my heritage was settled. My Yiddish and my odd logic placed me among his flock as sure as if he had attended my circumcision.

The *Rebbe* smiled with his wrinkled eyes and blinked in a way that made his face kind of twinkle, like an Irish gnome more than a Russian *Rebbe*. "Drink the tea. It was nice to come into a warm room. Thank you."

"I took the liberty of adding some coals to the fire. I came to talk to you."

"And why else would I suppose you would have come?"

"Yes, why else?"

"Some suspected you were a Jew. Not you actually, but your wife. Visiting a Jewish prisoner also made you suspicious. So you are a Yid as well. Interesting."

"*Rebbe*, I need a favor of you."

"Ah, so a question *and* a favor? But first, tell me what you look like."

"Why? Can't you see me?"

"Well, yes and no. I see images, but not details. They had me working in the snow for months when I was first sent here. My eyes were never so good. Since then I can only see outlines and such."

"I'm sorry. You must miss your sight for reading and study."

"Yes, but that's not the worst. I was a bird watcher. I always loved to go in the woods and see the birds. I still do, but now I only see their silhouette and know them by their songs."

"Is it like that with your interpretation of the law?"

"Ah, an intelligent young man. A good listener. Nu? So, what is it young man? What troubles you?"

"I thought you wanted to know what I looked like."

"No, not really. I just wanted to see what you thought like. So go on with your question and your favor."

"Thank you *Rebbe*. You see, my wife and I did not set out together. I had come alone to help my brother-in-law. She . . . well . . . she showed up, as it were."

"Women have their own way."

"Yes, apparently." And even here much was said between us. The Chassids ruled over their women, but for the rest of Jews women had status and were viewed with a kind of wonder. It is not that we did not wish to control them. We had no idea how, as we rejected either the violence we often saw between men and women of 'the others,' or the disdain, as we saw it, of the way Chassids treated their women.

"And what is your favor then? Surely if it is within my powers of what The Holy One has bestowed upon me, I will do it."

"We need to be married."

"Oh I see."

"There is more."

"There is always more."

"She is with child."

"Were you betrothed when she became with child?"

"Yes, we had received the families' blessings and we drew up a contract. It was a long engagement of two years or more, because of her father's wishes." I said by way of explaining.

"I'm afraid that is never good. Betrothals mean that *Hashem* has already intended you to be joined together. It is not good to tempt fate by waiting. It is not in keeping with human needs and feelings. It was not right of him to try to keep you apart in this way. His choices were to agree or to refuse, not to delay."

"Then we have not sinned?"

"Hm. An interesting question. If you have sworn your being together and intend to live a Jewish life, then let us say that *HaShem* understands. Or at least to the extent that I grasp the silhouette of He Who is Unknowable, I believe He understands. You have not sinned in any ultimate way. That is not to say that you have not transgressed the law. How many months is she from her time?"

"She has been ill. We must do it at her bedside."

"Is her illness mortal?"

"No, only she is on bed rest. And there's one more thing."

"Ah, there is always one more thing my child."

"Everyone here thinks we are Christians. We thought it would make it easier to deal with the authorities. So, you have to come disguised."

"And I suppose I should bring Jewish witnesses. And also disguised."

"Yes, I suppose."

"Is that all then?"

"Yes, that's all. I'm so grateful you will do it then. I'm indebted to you."

"And how do you know that I agree to all this young man?"

"Because you said that 'surely if it is within my powers of what The Holy One has bestowed upon me, I will do it.' This is within your powers?"

"Yes, you are a good listener and probably were a very troublesome student in *Cheder* with your Hebrew teachers. It will be a *groyseh simcha, a great joy*, to have a Jewish wedding for a change, even a secret wedding. I do too many burials here. My wife will come for the bride, and I will have to find another witness. She loves a wedding as well."

"Can't your wife witness? The fewer people that know about this the better."

"Of course not, *"Ahl pi shnayim aydim yakoom devar," "two witnesses are needed to establish something,"* and only a Jewish man may witness. Don't worry, there are many Jews here who would be glad to do the *mitzvah*. Jewish good deeds are hard to come by in Siberia."

So, that Tuesday, because on Tuesday all things are particularly blessed, we were to be married.

And on the third day, God made the two great lights in the firmament; the greater light to rule the day and the lesser light to rule the night, and the stars. And God set them in the firmament of the heaven to give light upon the earth, and to rule over the day and over the night, and to divide the light from the darkness; and God saw that it was good.

The Rabbi, his wife, and a young Jewish man who had been studying for the Rabinate before his exile were to be in attendance. We also asked our friend Captain Kerensky, if he would honor us with his attendance. He had been so kind and had become our one friend since arriving. He had used his influence and taken several risks in showing any possible connection on his part with a subversive prisoner.

"Lavr, I have a favor to ask of you."

"Are you short of money Jósef? I can certainly spare a little, but you see I've been gambling and . . . "

"No, nothing like that."

"What then? I will be glad to help out. I hope it is an adventure. I am totally bored in this hell hole."

"Well, Natalia and I are to be married."

"That's wonderful, Jósef. Glad tidings. I wish you both joy!"

He was such a hearty fellow, I was afraid to say something that might ruin our relationship, but I persevered.

"There is a small matter of which I need you to swear you will tell no one."

"I swear as an officer and a gentleman. Now tell me what it is. This is more intrigue than I've had in months. I can barely sustain my heart from beating out of my chest."

"We are to have a Rabbi marry us."

"A Rabbi, but why would you . . . ? Oh, I see. She is Jewish then. I thought that perhaps she had the look of a Jew about her. Not that I care a bit one way or another. I have always secretly found their women attractive. Those breasts! But then come to think of it Natalia doesn't . . . Oh, here I am talking this way and about your wife, I mean your betrothed. You sly devil you. But why not married in the Church? Surely your lives would be better if you lived as a Russian."

"But I am also Jewish you see. And we rather like being Jews. Well, at least most of the time."

"No, you're kidding me right? You're no more Jewish than I Jósef."

"Well, if your name is Goldberg that might be true. But otherwise, that leaves only one of us as Jewish, and that in this case would be me. I'm sorry we misled you."

"No. I understand. My family is Catholic and not Russian Orthodox. You can't imagine the prejudice I have run into even with that. I lie and say I'm Russian Orthodox. It must be much worse to be a Jew . . . I mean people must treat you worse. We are a small minded people for having such a vast nation."

"Actually, we wanted you to serve as sort of our family, support the bride, the whole thing. You are the only friend we have here."

"Then it is a great honor. I am proud and touched that you would ask. Deeply touched. I can't wait to congratulate Natalia."

"Actually, its Hadassah. And before you ask, I'm Tzvi-Yosef. The Apfel part is true, however. A German Jewish name."

"So, I can come to the wedding. And even be best man, and father of the bride, and all that! This is wonderful." And with this he gave me one of those huge Russian hugs that squeeze the very life out of you and leave you gasping for air and wondering how many ribs are broken. "Okay then, I'm off for a gift. Let me know when and where. Oh, and I have to polish my sword. That is if Jews don't have anything against swords."

"As long as they're not pointed at us, we can live with them."

"Well, of course I wouldn't point it at you. Oh! Ha-ha! Yes, of course, I see. That was one of your jokes. And now I understand where your odd sense of humor comes from. Good. Well, Tzvi-Yosef, what do you say to a drink to celebrate later tonight? Can you meet me at the tavern?"

"That would be my honor. But remember, drunk or sober, no one can know about anything, not even that there is a wedding or a party of any kind."

"As an officer and a gentleman."

So on Tuesday, a small group stood in our bedroom. Lavr had arranged for some flowers, and what this must have cost him or where he would have obtained them late winter in Siberia at any price and on short notice, I cannot imagine. Hadassah was thrilled by them and cried when he brought them into the room. Amidst the gray, stark room and white endless wilderness, they were a sign of life and restored Hadassah more than any medicine could. I stood next to the bed in which Hadassah lay, sitting up in her best dress with her hair carefully combed. The makeup did not completely hide her lack of color and the dark circles under her eyes, and I feared for her. Perhaps for this reason too, she was at that moment more beautiful than I ever knew her to be.

The nearly blind *Rebbe*, who saw deeply into people, his wife, who brought cakes, a young Jewish scholar-exile, who was well on his own way to blindness with his thick glasses, and a handsome officer of the Imperial Army, with polished buttons and sword and hair so stiff he would not have needed a helmet were all in attendance, circled around her bed.

And the Rabbi gave the benediction using our full Hebrew names, *"Hadassah bat Yaacov, Tzvi-Yosef ben Shlomo. Hadassah daughter of Yaacov. Tzvi-Yosef, son of Shlomo. Blessed are You, Lord our God, who has made us holy through Your commandments and has commanded us concerning marriages that are forbidden and those that are permitted when carried out under the canopy and with the sacred wedding ceremonies. Blessed are You, Lord our*

God, who makes Your people Israel holy through this rite of the canopy and the

sacred bond of marriage."

I sipped from the glass of wine and then the *Rebbe* offered it to

Hadassah via his wife, who held it to her lips. I repeated after the *Rebbe*,

"Behold you are consecrated to me with this ring according to the Law of Moses

and Israel." And then I placed a plain gold band on her index finger, because no

stone or break may mar the continuity of the marriage vows. So she too could

now point and say, "that one is mine." The glass, wrapped in a napkin, was

placed before me and I crushed it without hesitation. And with this we were

married and everyone congratulated us. They stayed for the cakes, and sat and

drank tea and schnapps I had bought for the occasion.

Everyone had brought gifts, which touched us deeply. The *Rebbe* and

Rebetzin brought a pair of small brass candlesticks that were dented and old, but

well made. *"Tzu machen Shabbes, und tzu machen an untershayd tzuvishin tog*

und nacht, to make the Sabbath and that you will know light from dark,"

meaning with these that we should live a Jewish life and know the difference

between good and evil, the right way from the wrong way, 'their' path from 'our'

path, kosher from treyf, marriage from adultery, a holy day from a day of work,

respect for wife and family, and love of God from walking lost in the world.

Because all this is wrapped in the words *to know light from dark* when spoken

from the lips of such a *Rebbe* as this.

"Thank you *Rebbe*. You have made this the most wonderful of

weddings. We will never forget your help and your understanding."

"It was a great pleasure Tzvi-Yosef. A wedding is the best part about

being a Rabbi, and this one I will always remember."

The young scholar-exile gave us a small *sidur*, a prayer book. "It is

small enough I thought that you could carry it and no one would know."

Even Reuven managed to send a gift by way of his various and sundry

connections. It was a silver kiddush cup, for blessing the Sabbath and holidays.

Inscribed on it were the words from the bible, *"Anee l'dodi, v'dodi lee, I am my beloved's, and my beloved is mine."* With this he added a note.

Just as you have come for me, God has come to join you.
Each of us is sent a messenger. Tzvi, we cannot pick our path. The
way the world is turning, it is possible that we may never return
home. You must carry that home with you. May this kiddush cup
make you ten thousand sweet Sabbaths together, wherever God
takes you. I shall never forget your kindness, and love, and the risk
you have both taken in coming here. Know that you have saved my
life. I was surely dead by now had you not come. I love you both as
a brother. May you be blessed with the love your sister Rachel and I
have. Who knows, we may yet bounce our children on our knees
Tzvi on a kibbutz in Palestine.

Love, Reuven.

But even amidst all this emotion, it was Lavr who touched us still more.

"I did not know what to give. So I brought this gift. I found it in a Jewish shop. I hope he didn't trick me. He seemed like an honest enough fellow."

And with this he handed us a small box, which when unwrapped revealed a delicate filigreed spice box in the shape of the Tower of David in Jerusalem. The box was silver and perhaps a full six inches in height. The work on it was exquisite and the *Rebbe* himself said he had never seen a finer one. We explained to Lavr that pungent spices were placed in it and that after the Sabbath it was smelled after some prayers, because there is a prayer for everything. The spices were to invite a sweet week and have the Sabbath sweetness linger.

And for this I gave him one of his own bear hugs, for he had taken our breath away.

Over the following weeks the winds howled and the temperatures remained so cold it was all we could do to keep our rooms warm. Hadassah complained that she would perish under the very weight of the covers. Although she tried to keep her humor, her health continued to deteriorate and the doctor came less and looked less hopeful when he did.

At first I asked no more questions, not wanting the answers. Finally, I confronted him, and asked for the truth.

"The answer is simply that I don't know. Her bleeding is only occasional, but I think that the baby may have already died. I can't hear a heartbeat. She says she feels it kicking occasionally, but I just am not so sure that she is not just wishing it so."

"What do we do in such a case?"

"She has to carry the pregnancy to term and deliver. But it is very hard on a woman to know that she may be carrying a dead fetus inside of her, so I prefer that she not know. There is also a chance that she will deliver the fetus early. I wish I had better news for you. I wish I even knew enough to be sure. I suggest you contact a Priest just in case."

"She might die?" I could barely say the words.

"Let's just say for the time being that a Priest might comfort her and prayer can only help. If she believes in prayer that is. She is a strong young woman, so she may well yet recover."

I was too stunned to even thank him for coming, and he let himself out. I looked in on Hadassah and found her asleep and breathing hard, her body fighting for life. Hadassah might not have known she was dying, but her body did. I sat beside the bed for a while, and held her hand, but the closeness of the room and the stale air made me claustrophobic. I had to get air, and so I dressed in my coat and went outside to walk, despite, or maybe because of the cold. I began to run as I came to an open field, as if I could escape into another place, and found myself yelling into the already dark early evening, haranguing God for his viciousness.

"If I have been so evil, strike me down. But not this way. Not through those I love. Not through Christina, not through Hadassah, not through my Bubbie. Not through my father. Deal with me. Are you afraid of me? Are you afraid of a direct fight? Do you have to wear me down this way? Please, please, I beg you. Heal her. Give her life. Spare her. I cannot live this way. I cannot survive . . . Are you even there? Are you listening? Do you care?"

And the ice cracked, and I plunged into the freezing water. I had only to allow the cold to soothe my pain and envelope me. There was no struggle left in me. And I sank into the ice cold water. I had no fight. I doubted that fight would matter. The past was a lead anchor, taking me deeper. It was a fitting end. No one would even know what occurred to me.

And at that moment Mameh grabbed at me. She would not allow me to betray my trust.

"You have my son in prison. You have my daughter laying dying. You have others yet to protect. For what do you think you have been forged? Do you believe that without these experiences you will be prepared for what awaits you? Do you believe that your father and I went through less? I lost two children in childbirth. I lost one child to pneumonia at the tender age of three. My own parents were lost to me and it was only your father and his family who gave me family again. In this life, and for what awaits your people, you must be tempered by these events. It is God's compromise to allow us to be strong enough to endure."

And there was nothing to do, but to rise up from the ice. I pulled myself up through the water and toward the surface. I had not descended so far, but as I reached the ice, I could not find the hole I had created. I fought panic and searched the surface. There was nearly no light but from the moon. I had perhaps a minute to live, thirty seconds of consciousness. I thought of wearing my tfelin one more time, of binding the leather bands on my left arm with the sign of God. A final tribute of recognition. It was the vision I had of my Zadie and my Papa, rising early before their work and saying their morning prayers. I had no choice but to choose left and as I looked left, there was the hole in the ice. I pulled myself toward it and strong arms lifted me up. I lay on the surface gasping for air, spilling up icy water that burned from my gut. And the arms returned me to my rooms and stripped me of my clothes and covered me in blankets. I do not know who these men were. They did not stay to accept thanks. They took with them the bottle of schnapps that was on the table. They robbed me of half the money in my clothes. Small payment for my life.

I slept through the night by Hadassah's side and was awakened by her calling out in pain.

"What is it dear? What hurts so much?" She had never shown any signs of pain throughout her illness and the obvious didn't dawn on me.

"Tzvi, Tzvi, get the doctor. I think I'm having the baby . . . soon. Oy Gottenyu!"

I ran for the landlady, who hastily fetched the doctor and he returned in less than a quarter of an hour. Hadassah's contractions had subsided, and she thought the whole thing might be a false alarm. In the midst of the doctor's examination, as I held her hand, her body again tensed, contracted, and she let out a scream that shook my soul.

"Do you have someone who can fetch the midwife? She will know more what to do than I. "

And I was off in a flash to find Lavr, who luckily was still in bed after a night's drinking.

"What is it Joséf? What's wrong?"

"It's Hadassah! She's having the baby. The doctor wants the midwife, but she lives in the next village. Can you help?"

"I am already there."

Minutes later, Captain Lavr Kerensky, of the Czar's Imperial Cavalry rode up to our house with a dozen fully dressed and uniformed riders. His jovial and boyish demeanor vanished, he sat ramrod straight in the saddle, demanding of the doctor where he would find the midwife. With practiced speed he yelled clipped orders to a sergeant to speed to the only other town in the region in case she was called away for another delivery during the night, and with five good horsemen was himself asaddle and away. He screamed at the sergeant, even as he rode, "Sergeant, bring her by force if need be, or I'll have your ears! All of you!"

Returning to Hadassah, I found the doctor cooling her with a wet rag and speaking to her softly. Hadassah continued to have contractions, but her screams became whimpers as her energy was quickly drained.

"Keep talking to her Joséf, or whatever your name is. Keep talking to her. Keep her conscious. She must be awake to help. I don't trust doing a surgery on her should the contractions end."

Time froze like everything else touched by the Siberian winter. I pleaded with Hadassah to stay awake. Told her stories of home, funny tales of our life in Warsaw. I described Yenta's antics at the restaurant, how she berated her customers, all the more the one's she loved. This brought a smile to Hadassah's lips. Someone had thought to bring the Rabbi and the Rebetzin and the Rebetzin was comforting and soothed her in the tongue of her mother and grandmother, with a *Yiddishe Mameh's* voice.

The sergeant returned with his men empty handed. I went outside for a breath of air, and to catch the little light of the days that were beginning to again be longer. It is so hard for a man to do nothing when a crisis occurs. Women are much stronger and more patient to wait for what comes.

The snow padded any noise of hoof beats, and the dim light and swirling snow masked vision beyond twenty meters. So, when Lavr arrived with his horse lathered, he was upon me before I had more than time to get out of his way. He dismounted in a single movement with a small, young woman wrapped in a blanket like a child and ran inside. Her feet never touched ground.

He deposited her at Hadassah's bedside and announced, "Here is your midwife. I'm sorry I took so long, but I grabbed her grandmother by mistake. I was expecting someone much older."

The midwife was all business and without even removing her coat (it was later apparent that Lavr had not allowed her time to dress), she examined Hadassah. She was a tiny woman, with wild blue eyes and dark hair braided in plaits and woven. She had strange hands that were joined by webs between the fingers, but did not lack agility despite the handicap. She appeared to be of mixed blood, probably descended from earlier days of Russian migration to Siberia, when the shortage of women led to many intermarriages with the native Tungus people. She felt Hadassah's body, smelled her breath, and without any notice of who was in the room, opened her legs and placed her face in close, demanding someone bring her more light.

"She is certainly giving birth. But I suppose she is in the fifth or sixth month. The baby is almost surely dead. If she can deliver soon, she may have strength yet. Otherwise, I will go in and take it out. She is a Jew, no?"

"Why do you say that?" I asked, paranoid that some prejudice might cause this woman to abandon her cause.

"Well, because she is calling out to you each time in Yiddish, and a Rabbi is standing in the other room!"

"Of course, yes. Does that matter?"

"Well, of course it matters. She needs to hear prayers. She needs your Rabbi's blessings."

Within the hour, a daughter was delivered, although they did not allow me to see her. The doctor said that she had probably been dead for a time. The midwife finished the delivery and, with the Rebetzin, cleaned and changed Hadassah. When all had done what they could, they drifted off, with promises to stay nearby in case they were needed.

"I suggest you stay with her Joséf. We will know by morning how it will go. I would tell you to hope for the best, but I'm afraid I must tell you to prepare for the worst. I am sorry that I couldn't do more. The midwife did all she could, I can tell you that. She begged the baby from her body. I never learned anything like that in medical school."

Lavr asked if he could do anything more. He stood there with his head down, shuffling his feet, looking like a child having disappointed his father too terribly for words to rectify. I hugged him and kissed him on both cheeks in the Russian style and sent him on his way.

"Come back in the morning Lavr, and thank you. You performed a miracle."

And he hugged me again, tears in his eyes, lifting me off the ground.

I was awake for most of the night sitting next to her, saying prayers, talking to God, asking forgiveness, pleading her case. In the morning I crawled into her bed. She was breathing slowly, and she spoke to me.

"Don't be afraid Tzvi-Yosef. I am happy. You've given me happiness. You've given me love."

"I love you so very much darling. You're everything to me. Your love has been a gift that I never thought I would receive. Never from someone like you."

Hadassah fell in and out of consciousness.

"I am so glad you returned, Tzvi-Yosef. You were gone. I was afraid."

"Don't be afraid. I'm here now."

"Is it a boy or a girl? I didn't hear a cry."

"It's a healthy little girl Hadassah. And she looks just like you, with dark curls and blue eyes."

"Will you bring her to me later? After I've rested. I already feel better now. Hold me tightly. I can barely feel you. Tell me how it will be for us. With our children."

And with my heart shrunken like an old gourd, dried so that its seeds rattle, I told her. "We will live on the kibbutz in Palestine. We shall have three children. Three is a good number. One for you, one for me, one to share." With this a small smile came to her face. "And we will make the desert bloom. In the evening we'll sit in our garden, in our garden under our grape vines. And the children will play in the grass. The evening breeze will blow air through the valley. We will be very tired and very happy. We'll put the children to sleep and make love. We'll make love every night that we can."

"But we won't be ones that forget God, Tzvi-Yosef."

"No my darling. We shall never forget God."

"Take off my clothes darling. Take off your clothes. Lay with me naked as we once did."

I hesitated for a moment, but sensed the desperation in her request. We held each other like this for several hours. For a time we stroked each other, feeling each other's bodies. We kissed tenderly. And Hadassah died in my arms as I washed her in my tears.

I would bury the kiddush cup with her, with the words inscribed, *I am my beloved's, and my beloved is mine.* She would know that this is what she was to me forever. I will not say after this that I never loved. But I was never from that moment open again. No woman, no man ever found a route to more than my silence and clipped intimacy. Most of the pain that I was able to experience was lost in those moments and Hadassah took my feelings, or at least my ability to express them, with her.

It is a cruel God who so imperfectly guards his flock.

Chapter 17

Flight

Awaking from nightmare into nightmare, we found it impossible to dig graves for Hadassah and our little girl in the frozen tundra. Funerals waited for spring and the mass graves that were ultimately created to bury the accumulated dead of winter. At first, hope was raised that perchance there had been enough thaw for a single grave, but the ground was unyielding. How could I place my tiny family in a warehouse of bodies? I tore a shovel from the men who came to report their failure. I fought the earth in a crazed panic, but could clear no more than a few centimeters of hardened clay. I collapsed in a sweaty heap, with bloodied hands, kneeling in supplication to God's great plan to break what little spirit still existed within me.

Upon learning from the Rabbi about the Jewish requirement for quick burial, Lavr would brook no delay on account of mere natural conditions. He hastily arranged for a soldier from an engineering unit to rectify the situation. The miner was versed in missions of military proportions. However much he tried to recalibrate the task, he managed to reduce by ten-fold, what should have been lessened one-hundred fold. In horror we witnessed his grotesque creation of a hole the size of a modest public building and Lavr had to trade more favors so that a full company of engineers worked through the night to scale it down to human dimensions.

There was to be no funeral for the infant, who was to be buried according to Jewish law with no name and no mourning period. Of all the wisdom and insight I have seen in Jewish law, I always found this one to be in error and testimony to either a flaw in God's greatness or the mistaken interpretation of men. I have hoped it was the latter.

So, I turned to someone knowledgeable in the law who was willing to argue with such points when he disagreed.

"Zadie, Zadie, how can I bury this child without a marker?"

"How would you mark the grave?"

"A name on a stone. A place to be remembered."

"Will someone ever come here to mourn her, to tend the grave?"

"No Zadie, her mother is buried beside her and I am leaving."

"So, you must carry her in your heart. That is to be her marker."

"Is this allowed in the law?"

"Of course. God does not forbid love for a child from your heart."

"But what shall I call her? We never spoke of a name."

"What is she to you?"

"She is loved Zadie. Hadassah and I already loved her very much."

"Then that will be her name, beloved, *Leebeh*. Now it is known between you and heaven. Her name is *Leebeh*."

"Thank you Zadie. I miss you. You are ever part of me, the good part."

"And you are part of me *zunaleh,* my child."

And so in silence, in a place deep inside me, I would forever call her *Leebeh*, *beloved* in Yiddish, as that is all she had time in this world to be.

For Hadassah I could offer little more. There was to be a ceremony, but so lonely, haunted by the emptiness of the wilderness. I brought her dishonor, burying her so far from her home, with so few to witness her departing this world. I complained to Lavr how in Warsaw a young woman of such a family would be surrounded by the presence of mourners, and what a poor showing I was able to offer her in this forsaken place where my fate brought her. Lavr was not a man of words, and left us, promising to return for the funeral procession, what that it was.

When Lavr returned, we departed the Rabbi's study for the funeral. We emerged to a retinue of all the men in his command in full uniform, brilliantly juxtaposed against the white snow and ice. I squeezed Lavr's iron arm that was looped within mine offering my deepest gratitude for this tribute.

Sixty men on horseback solemnly rode with the caisson, borrowed from the Czar's army. Their horses marched in ordered file, with soldiers holding drawn sabers pointed toward the earth in respect. Lavr offered a cannon and twenty-one gun salute, but the Rabbi convinced him that it was not exactly appropriate. Lavr and the *Rebbe* walked by my side, a pathetic figure with bandaged hands, requiring their support as my knees gave way every few steps.

With the Rabbi reciting, *Ayl malay rachamim, Lord who is full of mercy*, I screamed in protest against God in heaven. The last I recall, my legs gave way entirely and I was tumbling into the grave, glad that life was done with me as well. My heart stopped. There was no strength in me to draw breath. My eyes were without vision. I could hear no one about me. My only awareness was of a terrible burning and longing from within.

I refused to hold the traditional mourning period and instead insisted that Lavr take me to the tavern. If liquor was good enough for 'the others,' and if God was to turn his back to me, I would follow their tradition. After three days of drunkenness during which Lavr never left my side and matched me drink for drink, he deposited me with the *Rebbe* Smearson and his wife.

"You Jews are lousy drinkers, Jósef. You're far too depressing drunk. It doesn't even seem to ease your pain. So what good is it for you? Anyway, I love you too much to see you like this. Rabbi, maybe you have the magic elixir for his pain. The liquor doesn't seem to do anything but make it worse for him."

"Thank you Lavr. We'll do what we can here. You're a good fellow."

"For a goy, you mean, Rabbi."

"No, for a man Lavr. For a man."

Lavr's company soon received travel orders and in a quick farewell, we promised to meet again, but we knew it unlikely. In this life, it is not only in death that we are separated from those we love.

Indeed, I never saw Lavr after that. But I read about him. He rose rapidly in the field to the rank of general in the coming war, as officers above him were killed in quick succession of defeats. He was often in the newspapers where he led his troops to victory after victory in a war that saw more Russian retreat than advancing. I think it was in 1919 that he was executed for treason, along with many senior officers who were connected with the wrong party or feared for their leadership. They killed this man who was the essence of loyalty and devotion to his country. They always killed their finest. It is a Russian tradition.

We parted as brothers.

I spent many weeks with the *Rebbe* and his good wife, but was of little use to myself or others. I stopped drinking, as the *Rebbe* wouldn't hear of it. I refused to pray. I was back on strike with my God. To honor the Rabbi, I attended services at his home on Shabbes. I sat with the prayer book open in my lap or the *Chumesh, book of Torah*. I read and looked for insights in God's words, but uttered none of my own. He would not hear my prayers when they mattered, why would I bother to give Him the benefit of my grief and look to Him for consolation. Let Him know the sound of silence!

The days became longer quickly and although there were some cold days still, flowers emerged through the slush and endless, black mud. All of the houses leaked and there were buckets and pans everywhere, as the ice melted on rooftops and found any possible crevice in the claptrap housing. The furs that I had purchased during the winter fetched a high price as traders came to fill the fashions of St. Petersburg and Paris. So few people in this Eastern frontier had either the money or the freedom to make purchases and wait for spring, that I fell into somewhat of a largesse. I was amused, but it could have gone the other way and I would not have cared deeply.

My visits with Reuven sustained me. Having someone whom I loved and who depended on me, was a healing balm. Reuven's ordeal only made his soul wiser and gentler, and he had for years been more a father to me than my father. We received a letter finally from Rachel and we were heartened to know that she had received my letter telling her that Reuven was in good health and that there was hope. We had of course not spelled out what our hopes entailed, because we ourselves did not know exactly, but from her tone we knew she understood.

Early one damp Shabbes, the air still filled with the icy fingers of winter's chill, the *Rebbe* awakened me.

"Come Tzvi-Yosef. We have much to do."

"But it's Shabbes *Rebbe*, and much too early for prayer, even for you."

"Prayer-shmayer, prayer will have to wait today. We have a body."

"A body?"

"Yes, a body. Now stop asking questions. You must let the guard know."

"Know what? You're talking nonsense."

"Just get up quickly and get dressed. We're getting Reuven out of prison today."

Seeing that he would answer no more of my questions and sensing his urgency, I jumped into my clothes. Walking briskly, even had he been a young man, which he most certainly was not, I had a hard time keeping up with him or collecting my wits. He was in a half run, his hand holding his black hat to his head, ready to fly off like a kite as we leaned into the punishing wind.

"What is the plan, *Rebbe*?" I asked as we scurried across town.

"Well, it is not without danger. And it will cost money, in fact it already has, but I think we can save Reuven. In fact, I think that it is imperative that he leaves prison immediately, because with all the unrest there may be some severe sentencing tacked on to cases like his. I think they have been waiting for some men to put on show trials. As a Jew and a radical, Reuven fits the bill. It will be up to you to judge. We can always cancel the plan. It hasn't gone too far yet."

"So what is your plan?"

"Well, men die in the work gangs every day. I've had a Jewish guard waiting for a man who looks more or less like Reuven to die. I identified another guard in prison who was willing for a price to bring the body into the prison and substitute him for Reuven. That part is almost accomplished. If you agree, everything moves forward now, and quickly. If you say yes, the body will be placed in Reuven's cell. You will come now and verify that the body is Reuven's for the official record. They like to have someone who can verify that the man died from normal conditions. It doesn't happen to them very often that way. In the morning I will come and demand the body for a Jewish burial. Reuven will go free. No one will even look for him."

"Why didn't you tell me about this?"

"Well, for one thing, the fewer who know such things, the better. And what good would you have been in your state anyway? Now start acting like a *mench,* be a man. Enough of your self-pity. It's time for you to act."

"But won't they be missing the man from the work gang, *Rebbe*?" I could not believe this old scholar had thought of all this plan and set it into motion. The *Rebbe* looked at me, his fingers working his sparse beard with the same intense look he must have had when scouring over a book of Torah.

"Yes, they will think he took it on the run and we'll have to keep Reuven in hiding while they search the area. But we'll leave a trail of rumors that will have them looking all the way to Shanghai. And don't forget, I said they look similar. I've arranged for a man that is not nearly Reuven's height. No one will stand up a dead man and measure him. So, they will be looking for a man six inches shorter than Reuven. Reuven stands out because of his height, not because of his lack of it."

"It's a bold plan, but I don't want you to risk anything for us *Rebbe.* You have done more than enough and, after all, this is not your affair."

"It's too late for anything like that. The die is cast. Lavr actually made the contacts without exposing me before he departed. It's of little risk to me, because I will not be expected to know one Jewish corpse from another. I just need to move quickly and hope they don't ask too many questions. Okay, well I guess it is of some risk to me as well, but if Lavr can lend such help to a Jew, then who am I to turn my back?"

The guards had in fact not waited for my approval, and had moved forward, not wanting to lose their full payment. Even as we spoke, the body had

been placed in Reuven's cell, and he was being walked out of prison with a work

detail that had one too many, another guard earning what he could, and who

could fault a man for trying to earn a living? Once out of the prison, he was

taken to the home of a Jewish tailor who exchanged his prison garb for worker's

clothing and trimmed his beard and cleaned him up.

By the time we returned, my having identified the body as Reuven's, he

was in the Rabbi's rooms and part of the minyon reciting the Sabbath prayers.

I took my place next to him and we held hands beneath our *talaysem*,

glad for the warmth and cover of the large woolen prayer shawls. Looking down

at the one that had been given me, I recognized it as of my family's making. It

was my mother's stitchwork plainly in the collar and corners. There was no

mistaking it. Reuven saw it as well. It was the most direct sign from heaven that

I believe I ever received. I began to pray out loud.

Modim anachnu lach, sha ahta hoo adonai aloheynu. We gratefully
acknowledge that you are the Lord our God, the God of all generations. You are
the power that shields us in every age. We thank You and sing Your praises for
our lives, which are in Your hands, for our souls that are in Your keeping; for the
signs of Your presence we encounter every day.

As we prayed, a troop of armed police entered unceremoniously. They

showed no more care for the sanctuary then they would a barn. Less, for animals

they acknowledged as useful.

"You there. Jews, look this way. Come against this wall here. Let's

have a good look at you. We have a Jew on the run, and I wouldn't put it past

you *Sheenies* to guard him in your devil worship."

The Rabbi stepped forward in protest. "You may not do this. We have

permission from the Czar himself to observe our prayers."

For his disrespect, the Rabbi received a slap on the face that knocked

him to the floor. But he regained his feet as if only rising from a chair, so little

satisfaction would he give the man. This gained him another slap and then another. Each time he stood and each time he was knocked down. His men stood between us and the Rabbi, with guns pointed, so that we could only watch helplessly. Finally, the Rabbi could not rise again. The officer undid his trousers and urinated over him as he lay there.

Done with his business, he gave a cursory look at the rest of us. His eyes glanced back at Reuven and at me, but perhaps more for the hatred he saw in our eyes and the knowledge that in a fair fight either of us could break him in pieces and would if ever given the chance. He marched out, kicking the door from its hinges.

We ran to the Rabbi and carried him to his bedroom. The Rebetzin was beside herself with hysterics.

"Are you okay? Someone get a doctor." Reuven yelled to the men outside the bedroom.

"Hah, don't bother. That flea-bitten Jew hater couldn't hurt me if he tried. Just bring me a bowl of water, some soap, and a towel, so that I can clean myself. Then, please use the remaining warm water for what you can make of a bath." Even to bathe away his degradation, the Rabbi would not break the Sabbath and boil water.

"Are you sure you're okay?" Reuven insisted that a doctor be called despite the Rabbi's admonitions to the contrary.

"Yes, I thought I was rather good actually."

"Good! What are you talking about?" I asked incredulously.

"That Jew-baiter was so intent on beating me that he hardly looked at Reuven. What a fool, so easily taken from his task. Good that he is one of them. I couldn't suffer such a buffoon as a Jew."

"You provoked him on purpose?" Reuven asked, already knowing the answer.

"Of course. It's hard for a man to think clearly when he's enraged. Also, did you notice how Reuven stood out?"

"Well, now that I think about it, yes. He was a head taller than any other man there," I noted.

"I thought that was a nice touch as well," the Rabbi continued, bragging like a schoolboy. "Those were the shortest bunch of Jews in Siberia." This brought a wry smile to his lips, but also made him wince in pain. "That *grubyan* never thought for a moment that Reuven might be his man. He was looking for no giant. May he rot from the inside out, HaShem forbid."

Looking at the Rabbi, already sitting up in his chair, I could imagine the strength and power he must have had as a young man. I could also see how complicated it was to be such a Jew. Here he had called the man a *grubyan*, basically an uneducated lout. Now, that doesn't sound so bad, unless you know that there were no swear words in the Rabbi's vocabulary, outside of Russian, which he rarely spoke. As a Jew, the man being ignorant and coarse was in itself a serious diatribe. Then, although this man deserved worse curses for what he had just done to the Rabbi, he could not even wish him pain and torment, but had to soften his anger by asking God to cancel his curse, even as it was spoken.

Perhaps seventy years old now, he had sustained a beating that would have put a much younger man in bed for a week. I wondered what kind of a man he must have been that got him to Siberia. He was as strong in spirit as in body. Were our religion to have more of such Rabbis, who interpreted the silhouette of the law, its essence, with love and caring and such strength, we would have many more devout Jews today. When he had bathed, and we were satisfied that he was well enough, we left his side so that he could rest. He chose to do so with a book of the law in his lap, the print too small for his reading, for it was the Sabbath and his holy day had been disturbed.

We spent the day talking and worrying, watching the windows. Reuven slept quite a bit as well, being out of prison he was in a state of awe and shock and wonder. The fear of being caught and returned made him unusually fidgety when he was awake.

Unfortunately, a medical examiner was scheduled to check the body the next morning before it was to be released to the family and the Rabbi. We were aware that the prison had kept records of medical conditions, scars and various things that could help identify that they had the right body. We had hoped that with a family member to make positive identification this was not necessary, but Russian bureaucracy was not to be denied. We waited as the examination proceeded. I fully expected that even if the examiner did not bother to measure the corpse's height he would notice the lack of scars and then it came to me that we were indeed doomed. What of Reuven's one eye? Surely, even the most incompetent examiner would notice this.

When the officer of the guard entered the room with two guards I was resigned to being arrested and stood and placed my arms forward, as they handcuffed me and took me off. Instead, he handed me a bulk of paperwork for signing and release of the body for burial.

"Could you please, however, check the body one more time?" asked the officer. "Perhaps in your shock you made a mistake. You certainly seem very distraught. It's all so. . . . unexpected."

So, they did know, but wanted me to make my statement in writing and in front of witnesses. I had no choice but to follow them. In the medical clinic the body lay covered in a sheet. The examiner was next to the body and several orderlies were going about their work. At least the corpse was afforded a sheet, as patients in the clinics slept on dirty mattresses and just plain boards, with few blankets and a stench of infection mixed with lye to fight the worst of disease.

The examiner removed the sheet and if Reuven's life didn't depend on the small chance of our rue working, I would have recanted and stated that surely this was not my brother-in-law. I could tell them that it must have been the grief and shock that made me think so earlier, and just leave, and that would be that. Looking at the corpse, I was struck by how much the man did resemble Reuven. He was a Jew, of dark skin and hair, strongly built, with no lack of scars. And then I saw it. His eye had seepage. It was the wrong eye, but perhaps this was not even noted in the record, or was overlooked by the examiner. Still, I wondered why the need for this second check, if not to catch me in my lie.

"Yes, this is my brother-in-law. May God rest his troubled soul."

"You are sure?"

"Yes, of course."

"You are quite sure?"

"Yes, I am certain."

"Your are certain as well, Father."

"Yes," answered the Rabbi. "Quite sure." I was amazed at his calm. He was a master at deception and had nerves of steel.

"Good, then sign these papers and we can release the body."

We had hired two men to carry the stretcher and the Rabbi and I accompanied them to leave the building. At the last possible moment, as we were leaving the outer gate, the officer came running.

"Wait, wait. Guards, hold those two men right there!" he yelled.

So, that was that. We were found out. The trap was set and laid. The Rabbi for the first time looked worried, and turned his head from side to side, as if to make his escape, but there was none to be made.

"I have one more form for you to sign. And you need to take your copy to get by the outer guardhouse. There, now you can go. I'm sorry for your grief."

Later, after the burial we sat together with Reuven in the Rabbi's bedroom.

"That was close," I said. "It almost came collapsing down like a house of cards. I was impressed *Rebbe* with your choice of men. Besides the height, the man truly met Reuven's description."

"Indeed he did. *HaShem* provided."

"And how remarkable that his eye was injured as well, even if it was the wrong eye."

"Yes, we made a mistake on the eye."

"What, you even planned the eye? How many men would have had to die to find one that fit Reuven's description and had a bad eye?"

"He didn't have a bad eye."

"Oh, but I saw it myself."

"No, he had a bad eye then, but not when we found him. You see, we paid him to irritate his eye with chemicals the doctor provided as he was already dying. It was one of the most difficult things I ever asked of a man. He was already such a miserable fellow. We gave him something for the pain. He just did the wrong eye."

"What need does a dying man have with money?" I queried.

"Nothing, but his family did. He asked that I send the money to them. He was of course trusting that I would do so. He was thankful that he could provide some little something for them and to free a fellow Jew. He was a *guteh neshama, a good soul.* He actually enjoyed the idea of throwing one last wrench into the Czar's plans. You should include him in your prayers."

"What was his name?" Reuven asked.

"His name was Yankl Baranak. Remember him at *Yizkor* each year, as you say the prayers for your loved ones who have gone to the eternal spirit. I don't know his father's name, so you can call him Yankl ben Avraham, Yankl son of Abraham, for all Jews who are unknown are sons of our tribe."

The Rabbi's advice was that we dare not travel for several weeks when a search for Yankl Baranak was at all active. A minor prisoner of no real consequence to Russia, he was little more than a number. However, Reuven was to travel on forged papers and it was the Russian predilection when finding someone with forged papers to have him sit in jail for as long as it took to figure out who he really was. Someone might eventually put two and two together and uncover Reuven's actual identity. The Rabbi was certain that the Russians would not expect a fugitive to be able to lay low in the backyard of his escape for any period of time.

In the end of May of 1914, we were finally ready for our journey. We made our goodbyes to Rabbi Smearson and his wife. I had done very well in my trading, indeed I had done exceptionally well. As a final gesture, Reuven and I arranged from the nearest large town for the purchase of a small Torah. The scroll was worn and not in the best condition, but valuable nonetheless. His little congregation had of course gone without an actual Torah, as having a Torah was about as likely for such a congregation as having an automobile for driving the Rabbi around the town, and about the same price. As had been my history, I was not happy with the money I earned, always feeling it was somehow ill-gotten, even though this recent trading was entirely above board, or as above board as trading ever is. Hence, I felt much better providing the Rabbi with this gift.

The Rabbi broke down in tears when we presented him with the small scroll. At first, he would not touch it, but beheld it in wonder, pacing around the table. Examining it from all the angles, he avoided making contact. Eventually, seeming to come to a decision, he picked it up in his arms and sat holding it in a chair, rocking back and forth. Only after some time, he spoke.

"I have not held a Torah in nearly thirty years. It's the worst curse of my banishment. It was the punishment that I placed upon myself. I have never told you why I was sent to Siberia, although you Tzvi-Yosef, I think, guessed bits and pieces at times. Our town was attacked in a pogrom in 1884. It was not so bad as Odessa in 1905, where hundreds were murdered and thousands raped, but it touched me most directly. Men came on horseback and they rode the streets killing men, women, children, anyone in their path. They entered houses and violated our women, young, old, it didn't matter. I ran from my home to the Shul and when they came for the Torahs, to destroy them, I defended them with my life. With a pitch fork I killed one of the attackers and badly wounded two others."

"But *Rebbe*, it may be a sin to take a life, but you were in a dire situation. They might have killed you as well."

"Yes, but that is not the worst of it. I left my home to protect the Torahs. When I returned home, I found my wife and daughters murdered. The attackers raped my wife and my two daughters, not yet women. My wife and younger daughter they killed when they were done, but it must have been slow deaths. My oldest daughter . . . " and with this he broke down sobbing.

We tried to comfort him, telling him that he had said enough, that we understood. But he insisted on continuing.

"My oldest daughter, Frieda, only fourteen, was in her bed and covered from head to toe in . . . I can't even say the words. Her bowls were opened and yet she was still alive. She pleaded, "Tateh, Tateh, Tateh." I covered her small face with my body and smothered her until she was without life."

"Rabbi," Reuven tried to comfort him, "what could anyone have done?"

"No!!!" he screamed. "I should have been home protecting them. I worried first about the Torahs and didn't think about my family. As holy as this scroll is, it is secondary to life. I had lost that understanding. I am ready for Torah again. You two have helped me understand no less than the order of the world. Especially you Tzvi-Yosef."

"How could I do that *Rebbe*? I am hardly a teacher. I live my life in a constant turmoil with God."

"That is the special quality you have Tzvi-Yosef. You're in an ongoing argument with *HaShem*. You demand much of him and much of yourself. In your case, you expect too much of yourself or of Him. but I expected too little, and that is much worse a crime. You're also a leader Tzvi-Yosef, even though you refuse to lead. Men want to please you and to do your bidding. I myself was drawn to help you and Hadassah, *olehaw hasholom, peace be onto her*, and Reuven here. Did you ever think to ask yourself why? Many men have needed my help here in this wilderness, but I had never risked anything to do so, but gave counsel from the safer position of my pulpit. You showed me that to act one must throw oneself into the fray and trust in *HaShem's* plan. I had never understood that. Or I had become afraid to act. Maybe both."

And with this said, he embraced me and then Reuven with the small Torah held to his breast and then sat back in his chair and quietly rocked lost again in his own world.

Our journey to return home was to be circuitous, as the patrols watched the long-distance trains most of all. So Reuven and I set off by ferry, wagon, milk cart, foot, and the very occasional lorry. When we neared the Polish border, after over a month of travel we knew something was terribly amiss. The movement of troops and goods was enormous, and all was chaos.

Finding a peddler on the road, we heard the news. Archduke Ferdinand, heir to the throne of Austria-Hungary, had been assassinated on a peace mission to Bosnia. A man associated with the Black Hand by the name of Gavrilo Princip, almost certainly a Jew the man added, had killed the Archduke and his wife. War was coming. The news, all except the part of the assassin being a Jew, turned out to be accurate, and the next moves of the great powers would determine when and if, and on what scale, war would occur.

One thing changed to our benefit, however. The chaos meant that no one was bothering to check identification papers, at least not of men heading west. Young men, especially, were being welcomed wherever they went, their value having escalated immediately upon the very thought of war.

"So, what do you think, Reuven?" I asked. "Is this time all out war, or another fire in the Balkans? They never seem to get over their differences."

"Well, what do they have to gain by war?"

"Well, war may bring additional land and honor."

"Ahuh. Land where?"

"Why in Europe, of course."

"Of course, but where else?"

"I don't know and you, sitting in prison all these months, obviously do. So, let's stop playing teacher-pupil. I feel like I'm in *Cheder* again with Reb Pinchas and his herring and onion breath."

"Is my breath so bad then? ...no, no, just kidding. Okay then. Here's how I see it. Germany's the powerhouse. Austria's time has passed. Germany needs to strengthen herself and not only in Europe. She wants Africa especially, and maybe sites in the Far East. England wants the same. She's greedy for her colonies in India, in Africa, in the Far East. She doesn't care much about the rest of Europe. She's an island there."

"So I suppose the next question is Russia."

"Yes, and tell me what you think about that."

"Reuven!"

"Okay, okay. You know you were much easier to teach when you were younger. The Czar needs a war to divert attention from all the problems at home. Wars unite the nation. The Russians hate the Germans even more than they hate each other."

"So, it's war then."

"Yes, I can't see them backing out of this one. Germany will begin it, I'm sure. She is the most sure of what she has to gain and can't imagine herself losing. She feels invincible, superior in every way."

"And is she?"

"Yes, but that is because she is not figuring on America. It is America's time. American capitalism needs to grow outside America and to do that she must prove herself in war. America will enter the war sooner or later. She still identifies with Great Britain. She is the wayward colony that wants her mama's approval. Germany will lose. Millions will die."

I have seldom met a man who knew so much as Reuven. He understood how things worked. And the knowledge always hurt him. Reuven saw things as they were and so had nowhere to seek shelter from the truth. Others could imagine a short war with few deaths. Reuven saw that with modern weapons and old prejudices that war would be prolonged and horrible. Others imagined that Jews would be liberated by fighting bravely for their country. He knew that once their use was exploited, that anti-Semitism would rear its ugly head. Only about communism did he feel some kind of hope and I thought to ask him why.

"Why communism Tzvi? Because about communism we know nothing. Within a new experiment there is always hope. I will deny it if you quote me in the future, but to be truthful I think that even communism will fail because every other kind of government has."

And having eaten our meager lunch in the sunny field, we picked

ourselves up and walked on toward home, which was still weeks away as we

were mostly on foot, with transport being taken up by the army and those selling

to the amassing army. Indeed, the roads were already becoming crowded with

people walking this way and that, seeking their families, running to the

countryside, going to the cities for factory jobs.

As we neared Kalushin, I told Reuven that we would have to separate

for a time and that I would meet him in Kalushin. I gave him most of the jewels

that I had started out with on my journey, for the family's safekeeping. He tried

to convince me otherwise, that it was time for the prodigal son to return home. I

told him that was not from our bible. He resisted my argument, but accepted that

I had an obligation to go to Hadassah's parents and explain all that had occurred.

It weighed on me heavily, but they deserved to hear the details from my lips. I

had written to Nissan and Shifra so that they could tell his parents and they not

read it from cold paper, and had Rav Smearson write as well. But a letter was

one thing and a person was another.

I also was not quite ready to go home, even though I longed deeply to

see Rachel, Isaac, already with children, and little Rayzella and Jacob. Them, the

little ones, I hardly knew. And my aunts and uncles. I missed Aunt Miriam and

Uncle Mayer and his fish. Letters said he had his own shop now and was doing

better than ever. Aunt Eti, Aunt Naomi--was Eti still feeding and Naomi still

biting with her tongue? And what of Uncle Yosl, did he learn to talk back yet? I

had a special place for Uncle Yisrael and Aunt Leah, who had taken care of me

when I visited them in their small *shtetl* to get away from the grief of my home.

Aunt Rivkeh, with her limp and her love. And, of course, Tateh, who I could not

bear to see. In all my time away, he had never written to me, never asked me to

come home, never asked my forgiveness for what he had done.

It was with such thoughts that I was daydreaming later that week, sitting

by the roadside when a large group of soldiers came marching up the road. An

officer sauntered up to me, not a care in the world, as if war was as far off as could be.

"Good day, sir," I said.

"Good day," the officer smiled back at me. "Papers please."

I had switched to my real papers, given there was no more purpose in chicanery and the punishment it might bring if caught. I turned them over without a moment's hesitation.

"And from where do you come now Apfel, Tzvi?"

"Siberia."

"A long way then. Welcome back. We're glad to see you. Come with us."

"Come where?"

"To the army of course. You have just been conscripted. Don't look so glum and don't get any ideas about escape. It would be a shame to shoot you on such a lovely day. Anyway, all young men are being picked up. And if you're heading for Warsaw, don't bother. It will be lost to the Germans in the coming days. If you were captured there at your age, you would just become a German soldier. Germany declared war yesterday."

"And wouldn't that be better?"

"Maybe, but I guess you don't have the luxury of that choice now. You're a Russian soldier with us. Not to worry. The war will be over before it's begun."

Walking back to the wagons, the officer asked, "Do you speak the Jewish language?"

"Yes, of course," I answered.

"And Russian, having been in Siberia?" he asked switching from his rough Polish to Russian.

"Yes, Russian too," I answered in Russian.

And to a sergeant, the officer said. "This one looks fit and he's a Jew and speaks Russian. Make him a corporal of the group of Jews in the last wagon. God knows we need someone to make them understand orders."

And so I was to pass to the outskirts of Kalushin, as the conscription of
that town continued. Despite being bivouacked at the very outskirts of the town,
there was no chance of entering, because by this time we were well-guarded and
any attempt to leave would have meant arrest and summary execution. Two men
had tried and the Russians had been true to their threatened promise. I sat by my
tent and pondered the utter ridiculousness of my situation and the never-ending
irony God offered for our ongoing entertainment and unceasing amazement. I
had come to within a few hundred meters of my town after years of avoiding it,
and could not enter, just as Moses was not allowed to enter the promised land.

Part 3

War and Redemption

Chapter 18

Hardening of the Soul

We traversed the countryside over the next week, the soldiers rousting men from hay lofts and under floor boards. The officer was calm, calculated and effective. His uniform remained parade ready; the road dust did not encumber him as it did us. He had lists of men to recruit, but hardly referred to them. He had a quota to meet and no one would question his appearing with a full retinue. Some men were so sickly they died during that week of pneumonia, exposure, or sheer heartache at being torn from their homes and wives and lovers. He left them at the next town for burial by the local Priest or Rabbi and conscripted their replacements.

One day, he approached three men on the road, a father and his two sons. The man was too old to serve, the child too young. Like many of us they were caught off-guard by his warm demeanor. When he turned after ordering them into the wagons, the father gave his youngest a sign and the boy, he was not but a boy, bolted. The officer walked quickly back to the lead wagon and swung himself aboard. He took a rifle from a soldier, checked the bolt, and righted the weapon. He took aim into the distance and wounded the boy with the second round. We could hear the child's screams across the fields that separated us. The officer jumped down, and with the butt of his rifle struck the father unconscious. He left the youth to die in the fields or perhaps live to see another day. He didn't care one way or the other; his point was made.

"Zadie, is this my personal hell or has everyone joined me for the ride?"

"The world seems to be going mad Tzvi."

"Yes, I've noticed. God is showing us how bad the world can really be.

My pain and suffering are trivial. He is displaying the hint of horrors he can call forth."

"And how does this make you feel Tzvi?"

"I feel numb. This father lost in a moment what he has cherished for a lifetime. I lost what I treasured for a few short years, and what I did not raise. How can I compare my pain with his?"

"This is the thing with tragedy Tzvi. No two tragedies can be compared. One loses a child in his youth and another when the boy is already a man with his own family. Is one worse than the other? We can make no such comparisons."

"So, what are we left with Zadie?"

"We are left with what we have."

"And if that is not much Zadie?"

"Then you build more Tzvi. And you work to repair the world."

"A large task Zadie."

"A large task, *teekoon olam, repair of the world.*"

"Why are you chuckling Zadie?"

"Because at least in this, God gives us plenty."

"Not really very funny, Zadie."

"No, not really very funny *mein kind, my child.*"

After a brief period of training, with neither uniforms nor weapons, we were given orders to join our units. In my training I was allowed to fire three bullets; one went off inadvertently. My sergeant said two would do.

As a corporal, I was given an additional day of training on my special duties. This boiled down to listening to whatever my sergeant told me. Although I was technically responsible for the other men, the sergeant was so vicious that his orders were followed before I could carry them down the line. If left to dig a ditch or peel potatoes, I was entrusted to be sure the task was done. Only Jews listened to any small detail I might add in any case, and them only to fulfill their obligatory discussion of the finer points of whatever our assignment. So, the *goyim* did not listen and the Jews listened, but did not comply. I was better off with the *goyim.*

Except for the few who had been involved in the Jewish self-defense movement, the Jews were totally unsuited as soldiers. They abhorred their weapons, and only touched them out of necessity. Most were physically unfit and those that were fit, many of whom were porters from the cities, were anarchists. To Jews an order was a "suggestion." Everything after all for a Jew is debatable.

For myself, I could forget my own grief if kept active, but these menial tasks were moist ground for my pain and my insides churned with painful twisting. I often joined my Christian comrades in drinking, which alienated me from my Jewish brethren, but was often the only way I felt capable of making it through the days and nights. In the end, even this provided little solace. As Lavr had said, I was a poor drunk.

Being conscripted so close to home probably saved my life and most certainly saved my ebbing sanity. A few weeks into the training, two *shtetl* Jews entered our mess hall and one proceeded to fall over our sergeant's extended feet. The sergeant rose to give the fool a beating, but stopped short when he saw the behemoth facing him, with a neck the size of another man's thigh. The man-bear stared the sergeant down and, instead of the back of his hand and his boot, received only a stern reprimand.

The moment he turned to go about his business, I ran and leapt at the Goliath. He held me like a child at arm's length to see what kind of *meshuganeh,* the man after all was certainly crazy, would do this. Looking through my beardless face after all these years, recognition came to Shimon's eyes first and he called out my name, "Tzvi, it's really you." Gedalyeh could not find words, so instead he hugged me so hard I became faint and had to yell, "Enough, enough! Gedalyeh, you're going to kill me before the Germans can!" We three were united. Kalushin had come to me.

"Tzvi, I can't believe it's you. We heard you were back from Siberia. We saw your sister Rachel not long ago. She said there was good news about

Reuven. She was already packing to leave with the children."

"Thank you for that news Shimon. Do you know of the rest of my family?"

"Well despite the boycott on Jewish goods, Isaac has done well with the factory. He has four or five men now, quite an operation. His wife lost a baby in pregnancy last year. I know this from my sister, but word is she's already pregnant again. Your Uncle Mayer is doing well with his fish market. I know this personally because I often go there Fridays to pick up fish for my mother."

"How terrible of us Tzvi. We forgot what Rachel told us, here with the shock of seeing you," broke in Gedalyeh. "She told us about your tragedy. We share in your grief Tzvi. To follow you to Siberia. . .well, she must have been a special woman indeed, bless her memory."

"Yes Tzvi," joined Shimon. "We're sorry for your grief. Such a heartache. No words are enough. *Baruch Dayan emes, Blessed is the True Judge.*"

With this we shook hands manfully and stood silently. We were uncomfortable with so many years and no ball between us, not really knowing who each other was as a man, looking for the next words.

"And my father?"

"Funny that. When he heard we were on the list to be conscripted, he came to visit Gedalyeh and me at our homes. Tell him Gedalyeh."

"Yes, it was odd. How did he know?" Gedalyeh looked puzzled.

"How did he know what?" I didn't understand.

"Well, he said that when we should meet you in the war that we should tell you that you were in his prayers."

"He told you that?"

"Yes, he came to both our homes and that is what he said. I told him that it was probably a big war, but he seemed rather sure we would see you. He also gave me this letter to give you. I almost didn't bring it, but my father said that if by chance I was to run into you it would be a mitzvah. Here it's somewhere in my pack. . . Here, here it is."

I took the letter, but thought it better to wait to open it when I was alone. "He was probably just hoping against hope," I said. But still, I'm thankful for the *mazel* that we should run into each other like this. And he looked well?"

"He looked well enough I think. Yes, he looked well Tzvi."

And together we drifted off to get something to eat and share what news we had. They were serving pork in a kind of thick soup and many day old bread. Gedalyeh and Shimon were still keeping kosher, but this would only last some days because a man would starve to death if he didn't eat what was offered. So as not to make them uncomfortable I only ate bread and butter and some tea, but in truth I had been eating whatever was in front of me for some time now.

Later I opened the letter. It was like my father, dry.

Dearest son Tzvi,

Rachel is off to Galicia with the children to meet Reuven. They hope to drift down to Hungary, where Reuven has cousins. It will be a dangerous journey, but no one much cares which way a family goes in these times, so they should be safe. She told me ALL you did. Your mother, peace be onto her, would be proud of you. I also heard about your wife Hadassah. May HaShem bless her memory. I am sorry I cannot comfort you in your grief. Isaac is well and Razilla and Jacob are growing like weeds. You would not recognize them. If you can make it to Kalushin, know that you are welcome and always my son.

Your Tateh

The letter contained more than we had communicated in years. It was like him that he could not say directly that he was proud of me, only that my mother would be. He could not send words to comfort me in my loss, but could only say that he was sorry he could not comfort me. I should have seen his heart reaching out through the lines, but I was very much his son. He obscured his feelings in writing, I in reading. Who knows, had I been free I may have felt it was enough to return home. It was the closest I ever again came to that possibility. I intended to save the letter forever, so I know that it was important to me. I must have lost it in the battles that followed for when I looked for it to comfort me, it was gone. I am sure of each word to this day. That I did not write back was like me as well.

Platoons are grouped into companies, companies into battalions, battalions into regiments, regiments into divisions, and divisions into armies. Soon we were among a mass of men greater than I had ever seen together. We easily measured one hundred thousand and we could see campfires of other groups of men who from the light they emitted must have been of our size and more. Cities were created out of farmland.

Had it not been for the discrimination we encountered in everything we did, it was good to be a Jew in such a situation. The camp quickly became a place of danger with robberies and beatings and even a few rapes and murders. The rapes were usually of women, but not always. Many men did not even know who they were to be fighting. Luckily most of war is simple for the soldier. You face the direction that they point you in and you march. You aim your rifle across a field and you fire.

The vision that people have of the First World War is one of static trench warfare. This indeed quickly became the state of affairs on the Western Front, but this was the Eastern Front, and an entirely different war was fought here. On the Eastern front there was a rapid movement of armies and men and the taking and retaking of land in rapid succession. Germany and Austria had the equipment and the preparation for war. Russia had an almost endless supply of men that could be shot, with more taking their place. It made for a disjointed series of efforts, like two dancers who know none of the same steps and are following the beat of different music.

When orders came, we, now part of the Second Russian Army with seven army corps, were marched forward to the area around Locicz. The importance of throwing the Russians out of Poland was critical to Germany's war. The British were holding on by the skin of their teeth in Belgium at Ypres and in France at Calais, and Germany hoped for a quick victory in the East. Refugees streamed along the roadside, as the Germans advanced.

We had miraculously kept Warsaw from falling, even though the Germans had come to its doorstep. For some inexplicable reason that sometimes occurs in war, they just stopped, even with victory assured. Russia poured men and artillery back into the town, having all but abandoned it.

We were sent into a counterattack against an army made up mainly of Austrians (thank God) and some smattering of German troops. The Germans had committed most of her quality forces to the Western Front and left the Russians to the Austrians for the most part. A big mistake.

The Austrians had time to set barb wire and build trenches, but they were not prepared for the size of the Russian advance. No one was prepared for the snow. In the first minutes of the attack I thought I saw most of the men around me die. It is typical to lay down a large round of artillery to soften the enemy lines before sending troops forward. For Russia, with men available in quantity, and artillery and shells sparse, we were sent forward after only a short artillery burst. By nightfall we had taken a half a kilometer and a number of key bridges. The Austrians were retreating, but not chaotically and their rear guard action kept our further advance in check. They had time to clear their artillery and supplies, as well. Still, we had won the day and when the major came to make his inspection he was jubilant.

The next day was even more successful. Our advance and the carnage it wrought was steady and we captured thousands of Austrian soldiers who were already sick of war. They hardly needed guarding and we took their weapons and let them walk back to their imprisonment almost unattended. They saluted our officers as they went and were more disciplined as prisoners than we were as soldiers. Their officers were colorfully dressed and seemingly unmoved by the shame of their stainless uniforms, a fact that no Russian soldier failed to notice.

We were half the number we had been at the battle's beginning and had lost over fifty thousand men, but to have moved forward and to be congratulated by your officers, it felt good to be alive. It may sound callous, but by evening I hardly remembered the awful days that had passed, but wrapped them neatly within a multitude of horrors of the past weeks and let them go their way. It never really went away though, but leaks out like puss from a septic wound when least expecting it over the years.

The third day when we attacked, the Germans and Austrians held their ground only briefly and then fell into a rapid, disorderly retreat. Our officers screamed for us to quickly follow them and mop up their stragglers. It was a chance to take cannon and materiel and our officers were greedy for success after the earlier months of defeats. Our battalion was drawn into a farm among gently rolling hills. The others around me were running quickly after the enemy, blood lust in their eyes. As we overtook stragglers they were shot and our soldiers only slowed to rob the dead.

As I watched the retreating soldiers, they were barely stopping to fire. There were many officers among them still alive, but not one stopped to organize his men and fight a rear guard protection of the retreat. If anything, the officers seemed to me to be slowing their men's retreat, without offering resistance. The effect was that they were being funneled into a small valley farm area between a series of gently rolling hills where we could easily finish them off.

It reminded me of an alley not that many years earlier in Warsaw. It was too easy. There was too little resistance. It was too good to be true. I was sure it wasn't.

For myself, I did not care. I desired to throw myself into the fray and take on chance, and death. But I felt that I could not abandon Shimon and Gedalyeh, and they more than myself offered me a reason to live. I grabbed at Shimon who was still beside me and pulled him to a slower gait. He went to pull away, as caught up in the sport of victory as the next man, but he saw the look in my eyes and heeded my warning.

We kept moving forward and firing, but cautiously, allowing others to

overtake us. I kneeled as if my rifle was jammed in order to get it in working

order. Everyone was so confident of success that no one thought I was afraid to

go forward. I looked everywhere for Gedalyeh, but could not find him in the

chaos. We had begun together, but that was a kilometer back, and much fighting

and slaughter had occurred since.

I scanned the field and saw a stone building that must have served as an

earlier farmhouse, long abandoned. It stood at the first crest of the hill before the

lowered pitch of the land. I told Shimon over the roar of the guns to head in the

direction of that building.

"Shimon go that way. Head for that old house."

"But the enemy is that way," he pleaded, pointing ahead at the retreat.

"Shimon, the enemy is all around us. We have a chance with that farm

house and just hope that they didn't manage to close in behind us."

Still not fully understanding, he followed behind me as we fought our

way to the shelter. The building was still forward, but out of the way of the trap

that lay below. I noticed an officer leading a company in the same direction. I

was not the only man that had smelled the bait and seen the snare. The officer

was trying to alert soldiers to follow him as well. I called out in Yiddish to what

Jews I could. The "others" would no more listen to me than to a dog, as they

chased down the retreating enemy with frothing mouths. But a few Jews

responded to their mother tongue, as if no one would dare lie to them in Yiddish.

A number of others responded to the officer's call.

At that moment, the land itself exploded, with mines going off and

canons bursting. Where a great bulk of our men had been, was now a gaping

hole thirty meters across and deep, where a miner had killed several hundred men

in one fell swoop. Perhaps a thousand men were caught between criss-crossed

machine gun nests and deeply dug in men who had waited until the bulk of our

battalion was fully exposed.

In a scene straight from the Napoleonic Wars, a cavalry troop swept down across the field with lances, piercing to death men who ran for cover in the nearby trees. The lances left the men staked to the ground as they fell, half standing, some still moving in a vain attempt to remove the deep impalement. I often saw men recover from terrible wounds, but I never saw or heard of a man who was impaled by a lance live to see another dawn. In ten minutes I don't believe that fifty of us were alive.

The single able captain, the only officer I saw survive, rallied the remaining men to follow him. He led us in an orderly fashion to attack the farmhouse we were approaching, which in the end also held a bulk of enemy hiding below the casements. We lost several more men, but this key spot was not defended by a machine gun and we managed to outflank the defenders who either fled or were killed.

Shimon and I were among the living and by gathering the weapons and ammunition of the dead, we were able with a group of men to barricade ourselves into the stone building and mount a defense. Several waves of enemy attacked us, but by positioning men on the roof top and each of the windows, and several brave men outside the house in the brush, we were able to repulse their repeated attacks. This would only last as long as it took for the enemy artillery to liberate some firepower in our direction, and so we awaited nightfall and the possibility of escape.

"Where did you gain such battle experience, sir?" I asked the officer during a lull in the fighting.

"In the last weeks corporal, although I was trained at the academy in St. Petersburg. I'm surprised myself. I was more interested in the fit of my uniform and the women it attracted. You know you did well back there yourself. So, where did you learn to fight?"

I almost held my tongue, but the intimacy of our situation allowed me to speak out. "Fighting Jew-haters in Warsaw."

He looked at me for a moment thinking, but hardly shocked by my words. Then he looked forward as the enemy fire recommenced. "Funny, anti-

Semitism just saved your life."

With nightfall, we evacuated the building just as the shelling began. It was a dark night and several men were killed in the illumination of rocket fire, but most of us made our retreat. The captain kept a rear guard with eight volunteers. Shimon and I chose to stay with him, hoping still to locate Gedalyeh. After thirty men broke for the woods and safety, the captain signaled for us to follow him. A real fighter, his eyes glowed alert with the battle against the rocket fire. He waved us to move to the right and even a bit forward, which seemed into the mouth of the enemy. In a few hours he had earned our loyalty, and so we followed him to our certain deaths.

What he alone had seen was an outcropping of rocks just over a small crest. Although forward and closer to the enemy, the position also placed us nearer the woods. Several more small rock formations formed a checkerboard that could allow a small troop of men protection if the moon stayed behind the clouds. It did not, and we were again exposed.

The fighting was vicious and hand to hand. Most men on both sides were now out of ammunition. When one of the enemy attacked me, I parried and lunged with my bayonet, piercing his stomach. I could hear the gas escape and smell the odor of his insides. His eyes looked at me in surprise. We were about the same age and he too was a Jew; the recognition of our common bond isolated us for that frozen moment from the reality of the war that enveloped us. In that instant, our eyes communicated that if only he and I were there we could somehow between us take back this tragic moment. Just then, an Austrian came at me from the left, but I could not dislodge my rifle from the first's dying grip. He saw my coming death and released his hand so that I could defend myself, forgiving me this one sin.

Now only speed would save us, but running to the forest and probable safety, we came upon three of our men, dug into a small crevice, fighting for their lives. Each was wounded and one badly. I recognized him as Gedalyeh, his great bulk giving him away even in the night and tumult. They had been saved by being ordered to carry crates of ammunition, probably due to their size and strength. The crates had greatly slowed their pace. Their distance from the main point of slaughter, and their endless supply of bullets had kept them alive into the night. The officer would not leave the wounded behind, and Shimon and I were not about to abandon Gedalyeh in any case. The two of us took up Gedalyeh and begged him to use whatever strength he still possessed to run.

"Tzvi, Shimon I can't go on. Leave me so my parents will know to say *Kaddish* for me. It would be a comfort to them if they heard it from you."

"Live, damn it. You're not going to die on me." I screamed at him.

"I can't feel my legs, Tzvi. I can see my intestines."

I was blind with rage and fear and screamed at him over the battle's roar. 'Gedalyeh, it's a sin to give up. You won't be forgiven if you give up. Shimon, take his other side. Come on Gedalyeh, stay awake. We can't carry you if you collapse. Now live for God's sake! I want to dance at your son's wedding someday. Now let's go."

The captain and one other soldier fought our rear as we escaped. They most certainly died in the next minutes, but allowed our retreat.

With the last reserves of strength, we somehow got Gedalyeh to a wagon and made our way back to our lines. We were once again entrenched at the spot of the second day's assault, only being able to defend that marginal earlier advance. Much of the army had been fooled by the false retreat. Eighty thousand Russian soldiers were dead, wounded, or captured. The senior Russian staff celebrated the net gain as a victory.

As we waited in camp, the ragged troops flooded back. The wounds were terrible. Many we had witnessed occurring with our own eyes. But it is not the goal of the enemy to kill you. Death is inefficient. No, true success is causing wounds, because it takes no one to care for a dead man and five men to care for a wounded one. A severely wounded man breaks morale with his screams and the terror of the sight of the wound. The dead become other-worldly. One begins to think of them as the "lucky bastards." Nor was it a privilege to speak so many languages. Others only needed to hear dying men call out to their mothers in one language. I heard it in five tongues. But it was worst in Yiddish, even if each man in the end calls out to the one person who he knows would bring him comfort. "Mameh," "Mameh," "*Oy Mameh. Ich shtarbin. Helf mir.*" "*Oh mother, I am dying. Help me*" Only sheer exhaustion or death brought men sleep and escape.

Shimon and I waited the night with Gedalyeh. We promised each other that one of us would remain awake, but despite being on the floor of a tent and cold, we could not keep from drifting off. By the next afternoon Gedalyeh was sleeping soundly and still had no fever. He had a bad night, but the bullet had entered and exited cleanly through the muscles of his side and not interfered with any major organs. A second shrapnel wound from a grenade to his leg had caused the loss of three toes, but this was a lucky wound, as men were shooting toes off everywhere to avoid fighting. Gedalyeh's war had ended, thank God.

With our losses, discipline became more of a problem. As a Jew you did not walk alone in the camp. Nor was this a spontaneous outgrowth of ignorant men's prejudices. To avoid blame for their defeats, the military command spread rumors of Jewish traitors in the towns and among the ranks. Jews were placed on trial for treason and hundreds were arrested. Many were beaten, some were killed. Often at night I lay in my tent needing to urinate, but daring not go out alone. In the morning, the long line to the latrine was largely of Jews who had held their piss all during the night. It was a time to catch up on news and some had Yiddish papers and shared the world's events. Perhaps we had been more surprised by our earlier acceptance than this new surge of anti-Semitic vile.

But being a Jew had advantages for a soldier as well. The Eastern front was fought over Jewish Poland and hence many of the towns in which we billeted were largely Jewish. For the people of the town this was less a blessing. After the Russian advance over territory previously taken by the Germans, many Poles claimed that the town's Jews were collaborators. Nearby some Jews were

hung for such crimes and only later did it come out that these men were only
business competitors of the men that reported them.

Staying in one such *shtetl*, the Jews were glad to befriend the Jewish
soldiers for the protection it provided from other soldiers. A few men sleeping
on your floor was a small price to pay if it kept your home from being ransacked
or your wife and daughter raped. And rapes were everyday. This was all the for
the sheer sake of violence and disdain, as women were plentiful and could be had
for some food, Jewish women as well. The war had disrupted food distribution
and farms had not been allowed to make their harvest or had it confiscated. A
woman would offer herself for a stale loaf of bread. What mother would not
readily give of her body to feed her starving child? "Here my child, be
comforted, mother has brought you a loaf of bread. There now, don't cry."

As Shimon and I walked through the town's we came upon a group of
soldiers taunting two Jewish women who were attempting to find their way home
from the baker with bread in their arms. They were older women, or older for us,
perhaps forty, but still attractive enough to catch a soldier's eye, which is no
great task. It was a scene we had seen repeatedly and usually one we ignored, as
intervening often meant a beating for us and further abuse for the intended
victim. Something about these women, a dignity and perhaps their good looks
and handsome clothes, pulled at us.

"Leave them alone assholes. They could be your mothers," Shimon
shouted.

"And what bastard ass fuck is trying to tell me what to do," one of the
four answered.

I was always amazed at the combinations of profanity "the others"
invented, but now was not the time to wax on that issue. So instead I cocked the
bolt of my rifle and answered, "Both of us actually. And if you don't leave them
alone you'll find yourself on the wrong end of this."

This was a stupid thing for me to say, they with four rifles, we with two.
But the bravado and my being the only one with a bullet in the chamber paid off.

"Hell, let's leave these kike whores to these two if they want 'em so bad."

"Yeah, they probably have the pox already."

Of course, nothing ended so simply. As he passed her, the pimply one with the creative, foul mouth swung his weapon in an upward arc, hitting the women nearest him in the groin with the butt of his rifle. The vicious blow swept her into the air and then to the ground. When she attempted to stand, she lost consciousness, probably from the pain, and received a kick as the four marched off.

Shimon stepped forward to retaliate, but I held him back. The soldiers were leaving, and pressing his point might only cause the situation to escalate and bring no good.

With a few words we offered our help and carried the injured woman to their home. She slipped in and out of consciousness, but rest and getting her feet up was probably the best medicine available.

"Thank you for your help. Those monsters meant the worst I think. Let me make my sister comfortable and then get you some tea."

"We don't want to be trouble," I told her, but she would hear none of that, and perhaps also feared that the soldiers had watched for their home and would return if we left. In any case, after making her sister comfortable, she offered us some strudel that was the essence of home and hot tea with honey.

When we went to leave, she asked if we could stay the night. "I can only offer you the floor and the divan for one of you, but there are plenty of blankets. We would feel safer if you stayed."

And so we found friends, or two mothers was more the case, as they pampered us and fed us incessantly. In two weeks, Shimon and I had gained much of the weight we had lost and even laughter returned to us.

Yehudit and Esther were sisters who had come into an inheritance from their father and from Esther's husband had died a few years earlier in Lodz. Some nights we slept in our tent, but when we could we took advantage of the comforters and the warmth of the sisters' home.

One night during the third week, Shimon had guard duty and I came to the sisters' alone. After dinner, they insisted on my staying with them for the night. Not having to argue with Shimon as to who got the divan, I was more than happy to oblige, and soon was drifting off to sleep as the embers of the parlor's fine porcelain stove flickered in the dark night.

Perhaps I allowed the feeling to be part of my dream, and perhaps it was convenient that I believe so, but I was joined somewhere in the depth of the night by one of the sisters. She had let loose her chestnut hair and her nightgown was warm from her bed. Her thighs and breasts were warmer still. I was afraid her moans would wake her sister, but I didn't have the slightest idea which sister had her legs wrapped about me and which slept in her room. Their bodies were similar enough that only in the light of day could they be distinguished. Nor could I ask with whom I was entwined, as how can you say, "By the way, which sister are you?"

I wanted to push her away, as I thought the entire scene improper. Moreover, I knew I was entirely incapable of an erection. I felt deeply in grief over Hadassah's death and the women had not been objects of my desire. Her ardor and my youth proved otherwise and when she took my penis in her mouth I thought I would explode. I pulled back startling her, but it was no longer my intent to disengage, only to save myself to enter her. She would not release me and I finished with a groan into her mouth. I thought this might be the end of it, but she had different ideas and she continued to suck and play with me until I was hard again. She pulled herself on top of me and placed me inside her, all the time groaning as if to a tune to which she could not quite recall all the lines. She pulled me to her large, soft breasts and I sucked each in turn as she held me tightly. I held her waist in my arms and rocked her back and forth over me. In time, she orgasmed with a not small scream, nearly smothering me in her bosom until she ceased shuddering. When I regained enough air, my body responded in kind and she departed as I drifted to sleep.

In the morning nothing was said of the night and it was as if it had not occurred. I thought I sensed that Yehudit was more solicitous then before, and when she made a point of asking me about my night's sleep, and was I sure I slept well, I felt the secret answered.

The next few nights I was on guard duty, but the night following that Shimon and I were again with the sisters for dinner. I swore to myself that I would not repeat the earlier night's performance. I was filled with guilt over betraying Hadassah and although quite attractive, Yehudit and Esther were sixteen and twenty years my senior and the thought of taking either as a lover was simply uninviting. My body had other intentions. When Shimon was asleep my body slipped off to Yehudit's room and entered her bed and her waiting arms. She was a different lover this second night, quieter and less forthcoming. My hands found the wetness between her legs and she pulled me tightly to her. Her small moans excited me as had her near screams of the earlier night. She held me tightly until the tension and release came to us both.

In the early morning light I petted her breasts and squeezed her large, dark nipples between my thumb and forefinger. She moaned and aroused she pressed me once again to her, wrapping her legs about me and kissing me with a passion that I could feel held years of wanting. As she achieved her ecstasy her eyes rolled back into her head and I envied her the abandon that came to her with our entwining. My own fantasies were infiltrated by images of Hadassah and war and death. At times, these images of mangled bodies and rotting corpses with half faces haunted me and I would try to become lost in her body and the nurturance it offered. For moments it would work, but then the images would return, if less clear and defined.

For weeks our army sat in indecision, and we were often able to slip off into the night. With the lovemaking, the food improved appreciably as well and the sisters bought gifts for us where they could be had. With money they provided, we were able to purchase meat and vegetables and flour and sugar, for nothing was ever unavailable in the black market. We were rewarded with new socks, warm wool vests, new knives, the things soldiers needs. They dressed in their finest clothes when we visited and giggled like school girls. When I was alone without Shimon, she came to me. When Shimon was with me, I came to her. With Shimon gone, Yehudit was wanton and wild, with Shimon in the next room she was demur and sensual.

Most of the time we just played card games or sat and talked. Esther, it turned out, was a rather forward thinking woman, with ideas about women's suffrage and socialism.

"Palestine, New York, Warsaw, it doesn't matter. Men rule women until women will rise up and take control of their own lives."

"It's not like that with us Jews," Shimon argued and I agreed.

"Hah, so a Jewish man doesn't beat his wife, but he rules the house and decides if he will divorce her and toss her out. And the Rabbis back him up and never take a woman's side."

"Esther, you always exaggerate," said Yehudit, obviously having had this argument many times before.

"How many men want us for our money or our bodies? What man has ever asked you what you think?"

And so the arguments went, but as is the way with change, Esther's views did not keep her from cooking or picking up the plates and she protected her kitchen from any man's intrusion.

"You men just don't understand. It is not that I don't want to be a woman. I just want to be a strong woman."

As I thought I had mostly known strong women in my life, I did not understand her, but I conceded that she was the better arguer and that concession I suppose was a kind of respect that she wanted.

In the second week, Esther and I were alone in the kitchen and she breathed into my ear, "Come to me tonight, if Shimon is here. I want you inside of me. I need your tight body filling me."

I looked at her incredulously.

"So, now you blush. A little late for that, no?" she said, squeezing my leg and nibbling at my neck.

Only my blushing came with the realization that I had been lovemaking with two women, not one. Esther, wanton and wicked, Yehudit gentle and shy. Both images of propriety and, God save me from myself, of Yiddisheh motherhood come daylight. I swore that I could not defile two sisters. My body decided otherwise in the following nights.

It was all the harder to return to war, and when the call came we could only arrange a message be sent to the sisters, mothers, lovers. The message was simple and urgent.

Dear Esther and Yehudit:

You will be evacuated in days or even hours.

Make haste to hire someone to take you to safety in the East before the roads become impassable and you are left unsheltered with the hoards.

Our prayers are with you. Pray for us as well.

Gayte gesundt , go in health.

Love Shimon and Tzvi-Yosef

We were off to the newly emerging front in reaction to a major German push as the thaw of spring came. Worse, the entire area was being evacuated from civilians so that the Russians could destroy anything that might aid the enemy. We knew this meant that they expected this territory ultimately to be lost. The Germans had earlier in the war fought us staunchly and against our overwhelming forces over Prussia as every inch of German soil was sacred to them and they were protecting their families. For the vastness of Russia, what is the value of the territory of Poland, which is not where their ancestors or their families lived and live? So for Germany the strategy was attack and defend. For Russia now it was attack and slink back for the best place of defense. Giving up land was a part of their strength, stretching out the enemy's supply lines, bringing them beyond rail connections, drawing them nearer where Russian reinforcements could join.

We were force-marched at a grueling pace. Many fell to the wayside unable to go on and many died. Winter had brought the Spanish flu and thousands died of the fever and swelling, more than bullets and bombs could kill. Those still weak died on the march. Shimon himself had been ill, but I would not allow him to fall back as no food or shelter were offered to those who could not go on. Only forward into the mouth of war could life be found.

Everything was used to push men and material forward, trucks, horses, oxen, and even dogs pulling small improvised carts. In two weeks we covered a territory that our officers thought would not be possible in three. Our push against the Germans was forceful and effective. We came in unimaginable numbers and clearly caught the Germans by surprise.

Our battalion was well led, but only half of us had rifles. Men marched forward against German artillery and machine gun fire holding sticks and knives. Soldiers were ordered to attack and pick up weapons as their comrades fell, and this they did. Indeed, the smart ones ran forward unarmed most fervently, because the closer to the point of attack, the faster weapons became available. By night, we slept with our rifles under our bodies and our arms wrapped around them. No one ate, slept, or shat without his rifle slung around his neck and a tight grip on the stock. Our casualties were so great that no one had to wait long for a rifle! Such was the limitless terror we faced.

And then came the gas.

We had seen gas earlier in the war, but it had been ineffective as the Germans initially only used tear gas, an eye irritant. It was painful, but little more. Since then, the German scientists had been diligent. The new gas was a horror. Chlorine-based, it entered a man's lungs and caused them to fill with liquid. Essentially, he drowned. Watching such death was a scene out of hell, which Jews don't believe much in. I have seen it and know it exists. If it is possible to describe what is worse than such a death, it is living after being gassed. These men were perpetually drowning and nothing could bring them comfort as they writhed and struggled to gulp air into their lungs. Mercifully, many died of the exhaustion that followed such effort as their hearts gave out. Their bulging, pleading eyes haunt me and every man who witnessed it to this day.

When the gas came few of us had masks as they too were in short supply. One moment our battalion was moving forward and the next the gas enveloped the air and death was everywhere. We were saved by the shifting of the winds. The wind that day reversed itself, just as the gas came, bringing it back on the German lines with the accompanying torture and death. We could hear the Germans calling out in pain only a few hundred meters away. It was an inexact science.

The second thing that saved us was private Abramovitzky, a conscript in our ranks who was a professor of biochemistry and medicine from the academy at St. Petersberg. Private Professor Abromovitzky was *meshumed, a Jewish convert to Christianity*. *Meshumed* in Yiddish means destroyed and that is the term Jews applied to someone who converts from the faith. His was a typical case, as he said, it was either convert and be a professor or remain a Jew and teach little boys Talmud in *Cheder*. When war came, brilliant Abromovitzky, the Jew, was sent to the front with a rifle. Well, actually he was among those who came without a rifle, but by this day he was at least armed.

He was entirely unfit for soldiering. He was thin, myopic, frail, and nearing forty. He was so constantly confused in battle that others pulled him along so that he did not become lost. He became lost anyway, and would be brought back to us come morning by soldiers, not wanting him in their ranks and getting them killed. He was a pariah to us for his religious choice, to 'the others' as a Jew, and to everyone as he endangered all those around him. We grew fond of him.

As the gas came, our officers thought to shelter us in the trenches, as this is what a soldier does. It is an instinctive reaction to bore into the ground like badgers when threatened. For this perhaps it is called Mother Earth, as we seek its womb in the face of death.

As the gas came amidst shells and bullets, Abromovitzky ran from man to man and yelled at them to seek high ground. "To the top of that hill," he yelled, "or the gas will kill you." No one listened.

In panic, he ran to our major. Like a madman, he grabbed the officer by his coat and shouted into his face, barely holding on to his sanity. He had lost his glasses in the tumult and held the major face to face so as to be sure to whom he spoke.

"Major, listen to me. I know nothing about being a soldier, but I know everything about gas. This gas is heavier than air or it can't work. If it's light it just drifts up, so it must be made heavy. It will settle in the trenches. Our only chance is taking that high ground. The gas cannot drift up, only down."

The major's adjutant raised his revolver and was about to kill this mad Jew screaming at the commander, but there were two types of officers, those from the academy and those who advanced in the ranks. The major was from the latter, and he knew to judge war and this meant he knew to judge a man.

"You are sure of this private?"

"I'm as sure of this as you are that you were born from your mother."

"You're sure the gas fills the trenches and doesn't float up?"

"If you doubt me and the wind shifts, we're all dead."

The major hesitated for a few minutes. It is difficult to go against years of training and millions of years of instincts. Then, with no sign of indecision in his voice, he ordered us to the hill, sending word down the line to other officers to do the same. Perhaps five thousand of us moved to the hilltops and took up our defense among the rocks and sparse cover. Those who remained in the trenches, many more thousands, drowned in the sea of gas. We cried at the vision before us. We wept or buried our faces in our hands to shield us from the pain.

Abramovitzky received no official decoration for bravery. Thereafter, officers and men insured that he was kept out of harm's way so that he could live out the war and win his Nobel prize. From that day, he was passed from company to company to be sheltered and saved from death's path. He was unfit for war.

Following the gas came a major German advance and we were pushed back in disorderly retreat. Now weapons were available everywhere as men threw down their packs and weapons and ran for their lives, even with officers standing in their way and shooting many who fled. Thousands and then tens of thousands were taken prisoner. Shimon and I fought a retreat until August. Few of the men that began with us were still alive.

Near Vilna, outside of the town of Kelem we lay in pitched battle against the enemy. This was as much land as the Russians wanted to give and reinforcements from Siberia, hard men, joined the toughened souls who had survived five months of retreat and defense. War kills the best first, but those who survive are survivors for a reason. We were ruthless defenders with Russian soil to our rear.

I swear I saw the bullet that hit me. I saw it hit a stone in front of me some twenty meters ahead, and then everywhere there was blood. Yani, a good Russian comrade who had befriended Shimon and me looked at me as if seeing a demon.

"What?" I yelled. "What is it?" I was already certainly in shock.

"You're shot," he yelled back, crossing himself repeatedly.

"Where?" I asked panicking. I could not believe it. I felt no pain.

Shimon could not even speak, but in his eyes I understood that I was gravely wounded. I saw my death in his eyes. I reached up and felt the hole in my head, above my right eye, back on my forehead. Shimon called for a medic and when none came, and the attack was enveloping us, he and Yani took my hands and fled with me in retreat. Finally respite and a medic were found, and he looked at me incredulously.

"I will bandage him, but this doesn't look good. It's strange that his eyes are open."

"He's still alert," Shimon told the medic. "He listened to us when we told him to run. He looks at us as if he understands, but he hasn't spoken for a couple of hours."

"I've never seen anything like this. The bullet must have entered and exited, but it cut his skull wide open through the helmet. How could he not be dead?"

Other men came to gape and a Priest came to say last rites, but Shimon refused him for me. Even about this some of my Jewish comrades made jokes, such was our sense of the absurd.

"Why didn't Shimon call a Rabbi for Tzvi-Yosef?"

"What Jew would bother a Rabbi on a night like this?"

Chapter 19

Prisoners of Our Fear

Throngs of wounded covered the expanse outside the railway station.
The few surgeons were overwhelmed and the severely wounded were left to die
in peace, or not. I lay in a cot, not cleared from the waste of the last man's life.
The stickiness of his blood helped me grip the wooden plank upon which we
were both laid. It could not keep me earthbound.

Hovering above, I watched those around me. I saw Shimon holding my
hand speaking to me as I stared at him unresponsively. My old teacher at
Cheder, Rav Pinchas, appeared before me to share some undecipherable ancient
Hebrew text. I spat at him and he turned from me. "Shame on you," I yelled at
him in the fading distance. "Sending children to pain and war, destroying the
innocence of those sent before you."

Our soldiers abandoned the field hospital during the night, as the army
retreated in chaos from the swiftly advancing enemy. They stripped us of our
weapons, leaving us unprotected, but there was no choice. It was hoped that
without the ability to offer resistance, there was less excuse for a massacre.
Thousands of wounded men lay in utter silence, even the moans of the dying
were stilled.

The Germans overran the camp in the morning. Tens of thousands of
men were taken prisoner, mostly in orderly fashion with no unnecessary cruelty.
For us the war was over. Shimon was allowed to stay with me by a merciful
German medical officer, and was put to work in the prison hospital. I could
expect no medical attention as a prisoner of war, with German soldiers
themselves short of doctors, medicine, or morphine.

But Shimon, who knew nothing of science, sensed a secular breed of
Torah scholars among them. He recognized the scent of inquiry. He told them
about me, the common language of Yiddish again saving us. The German

doctors came to study my wound. They stood around me to unravel the secrets of God's work, as they understood him in the form of blood and sinew.

"He's alive by a miracle, but I think he'll be an idiot," one said to another. They did not know I spoke German and anyway were sure that I was beyond the capacity to understand speech.

"Yes, he can't talk and stares without blinking most of the day."

"But the orderly here says he sits up to eat and gets up to go to the latrine."

"Mechanical reactions. Remnants of his mind probably. He'll be vegetative. But it is a fascinating wound, isn't it? Be sure it's photographed and all his vitals recorded."

"You know he's one of you, a Jew."

"Yes, I noticed. Who else would have a cranium so thick?"

"As thick as you German Jews then?"

"No, Polish Jews have even harder heads then us. Did you learn nothing in medical school Volker? Living in Germany with the likes of you has made our German Jewish skulls soft. Now let's get on, there are some more interesting cases."

Throughout this time I understood what others' said. I tried to speak out or make signs, but was incapable. I refused to soil myself after once messing my bed. When the urge came, I demanded to go outside and find the latrine. I could eat if fed. But I was unable to speak or otherwise take control of my body.

I could not speak to my mother during the war, believing that she was too offended by what she saw. Or perhaps I sought wisdom of my Zadie, but could not accept the nurturing of my mother. In the prison hospital, wounded severely, she came to me.

"*Oy mein kleyne tataleh, father's little one*, what have they done to you?"

"Oy Mameh, they have shot me gravely."

"Poor little bird. Come to me. Let me comfort you."

"Why did you leave so soon Mameh? Why did you have to leave me?"

"You break my heart Tzvikaleh. If only I did not have to leave you, there's nothing I wouldn't have done."

"Am I to die Mameh? They say I'll surely die. That it's only a matter of time."

"What is your desire my child?"

"And if I desire to live?"

"Then I think you shall yet live."

"And if I don't desire to live?"

"I'm afraid you will die my little one."

"And what should I choose Mameh?"

"What would you choose my child?"

"I don't know Mameh. I want to come to you and to Hadassah. I'm so weary of this life."

"Then you will die."

"Is that the most hope you can give me Mameh?"

"You need to decide what there is to live for Tzvikaleh. That is the hope I can offer you. That and of course that I love you, that I have always loved you, and that I always will love you."

I declined rapidly because I could not choose. For what would I live? Everywhere was death and the dying. The ward smelled foul with the rotting of wounded bodies and spirits. Many were shell shocked and stared out into the day and the night without recognition. Others shook and called out. One pitiful fellow occupied his days putting together a comrade dismembered on the battlefield. It was an endless mission.

As the days passed many died, others recovered of their wounds, and newly wounded and dying were added. The doctors still came to observe me, but after their initial attention their interest declined. It was enough, however, that they allowed Shimon to administer clean bandages and he brought extra food when he could.

"Tzvi, you just keep getting well. The war will be over soon and we'll be able to go home. Listen to me Tzvi, you're strong and the wound is closing nicely. You'll have some scar, but think of the stories you'll be able to tell your grandchildren as they sit on your lap and you do that trick your Zadie used to do for us making his handkerchief into the shape of a rabbit. 'Zadie, got a bullet in his head from a nasty German, but that couldn't kill your Zadie.' Or you don't have to tell anyone anything; you can just let them wonder. Yes, the strong, silent type, that's you. Now here, eat this soup. It's not so bad today."

Poor Shimon was a wonderful friend, but a bad liar. He had no veil to guard his thoughts. I could see that although my wound was healing, that he saw my soul fading, and Shimon believed in souls. He also lied about the soup.

He could not heal me, but he could bring prayer. Over the next weeks he arranged a community of Jews with my bed at its center. He gathered what he knew, the breed of young men who were able to step a foot in the new world and keep a foot in tradition, those who salvaged faith even within the evil and death that encompassed us.

A routine of daily prayers and talks of home evolved around our common bond. Except for the man next to me who was so badly wounded; we only waited for him to die. His body was covered in bandages from burns to his torso and shrapnel wounds to his face. He ate through his bandages and looked out through haunting eyes that seemed empty, with no one behind them.

Something about this man both disturbed and attracted me and I laid in my bed and watched him. His voice called out with hushed sounds that spoke of terror, but formed no recognizable sentences–the incoherence of waking from a nightmare that continues in each dream.

But there was something else as well. Afraid as a lamb, scared and scarred, he was thankful for each kindness he received. He was already so close to his Maker, that he carried the dignity of the angels. As the others prayed, I stood nearby and held his hand, sharing my prayers for his recovery. He gripped tightly, only releasing me when the prayers ended. One night he woke us, crying out, screams of pain, as if his body was newly aware of the tortures that had

assaulted it. I rose from my bed and sat next to him and took him in my arms. I

could not speak, so I hummed to him, songs of my childhood, songs of his

childhood.

"You remember my songs, my child?"

"Yes Mameh, you sang them to me every night after Tateh came to hear

me pray the *Shema*."

"Yes, you didn't let me miss a night, even when I was exhausted. You

loved those songs."

"I sing them to sleep sometimes Mameh, when I'm afraid. They

comfort me. *'Tateh makes the shoes, Mameh makes the cakes.'*"

"I am glad they bring you comfort Tataleh. They are songs my mother

sang to me...and have you found hope my child?"

"I am not sure where it exists Mameh."

"Why, it exists in your arms my little one."

"But this stranger's dying."

"Is he a stranger? Look at him. Uncover his wounds."

"I know this man Mameh, but from where?"

"Look more closely. Look at his body. Feel who he is."

"But it's not possible Mameh. It can't be."

In agony I returned to my bed and buried myself beneath the covers to

avoid his screams and the reality of what new obligation had been set upon me.

What new tragedy was I destined to witness? "God, how could you do this to

him? How could you force me to see this?"

But by morning, with the coming light, I knew whom I had held and

whose life was entrusted to me.

I found my reason to live, even if it came unattached to any sense of

hope.

It was weeks more before I could communicate what I knew. I spent

the time trying to get well, to gain strength. I do not think that the doctors saw a difference, but Shimon did and I could sense that he was encouraged by my progress. So Shimon cared for me and I cared for Nisan and we all looked out for each other.

"Strange that you care for this one Tzvi. I found him in a back room with those just left to die. One of their Sisters brought me to him. She did not speak, but took my hand and guided me to his bed. Seeing him, I turned to leave. He looked beyond all hope. Then I saw he was a Jew, and thought, "well, at least he'll die among his own." So I brought him here. Looks like I was wrong, as he seems past the worst. At least his body. His eyes though . . . did you notice his eyes? There is no one there. Strange, she was so insistent."

In the end, I was not surprised by Nisan's appearance. I was sure he was brought by my mother and so clear that this was her gift for my life. This was her message as to what I should choose. This was her one chance to intercede in the world of the living, for it is said that even after life, a pious woman's hand reaches out yet once more to the living.

With time, I could write and thought that I might be able to speak. I went off alone and thought that I spoke, but doing so alone, I was unsure. This perhaps was part of my own madness, my being cut off from the world. It was a world to which I still had not made a commitment as to my participation. But the madness grew into a plan, and I thought maybe it was better that I appeared an idiot, without speech or reason.

Conditions at the prison camp deteriorated steadily. There was little food and men died of fevers and malnutrition. I saw little overt cruelty. Men cared for each other where they could, the Germans as well. Indeed, among our own army camp I had often seen soldiers treated worse, Jews especially. But the lethargy and lack of purpose, mixed with exposure, poor food, filth, and lack of medicine was an effective killer.

Men fought rats for scraps and the dying had to be watched, or the rats devoured them in their helpless sleep. It became clear that most of us would perish if we were to stay out the war in these conditions. Thoughts of escape were on everyone's mind, and in conversations, but no one actually had a plan. It was just talk. I had a plan, but no talk. So I set about it.

My first mission was healing Nisan. I brought him food and cleaned his bandages daily. I led him around the camp for exercise and he followed me like a puppy. He did not so much walk as trot, in slow motion, running almost in place. I knew that only speech would bring him back and off in corners of the camp, I spoke to him. I told him stories of his life. I told him of his family. I told him of Hadassah. I did not know if I was getting through, but it was all that I had.

"You are Nisan Eisen. You are from Warsaw. You are a Jew and studied in a Yeshiva. Your wife's name is Shifra. She is small, shy, fragile, and one of the most powerful women I know. At your wedding the waiters wore white gloves. You have one child, maybe even a second now. Remember when we fought those anti-Semitic bastards in the streets? That was when we met. I am Tzvi-Yosef, your brother-in-law. Your sister Hadassah was my wife and yes, she has left this world. You have been in a great war and you have been wounded. But Nisan, your wounds are healing, only you must wake from this deep sleep. I know that Shifra is alive. She needs you. Your *kinderlach, your children,* need you. You must get well and return to be a husband and a father. You are not like me. You have what to live for." He listened, but did not respond. Without his confirmation, I was unsure if I was speaking out loud.

In the end, all that was left to tell him was of the revulsion of war. At first I could not speak, but then the memories connected to my tongue. I recounted details of each atrocity I had seen, of each fear I had experienced, of each death I had witnessed. I spoke as if it was happening at that very moment, the sights, the smells, the sounds, the inner stirrings. As I spoke we held hands and I leaned toward him, and he clung to each word, tears streaming down his face and mine. I found my voice.

"Nisan, the bomb goes off and the flames spread like wildfire. I am somehow spared, but those around me, many men, have caught fire. Their uniforms melt off them and then their skin. Their screams pierce me. I dare not go near them to quench the fire, for it is everywhere and it would engulf me. This one holds his hands to his face and only removes them when he ceases to scream, but there is no more face, only seeping tissue. There are no eyes in his sockets. He is already dead, but he does not know it. I don't know if I knew him or not, but being so close to me, it must have been one of my comrades. It bothers me that I don't know who, that I can't even offer him that."

And as I spoke these horrors, both Nissan and I slowly healed. I could feel myself piercing a dense fog. My witnessing of the nightmare directly faced the demons that haunted our souls. From the prison of our fear we emerged together.

And then one day, as if he had never stopped talking, Nisan spoke. "Tell me about Hadassah. Tell me about how she lived and how she died." And I recounted her last days and did not spare him the joy or the anguish and together we wept as brothers.

"And there is a Russian officer who should be remembered as well. His name is Lavr Kerensky. In the end he could not save your sister, but he did everything humanly possible to do so. He moved heaven and earth. He was also the one who made Reuven's escape possible. He risked all that he had, all that he was, for us. If I die here, please remember him in your prayers."

"In the end Nisan, I sensed she was at peace. She seemed peaceful. I let her believe that her child was alive and would be there when she woke. In my arms she drifted off to sleep, believing she would wake. I am sure she did wake to the child in the next life. Leebeh, that is what I called her, was still one soul with hers and they died as one, only hours apart."

So now there were two of us who did not speak, who others treated as idiots, who could walk more freely, who could begin our escape from this slow, certain death.

Nisan thought that we could obtain clothes from the civilians who worked the camp, and pay someone to smuggle us out. I was dissatisfied with the plan. Oh, not that I did not think it would work. It would work because it was simple and because the hospital directly exited to a side of the camp that was almost unguarded. Nor did I think that finding shelter would be hard. This was a Jewish district, and there were those who would hide two Jews.

"So what is the problem?" Nisan demanded. He had little patience and was easily agitated. "Are you afraid?"

"Of course I'm afraid. But that's not the problem. I want twelve men to escape with us."

"Twelve? Are you crazy? Why twelve? Why are you always making things so difficult Tzvi-Yosef?"

"Because I can count twelve men who I killed, whose eyes I saw before their death."

"And how do you suppose we can get twelve men past the guards?"

"That would be the problem, *nu*? And don't forget me. Twelve and me. But, no, I don't know yet how to do it. But we'll think of something."

Nisan was not always lucid and slipped into nightmares that did not require sleep. He rocked back and forth, holding his arms crossed over his stomach. But then he would return to life. We both kept our silence. At times I think we were feigning madness, and at times the line between our poor play and the real stage blurred.

When I first spoke to Shimon he looked more shocked then if I had grown a third eye.

"What, you can speak?"

"For weeks now."

"Then why didn't you speak to me?"

"I wasn't sure words were coming out. Words that could be heard."

"And Nisan? He can speak too?"

"Yes, but I'm not sure he can speak to anyone but me yet. But he will."

"It's a *nes gadole*, a *great miracle*."

"Perhaps at least a small miracle. Yes, I think so. I believe your finding
Nisan was the miracle. I believe that my mother, *aleha hashalom, may she rest
in peace*, brought you to him and him to me."

With this Shimon's knees gave out, and he had to sit. He could not say
what he felt, but he also had recognized my mother, or the spirit of my mother,
for it does not matter that the woman was a goodly Nun who administered to the
sick in the camp.

"Shimon, there is something else. We're escaping."

"How Tzvi? It's not possible. Others have tried."

"Yes, but not from the hospital. They're not expecting the sick to be
capable. They expect our escape to the afterlife, not to this one."

"But how?"

"That's where we need you. You find ten men who can be healed,
whose wounds look worse than they are. Who are strong men beneath their hurt.
And we nurse them to health. We make them strong, as they pretend to be
drifting off from their injuries."

"But how do we get them enough food and medicine to do this? Even
those coming in with minor wounds fade fast."

"This is the danger in the plan."

"Yes, it will be hard to get medicine."

"No, that's not what I mean. We'll get them the medicine. But,
probably nearly everyone in the hospital will need to know. It will take nearly
everyone to save twelve. You see, we'll have to share our plan with those who
can live and those who will die." I let Shimon digest what I had said and then I
continued. "You see Shimon, we will have to ask two things of the dying. We
will need their food and need what money and jewels that some still have
somehow smuggled and saved. They will die more quickly or somehow survive
here on their own, but twelve will be saved."

It was a dreadful plan, but most came to see it as the only possible way
any would survive. For those who knew they were near death it was not so

difficult. They asked only to be remembered and gave up what they could. We would allow no man to starve to death, but giving up half one's food hastened the angel of death's journey. Some believed they would live, even though they would not, and we could not ask them to give up their food and what little medicine that could be obtained. Others believed they would die, but we did not, and we would not accept their food. The sacrifice had to be a choice by someone who could make the choice. And all was done in Yiddish, among Jews, because this plan was Jewish to its core.

Before, as men faded they were alone, with no one to share their end. Hope and life came with the plan, even to accompany death's waiting. As men lay dying, others spoke to them, held their hands, listened to their stories, cried, said prayers. The last to join this knitting of men were the chosen twelve. Their guilt over accepting the sacrifice of others had absorbed them and indeed four who originally accepted the sacrifice found themselves to be incapable of it and had to be replaced. Shimon himself wavered from day to day.

It was the dying that brought out the strength of the twelve, and they asked for them to sit at their bedside in many cases.

"Come my brother. Tell me your name. Let me tell you of my life. My name is Yehuda Ashkenazai. I was born in a village not far from here. When you escape, promise me that you'll try to find my family. Tell them I was brave and that even now I spoke of them. I wish I had a photo to show you of my children, although I guess they look like most children. The oldest, he is already bar mitzvah. My wife's name is Lena. Please, tell her that I really did love her, even if our parents chose her for me. You know, I never told her that. I was embarrassed for being forced to marry her, but I loved her since we were children. Please, remember to tell her that."

And such were the stories told between men. It was not only twelve who were to leave the camp with me.

With time I was able to ask Nisan the question whose answer I most feared.

"Nisan, do you blame me for Hadassah's death?"

He sat silently for a long time until he could gather his words, or wondering if I could hear them. "I wish I could say that I didn't Tzvi-Yosef, but I think you share the blame."

"I was afraid so."

"It's not what you did Tzvi-Yosef, but what you failed to do. You constantly underestimate the power that you have over people. Her going was her own doing. Your guilt lies in your not imagining that this is what she intended all along. Had you understood that, you might have made some provision."

We sat, as there was no response that I thought appropriate. I could see others love me. I could watch men follow me. It never overcame my self doubt.

"But Tzvi, don't think that you have all the guilt. Why couldn't she come to me with her pregnancy? I was her brother. I can understand her not coming to father or mother, but why not me?"

"You know, Hadassah came to me the other night in a dream for the first time. I had dreamed about her before, but only in death. The other night she came and danced with me. We were back in Warsaw and it was a Strauss Waltz. She so loved to dance. It was strange though. I never did dance with her like that, although she always wanted me to. Finally we danced. I felt she was forgiving me."

"Oh, on that you're wrong Tzvi-Yosef. She is one that would have never blamed you. She loved you too fully for that and was her own woman. I'm sure she felt she made her own choices."

And by opening this window, a flow of air drifted between us and I breathed more deeply. I was glad that what he thought was not worse. He was also wise enough to understand that if he put no burden of blame on me that my self punishment would be that much more severe.

In the coming days, I became stronger and was able to take some exercise. I walked about the yard and the hospital, always observing and watching the guards' routines and the comings and goings of the camp.

"*Vos vet zine fon mir*? "*And what will become of me?*" one of the 'others' spoke to me in clear Yiddish as I passed his bed.

I was no longer so surprised hearing Yiddish from a goy, as I had come to know several who had grown up among Jews, in their factories or in a town where more Yiddish was spoken than Polish.

"And what would you have it be with you?" I answered in Yiddish.

"I could tell the guards. It would be the end of your plans. You deserve it for including only Jews. It's an evil thing to exclude us."

"Is it us that have excluded you my friend? How many years have we been strangers in Poland?" I responded, letting my anger show. "Anyway, it's just easier this way," I continued more calmly. "There are no Jews among the guards, only a few doctors and we hardly see them anymore. This way we can plan without their knowing."

"A poor excuse. We could sneak as well as you."

"Then you wish to know the truth of it?"

"Yes, of course."

"The truth is that we do not believe that you could make the sacrifice. And if you could make it for each other, you couldn't make it for us. And we. . .we could not make it for you. Neither of us are convinced of the other's . . . I was going to say humanity, but we have come to know each other through this as human. No. . . . we do not believe in each other's divinity, and this sacrifice could only be made if one believes others are touched by God."

"So you believe that Christians would not give up their bread for another."

"No, that's not the hard part. The sacrifice is accepting the bread of another. Without believing this is God's will, one could not accept the sacrifice of so many other's lives."

"And you?"

"How did you know? You're right. I also can't accept the food from another. I will only go if I can become strong through my own rations. I cannot accept any more sacrifice of another. And in any case, it would not work if others thought I was gaining by this."

And I thought I saw in his eyes that he was satisfied. I would have to wait for time to know for sure.

The next day he produced two small jewels encrusted in mud that was baked over them so that they appeared like two pebbles in his boot, for who did not have rocks in his boot.

"I hope you have no Judas."

"I am haunted by the same."

"Was it you who came up with this plan?"

"No, there were three of us."

"But it was your plan."

"Yes, in the end I guess it was. What makes you ask?"

"Because I want to know who to remember. You know all of us will remember this forever whether it works or not."

"Do you think it is so evil or so brave?" I asked.

"That's the thing, I'm not sure and I go back and forth on it. I think that we all will for the remainder of our lives. It asks all the questions of God that I have ever asked. But for you it will be worse."

And, of course, he had recognized my fear. That I felt no choice in this creation, was never to be a consolation. I could have gone on no path. I could have died. I could have remained locked in my madness. I could have healed and waited with the others for God's choosing.

"By the way," he asked, "what's your name?"

"They call me Tzvi-Yosef. And you?"

"Kazimierz."

"After the Polish king who favored the Jews?"

"The same."

"Was he correct, or did he unleash a plague on your land?"

"Depends on the day I think."

We had hoped to go before winter, but men did not gain strength in time. Some wanted to postpone the escape until spring, but I did not believe enough would live through the winter. We bought clothing from peasants who worked the camp. We thought to purchase the use of wagons from among those who made deliveries to the camp, but the trick was to have several wagons, at least three available on a given day. But wagons were not forthcoming.

In one way it was fortunate that we had to postpone our departure, as finally the Red Cross brought a delivery of mail and I received a letter from my brother Isaac and Nisan received one from his wife Shifra. Shimon received no letter and became despondent, but I shared mine with him because it was news of home and mentioned his family. It was the only mail delivery the camp ever received and it raised what was to be false hope of an armistice, but still the letters brought news of home.

My dearest brother Tzvi,

I pray this letter finds you. We have been writing regularly, but we cannot know if the lack of answers means that you have not written or that you are not receiving our letters, or both. We are told by the officials that you are alive and a prisoner and they assure us if you were dead, G-d forbid, they would let us know. The Germans are nothing else if not efficient, so we trust this information to be true. I know that you must worry about us worrying about you, so know that we believe you to be alive.

Reuven and Rachel made it to Hungary with their children. He used money you earned to start a business making uniforms and writes that he is doing well, better than ever before. Rachel says that his injuries bother him, but that he never complains. They had a third child, Dina.

Our family is holding their own, but few people had extra money for prayer shawls.

We converted all the looms but one to make blankets and from this we are again earning a living. Most others are not doing so well, except for Uncle Mayer, whose fish shop is thriving with no meat available. Father is sick with worry for you, and if you can somehow write, he will feel better. Little Rayzella and Jacob are not so little anymore and blossoming into young adulthood. Both have sweethearts, even amidst all this, life does go on.

We were able to visit with Uncle Yosef. He and Aunt Hannah are making the best of it. He was not able to work in his profession, but had found work along with Hannah in a factory. It is not easy work, but again, it's better than for some. What's more, they had a tragedy, as cousin Chava's husband was killed in the fighting. He was decorated for valor, but what is that now, only it did get Uncle Yosef and Aunt Hannah their jobs.

Many in the town have died. Gedalyeh came home and told us of what you and Shimon did for him. In the Shul they said a special prayer for the two of you. Gedalyeh says that you're a hero. Shimon's family is doing well enough considering. He is also a prisoner and we are wondering if he was captured with you and that you are together. We hope you are, and at least have each other.

One funny thing occurred. When things were at their worst, the German authorities had shut down our looms, and we had no license to make goods. I can tell you now that there were weeks when we had almost nothing to eat, and what we had we gave the children. That Christian woman you used to see, Catherina, had her husband arrange a licence for us. It was truly an act of kindness and may have cost her a sizable sum, but she would accept no payment from us. She brought a boy with her. I know . . .

We are told that we can only use a page and no packages, or all your aunts would be baking into the night. G-d watch over you. You are always in our prayers and in our hearts. Survive!!!!!   Your loving brother, Isaac.

Finally, it was arranged. The men slipped into their clothing during the night, as deliveries came early in the morning. Each man said his goodbyes and his prayers. Mostly there was silence. I lay in my bed haunted by anxiety. Sleep would not come and I replayed all the possible sequences of failure. Death was not the worst ending. It was the shame of failure, of letting down my fellows that played large on my mind and caused me to sweat until my blanket was soaked.

How could I ever think that such a complicated plan would work? Why couldn't I be satisfied with saving six, or four, or two? Why did I have to lead at all? Since when did I think God's grace would look on to me? Were not all who I touched gored like those who come to loosen a bull from the fence wire?

Finally morning arrived. We were to make our way down to the kitchen where goods were delivered. When we made it to the meeting place, Abraham, Mayer, and Shimon were missing. I slipped back up the stairs, and found that the two guards were busy at cards outside their infirmary room to avoid their sergeant. The three could not move from their beds.

I returned once more to the kitchen, stumbling into a guard. I had a smuggled scalpel in my hand and was ready to strike, but he simply urged me to hurry to my shift in the kitchen. I went on with my head bowed in the practiced servility the Germans expected of Poles. We decided there was no choice except to return to our rooms and wait, as we could not be found milling about so early before breakfast was served. We had to accept that if this was not the morning that there would be another opportunity. As we made our way, back up the stairs, Shimon and the others finally appeared. Carefully, as the dim light of dawn was breaking, we made our way to the back door of the kitchen.

Only one wagon remained. A snowfall had made it late, but the other two had left probably sensing that the plan had gone awry. We argued whether it might be best to send six men who could be packed into the single wagon beneath the blankets and debris. Nisan was adamant against going. Shimon thought we must try now or we might never again have the chance. The others were evenly divided as well.

Shimon argued, "For six to live is a success. And how do we know any of us will survive the escape anyway? If we give up now, hope will be lost."

"No," Nisan said. "Men have chosen the twelve as the body on whom they have given their life. Twelve must at least begin the journey, and Tzvi of course, or the spirit of the men in the camp will be broken."

In the end we agreed with Nisan because we knew that like the camp itself, he was speaking from a spirit that was on the edge of broken or healed. Still, a sense of despondency set over the men, as many feared that the escape was now doomed. Winter, the lack of wagons, guards, waiting war outside the gates, were too much for many men whose spirit had already been burned to its last ember.

A week later as I lay in my bed, a Priest came and sat by me. As it was not known by many that I spoke and as I had nothing to say to him in any case, I sat up and waited for what he would have of me.

He waited for a time, just looking at me, taking my measure and perhaps gathering what he wished to say.

"I know you can speak and I know your name is Tzvi-Yosef. I have spoken with Kazimierz."

I stared and waited. I was afraid that there would be further grievance about our not choosing from among 'the others," and who better to argue their cause then a Priest, but again I had not judged men well. Not that my hunch would not have been correct most of the time, but that men often act far better or far worse than they would on average. In the end men do not act on average.

"I can see you don't trust me. But you must. Your plan was doomed. You had arranged for wagons that were making deliveries. You would have been caught. Those wagons are checked thoroughly outside the gates, which you did not think to ask. As they leave empty, they must be . . . well, empty. You need wagons that leave with things."

I felt the blood drain from my face. Overlooking this obvious detail shook me to my core. He was of course correct. We would have been caught ten minutes after we began. How could I be so stupid as not to see this?

He waited some moments for me to absorb what he said. Then he went on. "I have arranged for three wagons. They will come the day after tomorrow on Saturday if you agree. Each Saturday I bring six wagons. I bring them for the dead. Men from my parish are building false bottoms into the three larger wagons. Villagers in the morgue know of the plan too. They will hide you in the wagons and pile the dead above you."

I did not know what to say, other than "If this works you have saved our lives."

"That is for each man's heart."

As he did not part I waited for the rest.

"I can see you are a watcher of men, Tzvi-Yosef. You know that I have more to say."

"I have tried to know men, but I'm afraid I'm right about them in a rather random fashion."

"Well, this time you're right. I have spoken to the Rabbi in Kelem. He's arranged hiding among Jews in the countryside."

And so the other weak link in my plan was answered, as we had hoped to hide and make contact from the forest, knowing that we might be caught or starve or be killed by wolves.

"But you're still holding back, Father."

"And why do you say that my son?"

"Why not use the wagons for your own. Why not have Christians escape in our stead?"

"Because when Kazimierz told me your plan I knew what I had to do. You see, twelve Jews died here in a pogrom when I was a young priest. I did nothing to stop it. The carpenter who fixes the wagons and the man who owns them were part of the mob. They have waited in guilt all these years for a chance at penance. I have prayed for thirty years for this chance for mine. If we used your plan it would be murder again."

There was still one question I had, and the Priest was a good judge of men. "Yes, what is it?"

"Is the plan of heaven or hell?" I drew up courage to ask.

"It is of both Tzvi-Yosef. It is born of both. You will have to live with that. God has ceased their clear separation with this war."

On *Shabbes*, the men woke early to their prayers, as they did each *Shabbes*. Today it was simply charged with extra energy and fervor, as the chosen twelve and I were already in the morgue. Thirteen men from the camp had entered the hospital to displace the count and give us perhaps the day or two that would allow us distance. Kazimierz had donned a yarmulke to cover his head, and prayed to his own God to play his part filling the ranks.

When the wagons came, the floor boards were removed. There was barely room in my wagon, but in the last wagon the men were so tight that the four smallest had to be squeezed in head to toe. With the men in place, old nails were used to secure the floor boards. Then, we could hear the corpses being loaded above us. To prevent search, the Priest had set the bodies of men who had died of disease in our wagons. No guard would search such carts of misery.

Then, the wagons began to move and we could hear men's muffled voices. We stopped at what must have been the gate and I could sense the guards examining the wagons. Perhaps as a means of checking without risk to himself, perhaps out of mere malice, a soldier pierced his bayonet through a slat in the wagon's side. I heard the life's breath escape from Shimon as the long blade entered his back. He did not call out. I held him as he bled rivers in my arms, my hand covering his wound as if to keep his soul from escaping before its time. I tried to keep my weeping silent to share the bravery of his mute flight to death.

After we gained some distance, I tried to speak to him. "Don't be afraid Shimon. Stay with me. Don't leave."

"Not to worry Tzvi. You did what you could. We knew this could happen."

"Forgive me, Shimon."

"You take on too much Tzvi. None of us would be alive if not for what we did. And we did it together. Don't take away from me my part in it. I'm cold Tzvi, hold me....that's better. I always wanted to be a hero like you. Remember as children on the soccer field? We beat them again today. Tell my family I was a hero. Tell them I was finally proud of myself. They'll know what I meant. *Shema yisrael Adonai Aloheynu, Adonai echad, Hear O'Israel, the Lord is our God, the Lord is one.*"

Shimon kissed me goodbye.

In the graveyard, not far from the gate, men were buried in a common grave, in ground hallowed by the church. From there, the wagons rumbled on several miles and finally, when I thought there was no more air to breathe, we entered a barn and the floor boards were cracked open and we were lifted out. In the small wagon, one man had smothered. Eleven had survived. A group of women, some Jews and some from the Priest's congregation waited with wagons and we were immediately dispersed, one here, two there, and gone. I do not remember anything but asking the Priest to be sure that Shimon found his way to the Rabbi and that his name was known for the burial. He promised me he would get word to his family.

As Nisan and I rode in the wagon, beneath the hay and seed I heard my Zadie's voice mournfully.

"Eleven are alive Tzvi and gentle Shimon is dead. And yes my little one, I already know your question. How can you curse God and praise Him for the same act?"

....

Some months later, two Priests appeared at the door of a Jewish family in Kalushin. The man who opened the door recognized the Priest from the village, but not the other. Still, who looked much at Priests anyway?

"Yes, what do your reverences want here?"

"May we come in?"

"Of course. Forgive my poor hospitality."

"Is your wife here Reb Tobiansky? We need to speak to both of you."

Returning with his wife, Reb Tobiansky asked, "What is it? We mean no disrespect, but it is highly unusual for even one Priest to come to our home. I dare say it may never have occurred before."

"It's your son, Shimon I'm afraid. Forgive me for bearing the news, but he died in an escape from a prison camp. I know this is the most horrible thing for any parent to hear. But, I must tell you as well that he saved many lives. Not just the men that escaped with him either. He gave others' hope. I dare say hundreds lived because of the hope he gave. I met your son in the camp. I can tell you, if you trust me to say so given our differences, that he was touched by the Holy Spirit. His friend Tzvi-Yosef was with him to the very end. He told Tzvi that he wanted you to know that 'he was finally proud of himself.' That those were his exact words. And that you would know what he meant."

"We were afraid he might have died in the escape. The authorities only said he was unaccounted for. But we had hoped. Did others die in the escape?"

"It's a complicated business, but yes many also died. But understand, most would have in any case. The conditions were . . . well, you can imagine."

"Thank you for coming yourself. It must have been a difficult journey. Would you have something to eat?"

"No thank you. I'm sure you wish to be with family now in any case. We spoke to your Rabbi who told us where you lived. He's coming soon I'm sure. I must go now to the family of Tzvi Apfel. To them I have much to tell as well."

"Tzvi is alive we hope."

"Yes, and well hidden by Jews near my home town."

"*Geloybt is Gott, God be praised.* But, before you go I must ask you Father. What is your part in all this?"

"Penance."

Chapter 20

Finding a Path

After the initial weeks the intensive searches subsided. Little by little we came out of hiding.

I was hidden in a barn underneath the horse's stall. The cellar-like room was large enough for me to sit comfortably. I could stay hidden for hours and often did, only emerging to stretch my legs. The darkness was wretched, and the air fetid, but I slept off a tiredness that had been years in the making.

Jewish Lithuania was in many ways Poland, but more rural and traditional. Reb Weller, at whose home I was sheltered, was a stately man--tall, erect and powerful. He had organized our hiding throughout the countryside. Unusual for a Jew, he owned substantial land and had for years. Tzvi, his son, was a veteran of the Tzar's colonial wars, wounded and taciturn. They spoke to me as was necessary, but displayed little interest in whom I was or my past. It weighed on each of us that if I was found out they would be punished severely, perhaps losing everything.

In the early mornings with the dawn, I would emerge from my tomb to exercise. Walking one day near the house I came upon two women at the well, tending the sheep kept by the household. There was a pump placed to fill the trough for the animals. Some fools had placed an old millstone atop the well, effectively blocking the flow of water. It was probably the prank of some passing soldiers looking for harmless sport.

The women could not budge the huge stone. I startled them at first, but hearing my Yiddish they were no longer alarmed. My first efforts brought hard breathing, but little effect. Determined, I put my back into it and managed, barely, to roll the stone from atop the well. They were profusely thankful and offered me water.

The older woman was strong, with a warm smile. She looked at me as if she had poor sight, but wanted to carefully evaluate upon whom she gazed. The younger was a dark-haired beauty, with eyes aglow–the kind a religious family

watched closely. Beholding such beauty after my enclosure, I wanted to lift my

voice and weep. However, I only allowed whatever words were necessary to

pass between us. Had Reb Weller intended I meet these women he would have

surely introduced us. Since this had not been his intent, I did not dare to

disabuse his hospitality, given what he was risking for my safety. In any case, he

was not a man who appeared to suffer disappointment lightly.

In the second month of my hiding, Reb Weller came to me on Friday

afternoon. *"Nu*, you are a Jew you should prepare for *Shabbes*. You can't stay

with the animals forever," this said as if I lived in a barn out of preference. "You

know what it is to be a Jew?"

His reaction was not a surprise. I had come beardless. Perhaps more to

the point, the bravado that had come rumored with my escape hinted of some

wild warring barbarian and not a Jewish soul. Being alive with a bullet hole in

my head also produced a strange reaction. Since my physical appearance and the

stories of my escape shed doubt on my being touched by God, I likely had a

different sort of protector. Still, a Jew was a Jew, and *Shabbes* was *Shabbes*.

"Oh, and one more thing. It's too complicated with two Tzvis in the

house. From now on, if you'll permit, you're Yosef . . . Good then Yosef, come

prepare for *Shabbes*. Bye the way Yosef, what have you collected?"

"What do you mean Reb Weller?"

"Yosef, means '*to gather*,' so *nu*, what have you gathered?"

"I will have to think about that Reb Weller, until now I have been a

Tzvi, running like an antelope."

"Good, you'll let me know in time. Come. *Shabbes, Shabbes*."

I entered their simple, sizable home and found the large metal tub that

had been readied for me in the kitchen. Everywhere was a woman's touch,

curtains, embroidery, chair covers, so opposite of the army barracks and the

trenches. With soap, and a brush with bristles stiff enough for the horses, I

rubbed my skin to the bone, scraping the nightmare of these past months from my body. A mirror was set for me by the sink and scissors, but no razor, for a Jew does not touch himself with a razor. It is a sin to take a blade to one's body, and so only scissors may be used, hence the beard. Your body is not yours, but God's, even if God was allowing millions of his bodies to be torn, shredded, and burned.

You shall not round the corners of your heads, neither shalt thou mar the corners of thy beard. Ye shall not make any cuttings in your flesh, nor imprint any marks upon you: I am the Lord.

With several months growth, I trimmed my beard and donned the clothes with the *kittel*, a kind of half robe, left for me for *Shabbes*. They were satin and conveyed the relative wealth of the household.

Reb Weller entered and offered a nod of approval. "*Nu*, now you look like a *mench, a civilized man*, and not some beast of burden. Good. Very good. Come, you will meet my family."

Already at the table, his face reflected in the starched white tablecloth and the *Shabbes* candles flickering in his eyes, was Nisan, whose presence had been kept from me as a surprise. We hugged as brothers which brought tears to the family. "So," said Reb Weller, "I see you are Jews".

I was introduced to the household, Froi Weller and Tzvi, who I had already met on many occasions. Also, there were Reb Weller's two daughters, Chaya and Devora–the women of the well. Chaya was the serious type, no beauty, but carrying a certain countenance that said she knew her place in the world and was confident in herself in that place. Chaya, I guessed, was over thirty, old to be a single daughter living at home, but the war and the shortage of men conscripted to Russia for years or sent off to America to avoid the army made for many such women. Devora, the younger by many years, was a beauty, with fire in her eyes, and so nervous she could hardly stand still. At perhaps twenty she was already older than would have been normally allowed to remain single in such a household.

"You wish to perhaps say the *kiddush* and bless the wine?" Reb Weller asked of us.

I stepped forward, but *Zadie* interrupted. "Tzvi, it is the eldest who says *kiddush*, especially in his own home."

"He is not testing my Jewishness Zadie?"

"Of course, he is Tzvi."

"No, no, Reb Weller, it is your household," to which Reb Weller nodded approvingly and began the blessing.

As we sat and ate dinner, Reb Weller's wife and Chaya studied us with furtive glances, but the youngest was burning another hole in me, so intense was her gaze. Despite her beauty, or more precisely because of it, I avoided looking at her, and made conversation only with the men at the table. At first Devora looked at me as if asking a question, but this transformed to a smirk, which barely contained her swelling laughter. She refused to be chastised by her father's disapproving looks, or her mother's sending her every other minute back to the kitchen for something, and twice going back with her for an obvious scolding. Tzvi sat at the table void of mirth. Another son was off at war, and two were in America, Avraham, the oldest, and Yaacov, and doing well, "*Baruch HaShem,*" Bless His name."

Finally, the tension became too much for Reb Weller. "Devora, apologize to Yosef this instant. Your behavior's inexcusable. He's a guest in our home."

"But Tateh, it is not I who owe him an apology."

"And what does that mean?"

"This Yosef, as you now call him, is the young porter from Warsaw who I told you about. The young man I took care of in the hospital."

The memories flooded back to me. So far in time and out of context, I hardly recognized the young devoted girl who nursed me after my knock on the head, one of many over the years, that had sent me to a Warsaw hospital.

"But how did you recognize me?"

"Who recognized you? With that beard, I would have not known between you and Moses. I heard your name when all this was in planning months ago. I maneuvered with the Priest that you would come here. How many Tzvi-Yosef Apfels do you think there are in the world? And when he told me you had lived in Warsaw and what you looked like, I was sure it was you."

"So, you were *only* a porter then before the war?" Tzvi asked, emphasizing the word "only.".

"Well, I was many things, but yes, I was a porter for a time. Afterwards I entered studies, but then . . . well, it becomes a long story. In any case, when the war broke out I was conscripted and the rest is as you can imagine war to be . . . and worse."

"And your family?" Froi Weller asked. "Does your family know you're alive?" She was a kindly woman who looked at you with piercing eyes that asked questions beneath questions, allowing you to answer at what level you understood her. She was a match for Reb Weller and then some. "Your mother must be worried sick."

"My mother, *aleha hashalom, peace onto her,* passed away when I was a child. I believe that the Priest has gotten word to my father and brother in Kalushin."

"Kalushin, do you hear that Moishe? We have cousins in Kalushin. Do you know the Abromovitzs? Gittel and Ephraim?"

"Who on earth are these cousins Esther?" asked Reb Weller.

"They're my sister's husband's cousins of course. You met them at their wedding."

"I knew their son Yekheskel. We were in *Cheder* together," I answered. I remembered the boy well. "He was one of the few real scholars among us."

Had I been from anywhere within five hundred versts she would have found a Jew we held in common in order to make a bond. This cousin, so called, was hardly even a cousin of her brother-in-law, a cousin's cousin perhaps, and whether anyone had met him at the wedding was a bone of contention between the Wellers the entire time I stayed with them.

And so Froi Weller had made her family comfortable with me, as comfortable as they might possibly be with a young man living in the vicinity of their two unmarried daughters. Nor did I like the way Reb Weller now looked at me, as he cast his eyes toward me and then his spinster daughter.

In the coming weeks, I felt too fit to remain sedentary and began to work the farm. I had forgotten my strength, for the rifle makes all men equal. I did the work of two and Reb Weller was grateful, even if partially crippled Tzvi was not.

Still, in time Tzvi accepted me, and I could well understand his initial hostility, adjusting to his diminished capacity. He was not afraid of hard work either, and worked his part and more. As is often the case with an injury, the body compensates, and for his wounded legs, the power of his arms and tongue were amplified. By relying on his strength at critical times, I won him over day by day. Indeed, we were friends until his death many years later in America where he would wake early and stay late selling newspapers from his street corner kiosk in Chicago. His tongue always retained that bitter edge, but I was let inside his anger and he shared with me the parts of himself that he seldom allowed others to observe.

"Yosef, you know there is a Zionist group in town? We are looking for someone like you."

"I'm afraid I've almost forgotten the dream of rebuilding a Jewish homeland Tzvi. I've been so busy with keeping this one from collapsing."

"Well, just come to the meeting. We'll go after dark, and no one will recognize you. Many of your friends are coming and you'll want to see them anyway, yes?"

Of course, the hook was baited and I could not miss the opportunity to see Shimon and Nisan and the others. And then it hit me, there was no seeing Shimon. Being apart from him and the others, I would forget like this. The pain of remembering tore a fresh wound each time.

At the meeting everyone was full of ideas of Palestine and the promise of a Jewish homeland. These were men wounded from the war, or too sick to fight, too young, and too old. Except for the escapees who chose to return to the meetings, they had regained their full strength, each selected for his power and resilience. And so it was at the next meeting and the next.

I wrestled with myself. "Keep quiet. This is how you get yourself in trouble each time. Don't step forward. Don't volunteer. Leave them to their own path."

But at the next meeting I could no longer hold my peace. "When do you plan to leave for Palestine?"

"Soon." "When the war ends." "When we've formed a work group that can begin our own collective."

"Good enough," I replied, but what about now?"

"Now, we plan and prepare. What's your point?"

"My point is that there's much to do here. The Lithuanians are preparing for independence. If you're not strong, they will once again do it on our backs. And there are many families I see that are near starving and can't get their farms going or their shops in order. Girls can't go into town for fear of the soldiers."

"We're concerned about these things too Yosef, but we hardly have the resources to do anything about this."

"I don't know if that's true. Actually, I don't think it is. In the army I learned that a group can get much done that the same number of individuals can't. I suggest two committees, a defense brigade and an assistance brigade."

"But we'll never be able to do all that's needed," another remarked.

"That's right, there is just too much to be done and too few of us," another agreed.

"That's absolutely right," I answered.

"What do you mean they're absolutely right?" Tzvi blurted out, taken aback.

"What I mean is that I think at best we will only accomplish a little of what needs to be done. We will only scratch the surface. Indeed, we may well fail."

"Then why try?" asked one who seemed willing if only given a clear path.

"Because there is no other course that is acceptable."

A series of private conversations broke out as small groups argued among themselves.

"Why can't women also help? I mean . . . well, there are things that women can do," I heard from the back of the room.

And Chaya stood up at her chair side, barely overcoming her natural reticence. "I and the other women might perhaps be able to help. I mean, if you others agree. "

"Oh Chaya, you're being silly," chimed in Devora.

And Chaya, who looked almost pretty standing there, illuminated by courage, shrank back.

"Devora, be quiet," answered Tzvi. "What of the rest of you women? What do you think?"

And each answered for herself in turn, and the response was clear. "If not now, when? If not us, who?" And it was Chaya who was most resolute, although she never raised her voice, and other women gathered backbone from her demeanor.

Afterwards Nisan embraced me. "Shimon would be so proud of you Yosef. I'm so proud of you."

"For what? For opening my big mouth again?"

"No Yosef. Don't you see? This is the first time you ever acted. Always before you were reacting. Reacting out of guilt. Reacting in response to others. Reacting to avoid what you really felt. This is the first time you have ever acted, led, created. I always knew you had it in you. Shimon knew more than anyone. You always had the talent to lead, but avoided taking charge, accepting responsibility unless it was thrust on you. I even think . . . "

"What . . . what do you think? Don't start and then stop, it drives me crazy."

"I was just going to say that I think you may have created an idea that will spread well beyond this little *shtetl*."

And so it evolved, and committees from other towns came to hear about our accomplishments.   They came to learn our ideas and to be encouraged to take on tasks that they feared. And we became a force that the nationalists had to reckon with; they could no longer discount the Jews or trade them again for better terms. Nor did we really accomplish that much, but amidst the devastation that surrounded these communities, a sense of rebuilding emerged from the dust and ashes of war. And from the ashes of my own being, I accepted leadership– quietly, shared, powerful and far-reaching in its intent and consequences, even if it only moved the world ever so slightly.

Although I slept in the barn, Devora found excuses to seek me out. She would have to gather eggs from the hens, or milk the cow.

Of course, I knew just what she intended, but I was equally intent on avoiding any semblance of improper contact. I was happy in the home and a scandal would jeopardize not only my place, but that of the other men housed with families who were equally unsure of the wisdom of taking in rough soldiers, Jews or not. I threw many buckets of cold water on my head after coaxing Devora back into the house.

And so, I took it upon myself to become a righteous man. Certainly, I put the next year and a half into the Weller farm and was a good son. The time went quickly, marked by the Jewish holidays, with Pesach leading to Shavuoth, and the planting, summer leading to the High Holy Days and into Succoth and the harvest. Each holiday, major and minor was observed according to its tradition and to the fullest extent of the law. Except on holidays, I awoke early and was last to finish. If I finished early, I went into town or to another's farm to lend a hand and continue our Zionist work.

I did not participate directly in the defense committee, for fear that if I was too obvious in the town to 'the others,' I would be turned in to the authorities, but in the end I lead both committees and the work that grew out of them. As Nisan had said, I finally accepted leadership for what it was, and accepted my talent for it, even if I never understood its source.

I had always been a reader, and what free time I had I returned to study. On *Shabbes*, I joined the other men who came to Reb Weller's home, as the war raged on in the distance, petering out for Russia as revolution emerged in its stead. But we were far from that and Lithuania had gained a kind of tenuous independence. So, we read Talmud and Mishna and argued politics like Jews everywhere. I did not feign becoming a religious man, but I was observant in honor of the family's traditions. My only compromise was to return to be clean shaven, as I believed that the modern world held the most promise for Jews. And I set my sights on America.

"Mameh, do you think she is really the one?"

"She's a strong woman with heart."

"And beautiful Mameh."

"If you see her so. Her sense of God is deeply set in her will. She will be the mother of your children. In her your seed will grow in a new land."

"So you approve."

"She is the essence of my heart *tataleh*."

Finally, I came to Reb Weller as he tended the cows. I probably looked ludicrous, dressed on a weekday in my *Shabbes* clothes, but I felt it gave the occasion an air of the day's propitiousness.

"Good day Yosef. Is today your Bar-Mitzvah?"

"Yes, of course, Reb Weller, but before I'm called to the Torah, I have something to talk to you about."

"So, I'm stopping someone from talking?"

Already, whatever small composure I had attained was decimated, but there was nothing to do but go on.

"I've been here for eighteen months now."

"Has it really been that long? Humph."

"And I've worked hard."

"As we all do Yosef, but you have a point to make?"

As always, Reb Weller used his directness as a weapon to gain the upper hand, which was not how I intended the conversation to go.

"So, out with it Yosef. What is it you want?"

"I want to marry your daughter."

This caught his attention, and he looked up from the silage, with his pitchfork pointing at me, as if evaluating me for the first time. "And what does my daughter think?"

"I think she feels the same, but I have not asked her directly until I received your blessings."

"My blessings?" he asked with one eyebrow raised accusatively.

I sucked in my breath, realizing I had chosen the wrong words.

"I meant to say, your permission and, of course, your blessings. For you could of course not give your blessings without your permission first."

"Well, Yosef, I don't disapprove of you." I took this to be his way of saying that compared to those that were clearly objectionable--thieves, fornicators, defilers of the law, Samarians who worshiped the idol Baal--I was redeemable.

"However," he went on, "it is not clear where we will all be and when this war and now this turmoil will end for us and for you. Where will you go? What will you do? Without raising the *ayin horah, the evil eye*, you may yet have to run in the night. And where would that leave my daughter?"

"So, your answer is no then?"

"Life, I'm afraid, is not so simple. My answer is no in practice, at least for now. I do not wish to make for you another widow, *HaShem* forbid." And to complete the sentence banishing the evil eye, like my father he mimed spitting thrice on the floor, making the required sound, "phew, phew, phew."

"What then?"

"You'll be allowed to be with my daughter, but only with another present. That way there is no question of impropriety. We will continue to live, and....." Reb Weller took in a deep breath and let out a long deep sigh, almost a groan, "and we shall see what time brings."

"Oh, one more thing Reb Weller. In answer to your earlier question . . . I have gathered up myself. I have become whole."

"Yosef, whatever the outcome of all this, your *menchkite*, your being a good man, has long been clear to me. I'm proud to share my home with you . . . for what you've done here and before."

I did not speak because I did not want to cry.

"Good. So now that your Bar Mitzvah is here and gone, get out of those clothes and let's get some work done."

Clearly, Reb Weller also spoke to his family, giving me the new ennobled status of 'not rejected.' Froi Weller gave me the warmest of hugs the next time she saw me and took to calling me *Tzvikaleh, Tzvi my little darling*, in a voice that could have been my mothers. I obtained a room in the attic of the house and was able to spend more time with the family, but never with Devora un chaperoned, unless it was just around the yard or walking to town, but never in private. Devora, Chaya, Tzvi and I spent much time together, talking, eating, working, living life. I longed for Devora, but understood that our future depended on my following the family's intentions. We would brush up against each other, touch hands when passing a cup of tea, and capture each others' eyes in longing, knowing, fevered looks. I was determined to hold back, to be righteous.

Devora, unfortunately, was less resolute. One night, as I lay sleeping, she came to my bed, slipping quickly under the covers and onto the straw mattress beside me. I resisted, feebly.

"Devora this will be our undoing."

"I cannot sleep in the room below yours any longer without being close

to you. Tateh has designed this to test you, but it is me that can't stand the wait.
I am nearly twenty-one after all. Most of my friends have been mothers for
years."

"Shhhh, I think I hear someone."

"That's just Mameh using the night basin. Wild dogs couldn't wake
her."

"As soon as she goes back to bed, so do you *mein shayneh madeleh, my
pretty girl.* Enough of this foolishness."

"I will not. Okay then, you're right. We can just lay here. Just hold
each other."

And so by inches she had me, for I longed to feel the body that I had
only brushed up against in passing. Without her corset and clothes, her breasts
fell free. They were firm and large and she pressed herself against me, making
small humming sounds.

"Ummmm that feels so good Yosef." "What do you feel like Yosef?"

"To hold you, you mean?"

"No, to hold you."

"I can't really say."

"Let me try," and without waiting for my reaction, she took her hand to
my manhood and rubbed, finding the hardness."

"Oh my! That goes inside of me?"

"No, that doesn't. At least not now."

"I think you're wrong."

And with that, she brought her body touching mine. Two years kept
from a woman's body and each day with Devora boiling my blood, any
semblance of resistance evaporated like the morning mist on a hot day. We made
sweet, tender, innocent love, as quietly as possible. With each movement the
straw bustled, making a noise that sounded to my ears pressed against it like
crashing thunder. When I entered her, I placed my hand gently over her pouting
lips as she let out a small cry, but I finished so quickly that there was little for her

to endure, or enjoy for that matter. She lay in my arms for a while, and then, kissing me, snuck back to her bed.

In the morning, I caught her alone and scolded her.

"Devora, you cannot do that again."

"Me? I seem to remember you were there too."

"Okay, we cannot do that again. Your father would throw me out. We are so close to being married. We mustn't spoil it now."

"It was so bad for you?"

"Devora, darling, it was wonderful. But your father will have me slaughtered with the next sheep if they catch us."

"Good then we agree."

"Agree to what?"

"We'll meet in the woods."

"That's not what I said. I said . . . "

"Yes, it is. You said if they catch us . . ."

"Okay, but you know that's not what I meant. You're impossible. And anyway, what if you become pregnant?"

"Then *Tateh* will have us married by the following Tuesday!"

And so it was. At times we were unable to sneak away for days, but when we could, we met cautiously in the woods. Mostly, we only had time to kiss and hold each other. Devora brought me back to life and the ability to love again. It was a longer path than I had imagined possible. Often she would have me read to her, Yiddish poems, and demanded I even write some to her of my own.

Take me fully.
Hold me from this hurt inside.
Gather me in your arms with the softness of your touch
From the harshness I have known.
Open yourself to me
That I may become lost inside your love.

Her body was heaven, with full breasts and thighs, piercing blue eyes that ignited like the January sky when she smiled, and black wavy hair. Into the summer, we often made love standing, so as not to mark her dress and she would hold the tree trunk in rapture as I entered her from behind with her dress raised in my hands. Her breasts were so sensitive and if she would come to tease, I only needed touch her and she was mine. As for her power over me, she looked at me, and I was hers as well. She would peer into my eyes, then turn her gaze to the ground blushing, and my knees weakened. We both wished, without answer, for her pregnancy.

Nor was it only an attraction of bodies. Devora had a quick wit and an active mind. She had learned on her own to read and write, Reb Weller thinking that women did not need to know more than their prayers.

"You know Tzvi-Yosef, this war has changed us all."

"Yes, it has taught us about death."

"Yes, that too. But it makes life more tender too. I feel like a harlot making love outside, standing, for heaven's sake. I can barely say it. But at the same time the war has made it very beautiful. Even sacred. It would have never happened if not for war, and death, and well . . . all the time that war has taken from our lives."

"I don't think the world will ever recover from this war Devora. Long after it's over, and people don't even remember it, it will affect the world. The borders of what is right and wrong have collapsed. God himself has lost his high perch."

"Oh Yosef, don't say such a thing!"

"No? How can you not say it's true? Devora, I still believe in God. Even more strongly now than ever. But I always imagined Him as a flawless shepherd of His flock. He is an imperfect guardian."

"Don't be so hard on yourself Tzvi-Yosef. You've served your watch faithfully and more. You have guarded and saved many."

"I was talking about God."

"Yes, and that too."

During these days, I also came to know Chaya. It was sad that she did not have a betrothed. Often when sitting, I realized that Chaya was raised to be a mother, a *Yiddisheh Mameh*. She worked in the house or barnyard, whereas Devora was frail and kept mostly to light work in the house. When a crisis occurred in the family, it was Chaya who stood tall, who was the mainmast during the storm to which others clung, and this was much to be said in a household of strong figures. Above all, Chaya, was devout, and held her God close to her heart, and shared him in the form of love, caring, tenderness, and delight in others. She did not speak much, but was always in conversation. When you talked to her you felt to your core that she was listening, fully and intently, as if there was in that moment no one else in the world.

It was at this time that Devora fell ill. At first it looked to be a cold, but the Spanish flu was dreaded and many died in its wake, more than even the war killed. Devora lay dying in her bed. The doctors no longer came. It would go as it would go. One day she would make some gains, but the next she would be comatose and fevered. The *Melamed* came with wind cups to apply to Devora's body.

Her throat was almost closed. It was Chaya, more than anyone, who kept watch by her bed, staying up with her day and night. It was Chaya who read prayers to her, who begged her to live, who encouraged the family when everyone else was despondent. Devora, never strong, lacked the foundation to fight this sickness.

"Is she to die Chaya?" I asked, pleading.

"The doctors say they don't know Yosef."

"What do you think though Chaya? I believe you more than them."

"I believe in prayer. Pray Yosef."

And so I prayed, with all that I was. "Mameh, Zadie, please help me. Please save her. Don't let this happen again in my life. Not to her. Not to

Devora."

"And what would you offer God, our little one?"

"All that I am."

"Would you offer yourself to your people, to your family, to God?"

"I would offer my very life."

"Ah, but this is the question. Are you offering your life or your death?"

"No, no, my life. I will live as a Jew, for family, for my people, and for God."

"Do you know to what you commit Tzvikaleh? There is no going back from such an oath."

"I believe I know."

Who knows if our prayers are heard, but Devora rose from her bed. Slowly at first, but within weeks she returned to almost full strength. She was confined to the house, but active and again part of the household. Life had brought her back to be among its own. She was never to be fully healthy again, but the war had done that with so many, shortened their years, even those it left appearing whole.

It was a day like any other. I had finished my chores so as to go into town and help out with the family who had taken it upon themselves to absorb the Jewish orphans. There were many from the war, and few households could afford to adopt them, especially the girls.

The three young men were harassing a group of Yeshiva boys, pulling their sidelocks, slapping their faces. By the time I reached the group, they were holding the youngest, punching and kicking him. The boys were perhaps thirteen, spindly, with long side curls, young *Chassidim*, defenseless. What choice did I have?

"Leave him alone!" I yelled. "He has done nothing to you. He's just a boy."

"And will you stand in his place?"

"If I must." And with that the three released the boys who I motioned to scurry off, urging them in Yiddish, *Gayte, breng hilf. "Go, bring help."*

Already with sticks in their hands, they were on me in a moment. But the anger welled up inside me. Losing my mother, estrangement from my father, Christina, Hadassah, war, fights, Warsaw, Siberia, and lifting the weight of a world had prepared me--too well. With a stone in my hand, my first strike at the biggest fellow dropped him to the ground. Surely dead.

In the tumult that followed, a group of *Chassidim* hurried me off, before the dust of death fell, and into hiding.

In the night, Nisan came to me at the home of the *rebbe*, a house smelling of books, deathly stale odors, and stout devotion. It was the *Rebbe*'s grandson I had saved. "There is no going back Yosef. The man you killed was the son of the nationalists' leader here, a Jew-hater through and through. They know who you are."

"Is the Weller family safe?"

"For now. It's not clear to them where you were staying. When you lost your cap, your bullet hole tipped them off. That and your strength. It seems you're more legend than any of us knew among them. They thought it was you fighting off the toughs in the town all this time. Funny, at the only time I have known you that you were not fighting...till now."

"I must run then."

"I'm afraid so. But it's not so simple. You can't stay here in Lithuania and you can't go back to Poland. Russia is out of the question."

"*Nu*, so what then?"

"We've arranged for you to go to America. But it will take hiding as much as travel. It will be an arduous route."

"I will never see Devora again."

"Well, perhaps that's not true. Reb Weller says he's sending you his daughter. They're looking for a single man, not a man and wife. He says his daughter has the strength to save you, and there's nothing now for her here."

"Nisan, I don't know when we will ever see each other again. Will you go to my family? Tell them I love them. Ask my father to forgive me?"

"Of course."

"Thank you for being my brother."

And so I was off the next night, and delivered from house to house, *Shul* to Yeshiva, across the countryside, this time by great *Rebbes* and *Chassidim* and Yeshiva students, dressed in a caftan with a beard and fur hat. Already far from Kelem, with no turning back, she came to me. Reb Weller had delivered unto me his daughter, the mother of my children, my savior, the source of my future devotion to God, his daughter, Chaya. The daughter strong enough to save me. The years to work for the hand of his younger daughter, Devora, were not to be.

The Letter Opened

Chicago, 1956…So, many years, so much distance of so many kinds, it's hard to measure. My own children grown, two of Chaya's. Chaya died not many years after coming to America. She refused to carry an umbrella to *Shul* on *Shabbas*, always devout. And then she insisted on doing laundry in the damp basement. Pneumonia took her quickly. And this letter weighs heavy with her family's names as well. Tateh died well before the war. Thank God we began to write and our relationship was easier by infrequent letter. Chaya's father died in 1924, and her mother Eti died in 1935 or 36. Devora had stayed with them, each feeling the other would be unable to make the trip to America. Tzvi, who in America became Harry, came not long after us to Chicago and together with Chaya's brother Jack and later her brother Louis, we reestablished the family here in the *Goldeneh Medineh*, this *Golden Land*. And so, finally, I opened the letter . . .

The Jewish Agency

Dear Mr. Apfel,

It is with sad heart that I write such letters. We have used the most exhaustive means available to us to identify the whereabouts and final resting place of your loved ones. Understand that not all records are complete and that some are only the product of eye-witness testimony, and not officially recorded with proper certificates. In years to come, more exact information will hopefully become available. Not to give false hope, there is an occasional error, such that someone believed dead is living, sometimes under another name. The records from Treblinka and Auschwitz

The Imperfect Guardian

are unfortunately most clear, as the Nazis kept careful books. Records from massacres are generally supplied by the handful of survivors and verified only by the lack of appearance of the same individual under records of those found living after the war.

The general records of the Kelem massacre are well-established. The Nazis huddled the Jews together for a few days. They marched them to a nearby woods where a pit was dug. They were shot, point-blank and thrown into the pit. The mass grave has been marked and may be visited if you ever wish. The land has been sanctified by Rabbinical authority and a stone marks the grave.

Thank you for the generous donation in aid of our work. Please let us know if we can be of any further service.

Baruch Dayan Emes. Blessed is The True Judge.
Sincerely,
Chana Wolinksy,
Identification Division

Apfel-2

Records of the Martyred

Yosef and Hannah Apfel, Warsaw Ghetto, 1942

Chava (Apfel) Litman, Auschwitz, 1944

Mayer Apfel, Treblinka, 1943

Miriam Apfel, Kalushin, 1942

Of your mother's family.

Yosl Leiterman, Kalushin 1940

Yisrael and Leah Leiterman, Treblinka, 1943

Revkah Leiterman, Treblinka, 1943

Shmuel and Eti (Leiterman) Levy, Treblinka, 1943

Reuven and Rachel (Apfel) Applebaum, Auschwitz, 1945, as a result of the last-minute annihilation of the Hungarian Jewish Community at the war's end.

(there is no record of the deaths of their children, Noami, Leon, and Shandel, we have had inquiries about the deaths of Reuven and Rachel Applebaum from a Naomi Apel of Budapest)

Isaac and Chana Sarah Apfel, Treblinka 1943

their three children, Asher, Yahonaton, and Naomi, Treblinka, 1943

Avraham and Razilla (Apfel) Kolinsky, Treblinka, 1943

their two children, Nachmon and Chanah-Sarah, Treblinka, 1945

Jacob and Sarah Apfel, Treblinka, 1943

their four children, Avraham, Pinchas, Aaron, and Leya, Treblinka, 1943

Friya Apfel, enroute to Treblinka, 1942

Benjamin Apfel, Treblinka, 1943

Rezl (Apfel) Chernikoff, Treblinka, 1943

The Imperfect Guardian

Devora Weller, Kelem, 1941

Records of the town indicate no marriage or children for Devora Weller.

Nisan and Shifra Eisen, Auschwitz, 1945.

Records indicate that Christina Sienkiewicz died a Righteous Gentile. Survivor testimony indicates that she harbored Jewish families during the war. Her home was used as a half-way house for Jews going underground. She was caught and executed in 1944.

Her son, Jozef Sienkiewica was a partisan leader. He was executed in 1945 and later decorated by the Polish government for repeated heroism. He claimed to be Jewish on his father's side. He is also listed as a Righteous Gentile in Jerusalem for saving of Jews.

And so it is. Each name, burned into print. And yet, three children of my sister Rachel and dear Reuven unaccounted for. From Hungary they had a chance, so quickly did the German machine execute its final solution there on the eve of the war's end. Being behind the Iron Curtain would also explain how hard it would be for them to find out about where I was or get word to me. And now the new task of finding them if possible. No, I must act as if they are alive. Getting them what aid I can. Reaching across the ocean and into a world cut off from us.

And now it is the evening of the first Seder of Passover. On the credenza lies an old *tallis*, the prayer shawl carefully embroidered by six women

The Imperfect Guardian

who loved me. Beside it tiny silver traveler's menorah, ready to be lit for the holiday, and a Moroccan Jewish Amulet. Encased on the wall is a small traveler's prayer which Krzysztof had given to me so many years ago. As it turns out, I could have sold it or the tiny menorah at any time to a collector for a fortune, which had been Krzysztof's secret intent all along, thinking I would one day need to pawn my last possessions to live. I am glad it never came to that.

The family is here, as always for the holidays. The table is full and extended, seating for twenty. The white starched tablecloth, the gleaming candles, the light reflecting in their eyes as they look toward me to lead. On each face of my children, their husbands and wives, my grandchildren, I see my family here...and there in the ashes of Europe. And now I am *Zadie*, and I pray for the power to guide them.

How imperfect we are. How fragile. How we attempt to live our lives by high ideals. How much we miss the mark. How we seek to protect those whom we love and fulfill a multitude of obligations. We endeavor with each step to raise our children well, to give them love, to create family and community. How God guides his wayward flock. How difficult our task . . . and His.

Acknowledgement

Many people aided me in the writing of the book. Petra Buchwald (Germany), Yael Caspi (Israel), Richard Hirschman (U.S.A), Krystof Kaniasty (Poland & U.S.A.), Evie Papacosma (Greece & U.S.A) are scholars from around the world who read and critiqued earlier drafts. My Yiddish and Hebrew references received the watchful eyes of two rabbinical authorities, Rabbis Stanley Schachter and Rabbi Stephen Weiss. My wife provided unfailingly biased support, yet managed to gently offer suggestions that speak to her great depth of spirit. My brother Jerrold Hobfoll read the book with thoughts of our grandfather in mind. My dear cousin, Joel Schwartz (z"l), a physician and Torah scholar, suggested helpful revisions. He died as his life was flourishing, but in a moment of joy. I miss our phone calls very much. Although each of them contributed to the book, I take full responsibility for any failings within. I assure you that they tried often to save me from the error of my ways.

Made in the USA
Charleston, SC
29 March 2011